DAMAGE NOTED

scribble marks
6/6/18 DN.

SO-BEZ-075

W
9.15

DE -- 12

Get a Clue!

Camp Club Girls

DISCARD

Get a Clue! © 2012 by Barbour Publishing, Inc.

Camp Club Girls & the Mystery at Discovery Lake © 2010 by Barbour Publishing, Inc.
Sydney's D.C. Discovery © 2010 by Barbour Publishing, Inc.
McKenzie's Montana Mystery © 2010 by Barbour Publishing, Inc.

Edited by Jeanette Littleton.

Print ISBN 978-1-61626-917-3

eBook Editions:
Adobe Digital Edition (.epub) 978-1-62029-554-0
Kindle and MobiPocket Edition (.prc) 978-1-62029-553-3

All rights reserved. No part of this publication may be reproduced or transmitted for commercial purposes, except for brief quotations in printed reviews, without written permission of the publisher.

Scripture taken from the HOLY BIBLE, NEW INTERNATIONAL VERSION®. NIV®. Copyright © 1973, 1978, 1984, 2011 by Biblica, Inc.™ Used by permission. All rights reserved worldwide.

Additional scripture quotations are taken from the King James Version of the Bible.

Scripture quotations marked CEV are from the Contemporary English Version, Copyright © 1991, 1992, 1995 by American Bible Society. Used by permission.

This book is a work of fiction. Names, characters, places, and incidents are either products of the author's imagination or used fictitiously. Any similarity to actual people, organizations, and/or events is purely coincidental.

Cover thumbnails design by: Greg Jackson, Thinkpen Design

Published by Barbour Publishing, Inc., P.O. Box 719, Uhrichsville, Ohio 44683, www.barbourbooks.com

Our mission is to publish and distribute inspirational products offering exceptional value and biblical encouragement to the masses.

 Member of the
Evangelical Christian
Publishers Association

Printed in the United States of America.
Bethany Press International, Bloomington, MN 55438; October 2012; D10003589

PROPERTY OF C L P L

Get a Clue!

Camp Club Girls

3 STORIES IN ONE

BARBOUR
PUBLISHING

Contents

Camp Club Girls

Mystery at Discovery Lake

Renae Brumbaugh

Cabin 12B

"Shhhhhhh!" Sydney told Bailey. "What was that noise?"

"What noise?" asked Bailey.

"Shhhhhhhhhhhhhhhh!" commanded her new friend.

The two listened with all their focused energy. Then, there it was. Footsteps. Large, heavy footsteps.

The girls stood in terrified uncertainty.

Aaaaaaaaaarrrrrrrkkkkk!

Sydney gasped as the eerie shrifi filled the air.

Yahahoho-ho-ho!

Bailey trembled uncontrollably as the crazy, other-worldly laugh followed.

"Run!" Sydney screamed. The two dashed as fast as their legs could carry them back toward the camp. Sydney stopped twice, waiting for Bailey's shorter legs to catch up.

●—■—●

Fourteen-year-old Elizabeth sat in the middle of the dusty road, trying to cram her undergarments back into her suitcase before anyone saw. *I thought wheels were supposed to make a suitcase easier,* she thought. Instead, the rolling blue luggage had tipped over three times before it finally popped open, leaving her belongings strewn in the street.

Suddenly she was nearly barreled over by two girls running frantically. "Run for your life!" the smaller one cried. "It's after us!"

"Whoa, calm down." Elizabeth focused on the terrified girls. The taller one panted. "Something's back there!"

Elizabeth looked toward the golf course but saw nothing. She noticed that the smaller girl seemed to struggle for air, and her protective instincts took over. "Calm down. You'll be okay."

"Need. . .inhaler," gasped the girl.

Elizabeth sprang into action, digging through the girl's backpack until she found a small blue inhaler. Then she helped hold it steady while the slight girl gasped in the medication. The taller girl kept looking toward the miniature golf course they'd just left. "Sorry," the small girl whispered. "I'm supposed to keep that in my pocket, but I got so excited I forgot."

"I'm Elizabeth. Why don't you tell me what happened."

"I'm Bailey," said the short, dark-haired girl. "Bailey Chang."

"And I'm Sydney Lincoln," said the tall, dark-skinned girl with beaded braids. "We were at the golf course, and. . .and. . ."

"And something came after us!" exclaimed Bailey.

Elizabeth looked skeptical as she tucked a strand of long blond hair into the clip at the base of her neck.

"Is this your first year here? This is my third year here, and the most dangerous thing I've seen is a skunk."

The girls giggled but didn't look convinced. "Come with us. We'll show you." Bailey pulled Elizabeth back toward the golf course.

"I thought you were afraid of whatever it was! Why do you

want to go back there?" Elizabeth asked.

The young girl stood to her full height. "Because I am going to be a professional golfer. And I'm not going to let whatever that was bully me. I plan to practice my golf strokes while I'm here."

"Will you tell me exactly what happened?" Elizabeth asked Sydney.

Sydney looked each girl in the eye and spoke slowly. "Something or someone is in the woods by the golf course. And it wasn't friendly." She paused for dramatic effect. "And. . .it came after us."

●—●—●

Kate Oliver leaned back on her bed and smiled. *Yes! I got the bed by the window!* she thought. *Hopefully, I'll be able to get good reception for my laptop and cell phone.* She tucked a strand of blond hair b›ind her ear. It was too short to stay there and just long enough to drive her crazy.

Bam! The cabin's outer door slammed, and Kate heard voices. Pushing her black-framed glasses up on her nose, she sat up. Two girls entered the room giggling and talking.

"I can't believe I'm finally here! This is so cool. And look at this cute little dorm room! It's just like the cabin in *The Parent Trap*! Oh, hello!" The fun-looking brunette with piercing blue eyes greeted Kate. "I'm Alex Howell. Alexis, really, but nobody calls me that except my mother. I am so excited! This will be the best two wefis ever!"

Kate smiled and reached to shake the girl's hand. "Kate Oliver," she said. "Welcome to cabin 12B." She looked at the other girl.

The girl's freckles matched her curly auburn hair, and she offered a friendly smile. "Hi there. I'm McKenzie Phillips."

•—•—•

The two girls looked at Elizabeth stubbornly, as if needing to prove their story to her. Hearing another bus pull up, Elizabeth remembered her belongings, which were still lying in the middle of the road.

"I'll tell you what. You help me get this awful suitcase to cabin 12B, and then I'll walk to the golf course with you. Deal?"

Bailey's mouth dropped open, and Sydney's eyes widened.

"You're in cabin 12B?" asked Sydney.

"That's our cabin!" exclaimed Bailey.

Now it was Elizabeth's turn to be surprised. "You're kidding! Wow. It is a small world. Okay, roomies, help me hide my underwear before the entire camp sees, and we'll be on our way."

The girls gathered the strewn articles of clothing. Bailey held up one particular article of clothing and giggled. "Tinkerbell? Seriously, you have Tinkerbell on your . . ."

Elizabeth snatched the unmentionables from Bailey, crammed them in her suitcase, and snapped it shut. "Not another word, shorty!" Elizabeth scolded, but with a twinkle in her eye. The three girls chattered all the way to cabin 12B. As they approached the cabin, the two younger girls pulled their luggage out from b›ind some bushes.

"We sat together on the bus from the airport, and we both wanted to see the golf course before we did anything else. So we stowed our suitcases here until we got back," explained Sydney.

Elizabeth laughed. With these two as roommates, this year's camp experience would be far from dull.

The girls entered the cabin and located room B to the right. Three girls were already there, smiling and laughing.

"Hello, I'm Elizabeth. I guess we'll be roommates!" She tossed her things on the lower bunk closest to the door, and Sydney placed her things on the bunk above that. Bailey took the top bunk next to Sydney. After an awkward pause, McKenzie stepped forward.

"I'm McKenzie Phillips," she said. "I'm thirteen, and I'm from White Sulphur Springs, Montana."

Alex bounced forward. "I'm Alexis Howell, Alex for short. I'm twelve, and I'm from Sacramento."

"Sydney. Twelve. Washington, D.C."

"Oh, that is so cool. Do you know the president?" asked Bailey, and everyone laughed. "I'm Bailey Chang. I'm nine, and I'm from Peoria, Illinois. And just so you'll all know, I plan to be the next Tiger Woods. I'll be glad to sign autographs, if you want. They'll be worth money someday."

Elizabeth stepped forward. "I'll take one, Bailey. I'll sell it and use the money for college. I'm Elizabeth Anderson, fourteen, from Amarillo, Texas."

"Well, I guess that leaves me," said Kate. "Kate Oliver, eleven, Philadelphia."

Alexis jumped up and down. "Oh, this will be so much fun! Kate brought her laptop with her. I have the coolest roommates ever!"

Everyone's attention turned to Kate's bed, which was covered with a laptop and several small gadgets. "What is all that stuff?" asked Sydney. The girls gathered around Kate's bed and watched her pull items out of a black backpack.

"It's like a magician's bag. It has no bottom," mused McKenzie.

Kate laughed. "My dad teaches robotics at Penn State, so he's always bringing home little devices to test out. Some of them are really helpful. Some of them are just fun to play with."

One by one, she pulled the oddly shaped gadgets out of her bag, describing the functions of each.

"This is my cell phone. It can take pictures and short video clips, has a GPS tracker, a satellite map, Internet access, a motion sensor, a voice recorder, and about a zillion other things!" Aiming it at the others, she said, "Say cheese!"

The other girls leaned together and smiled. "Cheeeeeeeeeeeeese!"

Kate saved the picture then passed the phone to the others and dug through her backpack again. "This digital recorder can record conversations up to thirty feet away."

Sydney squinted her eyes. "You're kidding! That thing is the size of a contact lens! Let me see!" Kate handed her the recorder and kept digging.

"This is a reader," she continued, holding up a small penlike device.

"A what?" asked McKenzie.

"A reader. You run it across words on a page, and it records them to memory. Like a small scanner."

"That is so cool! I had no idea stuff like this existed!" McKenzie examined the reader.

"Here, I have my Bible. Will you show us how the reader

works?" Elizabeth grabbed a worn Bible from her bag and handed it to Kate.

"Sure. You turn it on by pressing this button, and. . ." She ran the pen over a page in Psalms.

Elizabeth giggled. "I've heard of hiding God's Word in your heart, but never in your pen!"

The gadget girl suddenly stopped her display to announce, "Hey, I'm starved. Is anybody else hungry?"

"It's almost dinnertime," announced Elizabeth. "But first, we have some business to take care of at the golf course."

The girls listened as Sydney and Bailey described their experience.

"Whoa, cool!" exclaimed Alex. "We have a mystery on our hands! Why don't we go right now and check it out?"

"Why don't we eat first?" called out Kate. "Starving girl here, remember?" The others laughed at the petite girl whose stomach was growling loudly.

Since it was almost dinnertime, the group decided to head to the dining hall first. Bailey led the way, taking over as tour guide.

"Wait for me," called Alex. "I need to grab my lip gloss!" She shoved strawberry Lip Smackers into her pocket.

The group wandered through the camp, with Bailey pointing out different sites. Suddenly, she stopped. "Well, guys, I hate to tell you this. . .but I have no idea how to get to the dining hall from here."

"It's this way," stated Elizabeth. "You'll get your bearings. My first year here, it took me the whole time before I could find my way around. But I get lost in a closet."

McKenzie spoke up. "Come on, girls, let's go. Remember, Kate's about to starve. We wouldn't want her to waste away to nothing."

Everyone laughed at Kate, who pretended to be nearly fainting. "I need sustenance, and I need it now!"

The group arrived at the dining hall with seven minutes to spare. They stood near the front of the line, and Elizabeth said, "Get ready for a long meal. The camp director will explain all the camp rules, introduce the counselors, and tell us more than we want to know about Camp Discovery Lake."

"Terrific." Bailey sighed. "I wanted to visit the golf course before dark."

"Don't worry," said Alex. "After the story you and Sydney told, I think we all want to find out what's down there."

"Really?" Bailey asked. "You'll all come?"

"You bet!" said McKenzie. "The girls of cabin 12B stick together!"

—•—•—

The sun was dipping b›ind the horizon by the time the girls left the dining hall.

"Hooray! We can finally go to the golf course!" Bailey called.

"We'd better hurry. It's getting dark," said Elizabeth.

"Yeah, and after the story you and Sydney told, I certainly don't want to be there after dark," added Kate.

The girls scurried while chattering about the different camp activities they wanted to try. Before they knew it, the sun was gone and they could barely see the road. "Why is the golf course so far away from the main camp?" asked Alex nervously.

Sydney laughed. "So nobody will get hit on the head with a stray golf ball!"

Suddenly, a voice called out from the woods.

"Who? Who? Who?"

"What was that?" whispered Bailey.

"Who?" came the voice again.

McKenzie giggled. "You city girls don't know much about the country, do you? That was an owl!"

The others burst into laughter as the voice called again, "Who?"

"I'm Sydney! Who are you?" Sydney shouted, and the laughter continued.

"It sure does get dark here, doesn't it?" said Kate. "It never gets this dark in the city."

"Are we close to the golf course?" asked Alex.

"It doesn't seem nearly as far in the daytime," Elizabeth told her.

They continued, each trying to seem brave. The trees that had seemed friendly and protecting in the daytime now loomed like angry giants. The girls' steps became slower and slower as they struggled to see where they were stepping.

Finally, Kate stopped and looked at the sky through the trees. "Look, everybody! It's the Big Dipper!" The other five girls looked to where she pointed.

"Wow, the sky is beautiful. It's so dark, and the stars are so bright," whispered Sydney.

"The stars are never this bright in Sacramento," Alex

commented. "The city lights are brighter. Hey, this reminds me of an episode of *Charlie's Angels,* where the Angels' car broke down in the middle of nowhere and they had to use the stars to find their way home."

The girls were so focused on the sky that they didn't notice the image moving toward them. Kate was the first to lower her eyes, and she blinked in confusion. Adjusting her eyeglasses, she whispered, "Uh, guys?"

The girls continued pointing out the brightest stars.

Kate tried to make her voice louder, but terror kept it to a soft squeak. "G–g–guys?" The image moved closer, but still no one heard her. Finally, Kate grabbed Sydney's sleeve. "Wh–wh–what is that?" she squeaked.

Sydney looked. "Oh, my word! What in the world is that?"

The girls saw a white stripe in the road, moving slowly, steadily toward them. They were frozen, until Elizabeth yelled, "Skunk!"

Camp Discovery Lake resounded with shrifis and squeals as the girls ran back toward the cabins. McKenzie led the way with Alex close on her heels.

The girls didn't slow down until they had burst through the door of cabin 12B. Falling onto the beds, they panted then soon began giggling.

"Can you believe it? A skunk! We were scared of a little bitty skunk!" howled McKenzie.

"I don't know about you, McKenzie, but I wasn't about to smell like Pepé Le Pew out there!" retorted Alex, and the girls laughed even harder.

"Hey, Sydney, is that what scared you today? Some forest creature?"

Sydney and Bailey stopped giggling and looked at one another. "No," they replied.

"Whatever we heard was not small," said Bailey. "And it wasn't friendly."

"And it definitely came after us," added Sydney.

CHAPTER 2

Dan Ger?

"No! Make that noise go away!" Bailey groaned, pulling the covers over her head as a loud trumpet sounded reveille over the loudspeaker the next morning. "It's still dark outside!"

The wretched music continued. Apparently the unknown trumpet player was committed to torturing the entire camp.

Sydney threw back her covers. "I'm taking a shower before all the hot water is gone," she told her roommates.

"Good idea. I'm coming, too," called Kate. Alex sat up and stretched, while Elizabeth began making her bed. McKenzie remained a motionless lump.

Alex tossed her dark curls, smiled, and began singing with an off-key voice. "It's time to get up. Get out of bed. It's time to get up, you sleepyheads!"

A pillow flew at her from Bailey's bed, but this only encouraged the perky brunette. She stood to her feet and stretched close to Bailey's ear. "It's time to get up. Get out of bed. It's time to get up, you slee—"

"Okay! Okay! Promise me you will *never, ever* sing again, and I'll get up!" Bailey sat up and rubbed her eyes.

Elizabeth, spotting McKenzie's motionless form, laughed. "Alex, I think your services may be needed elsewhere."

The vivacious songbird stooped to McKenzie's level. Just as she poised her mouth to sing, McKenzie's eyes popped open. "Don't even think about it!"

They all laughed, and soon they headed toward the dining hall.

"Food at last!" Kate exclaimed as they took their places in the long line. "I feel like I haven't eaten for days!"

"You look like it, too!" announced a sneering voice. "What's the matter? Don't your parents feed you?"

The whole group turned around. "And those glasses. . . Maybe if you'd eat a carrot once in a while you could get rid of those," the very pretty, very mean-looking girl announced.

Sydney stepped forward, towering inches over the girl. "Excuse me?"

"It's okay, Sydney. I can handle this." Kate stepped forward, adjusted her glasses, and stared into the eyes of her unpleasant opponent. "It's a common misconception that small people don't eat much. However, the genealogical consequences of the high metabolic rates of both of my parents have resulted in similar metabolism in each of their offspring."

The girl stared at Kate, clearly baffled by her words. Kate triumphantly smiled.

Ever the peacemaker, Elizabeth stepped forward. "Hi! Aren't you Amberlie Crewelin? You were here last year. I'm Elizabeth, and these are my roommates: Sydney, Kate, McKenzie, Bailey, and Alex. It's nice to see you again. Oh look! They've opened a new line. I guess we'll see you later!" Elizabeth guided the group to the other line. "We probably want to steer clear of her," she murmured to the others.

"She has some. . .issues."

"Don't let her get to you," McKenzie added. "People like that are miserable, and they want to make everyone else miserable."

"Well, I don't know about the rest of you, but I'm not hungry. All I can think about is that miniature golf course and those noises we heard last night!" Bailey announced.

"Not hungry? Speak for yourself," said Kate.

Alex jumped up and down. "Let's check it out after breakfast! If we hurry, we'll have almost an hour before our first session begins. Oh! I just love a good mystery!"

"And I just love a good meal," Kate stated.

The small band of detectives moved hastily through the line and chose foods they could eat quickly. Kate loaded her plate with five fluffy biscuits and five sausage patties, drawing amused stares from her roommates. She grabbed two cartons of chocolate milk, a carton of apple juice, and a banana. She started toward the table but paused again to add an orange to her tray.

The girls settled at a table by the door and ate quickly. Kate was only half finished when the others began picking up their trays. "Hey! I'm not done yet!" she protested.

"Bring it with you," replied Elizabeth. "Here, wrap it in this napkin and stuff it in your pocket. The golf course is at the other end of the camp, so we need to hustle."

The group hurried past the chapel and around the stables on their way to the site of last night's mystery noise.

"Hello, girls!" called a man from the stables.

"Hello, Mr. Anzer," Elizabeth called back. "You all will love him," she told her friends. "He's the camp grandpa." Then, looking at her watch, she said, "We have forty-seven minutes. Last year a group was late to the first session, and the camp director made them clean the kitchen in their free time!"

"Hmm. Did they get to eat the leftovers?" Kate asked.

"*Shhhhhh!*" Alex hushed them as they neared their destination. "Listen! I think I hear something!"

The young sleuths stopped in their tracks, afraid to move. Sure enough, they heard a distant howling noise.

"Is that what you heard last night?" Alex asked.

Sydney and Bailey both shook their heads. "No. What we heard was more. . ." Sydney searched for the correct word.

"Creepy!" Bailey interjected. "What we heard was like creepy laughter."

"That noise sounded pretty creepy to me," whispered McKenzie.

"Well, I don't know why we're standing here. Nancy Drew would already be investigating!" Alex exclaimed.

No one moved. "Okay. I'll go first!" said Alex. The young investigator led the way, and the other detectives reluctantly followed.

Elizabeth stopped the group as they reached the gate to the miniature golf course. "We need to stay together. We don't know what we'll find, and we're a long way from the main camp."

The girls all nodded their heads. Bailey unlatched the gate, and it swung open with a low creak. The girls moved inside and slowly approached the howling noise, which was getting louder.

"It sounds like a wounded animal," said Sydney. "Not scary, just. . .sad."

As the girls tiptoed through the golf course, they noticed the worn attractions.

"Wow! Look at this place! We don't have anything like this back in Peoria." Bailey said. "Look, there's a windmill and a clown and a castle. . . . It's not nearly as scary in the daylight. I'm going to come here every day to practice my Tiger Woods strokes."

Suddenly a high-pitched, mechanical-sounding laugh came from the direction of the clown.

The girls squealed and banded together more tightly. "Or maybe I won't," continued the group's youngest member.

"What was that?" asked McKenzie. "It sounded so. . . fake."

The howling turned to a whimper, and the group froze. "That doesn't sound fake!" said Kate. Forgetting her promise to stay with her friends, she ran ahead. "Hey, get over here! Come look at this!"

The girls ran to join Kate at the windmill. They found a skinny puppy caked in mud. His paw was caught in the golf hole, and he whimpered pitifully.

Kate knelt to help the puppy. With the help of the others, he was soon free of the trap.

"Here you go, little fellow! You're okay now." Kate held the small dog close, then at arm's length. "Whoa! You stink!"

"Awww, look at him! He's hungry," said Elizabeth. "Kate, where's the rest of your breakfast?"

Kate pulled a biscuit from her pocket, and the dog

swallowed it in two bites. Then, tail wagging, he attacked his rescuer with puppy kisses, knocking her glasses askew. She offered him half of a sausage patty and another biscuit.

"Look at that. He loves you, Kate! You're his hero," said McKenzie.

"He sure ate those biscuits in a hurry. I think we should name him Biscuit!" suggested Bailey.

Biscuit wagged his tail in agreement.

Suddenly the girls were startled by a man's voice.

"Hey! What are you girls doing? Get away from that mutt!"

An angry-looking man walked toward them. His green, collared shirt showed that he was a Camp Discovery Lake staff member.

McKenzie stepped forward. "Oh, we were just looking around, and we found him. His paw was stuck in a—"

"You girls need to stay away from here. Give me that dog and get to class!" He reached for Biscuit, but the small dog wiggled out of Kate's arms and ran toward the woods.

"But, sir, he's just a puppy! He was stuck and hungry and we had to help him," Elizabeth told the man.

He glared at her. "You girls aren't here to rescue dogs or to poke around an old golf course. Stay away from here, you understand?" The girls backed away a few steps.

"What are you waiting for?" he shouted. "Get out of here!"

The girls turned and ran through an open side gate, into the woods.

"And don't come back!" the angry man yelled.

They ran frantically, not stopping until they were deep in the woods. Finally, out of breath, they halted.

"Why was. . .he so angry? . . . We weren't. . .doing anything wrong," said Sydney, catching her breath.

"He seems like a. . .very unhappy. . .person to me," replied McKenzie.

Alex sank to her knees, while Bailey propped herself against a tree. Gradually their breathing slowed, and they began to look at their surroundings.

Elizabeth leaned toward Bailey. "You okay, Bales? Got your inhaler?"

"It's in my pocket. Umm, does anybody know where we are?" asked Bailey.

"Does anybody know where Biscuit is?" asked Kate, her voice shaking.

"Biscuit! We've got to find him!" exclaimed Elizabeth. "If we don't, that horrible man will probably send him to the pound!"

The girls started yelling, "Biscuit! Come here, Biscuit!"

"Wait!" Elizabeth stopped them. "We have to stay together. The last thing we need is for one of us to get even more lost!"

"Yes, Mother," teased Bailey.

All of a sudden, a bloodcurdling scream pierced the air, followed by a rustling sound in the trees above them. The girls shrified and huddled together.

"Wh—wh—what was that?" whispered Bailey.

"I don't know, and I d—don't want to find out!" McKenzie responded.

Elizabeth craned her neck, trying to determine the source of the alarming sound. "It sounded like a woman. A terrified woman!"

"It sounded like a cougar," said Sydney. "We studied them in my Wilderness Girls class."

"A cougar! Yikes! Let's scram!" exclaimed Alex.

"We do need to stay together," Sydney continued. "Cougars probably won't attack a group, but they sometimes attack individuals. I think we scared it."

"But Sydney, what about Biscuit?" asked Kate.

A worried silence fell over the group. Then they began calling for the lost puppy again. Just a few minutes later, they heard the rustling of dead leaves, followed by a whimper.

"Biscuit!" Kate followed the sound and pulled the bedraggled puppy from a pile of leaves. "I'm so glad you're safe!"

The girls surrounded their wiggly, smelly treasure and took turns holding him. Then the cougar screamed again in the distance.

"Let's get out of here," McKenzie urged, wide-eyed. "We may have scared that cougar, but it scared me, too!"

"You and me both," agreed Alex. "But we have a problem. I have no idea where we are or how we got here!"

The frightened young campers all looked to Elizabeth, the oldest. "Don't look at me!" she told them. "I'm directionally disabled."

"I have a compass," Kate told the group as she struggled with her wiggling bundle. They all looked at her hopefully until she added, "In my backpack. Back at the room."

"We can figure this out," asserted Sydney. "Let's think about this. The golf course is south of the main camp. We came into the woods from the right, which would be east. So, we were heading west."

"Maybe so, but we've turned around so many times, I don't remember which way is which," said McKenzie.

Five pairs of eyes remained glued to Sydney's face as she continued to work things out in her mind. She muttered under her breath, reminding herself of things she had learned in her nature studies. The others listened, not wanting to interrupt the girl who seemed to be their only hope for escape from these dark, menacing woods.

Sydney walked around trees, examining the bark, scrutinizing the branches. Her beaded braids jangled as she moved from tree to tree. Finally she addressed her fellow campers. "To get back to the golf course, we need to head east. Look for moss growing at the base of the trees, and that will be north. Also look for spiderwebs, which are often found on the south sides of trees."

The group began to examine the details of their surroundings.

"This is fun," said Bailey. "It's sort of like a treasure hunt!"

Elizabeth stopped her search and looked thoughtful. "That reminds me of something in the Bible. Several times in Deuteronomy, God said His people are His treasured possession."

Just then, the girls heard the screaming once more in the distance. "Will you hurry up, already?" Bailey urged Sydney. The other girls tried to remain calm.

"You sure know a lot of Bible verses," McKenzie said to Elizabeth. "Let me guess. . .I'll bet your dad is a preacher!"

"Close," Elizabeth said, smiling at the insightful redhead. "My grandpa's a preacher. My dad teaches Bible at the local seminary."

"This way!" Sydney called, and the group anxiously followed her. "I see the windmill up ahead!"

Moments later, they approached the now-abandoned golf course.

"Any sign of Oscar the Grouch?" asked Bailey.

The group chuckled, and McKenzie stood on her tiptoes and scanned the area. "I don't see anyone."

"Probably couldn't find a job anywhere else," muttered Sydney. "But look—someone has been digging over there, by the castle!"

The amateur sleuths walked to the fresh pile of dirt.

"It had to be the Grouch! Why would he dig here?" Alex knelt for a closer look.

"I don't know, but we'll have to figure it out another time. We'll be late for our first session," Elizabeth informed them, looking at her watch.

"What can we do with Biscuit?" asked Kate.

"If we hurry, we can take him back to the room. We'll hide him there for right now," Elizabeth told her.

As the group headed out the gate, Alex and McKenzie lagged b›ind.

"I have a feeling there's more to the Grouch than meets the eye," McKenzie told her friend.

The two began to follow the others until Alex spotted a small piece of paper near the pile of dirt.

"Oh my!" she exclaimed as she read it. She held it out to McKenzie.

The torn paper issued a warning: *Dan Ger.*

The girls looked at each other, then took off running, full speed ahead.

Keep Out!

The two girls caught up with their friends in no time.

"Look what we found. By that pile of dirt," Alex panted. She passed around the wrinkled piece of paper.

Then they all spoke at once.

"What does this mean?"

"Who is this for?"

"Do you think this was meant for us?"

"I wonder if the Grouch had anything to do with this."

Sydney paced back and forth, hand to her chin. "Why do you think he was so mad at us? We weren't doing anything. That was our free time. We haven't been told to stay away from the golf course."

Elizabeth jumped in. "Speaking of free time, we may not have any if we're late. We can talk about this later. Let's go! Kate, I'll go with you to take Biscuit back to the cabin, and the rest of you get to class."

The small group of sleuths scattered.

In the cabin, Kate laid Biscuit gently on her bed. He licked her hand, curled into a ball, and promptly went to sleep. "Poor little fellow," she said. "He's had a rough morning."

"Let's just hope he stays asleep while we're gone," said

Elizabeth. She grabbed Kate by the arm and led her out the door. "I'll meet you back here as soon as this first session ends."

The two girls hurried to their classes and scooted into their seats without a moment to spare.

●—●—●

Awhile later, Elizabeth sat in the end chair on the back row, trying to focus on the camp counselor's words. Her mind was crowded with thoughts of puppies and cougars and cryptic warnings.

"My name is Miss Rebecca. For the next two wefis of camp, you will compete with your other five roommates as a team. Each group needs to create a team name, and whoever has the best name will receive points. You will also earn points for cleanliness, punctuality, and attitude. These points will be given at the discretion of the counselors.

"Your team will also compete in various categories in a camp-wide competition. The categories are scripture memory, nature studies, horseback riding, rowing, and a few others we'll tell you about in the next few days. On the last day of camp, the team with the most points wins the title Team Discovery Lake. Each girl on the winning team will receive a blue ribbon and a partial scholarship to next year's camp."

Elizabeth looked around at the other girls. There, on the front row, smiling sweetly at the counselor, was Amberlie.

Now that girl is trouble! Elizabeth had never gotten to know her very well, but she knew enough. All sugar and spice and everything nice around the counselors. But the minute she was away from adults, her sugar and spice turned to vinegar.

Amberlie's hand shot high into the air. "Will there be

daily winners?" she asked.

"Good question, and yes. Each day, the team with the most points earned on the previous day will be first in all meal lines. Teams will receive daily points for attitude and for the cleanest rooms."

This announcement was followed by an enthusiastic buzz from the campers. First at mealtime—now *that* was worth competing for.

Miss Rebecca smiled as she gave the girls time to absorb the information. "Now that we've got that out of the way, let's begin our Bible Explorers class! We'll memorize a lot of scripture in the next two wefis. Let's start with a game. . . ."

Elizabeth settled back in her seat and smiled. She was good at scripture memory. This class was right up her alley.

•—•—•

McKenzie and Sydney stood with the other girls by the stable door, listening to the counselor talk about basic horsemanship. The horses all seemed gentle and trustworthy, unlike some of the stallions back at McKenzie's ranch in White Sulphur Springs.

"During your time here, you will learn basic horse care and riding techniques. These horses are used to young ladies and are calm, so you don't need to be afraid of them. However, they are very large animals, so you need to be gentle with them as well."

Sydney elbowed McKenzie. The auburn-haired girl looked at her new friend and saw her motioning to a large oak tree at the edge of the paddock. In the shade of the tree was the grouchy man from the golf course talking to the older man

Elizabeth had pointed out earlier in the day. From the abrupt gestures of the grouchy man, Sydney guessed he wasn't too happy.

The girls watched and strained to hear the words, but it was no use. The men were too far away, and the counselor's words drowned out any chance of eavesdropping.

They continued to observe the exchange. The older man— Mr. Anzer—put his arm around the Grouch's shoulders, and the Grouch seemed to calm a bit. The two then walked away, continuing their conversation as they moved toward the offices at the east end of the stables.

● — ● — ●

Kate had signed up for the nature studies class right away. In her concrete world of Philadelphia, she didn't get much exposure to the rugged outdoors. The closest thing she had back home was the well-groomed city park or the beautiful college campus where her dad taught. She had been excited to learn about various trees and flowers and wildlife. She had even brought her cell phone so she could take pictures.

But now she could only think of the muddy black-and-white puppy asleep on her bed. *He likes me,* she thought. *I've never had a dog. I wonder if Mom and Dad would let me keep him.*

"That's about it for today, girls. As you're walking around the camp, remember to pay attention to the shapes of the leaves you see. Try to identify the ones we talked about."

Kate jerked to attention. Had she really daydreamed the whole class away? Staring at her blank phone screen, she wondered how the hour could have passed so quickly. She couldn't remember a single thing the counselor had said.

Snapping her phone closed, she remembered Elizabeth's request to meet back at the cabin. *Immediately after class.* Besides, she was eager to check on Biscuit.

Slipping the small phone into her pocket, she ran as fast as she could, nearly crashing into Bailey and Alex as she reached the crossroad that led to their cabin.

"Whoa, Kate! Slow down! At that rate, you'll have a major collision!" Alex laughed.

Kate caught her balance and smiled. "Sorry! I just can't wait to get back to the cabin. Biscuit was asleep when we left him, and I. . ." She was interrupted by a low, mournful howl.

The three girls looked at each other and exclaimed, "Biscuit!"

They ran to cabin 12B in record time. Bursting through the door, they stopped short at the sight before them.

The dirty, round-eyed puppy sat in the center of the room, tail wagging with excitement. A pair of green shorts hung off his back, and he held a dirty sock in his mouth. Undergarments, nightgowns, and T-shirts were scattered from one end of the room to the other.

"Oh, Biscuit. What have you done?" Kate scooped up the puppy and he licked her face. "Hey, stop that!" She laughed and held him out of face range. "I don't mind the kisses, but we've gotta do something about your breath!"

"Uh, girls. . .we'd better clean up this mess. The counselors are coming before lunch to check our rooms!" said Alex.

"But first. . ." Bailey dug through her pockets. "Look what we made for Biscuit!" She pulled out a colorful ribbon-braided rope and attached it around the dog's neck. "Alex and I worked on it in class. Now he has a collar!"

"Perfect!" exclaimed Kate. Alex and Bailey looked pleased.

"What in the. . .world?" The girls turned as Elizabeth stepped into the room. "Oh my." The older girl just stood, taking in every detail of the disastrous room. "Oh my, oh my."

●—●—●

Sydney and McKenzie lingered after class, pretending to admire the horses. "Do you think we should go find out what they're talking about?"

"I think we should at least see if the Grouch has an office over here or something," Sydney urged.

"That older man he was talking to, Mr. Anzer, seemed nice. Elizabeth seemed to really like him. Surely he's not like. . ." McKenzie paused. "No, it looked more like he was trying to calm the Grouch down, didn't it?"

The two girls walked toward the office area, pausing to look at the horses when a counselor passed.

"I want to ride the bay over there," exclaimed McKenzie.

"I think I'll stick with the pony," replied Sydney.

When the coast was clear, the girls continued to the east end of the building, pausing outside an open window. Hearing voices inside, they grew still, straining to hear the conversation.

"I'm telling you, Dan, you can't post a KEEP OUT sign at the golf course. It may be old, but the kids still love it. You can't keep them from playing a few rounds of miniature golf if they want to."

"But William, I'm trying to get my work done. I can't make the repairs if a bunch of little girls are running around everywhere."

This was followed by a long pause.

Finally, Mr. Anzer spoke again. "Just do what you can while the girls are in their classes. I'll see if I can come help you."

"No! That won't be necessary!" Dan spoke up quickly. "I'll just figure out a way to make it work."

The two girls looked at each other, wide-eyed, but didn't move. Suddenly, the man they now knew as Dan burst through the door and nearly barreled over them. He stopped, clearly surprised to see the sleuths, and opened his mouth as if to speak.

McKenzie spoke first. "Pardon us, sir! We didn't mean to get in your way. We were just headed back to our cabin. You have a very nice day, sir! Umm. . .good-bye!"

The two girls dashed toward the cabins.

As soon as they were out of earshot, Sydney spoke up. "Whew. That was close. I wonder if he knows we were listening."

"I don't know. I just can't figure out why he doesn't want anyone at the golf course. I mean, this is a kids' camp," McKenzie responded.

Sydney's voice rose. "Yeah. Of course kids will be running around—that's kind of the point. If it weren't for us, he wouldn't have a job here in the first place!"

"Shhhhh. We don't want the whole camp to know. Something tells me that the Grouch doesn't care much about his job. He doesn't keep the golf course tidy. He must have some other reason why he doesn't want anybody down there," McKenzie told her friend.

"I think you're right. Let's go tell the others what we heard."

The girls jogged back to the cabin, where they found the others making piles of clothing. "What in the world? What are you all doing with my shorts? And my headband? And my. . ." Sydney's bewildered gaze landed on the innocent-looking puppy sitting at Kate's feet. "Biscuit! What did you do?"

The puppy answered her with a bark and a wag of his tail.

●—●—●

The young detectives sat in a circle on the floor examining the wrinkled piece of paper.

Dan Ger.

"Why is it written that way? You know, with a space in between, and the *D* and the *G* capitalized?" asked Bailey.

"I think the way it's written must be a clue of some sort. Maybe the space in the *middle* means *we* are in the middle of danger!" Sydney added.

The girls passed around the small paper, trying to find further clues. Elizabeth held the paper up to the light. "This looks like envelope paper. If you hold it up, it has a pattern, kind of like the business envelopes my parents use."

Alex reached for the paper. "May I see that?" Then, holding it up, she said, "Elizabeth is right! This may be. . . Hey! Maybe Dan is someone's name!"

McKenzie and Sydney began talking at once. "I can't believe we haven't told you yet!"

"We got so caught up in cleaning up Biscuit's mess that we forgot to tell you what happened!"

The other four sat up straight, all ears, listening to the two girls tell what they knew.

"So. . ." Alex stood, still holding the paper. "We know that the Grouch's name is Dan, so maybe this paper belongs to him. Elizabeth, can you find out Dan's last name?"

"Sure. I'll go talk to Mr. Anzer. I've been meaning to visit with him, anyway."

"Great!" Alex continued. "Kate, what else do you have in that bag of yours? Surely you have some kind of gadget to help us get to the bottom of this."

Kate sprang into action, going through her treasures and evaluating each one for its possible mystery-solving potential.

"Here's my robot spy-cam." Kate held up what looked like a remote-control four-wheeler. "We can hide and make this baby go wherever we want. The only problem is, the sound isn't that great. So we can watch what happens, but we might not be able to hear it."

"What about the tiny recorder you brought?" asked Sydney.

"I've tried that. It will work, sort of. But it's hard to get the recorder to play at the same time the video plays. So you end up watching something happen while listening to the thing that happened a minute or two before, and it gets confusing."

Elizabeth laughed. "Sort of like watching a foreign film with the words at the bottom of the screen! I can never keep up with those movies."

Alex seemed a natural fit for the role of lead detective, and the other girls listened to her instructions. "Okay, here's what we'll do. Elizabeth, you and McKenzie go back to the stables. See what more you can find about this Dan fellow. The rest of you come with me. Kate, bring the robot."

"Sounds like a plan," said Elizabeth. "Let's go!"

Kate quickly put Biscuit into her oversize backpack and zipped it, leaving a small air hole.

Just then, Miss Rebecca poked her head around the door. "Hi, girls! I'm Miss Rebecca—oh, hi, Elizabeth! Good to see you! I'm the counselor for cabin 12. My room's at the end of the hall, in case you need anything."

"Thanks!" the girls replied, trying not to look guilty.

Miss Rebecca stood looking at the group. "Umm. . . okay then. Don't forget that now is your Discovery Time. For the next half hour, find a quiet place and study today's Bible lesson."

"Yes, ma'am," said the angelic-looking group. Biscuit whimpered, and Bailey began sneezing to cover the sound while Kate used her foot to gently push the wiggling backpack under her bed. The counselor stepped into the room and looked around with a suspicious gaze.

Discovery Time

Bailey sneezed several more times.

"Bless you," Miss Rebecca said. She lingered a few moments, looking each camper directly in the eye. Then, with one last look around the room, she said, "Remember, I'm right at the end of the hall!" With a smile and a wave, she was gone.

"Whew! That was close!" exclaimed McKenzie as she closed the door.

Once again, Alex took charge. "Okay, you heard her! It's *discovery* time. And we have a lot of discovering to do. . . ."

"Wait! Before we go, let's read our Discovery Scripture. That way we can talk about it while we're walking. Then we'll be doing what we're supposed to be doing," Elizabeth said as she grabbed her Bible. "Today's verse talks about wisdom. Hmm. . .let me find it. . . . Here it is! Proverbs 2:4–5 says, 'If you look for it as for silver and search for it as for hidden treasure, then you will understand the fear of the Lord and find the knowledge of God.' "

"That's perfect!" Alex exclaimed. "We are going on a treasure hunt to find clues, which will give us wisdom and knowledge about what is going on around here!"

The group laughed at Alex's enthusiasm. Elizabeth smiled at the girl as she put her Bible away. "Or something like that. . ." She chuckled. "Just remember, if any camp counselors ask what you're doing, talk about that verse."

"Okay, let's go!" The group split up, with McKenzie and Elizabeth headed toward the stables and the others toward the golf course. Biscuit poked his head out of Kate's backpack and enjoyed the ride.

As they approached the golf course for the second time that day, the girls walked cautiously and stayed in the shadows of the trees lining the road. Sure enough, Dan the Grouch was digging away.

"Why is he digging?" whispered Alex. "It looks like he's trying to find something."

"He should be trying to clean up, not making a bigger mess," added Sydney.

"Here. I brought my robot-cam. Maybe we can get a closer look," said Kate, setting down her backpack. Biscuit, glad to be free, began sniffing around the trees. The other three watched as Kate pulled out the small remote-control gadget. "I have it set to deliver the images to my phone, so we can watch from here. I'll drive, and you all can hold the phone."

"Okay, but be careful. We don't want Grouchy Dan to catch us. I've been yelled at enough for one day. He scares me," added Bailey.

The girls crouched at the edge of the golf course, hidden b›ind an overgrown bush. Kate held the remote, flipped the ON switch, and pressed buttons. Slowly the car moved forward.

The other girls started whispering, giving Kate directions.
"To the left!"

"No, to the right!"

"All we can see is dirt and leaves!"

"Hold it!" Kate whispered with a hint of frustration. "One person at a time, please. Sydney, you direct me."

The other girls remained quiet, and the only sound was Sydney's soft whisper, "Left. Now forward. A little to the right. . ."

Finally she whispered, "Stop! That's perfect. We can see him. What is he looking for? He shovels then stops and digs with his hands then shovels some more. What does he think he's going to find?"

"Maybe he's looking for electrical wires or water pipes or something," said Kate.

"It looks like he's. . .he's. . .he's moving."

"Where did he go?" The girls didn't look up until it was too late. An angry-looking Mr. Dan glowered at them. "I thought I told you girls to stay away from here! Aren't you supposed to be somewhere right now?"

The girls sat frozen, not knowing how to respond. Finally Bailey, remembering the Bible verse, spoke up in her sweetest voice. "We're searching for treasure, sir."

●—●—●

Elizabeth and McKenzie approached the stables, stopping to admire the horses. "That one reminds me of Sahara, my horse back home. I can't wait until I can ride the trails here," McKenzie said.

"I've always wanted horses," Elizabeth responded. "I look

forward to coming here every summer just so I can ride."

"I thought everyone in Texas had horses!" said McKenzie with a laugh.

The girls continued around the stables, heading toward the office area. "This is where Sydney and I overheard the two men talking. The Grouch, or whatever his name is, seemed determined to keep people away from the golf course."

"Well, I don't know anything about him, but I know Mr. Anzer has a heart of gold. He would never let anything bad happen here at Discovery Lake," said Elizabeth.

"Did I hear my name?" Mr. Anzer asked as he walked around the corner. "Oh, hello, Elizabeth! Who is your friend?"

"Hi, Mr. Anzer!" said Elizabeth with a smile. "This is McKenzie. She's one of my roommates, and she has her own horse!"

"Is that right?" asked Mr. Anzer. "Well, feel free to hang out at the stables while you're here. We can always use an extra stable hand!"

McKenzie laughed, and Mr. Anzer motioned the two girls to join him on a long, low bench.

"Mr. Anzer"—Elizabeth looked at the gray-haired gentleman—"McKenzie and I wanted to ask you something. This morning we got in trouble by one of the staff members for being at the golf course. We didn't think we were doing anything wrong. Have the rules changed? Are we not allowed at the golf course anymore?"

Mr. Anzer looked concerned. He leaned back against the rough wooden wall. Finally he answered, "Mr. Gerhardt is the groundskeeper for the golf course. He's a new staff member. I suppose he's just trying to figure out his job. I'm sure he didn't mean any harm."

McKenzie spoke up. "Mr. Gerhardt. . . Is his first name *Dan*, by any chance?"

"Why yes, it is," answered the old man.

Elizabeth spoke up. "Well, he seemed very upset that we were there. To tell you the truth, he was pretty scary."

"Mr. Gerhardt is a good man. He just has a lot on his mind. I'm sure he didn't mean to scare you," said Mr. Anzer.

Elizabeth and McKenzie looked at each other but said nothing. Standing up, Elizabeth told her old friend, "Thanks, Mr. Anzer. It's always great to talk to you. Maybe I'll come by for a ride this afternoon."

"That would be nice, Elizabeth. You girls go have fun. And stay out of trouble!" he said with a twinkle in his eye.

◆—●—●

At the mention of the word *treasure*, Mr. Gerhardt's face went white, his eyes grew wide, and his hands balled into fists. "What do you know about a treasure? Have you found something? If so, you need to tell me about it right now!"

The girls scrambled backward.

"Tell me what you know!" the man yelled.

"Bailey was just talking about our Bible verse for today. God's wisdom is like treasure, and we have to search for it," said Kate. The other girls nodded.

Mr. Dan seemed to calm down a bit. He looked into the distance and ran his fingers through his hair. Taking a deep breath, he spoke slowly. "I didn't mean to yell at you. But you girls need to be careful around here. You shouldn't be down here yet; free time isn't until this afternoon. You need to stay in the main part of the camp until your free time. You never know what might happen."

The girls stared at the man, not knowing what to say. He looked at them a moment longer then turned, walked to his golf cart, and drove away.

The girls collectively let out their deep breaths. "Something is definitely going on down here," said Alex.

"Yeah, that was strange. Why did he get so mad?" asked Sydney.

"He seemed almost normal until. . .until. . ." Bailey stopped. "Until I mentioned treasure!"

The other girls looked at Bailey. "Think about it," she continued. "We were hiding and spying on him. He asked us what we were doing, but he didn't freak out until I mentioned—"

"Treasure!" they exclaimed.

"That's it!" said Sydney. "He must be looking for treasure!"

"But why would he look for treasure in an old miniature golf course at a kids' camp?" asked Kate.

"That's what we're going to find out." Alex looked to be deep in thought. "I remember watching an episode of *Murder, She Wrote*, where—"

"Murder!" Sydney exclaimed. "Who said anything about murder?"

"Don't be silly. Nobody is going to murder anybody. Just listen to what happened in this episode, okay?" Alex continued. The girls leaned in to listen to the animated brunette describe the television mystery. "In the episode 'Dead Man's Gold,' all of the suspects are searching for buried treasure. One of the suspects owes money to a loan shark, and he doesn't want anyone else to find the money before he does!"

"You think Mr. Gerhardt owes money to a loan shark?" asked Sydney.

"I think he's a suspect and doesn't want anyone else to find whatever treasure he's sefiing," said Alex.

— • — • — •

McKenzie and Elizabeth headed toward the golf course to meet the others, each absorbed in her own thoughts. Finally Elizabeth spoke. "Well, at least now we know what the *Dan Ger* paper meant. It was just part of Mr. Gerhardt's name."

"Yeah. But, Elizabeth, I don't care what Mr. Anzer says. That man gives me the creeps!"

"Me, too. Something definitely isn't right. But I also trust Mr. Anzer. I think he'd know if we were in any danger. I guess we should just stay away from Mr. Gerhardt."

"That will be hard, since Bailey's determined to be a golf pro by the time she leaves camp!" McKenzie said. The girls laughed.

Suddenly Biscuit loped toward them with what looked like a large metal stick in his mouth. "Biscuit!" cried Elizabeth. "Where did you come from?" She bent and retrieved a small golf club from his mouth.

"That's funny," said McKenzie. "He wants to play fetch."

Elizabeth picked up the puppy and turned her face away. "Oh Biscuit! You seriously need a bath!" The girls continued on the path to the golf course and met the other four girls coming around the curve.

"Oh good, you found Biscuit!" exclaimed Kate. "We thought he'd gotten away!"

"He was carrying this golf club like he wanted to play! Isn't that funny?" McKenzie held up the club. "I'll just go put this by the fence. I'm sure Mr. Gerhardt will find it."

The four spies looked at each other, and then Sydney said, "Mr. Gerhardt?"

"Yeah, that's the Grouch's name. Dan Gerhardt."

The six sleuths exchanged information and tried to fit the clues together. They didn't notice that Biscuit had gotten ahead of them. They also didn't notice the group of girls headed right toward Biscuit.

Suddenly, their conversation was interrupted by screeches. "*Eeeeewww!* Get off of me, you filthy creature! *Help!* This dog is attacking me! Help!"

The girls ran forward, Kate in the lead, and pulled Biscuit off Amberlie Crewelin. "Sorry about that," Kate told the terrified girl.

Amberlie's fear quickly turned to disdain as she said, "Is that *your* dog? Pets aren't allowed here. I'm going to report you."

Kate dropped Biscuit. "Oh no, he's not mine. I guess he's just a stray. Go away, little dog!" she yelled at Biscuit.

Confused, the poor dog headed toward the woods. Elizabeth spoke up. "We should go report this. Don't worry, Amberlie. We'll take care of everything. I can see you've been through enough. . .trauma."

With a snort, Amberlie gathered her group and turned. "Come on! I'll have to go back and change clothes now. That horrible creature got me all muddy."

As soon as the girls were out of sight, Kate ran toward the woods, her five roommates close b›ind her. "Biscuit!" they called. "Biscuit, come back!" Within moments, the puppy charged back at Kate, bounded into her arms, and gave her his slobbery greeting.

"Oh Biscuit, can you ever forgive me?" asked Kate.

"It looks like he already has," said McKenzie.

Elizabeth looked at her watch. "Come on. We need to give this dog a bath, and if we go now, nobody will be in the showers at the cabin."

●—●—●

Sydney and Bailey peered around the cabin door to see if it was safe to exit. After a group of laughing girls wandered out of sight, they gave the signal. "Take him to the back of the cabin before you put him down," suggested Sydney.

Kate held a wet, clean Biscuit at arm's length, and the other five girls circled her to shield the dog from view. Once out of sight of the main road, Kate let Biscuit go. The dog immediately shook himself, splashing his protectors and causing them to squeal.

The puppy took their squeals as an invitation to play and began running. He ran a few yards then stopped to see if they were chasing him. Satisfied that his playmates were following, he ran more. This continued as the girls tried to catch the damp puppy without drawing attention to themselves.

They finally cornered the dog, dried him, and combed his hair. Then they stood back to admire the handsome dog before them. No one would ever recognize him as the muddy stray they had found that morning.

Biscuit took their looks of approval to mean that they wanted to play some more, and with a bark and a wag of his tail, he was off. The girls kept him cornered, but no one could catch him.

Finally Kate disappeared into the cabin and returned with a handful of cheese crackers. "Here, Biscuit! Here, boy! I don't have a biscuit, but trust me—you'll love these!"

Instantly the dog bounded to her, and she knelt to feed him. "That's a good boy! Now, we have to leave you b›ind while we go to our next classes. If you're good, we'll have more food for you!"

The girls once again hovered close together to hide their new pet from view. They placed him inside the room and closed the door. Almost immediately, the howling started.

"Shhhhhhh! Make him stop!" Alex whispered. "I think I see Miss Rebecca coming up the road!"

Elizabeth opened the door, and the howling stopped. She closed it, and the noise started again. She and Kate slipped inside.

"What are we going to do?" whispered Kate. "We can't leave him here! We'll have the whole camp investigating our cabin!"

"I know," said Elizabeth. "We'll just have to take turns taking him with us. I know you're pretty attached to him, and he fits perfectly in your backpack, so you take him with you now."

"Uh, I don't think that will work," responded Kate.

"Why not?" asked Elizabeth, surprised.

"Because my next class is a cooking class. He will never stay still and quiet if he smells food!"

"Hmm. . .you're right about that. I'm going on a nature walk, so I guess I'll take him with me. I think Bailey is in that class, too. We'll stay at the back of the line. Here, let me borrow your backpack."

Outside, the girls greeted their counselor, chatting to cover their nervousness.

"Hi, Miss Rebecca! How are you?"

"Do you like being a counselor here?"

"We're so glad you're in our cabin. You're the coolest counselor."

The pretty young woman laughed and again eyed the group with gentle suspicion. "What are you girls up to? Don't you need to get to your next classes?"

Then she noticed that they were all water splashed. "What in the world have you been doing? Swimming isn't until this afternoon! And, ew! What is that smell?"

The girls exchanged panicked looks. Would Miss Rebecca figure out their secret?

Moans, Howls, and Growls

The girls stood in silent guilt, wondering how to respond.

Miss Rebecca laughed. "I'll tell you what, girls. I don't even want to know what you've been up to. But I want you all to march right back into your rooms and get some clean clothes on. Come with me."

Sydney began speaking loudly, hoping that Elizabeth and Kate, still inside the room, would hear. "Yes, Miss Rebecca! We'll go inside this very minute to change our clothes! We are coming inside right now!"

The girls stood in front of their door, none of them wanting to open it while Miss Rebecca was with them. The counselor, with an expression of confused amusement, stepped forward and opened the door herself.

As the door groaned open, Kate and Elizabeth stood there innocently, ready to head out the door. "Oh hello, everyone! We were just leaving. See you all later!" Elizabeth called as she and Kate left the room. The counselor just shook her head and continued down the hall. The girls all sighed in relief that she didn't notice what the rest of them saw clearly. The backpack draped over Elizabeth's shoulders was *moving*.

The four girls quickly changed their clothes and hurried

to their next classes.

The next few days passed in a whirlwind of camping activity and Biscuit training. Before long, the young dog knew how to sit, stay, fetch, and roll over. The girls learned that as long as he wasn't left alone, he wouldn't howl. But keeping him with someone at all times was becoming more and more difficult.

"I have an idea," said Bailey one evening as the girls prepared for bed. "I've visited the golf course several times a day to practice, and I haven't seen Mr. Gerhardt there since that first day. But every time I go, I see new places where someone has been digging. He must dig at night. . . . Anyway, why don't we leave Biscuit at the golf course during the day? It's far enough away from the camp that if he howls, no one will think anything of it."

"That's a great idea, Bailey!" said Elizabeth, combing out her blond tresses. "That would sure make things easier. I don't know about the rest of you, but I've had some pretty close calls with the little guy."

"Me, too!" said the other five girls.

"Hmm. . ." Alex fluffed her pillow and crawled under her covers. "I wonder why the Grouch has disappeared during the day. And why in the world would he dig at night?"

"I don't know and I don't care," said Bailey. "I kind of like having the golf course to myself. I stay away from him, he stays away from me, and everything's good."

The girls turned the light out and stopped talking, until Bailey broke the silence. "But then, there are still those noises."

Sydney sat up, flipped on the lamp by her bed, and asked, "Noises?"

Bailey covered her eyes with the pillow and said, "Turn that thing off!"

"Bailey, what noises?" McKenzie asked.

Bailey rubbed her eyes. "Well, there's that weird laughing thing that happened on the first day. And sometimes I hear moans and howls and a deep, low growly thing."

The other girls were wide-awake. "Bailey, what are you talking about? Why on earth would you keep going down there?" Elizabeth asked her.

"Well, the first couple of times it happened, it scared me. Good thing I had my inhaler with me! But I finally figured out that it must just be the golf course. Those noises are wired up som›ow—probably to make the course more interesting. They don't even bother me anymore."

Alex dangled her feet from her bunk and asked, "Do you hear the noises every time?"

"No," Bailey answered. "A couple of times I've been there and nothing has happened. But I think the digging must have tripped a wire or something."

"Why do you say that?" asked Kate.

"Because every time I go near a hole, I hear one of those freaky noises. As long as I stay clear of the holes, everything stays quiet."

The girls thought about that for a moment, and then Alex piped up. "I remember an episode of *Scooby-Doo* where—"

The other five moaned, and Kate threw her pillow at the pretty brunette. "Not again, Alex! You and your Hollywood mystery solving. . ."

"Seriously, you guys! Listen to me! In one episode. . .

actually, in several episodes, there were these spooky noises! They almost always turn out to be someone hiding and making the noises go off when the characters are close to solving the mystery! The noises are a fear tactic. Whoever is causing them doesn't want Bailey near those holes!"

The room grew silent as each girl digested Alex's information. Once again, Bailey broke the silence. "Well, that's just great. I was getting used to the noises. Now I'm going to have to use my inhaler again."

"You could just stay away from the golf course," Elizabeth told her.

"Are you kidding? I have to practice my strokes! You'll be glad, too, when I'm rich and famous. You'll be able to say, 'I knew her when. . .' "

The girls laughed, and Sydney turned off the lamp. "We'd better get some sleep," she said. "We'll talk about this more in the morning."

●—●—●

Early the next morning, before the trumpet wake-up call, Alex sat up in bed. "I have a great idea!" she called to her roommates.

The girls groaned and moaned, but Alex didn't let that stop her. She hopped out of bed and continued chattering. "We can attach Kate's tiny recorder to Biscuit's collar, and we'll leave him at the golf course. Then we can hear the noises Bailey told us about. If they go on and off all day, we'll know they're just random. But if they only sound when people are there, we'll know someone is making them go off."

"Yes, but what if it's Bailey making them go off? What if she's just accidentally stepping on something?" asked Sydney.

"We'll figure that out later. First let's just find out if they happen all the time or just when people are around," Alex told her.

"Uh, guys, you're forgetting one thing." Everyone looked at Kate, who was still in bed. Her muffled voice came from under the covers. "If we leave Biscuit alone at the golf course, he will howl all day. That's all we will hear."

Alex sighed. "You're right. I didn't think about that."

The conversation was interrupted by the wretched trumpet music, and the rest of the girls began crawling from their beds. When the song ended, Elizabeth spoke. "We could try it anyway. Maybe we'll hear something in the background, even over Biscuit's howling. It can't hurt to try."

Hearing his name, the puppy poked his head from beneath the covers at Kate's feet and barked.

"Come on, boy. I'll take you outside." Elizabeth scooped up the small dog and tucked him into the folds of her robe. She carried him outside, b›ind the small cabin, and waited for him to do his business. Biscuit had just disappeared b›ind some trees when she was startled by a voice b›ind her.

"Elizabeth, what are you doing out here?" Mr. Anzer called from the road. He was making his morning golf-cart drive through the camp.

"Oh! Mr. Anzer, you startled me! I was, uh. . . I was just out enjoying the sunrise!" Elizabeth smiled at her old friend.

Mr. Anzer gave her a puzzled look. "Elizabeth, how many years have you come to this camp?"

"This is my third year, sir."

"Then you should know that the sun rises in the east.

You are facing west."

Elizabeth giggled nervously. "Oh, I guess that's why I missed it. I never was very good with directions."

Mr. Anzer shook his head, waved good-bye, and drove away. The girl breathed a sigh of relief and scooped up the puppy, who was now at her feet. "Biscuit, you are a lot of trouble, you know that?" she scolded the dog then kissed him on his cold, wet nose. "But I suppose you're worth it."

•—•—•

The girls hurried to the old golf course before breakfast. When they arrived there, Kate knelt to check Biscuit's collar. "The recorder is attached securely, and. . .there. I turned it on. So now we'll just wait and see what happens." She gave the little dog one last hug, placed him inside the gate, and closed the latch.

Sydney and Alex jogged around the course to make sure no other gates were open. When they were convinced that all was secure, they called good-bye to the little dog, who had retrieved a golf club and sat expectantly wagging his tail. When the girls turned to walk away, his tail sank. He dropped the golf club, gazed after them with sad eyes, and began howling.

"Just keep walking," said Elizabeth as Kate and Bailey paused. "Going back will just make it harder."

"This is breaking my heart," said McKenzie, trying not to turn around. Som›ow they ignored the dog's soulful cries and kept walking to the dining hall.

As the six roommates stepped into line, they were rudely pushed aside by Amberlie and her crew. "Pardon me, excuse me, step aside, please," said Amberlie in a commanding voice.

"Make way for the Princess Pack. We won the clean cabin award yesterday, so we go first. Move out of the way."

Elizabeth stifled a laugh; Bailey let out an exasperated moan; and Sydney tried to keep from rolling her eyes. "Oh my, my," said Sydney. "The *Princess Pack*? We cannot, and I repeat, *cannot* let Amberlie win this competition. What are those counselors thinking, awarding her more points than the rest of us?"

"Don't worry, we can catch up," Elizabeth told her friends. "So far, the only real points awarded are for clean cabins. Let's just make sure ours is really clean today. But first we need to come up with a team name."

"I've been thinking about that," said Bailey. "I think it should have something to do with the fact that we're at camp."

"Let's make it a name to reveal that we are members of an elite group," said Alex.

"How about the Discovery Lake Discoverers?" suggested McKenzie. "No, it's too much of a tongue twister."

"I think we should keep it simple," said Elizabeth. "Something easy for everyone to remember."

"So. . .we want to have a camp club or something like that," said Kate.

"I've got it!" said Bailey. "We can be the Camp Club Girls!"

"I like it! It's simple and to the point," said Sydney.

"Very well, then. We are the Camp Club Girls!" said Elizabeth, and the group let out a cheer.

●—●—●

After breakfast, the Camp Club Girls hurried back to their cabin and cleaned it to a high shine. "I love Biscuit, but he sure is messy! It's a lot easier to clean without him dragging everybody's socks out!" said McKenzie.

"Tell me about it! He thinks my panda is an intruder! Every time I take it off my bed to make it up, he attacks it!" said Bailey.

"We need to decide who will compete in which camp event," Elizabeth told them. "McKenzie is the natural choice for horseback riding. We'll also need a team for the canoe races and someone to compete in the nature studies quiz. And, of course, the talent competition."

The girls talked at once, discussing who wanted to do what.

"Kate, why don't you do the nature studies quiz, and I'll do the scripture memory competition," Elizabeth suggested as she helped Bailey straighten the covers on her bed.

"I think this competition is in the bag!" exclaimed Bailey, heaving her giant panda back onto her bed.

"I do think we have a good chance, but it will be tough. Amberlie seems pretty competitive. She really wants to win," McKenzie told her friends.

"She can want it all she wants," said Sydney, "but we want it more. And we're gonna win!"

●—●—●

Kate left her nature studies class, pressing past campers returning to their cabins. When she was halfway to the golf course, Elizabeth caught up with her.

"I'll bet I know where you're headed," said the fourteen-year-old.

Kate sighed. "I feel guilty about leaving Biscuit alone. But I know it's best this way. I've just never had a pet before. I wish

I could talk Mom and Dad into letting me keep Biscuit."

Elizabeth smiled. "'Take delight in the Lord, and he will give you the desires of your heart,' Psalm 37:4. That's today's Discovery verse. I guess you could say that a dog is one of the desires of your heart."

"Yes, it is. I guess I'll have to think more about that verse. Maybe there is hope, after all," Kate responded. "Come on, let's go. I miss Biscuit!"

They jogged the rest of the way to the golf course. As they approached, they heard the low, mournful howls that told them two things: Biscuit was safe, and Biscuit was very, very sad.

The little dog lunged at Kate, nearly knocking her to the ground as soon as she slipped inside the gate. "Biscuit!" she exclaimed. "I've missed you, too, boy! I'm sad when we're apart!"

The dog attacked her with slobbery kisses and muddy paws.

"Hey! Stop that!" Kate laughed at the dog's enthusiasm.

Elizabeth smiled at the girl and dog who were so in love with each other. "Boy, that bath didn't last very long," she said. "Now be still, Biscuit, and let us listen to your collar."

●—●—●

Alex and Bailey returned from their crafts class, each holding a small wooden treasure box. Bailey's sparkled with glitter and plastic jewels, while Alex's was painted with bold stripes. Arriving at their room, they stopped. They stared. Then the girls jumped up and down, cheering.

A cardboard trophy with the glittered words CLEAN DORM WINNER—25 POINTS hung on their door.

"We won!" The two girls squealed.

59

That is how Kate and Elizabeth found their two friends moments later. They had run all the way from the golf course, and now they were panting. "Girls, listen. . ."

Kate stopped and fell onto her bed, trying to catch her breath. Holding up the small recorder, she said, "Listen."

They were interrupted by Sydney and McKenzie, who had seen the trophy on their way in the door.

"Hey, cool! We won! Now, unless Amberlie can rack up some serious character points, we'll be first in line all day tomorrow," said McKenzie with a grin.

"I can't wait to see Amberlie's face when we pass her," Sydney said.

"Well, don't act too smug. The Princess Pack is still way ahead of us in overall points. Remember, they've won three days in a row! We still have some serious catching up to do," said Elizabeth.

Kate, now recuperated from her run, waved her arms. "Guys," she called out. "I think this is more important than standing first in line. Listen to what was on Biscuit's recorder!"

The girls gathered around Kate's bed and leaned in to hear the tiny device.

"Sounds like howling, just like you said," McKenzie told her.

"Shhhh! Just listen."

The girls strained to hear something, anything, over Biscuit's desperate howling. Then, after about thirty seconds, the howling stopped.

Digging for Treasure

The girls looked at each other and continued listening. In the background, they heard what sounded like the low rumble of a truck's engine. Then the engine died. They heard a door slam and heavy footsteps approach.

The footsteps ended with what sounded like a cell phone ringing then a man's voice. "Hello? Oh hi, Dad. Yeah, I've been digging. No, I haven't found anything. No, no sign of any treasure. But I'm not giving up. Don't worry, I'll find it. I'll call you as soon as I know something."

The talking ended, and then the footsteps started again. Only this time, they seemed to be going away from the recorder. A car door slammed, an engine revved, and then it seemed the truck drove away. When the noise from the vehicle faded, Biscuit started howling again.

The girls sat in silence.

Finally Alex spoke up. "Well, girls, the plot thickens."

"I'll say," said Bailey. "I guess that explains all the holes."

"So, Mr. Gerhardt *is* digging for treasure. . . ." McKenzie looked thoughtful. "I wonder what his dad has to do with all of this."

"Yeah," said Sydney. "And if his dad is in on it, does he come here and help his son?"

Elizabeth just sat quietly, soaking it all in. Finally she spoke up. "Well, we have a full-blown mystery on our hands. And it's up to us to get to the bottom of it. But for now, let's only go to the golf course in groups of two or more. No more going down there alone, okay Bales?"

"No problem! I almost needed my inhaler just listening to the recording!"

●—●—●

Elizabeth dangled her feet over the side of the dock and watched the ripples from the rock she had just thrown. Her Bible was open on the dock beside her, and her eyes focused on the verse she had read three or four times. She read it out loud, as she often did when trying to memorize something:

"Matthew 6:19–20. 'Do not store up for yourselves treasures on earth, where moths and vermin destroy, and where thieves break in and steal. But store up for yourselves treasures in heaven, where moths and vermin do not destroy, and where thieves do not break in and steal.' "

Lord, there sure is a lot of talk about treasure here at camp this year. I want to have the right kind of treasure—the kind that will make You happy. But what about the mystery at the golf course? Is a treasure really buried there or somewhere around the camp?

When she heard the soft murmur of a golf cart drawing near, she knew it was Mr. Anzer. He faithfully made the rounds in that golf cart, watching over the camp, making sure everything was running smoothly. She smiled at the man who reminded her so much of her grandpa.

"Hello, Elizabeth. I had a feeling I'd find you here in your old spot. Don't let me disturb you. I'm just going to check the pedals on these paddleboats. They've been sticking. I'll bet they just need some oil." The old man pulled an oil can from the toolbox in the back of the cart.

"Oh, you're not disturbing me. I was just thinking about this morning's verse. I've noticed all of our verses so far have talked about treasure, and I think it's funny."

"Funny?" Mr. Anzer's eyebrows lifted.

"Oh, not funny, ha-ha. The other kind of funny."

The old man began examining the pedals of a boat banked along the edge of the lake. "Tell me why it's funny," he said.

Elizabeth leaned back and looked at the sunlight glistening through the branches. She didn't want to reveal too much of the mystery, but she did want some answers. Something told her that Mr. Anzer was a good source of information.

"Oh, my roommates and I have just been playing sort of a. . .a mystery game. We're pretending a treasure is buried somewhere in the camp. It's silly, really. But we're having fun."

The old man stood and looked at her. "Well that is funny. Just where do you think this treasure may be hidden?"

Elizabeth laughed nervously. "Oh, it could be anywhere— the stables, the nature trail. . .the golf course. . ."

Mr. Anzer turned his attention back to the pedals. "I've been working here for a long time, and I've never run across any buried treasure. But that doesn't mean it's not here!" The man chuckled. "If anybody can find treasure in this old camp, I'm sure it will be you."

Elizabeth smiled. "How long have you worked here, Mr. Anzer?"

"Oh, longer than you've been alive. Years ago, I was the manager of camp operations. All three of my children attended this camp every summer, and my wife used to oversee the cafeteria. She died a few years back, and my kids are all grown and married. I just can't bring myself to leave this old place. . . ." He paused and smiled. "So now I just putter around and fix things."

"It sounds like a fun job to me," Elizabeth told him, and he smiled at her. "I have a question, though. This is such a great camp, and everything is kept in top shape—except for the golf course. It seems kind of run-down, and that doesn't fit in with the rest of the camp. Why?"

Mr. Anzer moved to the next paddleboat and knelt to check the pedals. "The golf course was a main attraction when the camp was new. But years ago, it turned out that a gang of thieves had their hideout on the old Wilson farm—just on the other side of the golf course. When they were discovered, we increased the security here at the camp. For a couple of years, we didn't let any campers go down that way—the golf course was off-limits. Then, even when we reopened it, most of the campers were a little spooked by the idea that thieves might have hidden there. It just never became a popular attraction again. And with a tight budget, maintaining the golf course never seems to become a priority."

"Wow, that is kind of scary. Any chance the gang is still there?" Elizabeth asked.

"No. This happened a long time ago. I don't know what happened to the thieves, but I'm sure they wouldn't come back to the same place where they got caught," he told her.

Elizabeth picked up her Bible and stood. "I need to do something before my next class, Mr. Anzer. It's been really nice talking to you."

The old man waved good-bye and continued on to the next paddleboat. "See ya later," he called.

Elizabeth hurried toward the cabins. *Wait till the others hear about this!* she thought. *This is more complicated than we thought.*

A few minutes later, she flung open the door to find her roommates getting ready to leave for their next classes. "You will never believe what I just found out!" Elizabeth announced.

●—■—●

That afternoon, the girls used their free time to explore the golf course. They greeted a very excited, muddy Biscuit, and slipped through a small opening in the far side of the fence.

"The old farmhouse has to be this way," said Sydney. The six young detectives, with their four-legged sidkick, tromped through thick trees and brush until they arrived at a clearing. There, just beyond a trickling creek, was an old farmhouse.

"This is it!" said Alex. "This is just like in *Dragnet!* I watch those reruns all the time with my grandpa. Once they were looking for—"

"Shhhh!" whispered the other girls in unison.

"We don't know what we'll find," said Elizabeth in a hushed voice. "Whatever happens, let's stay together."

The girls nodded, gingerly walked through the shallow creek, and approached the old house that was falling apart. The only sounds were the gentle rustle of trees swaying in the breeze and Biscuit's steady panting.

They noiselessly drew closer to the old farmhouse until they were close enough to pefi through a broken window. Old newspapers and discarded fast-food containers littered the floor, and tattered furniture was flipped this way and that in careless disarray.

Biscuit began to growl, and the girls froze. The dog's growl grew louder, until finally he dashed toward the trees. Standing on his hind legs, he looked ready to scale the tree.

A squirrel chattered angrily from its branches. The girls sighed with relief and continued exploring.

Alex motioned for the group to follow her. "This way," she whispered, and the band of detectives stepped carefully around the corner of the house, onto the steps of the wide porch, and through the door, which hung only partially on its hinges.

"Wow, this looks like something out of a scary movie," said Bailey.

The girls spread out through the small downstairs area, turning chairs upright and peering in closets.

"Whoa! Bad move!" they heard Sydney call from the kitchen. She had opened the refrigerator, and the foul stench spread through the rest of the house in moments.

"Ugh! Gross!" The other girls covered their noses. Kate and McKenzie pulled their T-shirts up over their faces, leaving only their eyes visible.

Elizabeth rushed to open a window, but she found it painted shut. Then, spying a back door in a corner of the kitchen, she opened it wide. "At least there's a breeze. Maybe it will blow the smell away." Sure enough, the odor began to die down.

Alex stood at the foot of the stairs, looking into the shadowy hallway above. "Hey, let's go upstairs and look around."

The girls looked at each another, waiting for someone else to go first.

"Uh, you go on ahead, Alex," said Sydney.

"Awww, come on, guys. You're not scared, are you?" she prodded them.

"I'm not scared. Are you scared?" Sydney retorted.

"No, I'm not scared," Alex shot back. She remained glued to her spot.

Finally Kate led the way. "Okay, Alex. Come with me." Then she said, "If we're not back in ten minutes, run for your lives!"

The other girls laughed nervously then followed Alex and Kate up the stairs. "We might as well stick together," said Elizabeth, bringing up the rear. Biscuit bounded up the stairs ahead of them and rushed into a dark room.

The girls followed their beloved mascot into a dusty bedroom. McKenzie pulled back the curtains and lifted the shades, and sunlight flooded into the room. Biscuit sniffed here and there and then dove under the bed. A moment later, he reappeared with an old sock in his mouth.

"What is it with you and socks, boy?" asked Kate, kneeling to scratch him b›ind the ears. The girls opened drawers and closets, finding a moth-eaten coat, a muddy pair of brown work boots, and more old newspapers. The small connected bathroom revealed a rusty drain, a dried-up cake of soap, and a roll of yellowed toilet paper.

Together, the girls moved to the next bedroom, and this time Elizabeth opened the curtains. As the other girls snooped around, Elizabeth stood at the window. She noticed a ladder propped up against one side of the window. Then her gaze went to the driveway leading to the farmhouse. The mud showed fresh tire tracks, but she saw no v›icles. Funny, she hadn't noticed those earlier. The house certainly looked like no one had been inside for a very long time, so why the tire tracks?

She turned from the window, not wanting to frighten the younger girls. "I think we should head back," she told the others. *I'll tell them about the tire tracks after we're safely back at camp,* she thought.

"Hey, look at this!" said Kate, pulling a faded spiral notebook from a drawer in the bedside table. "It looks like an old journal of some sort. But it must have gotten wet, because most of the words are washed out."

The girls crowded around, looking at the cryptic notebook. Biscuit, still carrying the old sock, hopped onto the bed beside Kate and made himself comfortable.

Bang! The girls jumped at the noise from downstairs. Their eyes filled with panic as they heard heavy footsteps. Bailey opened her mouth to scream, but McKenzie clasped her hand over Bailey's mouth. The girls remained frozen as the footsteps got louder. Quietly Elizabeth tiptoed to the door, shut it softly, and turned the lock. Then she looked at the girls, held a shushing finger over her lips, and tiptoed to the window.

No one moved except Elizabeth, who skillfully opened the window. In a soft whisper, Elizabeth said, "We need to stay calm. Here's a ladder, but we have to be extra quiet, or whoever is downstairs will catch us. Sydney, you go first and help the others down. I'll stay here and go last."

Sydney's eyes widened, but she tiptoed to the window, slipped over the ledge, and scurried down the ladder. Bailey went next, then Kate, holding the notebook. After that, McKenzie descended with Biscuit. Alex grabbed an old newspaper before heading down. Finally, with one last look around, Elizabeth started out the window.

Just after Elizabeth's feet hit the ground, the ladder tipped. Before the girls could catch it—*crash!*—it landed on the ground.

"Hey!" a man's voice yelled.

"Run!" shouted Elizabeth. The girls took off. Through the crefi they splashed, as heavy footsteps followed.

Just when it seemed they would escape, Bailey tripped over a large root. The others stopped to help her, but Elizabeth shouted, "Go, go, go!" She helped Bailey to her feet.

The girl gasped for air. Elizabeth felt in her friend's pockets until she located the inhaler. She looked around but saw no one. She stood with Bailey, holding the inhaler in place and coaxing her friend to breathe slowly.

Finally Bailey pushed the inhaler away. "I'm okay," she said. "Come on, let's get out of here."

The girls jogged after the others. As they reached the fence line for the golf course, Elizabeth stepped into the shadows of a large tree, turned, and looked.

Missing Jewels!

Elizabeth caught up with the other girls. They lingered by the golf course gate, making sure Bailey was okay, all talking at once and trying to make sense of what had just happened.

Biscuit stood patiently with a golf club in his mouth until Kate finally threw it. He immediately retrieved the club and begged her with soulful eyes to throw it again. The other girls chattered on with frightened, excited exclamations.

"Did you get a look at him?"

"No, but he sounded big!"

"How do you know it was a man?"

"Well, the footsteps sounded big. I don't think a woman would walk that loudly."

"Well, I think it was the Grouch," said Bailey.

Finally Elizabeth spoke. "I saw him."

Everyone looked at her. "Bailey is right. It was Mr. Gerhardt."

"I knew that man was trouble! He is definitely up to no good," exclaimed Alex.

"I don't know," Elizabeth mused. "He walked back toward the farmhouse, but he didn't look angry or scary. His shoulders were down, and he just looked. . .I don't know. I thought he looked sad."

"Well, I think you have too much compassion. He nearly scared us to death, remember?" Sydney reminded her.

"Yes, but perhaps he didn't mean to scare us. He couldn't have known we were there. Maybe we scared him!" Elizabeth countered.

The other girls stared at Elizabeth as if she'd lost her mind. Finally McKenzie spoke. "Let's get back to the cabin. I need some time to relax. I think I'll change into my swimsuit and head down to the pool."

"Now that sounds like a great idea!" Alex agreed. The group said good-bye to their puppy and headed back toward the main camp.

That evening, Sydney and Alex wandered to the front of the dinner line, where Elizabeth was holding their place. They smiled in response to congratulations and good-natured "Just wait until tomorrow! We'll win!" from other campers.

They were almost to the front when Amberlie blocked their path. "Enjoy your short-lived victory, girls," she sneered. "Tomorrow, you all are toast!"

The two girls scooted around their ill-tempered rival and greeted Elizabeth at the front of the line.

"What was that about?" Elizabeth asked.

"Oh, nothing. Just Amberlie being herself," said Sydney.

When the girls had their food and sat down, talk quickly turned to business. "We have to get to the bottom of this mystery," said Alex. "Elizabeth, I know you think Mr. Gerhardt is some poor, sweet man, but I think he's looking for something. I think he's one of the thieves!"

"I didn't say he is poor or sweet! I just think there is more to him than meets the eye," said Elizabeth.

"I agree with Elizabeth," McKenzie announced. "And I agree with Alex. Mr. Gerhardt definitely has something to do with this mystery, but we need to find out more facts before we accuse him of anything."

The conversation halted as a shadow fell over the table. The girls looked up to find—of all people—Mr. Gerhardt. He stood at the end of their table, looking at Bailey, not saying a word.

They all remained still, waiting for him to say something. Bailey squirmed.

Finally the man spoke. "Are you enjoying camp?" he asked. They nodded.

"That's nice," he said. Then he turned and walked away. No one spoke for a moment.

"What in the world was that about?" Sydney asked.

"That man gives me the creeps," said Bailey.

"My point exactly," said Alex, picking up where the conversation left off. "Let's hurry and go back to the room. Kate, can you do an Internet search?"

Kate, mouth full, looked longingly at her heaping plate. She swallowed then answered. "I'll do anything you ask. Just don't rush me!"

Later that evening, Elizabeth leaned over Kate's shoulder, watching her type various phrases into the search engine. "Try 'thieves near Camp Discovery Lake,' " she suggested.

Kate typed in the phrase. The words "Sorry, but there are no results for that term" appeared on the screen.

Kate breathed a frustrated sigh. "The problem is that all of this took place before everyone had access to the Internet. So, unless someone has written about it on the Web, we won't find anything."

Bailey and McKenzie lay on the floor, flipping through the water-stained notebook Kate had found. "This is useless, too. The ink is too faded to read," complained McKenzie.

Alex and Sydney had divided the old newspaper, and each scanned through the stories. "This newspaper is over twenty years old. It's crumbling in my hands," said Sydney.

"Surely we'll find some kind of clue here. Let's keep looking," Alex encouraged the group. She gently turned the pages, reading headlines.

"Wait, I think I found something!" exclaimed Sydney. "Look! It's only one paragraph, but it says that a jewel thief has been convicted. And, oh my goodness. You are not gonna believe this. . . ." Sydney continued to stare at the page.

"What? Tell us!" the girls urged her on.

"The name of the man who was convicted. . ." Sydney looked at her roommates.

"Come on, spill it!" Alex nearly shouted.

"William Gerhardt!"

"I knew it, I knew it, I knew it!" exclaimed Bailey. "I knew that the Grouch was no good!"

"There's more," continued Sydney. "It says the jewels were never found."

"Maybe the thief was Gerhardt's father!" said Alex. "And now Dan is trying to recover the jewels!"

Kate began typing on her computer again.

"Jackpot!" she cried, and the girls gathered around her. "The search for 'William Gerhardt, jewel thief,' turned up six, seven, eight different articles! Looks like we may solve the mystery, after all!"

"And look what I just found," said McKenzie. "It's hard to read, but it looks to me like an address. And right above, it says, 'Manchester Jewels.' Is that the name of the jewelry store that was robbed?"

Kate clicked on an article and lifted her arms in victory. "Mystery solved. It says right here—William Gerhardt was convicted of grand theft for robbing Manchester Jewels, a large jewelry store in Springfield. That's about an hour from here."

They all chattered at once, celebrating this new information. Then Kate lifted her hand. "Not so fast. It says here that the jewels were never found. He was convicted by a jury with a seven-to-five vote. Nearly half of the jurors didn't think he was guilty."

"Of course he was guilty. Why else would his son be digging for the jewels? He must know they were hidden somewhere at the golf course," said Sydney.

The girls sat in puzzled silence. Finally, Alex spoke. "Kate, you come with me. We need to go get Biscuit. And we have a little more discovering to do."

"I'll come, too," said Elizabeth.

"Not me," said Bailey. "I'll save my trips to the golf course for the broad daylight!"

Sydney and McKenzie, tired from a long day, decided to stay with Bailey.

• — • — •

The three girls approached the golf course, using Kate's cell phone as a flashlight.

"Shhhh! Listen," Kate whispered just before they rounded the curve leading to the gate.

"What is it?" asked Alex.

Kate motioned for them to scoot into the woods b›ind a thick crop of trees. "Biscuit is either gone or he's not alone. He's not howling."

"You're right," whispered Elizabeth.

"Well, we can't just stand here. I'll tell you what. . .I'll go on around through the gate, and you two stay here in case something happens," suggested Alex.

"No, I don't like that idea. We need to stay together," said Elizabeth.

"Shhhh! What's that?" Kate interrupted.

The girls quieted, straining to pinpoint the sound. "It sounds like digging," said Elizabeth. "Let's sneak to the fence and see what we find. Kate, snap your cell phone shut, or whoever that is will see us for sure."

Kate closed the phone, and the only light left was the soft moonlight. Slowly the girls crept through the brush until they arrived at the fence line. A twig snapped beneath Elizabeth's feet, and the girls froze. Then a soft whimpering moved toward them. "Biscuit!" whispered Kate, and the little dog lunged at her face, kissing her with wet, sloppy kisses. She stifled a giggle, and the other two girls shushed her.

"Be quiet! I think I see someone," Alex whispered. Sure enough, the girls could just make out the figure of a man. The digging had stopped, and the man stood still, looking their way.

"Who's there?" he called.

The girls crouched in the shadows, holding their breath and praying Biscuit didn't make any sudden moves. The dog wiggled in Kate's arms, but his preoccupation with kissing her kept him from making much noise.

"Hello?" the figure called again. Suddenly a bright flashlight snapped on. The girls remained still as statues, praying the man wouldn't see them. Slowly the beam passed through the woods to their left, traveled in front of them, and then continued to the right.

Finally, after many long moments, the light was snapped off, and eventually the digging resumed. Still, the girls remained, partly because they were too frightened to move, and partly because they wanted a better look at the man's face. They thought they knew who it was. They just wanted to be sure.

A cloud passed in front of the moon, leaving them in complete darkness. Then the cloud moved away and rays of moonbeams fell directly on the man's face.

Mr. Gerhardt was digging.

Noiselessly the girls tiptoed back through the brush to the road. As soon as they were out of sight of the golf course, Kate snapped her cell phone back on, casting a soft blue glow around their path. They remained silent all the way back to the cabin.

An hour later, the girls were still awake, talking about the mystery.

"Well, we know Mr. Gerhardt is guilty. We just have to

prove it," said Sydney.

"I'm not sure I agree," said Elizabeth. "Sure, he's looking for the jewels. Sure, he has some kind of interest in this case. But I keep thinking about that Internet article Kate found. Surely there must have been some reason why the jury was so divided."

"I'll research more tomorrow," said Kate. "But I'm tired of thinking about it. Biscuit and I want to go to sleep." She pulled the covers over her head then started giggling. "Biscuit, stop it! Biscuit, quit licking my toes! Stop!"

Before long, the whole group was laughing at Kate and the small dog.

"Well, I do have one more thing I want to talk about before we go to sleep," said Bailey. "Who wants to be in the talent show?"

The giggles turned to groans, and Bailey sat up. "Come on, you guys. We need those points!"

"I think you should do it, Bales. You have Hollywood written all over you," said Alex.

Bailey's face lit up with a smile. "Well, okay, if you insist! I was in the spring talent show back home in Peoria, and I can do my singing and dancing act. I did happen to bring the music and props with me in case they had talent shows here. But I need someone to play the piano for me," she said.

No response.

"I need someone to play the piano for me," she repeated.

Silence.

"Elizabeth, don't you play the piano?" Bailey continued.

Elizabeth leaned up on her elbows. "I don't like to play

in front of people."

"Awww, come on, Beth! Pleeeeeeeaaase? Pretty please with a cherry on top? For me?" Bailey begged.

More silence.

Finally Elizabeth sighed. "Okay."

"Hooray! Oh thank you, thank you, thank you! You're the greatest! I know we'll win. We have to start practicing tomorrow. Isn't there a piano in the dining hall? I wonder if they'll let us use that. How about during our free time? Or maybe sooner. Maybe we should wake up early and go practice. I have this great tap dance I do, and the song is so fun. It goes like—"

"Go to sleep, Bailey!" chimed five voices in unison.

Early the next morning, Bailey and Elizabeth walked to the dining hall. The sun was barely peßing over the trees, and Bailey was humming and singing her song so Elizabeth could learn it.

"It goes like this, Beth:

I love being beautiful,
Being beautiful is grand,
With my hair just so, and my eyes all aglow,
A new dress, and my nail-polished hands!

"I have some pink spongy rollers for my hair and some of my mom's face cream! Won't that be hilarious? I'll be out there, my face all creamed up, rollers in my hair, tap-dancing and singing about being beautiful!" Bailey's excitement grew as they entered the dining hall.

Elizabeth laughed at Bailey's enthusiasm. "You will be the star of the show," she told her. "Now, where is the music?"

Bailey pulled the sheet music out of her backpack and handed it to Elizabeth.

Sitting down at the old piano stationed to one side of the stage, Elizabeth began flipping through the pages, becoming familiar with the chords and the key changes. "This music has several key changes. I'm not sure I can play it like it's written; I'd need to practice this for wefis. But the chords are listed, so in some parts I'll just play those. I'll jazz it up here and there. I think it will be fine."

Bailey smiled. "I know you can do it!" she encouraged.

Elizabeth began playing with Bailey singing along. After a few rough starts, she finally sang through the piece.

"Okay, now let's try it with me on stage. We'll go all the way through without stopping," Bailey instructed. Elizabeth began to play, and Bailey began singing and dancing her heart out. She performed to the empty room as if it were an audience of hundreds. At the close, she held out her last note, arms high in the air, and then finished with a grand curtsy.

Both girls were surprised when applause came from a corner of the room. Amberlie stepped out of the shadows.

"Very nice, for an amateur. Your little act will add some good variety to the show. But you certainly won't win the grand prize. Your talent doesn't even come close to mine. Sorry to break it to you, kiddo, but you don't have a chance."

Bailey's smile turned into a frown as she responded, "How dare you! You are so. . ."

"Amberlie! We didn't know anyone was here. So great to see you. Did you want to practice? Here, we were just finishing. Come on, Bales. Let's go." Elizabeth gathered the music, grabbed Bailey by the arm, and walked past Amberlie.

When they were outside, Bailey let loose. "How could you just let her talk to us like that? She is so mean! I'd like to give her a piece of my mind!"

"Bailey, that's exactly what she wanted us to do. If we act like her, she wins. She knows she got to us. Sometimes it's best just to play dumb," Elizabeth said.

"Play dumb?" Bailey questioned.

"Pretend you don't know she's being mean. And keep being nice. Then she looks bad, and you look like a saint. Eventually she'll go away and be mean to someone else," Elizabeth explained.

"But then she wins!" complained Bailey.

Elizabeth laughed. "That's where you're wrong. Right now, she's back there trying to figure out why she didn't intimidate us. We won."

As they rounded the corner leading to the cabins, they nearly collided with Sydney, who was running at full speed. "Elizabeth! Bailey! Come quick!"

Into the Darkness

The girls rushed back to their cabin, where Alex and McKenzie leaned over Kate's shoulder, reading something on the Internet. "Unbelievable," Kate was saying.

"But that doesn't mean anything. I still say he's guilty," Alex responded.

"I don't know. I just don't know," said McKenzie.

Elizabeth jumped in. "Would somebody please tell us what is going on?"

"Yeah," added Bailey. "What's so unbelievable?"

Kate looked over her shoulder and said, "Listen. 'William Gerhardt was convicted of grand felony theft and sentenced to twenty-five years in prison,'" she read aloud. "'The conviction came beneath a shroud of doubt and questionable evidence, with a seven-to-five jury convicting him. Gerhardt, an employee of Manchester Jewels, is accused of selling the jewels on the black market. The jewels have not been found. In a post-trial interview, jurors continue to debate the legitimacy of the evidence presented.'"

The girls listened eagerly.

"If he sold them, why is Mr. Gerhardt looking for them?" asked Elizabeth.

"Well, I still say Gerhardt is guilty. I mean, look at his son, the Grouch. That man is digging, breaking into abandoned houses, chasing little girls. . . .That's not exactly normal, innocent b›avior," said Sydney.

"Perhaps we should wait until we know more before we make up our minds," Elizabeth told her friends.

"I agree with you," said Alex as she smoothed on her strawberry lip gloss. "As a matter of fact, I think we should do a little more investigating of our own as soon as possible."

"Well, I think we should eat," said Kate. "It's time for breakfast, and if we don't hurry, they'll start without us. That would be a waste of a perfectly good front-of-the-line pass."

"You're right," said Bailey. "Is the room ready for inspection? I'd love to win again today."

"Yep," said Sydney. We delivered Biscuit to the golf course and made sure everything was perfect before we started the Internet search."

"Hello! Starving girl here, remember?" called Kate. "You all stay here and gab all morning if you want. I'm leaving!"

The other girls laughed, and then they followed their tiny, hungry roommate to the dining hall.

●—■—●

During breakfast, Alex brought up the mystery again. "Nancy Drew always says, 'Drastic times call for drastic measures.' I think we need to snoop around Mr. Gerhardt's office."

Elizabeth held her fork in midair, deep in thought. "When did Nancy Drew say that?" she asked.

Alex giggled. "Well, come to think of it, I'm not sure she did say it. But somebody said it, and I agree."

"Okay, Miss Hollywood. What do you think we should do? Just waltz into Mr. Gerhardt's office and snoop through file cabinets and desk drawers?" asked Bailey.

Alex smiled. "Yes, that's exactly what I'm suggesting. And I think I may have the perfect plan. . . ."

The girls leaned together and began making plans, when suddenly Amberlie fell in front of their table, sending scrambled eggs, orange juice, and dishes in every direction. The girl began crying in a loud, dramatic voice, "They tripped me! Those mean girls tripped me!" She pointed at the Camp Club Girls.

The girls were caught off guard, and when a counselor rushed over to help Amberlie, she looked at the six roommates with a disappointed expression. "Is this true?" she asked.

"Yes, it's true. I saw it," said one of Amberlie's sidfiicks.

"I saw it, too," testified another of Amberlie's friends.

"I'm not sure which girl it was, but I definitely saw a leg stick out just as Amberlie walked by," said one of the girls.

"Yes, and just before that, they were all whispering together, like they were planning something," said the other girl.

"I saw that, too," said the counselor. She turned to the six roommates and asked, "Which one of you tripped Amberlie?"

The girls just looked at her in stunned silence.

"Okay then, if none of you will tell the truth, I'll have to punish all of you." Then, zoning in on Elizabeth, she said, "I'm disappointed in you. You know we don't put up with that kind of b›avior here."

Elizabeth found her voice. "But we didn't trip her! We were talking about something totally different!"

The counselor looked at her. "Then tell me what you were talking about."

The six girls looked at each other. They certainly couldn't tell her they were planning to sneak into Mr. Gerhardt's office and snoop.

Their silence sent the wrong message. "That's what I thought," said the counselor. "All six of you will be on clean-up duty for two days. You can start right now."

The girls began gathering their trays as Amberlie and her two buddies stood looking innocent. As the counselor walked away, Amberlie gave the group a smug grin.

Sleuthing would have to wait. It looked as if the girls would spend every free moment of their next two days in the dining hall.

●—●—●

After lunch on the second day of their punishment, Elizabeth scrubbed burned goo from the bottom of a pot with furious determination. Her roommates worked around her, talking, laughing, and flicking soapsuds on each other. But Elizabeth worked in silence.

She was too angry to speak.

I don't understand, Lord, she prayed silently. *We didn't do anything, and Amberlie is so awful. Didn't You say You would not let the guilty go unpunished? So why are we scrubbing pots and mopping floors, when the guilty one is probably out riding horses and having fun right now? It's not fair. We should be enjoying our camp experience. Instead, we are stuck here.*

Bailey interrupted her thoughts. "Elizabeth? Did you hear me?"

Elizabeth jerked to attention. "I'm sorry. Were you talking to me?" she asked.

The other girls laughed. "That pot doesn't have a chance against you," McKenzie said. "You're attacking it like it is your worst enemy."

Elizabeth smiled, but inside she still felt mad. She knew she had to forgive Amberlie. But she wasn't quite ready to do that.

"They want to hear our song, Beth. I was asking if you'd play for me. C'mon. We need the practice, and it'll be fun. We are allowed to take breaks, you know." Bailey spoke with a pleading voice. "Pleeeeeeeeeeeeeeaase?" she begged.

Elizabeth nodded, set down the pot, and wiped her hands on a dish towel. She walked to the piano and sat down.

Bailey scrambled to get the sheet music out of her backpack then placed it on the music stand. She described her crazy costume to the girls then nodded at Elizabeth to begin.

Before the song was halfway through, each member of the four-person audience was on the floor in fits of giggles. "That's the funniest thing I've ever seen!" laughed Alex. "I think you two should go to Hollywood for an audition!"

Sydney held her side; she was laughing so hard she couldn't speak. Tears streamed down Kate's chefis, and McKenzie let out a giggling sound that sounded partially like a monkey and partially like a chicken. The silliness of it all, paired with the girls' tiredness, made everything funnier. Before long, Elizabeth and Bailey had joined the laughter.

This was how Miss Rebecca found them. She silently stood in the doorway, and one by one, the Camp Club Girls noticed her. Slowly the laughter died as the girls waited to see what their counselor had to say.

An amused smile spread across the young woman's face. "Carry on," she told them then turned and walked away.

After a few moments of stunned silence, the silliness continued. After all, Miss Rebecca had told them to carry on. Who were they to disobey a camp counselor?

●—●—●

After dinner that night, the girls moved slowly, mopping, sweeping, and scrubbing dishes. Bailey stifled a yawn and brushed a wisp of hair out of her eyes. "I am going to sleep well tonight," she said.

"I still can't believe we've been stuck working here for two days," said McKenzie. Then she chuckled. "It has been kind of fun, though."

"Yeah, sort of like in those *Facts of Life* reruns, when Jo, Blaire, Tootie, and Natalie had to paint the dorms," said Alex. "Or when they had to work in the cafeteria serving line."

"Oh, I remember seeing that show. Yeah, I guess we are kind of like those girls," said Sydney.

Once again, Elizabeth remained quiet. Yes, she'd enjoyed some fun moments during the two days of clean-up duty. But she was still angry at Amberlie. She would need a little more time to get over this injustice.

The room fell into a comfortable silence as the tired girls finished their final duties. Suddenly they heard voices from the office next to the dining hall. They didn't think much of it—counselors came and went from the office all the time. They had a special area there where they could relax away from the campers.

Then the name *Gerhardt* caught their attention. They looked at each other then strained to hear the words.

"Such a shame, really. It has taken over his entire life," said a high-pitched voice.

"How much longer until he gets out of prison?" asked a lower female voice.

"I don't know. He must be getting close to the end of his time. But Dan is still obsessed with finding new evidence."

"Do you think his dad is really innocent?" asked the lower voice.

"Who knows. But it's sad. Dan talks to his father every chance he gets. And Tiffany said he gets a letter almost every wefi postmarked from the prison. She delivers them to his office, and he keeps them all in a desk drawer, tied with brown string."

"What if his dad is guilty, and Dan's trying to. . ."

"Don't even say it. I've said too much as it is."

With that, the distant conversation turned to which flavors of ice cream were stored in the lounge freezer.

●━●━●

Back at the cabin, the girls practically fell into bed. "I don't think I've ever been this tired!" groaned Bailey.

"Me neither. But now I won't be able to sleep. We've got to get our hands on those letters!" said Alex.

"I'm starving." Kate sighed. "All that work has really built my appetite."

Elizabeth reached under her bed. "Well, I have just the cure. I've saved these for an emergency. After all we've been through, I'd say we've earned them." She pulled out three boxes of Ding Dongs, and the girls suddenly found new energy as they pounced on her bed.

"You've been holding out on us!" chided Kate. "I'm surprised Biscuit didn't find these."

Elizabeth laughed and passed out the treats. "I had them zipped inside two plastic baggies then locked inside my suitcase."

Kate sat up suddenly. "Biscuit! We were so tired we forgot him! We can't leave him there all night!"

"Kate, don't you think he'll be okay? I love the little guy, but I'm sooooo tired!" said Bailey.

Kate reached for her flashlight and stood. "It's okay. I'll get him."

"Oh no you don't," said Elizabeth and Alex together.

"You can't go out there alone at night. I'll go with you," said Elizabeth.

"And this is the perfect time to snoop around Gerhardt's office. I'm coming, too," said Alex. "Kate, grab that reader-pen-thingie of yours, the one you showed us on the first day of camp."

The other girls looked at Alex as if she'd lost her mind. "Are you kidding?" asked Sydney.

"No, I'm not. We're going down there anyway, so why not make the most of it? It's dark, so no one will see us," Alex persuaded. "If Gerhardt shows up, well. . .we'll just cross that bridge when we come to it."

The other girls stared at her. Finally, Kate dug through her backpack. "She's right. We might as well kill two birds with one stone," Kate told them.

Elizabeth spoke up. "We don't all need to go. That will just increase our chances of getting caught. Sydney, McKenzie, and Bai—" Stopping, she looked at Bailey's bed. "Look. She's out like a light."

Elizabeth continued. "Sydney and McKenzie, you stay here. My cell phone is in my suitcase, and we'll take Kate's cell phone. If we get into trouble, we'll call."

The girls looked at each other with fear and excitement. Finally McKenzie spoke. "Be careful."

With a wave, the three girls stepped through the door and into the darkness.

• — • — •

The howling got louder the closer they got to the golf course. "Well, at least we know he's okay," said Alex.

"Poor little guy. We've really neglected him the last couple of days," said Kate around a mouthful of Ding Dong. "Remind me to bring him an extra sausage in the morning."

The little dog pounced on them as they entered the gate. Kate scooped him into her arms. "We're so sorry, boy. We'll make it up to you, we promise."

Suddenly Biscuit jumped out of her arms and bounded into the darkness. He returned a moment later carrying a golf club in his mouth, and the girls laughed.

"He likes to play fetch more than any dog I've ever known," said Elizabeth.

"Well, we'd better get down to business and get out of here. Let's see if Mr. Gerhardt's office is unlocked," said Alex, drawing them back into detective mode.

Kate shined the light of her cell phone, and the girls tiptoed to the small building that housed the golf clubs, balls, and a small office for the groundskeeper. Rattling the door, they discovered it was locked.

"Let's try the window," Alex suggested. They moved to the side of the building. Biscuit stayed close to their feet, sniffing the area protectively.

The window was small and high off the ground. Elizabeth, the tallest, pushed on the window pane, and it easily opened.

"You're the smallest," Alex told Kate. "We'll push you through, and you can look around."

"Okay, but you guys are gonna owe me big-time for this," Kate said. Then, looking straight at Elizabeth, she said, "I'll take my payment in Ding Dongs."

The two taller girls hefted Kate through the window. She landed on the floor with a loud thud. "I'm okay," she reassured.

"What do you see?" asked Alex.

"Nothing," Kate replied. "You still have my light."

"Oh, sorry," called Elizabeth, standing on her tiptoes. "Here, I'll drop it down." She held the phone through the window and released it.

"Owwww!" came Kate's voice. "Right on my head!"

"Sorry!" Elizabeth called out.

They heard Kate moving inside. "Okay, here is the desk. Now, I just have to—"

Her voice was cut off by the sound of a truck's motor. Elizabeth and Alex ducked b›ind a bush just before two headlights flashed onto the building. The motor died. A door opened and closed. The girls heard footsteps and then keys jangling. They heard a click, a door opening, and then the window lit up as the person inside switched on the light.

CHAPTER
9
★ ★ ★ ★

"Prince"

Kate had just removed the stack of letters from the desk drawer when she heard the truck's motor then saw a flash of headlights through the window. Thinking quickly, she noticed a small closet in the corner of the room. Clutching the letters, she moved around a couple of large storage boxes, slipped into the closet, and shut the door. Her cell phone light revealed a large pair of men's boots with a long overcoat hanging above them. A couple of dirty shovels rested in the opposite corner. She stepped into the boots and slid her body into the middle of the coat, hoping to disguise herself in case someone opened the closet door.

She tried to quiet her breathing and wished she could soften the pounding of her heart. She heard the click of the office door opening then saw light beneath the crack in the closet door. Heavy footsteps were accompanied by whistling... was that a praise song?

The footsteps came toward the closet, and the door creaked open. Kate held her breath and prayed like she had never prayed before. *Please, Jesus, don't let me die. I'm too young to die.*

Large hands reached into the closet, grabbed the shovels,

and then shut the door. She then heard rustling outside the door and assumed the person was searching through the boxes. She heard a scooting sound, and the light from the crack in the door was covered. After more rustling, the footsteps retreated. The light clicked off and she heard the outer door close. Slowly, quietly, she let herself breathe.

Thank You, God; thank You, God; thank You, God, she prayed. Then she reached for the door handle and pushed. The door wouldn't budge. Apparently, one of the boxes had been moved in front of the closet door. She was stuck!

Kate took a deep breath and told herself not to panic. She slid to the floor and pulled out the letters. If she was going to be stuck in a dark closet, she might as well make the most of it.

•—•—•

Elizabeth reached for Alex's hand in the dark. Biscuit nuzzled between the two girls, and Alex scooped him up. Neither girl made a sound as they peered through the small shrub. They watched the truck park. The headlights died. They heard the truck door open, then footsteps, accompanied by whistling. Elizabeth recognized the tune—the campers had sung it that afternoon at the worship service.

The girls heard a door opening. Suddenly light flooded out of the window above them and Alex gasped. Elizabeth held a finger to her lips. The girls remained still as opossums, staring at each other and squeezing hands.

After what seemed an eternity, the light disappeared, the office door opened and closed again, and the footsteps retreated. The two girls sat, afraid to move. Finally Alex whispered, "What do you think happened to Kate?"

"I don't know. I guess she found a place to hide," Elizabeth spoke softly. Then she stood to her toes and strained toward the window. "Kate!" she whispered urgently.

No answer.

"Kate! Answer me!" Elizabeth urged.

Still no answer.

The clouds shifted, casting moonlight on the area. Elizabeth looked at Alex and said, "I'm going in. Help me up."

"What? You can't leave me out here alone!" whispered Alex.

"I have to. We have to find out if Kate is okay!" Elizabeth answered.

"Well, let's both go," Alex whispered back.

"We can't both get in. Besides, one of us needs to stay here in case something happens," Elizabeth said firmly. "Now help me up. Please."

"Okay," said Alex. "But this is not going like I thought it would." She clasped her hands and held them down so Elizabeth could use them as a step.

Struggling, Elizabeth wiggled through the window, landing with a thud on the other side. She stood, rubbed her sore backside, and groped through the dark.

"Kate!" she called desperately.

"Elizabeth! Is that you?" Kate's muffled voice came through the darkness.

Elizabeth stumbled around the room, feeling the wall, trying to find her friend. "Kate, where are you?" she called.

"I'm in the closet. Something is in front of the door!" she called out.

Elizabeth felt around until she located the boxes and the door. It took all of her strength to push aside the large box, but soon the closet door was free. Kate stepped out, and the light of her cell phone cast a soft glow around the room. The girls pefied in the box to see hammers, wrenches, and a pile of oddly shaped metal tools. The girls breathed deep sighs of relief.

"What ha—"

"I was so sca—"

Both girls started whispering at once, and this started them in a series of nervous giggles.

"I can't believe this is happening. Did you get the letters?" Elizabeth asked.

"Yes, but we need to put them back and get out of here. I used my reader pen and recorded about a dozen pages, but it was dark, and I had a hard time seeing the lines. We may end up with a bunch of gibberish, but hopefully we'll have something we can use," Kate told her.

The girls jumped when they heard a voice through the window. "Hey! Are you two okay?" Alex frantically whispered.

"Yes, we're fine. We'll be right out," Elizabeth told her.

Elizabeth turned to Kate, "We'd better go out the window so no one knows we've been here."

Kate hurried to the desk and replaced the letters. They scooted the desk chair beneath the window and climbed back through the opening. Each of them stifled cries of pain as they landed on the scratchy branches of the small shrub.

"Finally!" Alex exclaimed. "I was starting to think you were going to have a slumber party in there!"

In the excitement, they hadn't heard the sound of footsteps drawing closer. Suddenly, a flash of light shined through the window. "Hey! Is somebody in here?" Mr. Gerhardt demanded from inside the office.

The girls paused. Then, without saying a word, they ran full speed through the darkness. Alex still clung to Biscuit, and they were just rounding the corner when they heard, "Hey! You girls! Come back here!"

The girls ran faster than any of them had ever run in their lives. They were too afraid of what might happen if they stopped!

Finally they arrived back at cabin 12B. Sydney and McKenzie sat on the front steps in their pajamas.

"Oh thank goodness you're back! We were just trying to decide if we should come after you!" whispered McKenzie. The five girls entered the cabin, three of them holding their sides from the pain of the long sprint. The clock read 12:33 a.m. when the whispers stopped and the girls finally slept.

●—•—●

During Discovery Time the next morning, all six girls dangled their feet from the dock. They had elected Elizabeth to lead them in their devotions, and now they listened to her read the scripture from her Bible.

"Proverbs 10:2, 'Ill-gotten treasures are of no value, but righteousness delivers from death,' " she read.

"I definitely agree with the first part!" said Kate.

"Why?" asked Elizabeth.

"I guess you could call those letters last night, 'ill-gotten treasures.' We could have been arrested for breaking and entering! We had no business going through Mr. Gerhardt's letters, and now they have no value."

The girls nodded. They had been disappointed that the reader pen hadn't delivered more information. The closet had been too dark for Kate to run the pen evenly along the lines. Most of the lines were scrambled, and what little they could read was just about prison life.

"Well, we may not have acted in 'righteousness,' but it sure felt like we got delivered from death!" exclaimed Alex.

"Oh I know it! I was so scared! I just knew we were going to. . ." Kate was interrupted by loud squeals from Bailey.

"Eeew! Gross! Get that thing away from me!" she yelled. The other girls laughed when they saw the source of panic. It was a tiny green lizard that had climbed onto the dock and almost into Bailey's lap.

"Awww, look at him! He's cute," said McKenzie. She scooped up the lizard and held him for the others to see.

"Step back, Mac!" squealed Bailey to McKenzie.

Alex, Elizabeth, Sydney, and Kate crowded near McKenzie for a better look, while Bailey kept her distance.

"I wish we could keep him," sighed Kate.

"No!" said all five roommates. But Elizabeth took the lizard from McKenzie and studied it.

"We can't keep him. But maybe we should hang on to him for a few hours. I have an idea. . . ," she said with a mischievous grin.

●—●—●

McKenzie helped Sydney into the saddle of a gentle-looking mare. "This will be fun," she told her friend. "This will be the first time I've gotten to ride the trails since camp started."

Sydney looked at her freckle-faced friend. "He seems pretty gentle. I've always wanted to ride a horse."

McKenzie chuckled. "She. The horse is a she. Her name is Sugar. I've helped Mr. Anzer a few times with the grooming, and she's a sweetie. You'll like her." She then adjusted the saddle on a strong black quarter horse, stepped into the stirrup, and pulled herself into place. "This is Spirit. He's well trained and full of energy. He reminds me of Sahara, my horse back home."

The two girls were about to hit the trails when Mr. Anzer and Mr. Gerhardt rounded the corner and approached them. The girls avoided Gerhardt's eyes and focused on Mr. Anzer.

"Hello, girls," Mr. Anzer said. "Headed out?"

"Yes, sir," they responded.

"That's nice. It's a lovely day for a ride," he said with a smile. Then his expression changed to one of concern. "Say, girls, Mr. Gerhardt told me that some campers were fooling around at the golf course late last night. He said he thought it might have been some cabin 12 girls, though he didn't get a good look. Were you at the golf course after dark last night?" He looked straight at McKenzie then at Sydney.

The two girls looked at each other then back at Mr. Anzer. "No, sir," they answered.

He eyed them steadily then said, "That's good to know. You two be careful and have fun!" The smile returned to his face, and he waved as they rode through the gate and toward the trails.

"That was close," said McKenzie as they got out of earshot. "I wouldn't have lied to him."

"Me neither," said Sydney. "My mom says withholding information can be like lying, though."

The girls grew quiet, enjoying the beauty of the trails. Suddenly they heard giggling from the trees. Out of nowhere, a fat water balloon exploded on the trail in front of them, spooking Spirit and causing the horse to whinny, rear back, and then take off in a full-speed run. Red hair streamed in the wind as the horse rounded the curve and sped out of sight.

Sydney turned to see Amberlie and her friends running away. She decided she would deal with them later. Right now she had to help her friend.

●—●—●

McKenzie clutched the reins. After a brief scare, she realized the horse was staying to the trails. Eventually they would circle back to the stables. She held her head back, enjoyed the wind on her face, and let the horse run. After a few minutes of a thrilling ride, she felt the horse getting winded. Tugging gently on his reins, she guided him to slow down.

"I don't know where that balloon came from, Spirit! I'm sorry it scared you," she told the horse, rubbing him gently b›ind the ears. "Sydney will be worried. We'd better go find her."

She gently guided the horse to turn around and head in the opposite direction. Before long, she met Sydney, who was coaxing Sugar into a slow, labored gallop. McKenzie had to chuckle at the sight of her friend bravely coming after her on the slow horse. "I'm okay," she announced.

"Well, that's good," said Sydney. "I didn't know whether to come after you or to go back and get help. Either way, Sugar doesn't know the meaning of 'Hurry up'!"

McKenzie guided Spirit to turn around once again, and the girls continued down the trail. "Did you see who threw the balloon?" McKenzie asked.

"Do you even have to ask?" Sydney responded.

McKenzie nodded. "It's a good thing Spirit is well trained. That could have been really dangerous."

"I don't understand that girl. She's so fake around the counselors. But she's the meanest girl I've ever seen. I almost feel sorry for her," said Sydney.

"Yeah, I'd love to know what's going on inside that head of hers. She obviously has some problems." McKenzie looked thoughtful.

The two girls settled into a comfortable silence; then Sydney started laughing.

"What's so funny?" McKenzie asked.

"Elizabeth's plan. Never in a million years would I have thought Elizabeth was capable of coming up with something so. . .so. . ." Sydney searched for the word.

"Naughty?" McKenzie helped her out.

The girls chuckled and talked about the plan for the rest of the trail ride.

●━━●━━●

The campers had just been released from the evening meeting, and groups of girls were ambling toward the cabins. No one was ever in a hurry to get ready for bed. Amberlie and her roommates were about to turn down the path leading to cabin 8 when Bailey and Alex stopped them. "Amberlie, could I talk with you for a minute?" Alex asked sweetly.

Amberlie looked at the two with a mix of curiosity and suspicion. "What do you want?" she asked. Amberlie's roommates stood by, listening.

"I was just wondering if you are a cheerleader," asked Alex. Amberlie was taken off guard. "A what?" she asked.

"A cheerleader. Are you a cheerleader at your school?" Amberlie paused. "No," she said.

"Oh, that's a shame. You've got the perfect build to be a cheerleader. And you're so pretty. You should think about trying out," Alex told her.

"Uh, okay," Amberlie responded. She clearly wasn't sure how to take the compliment.

"If you'd like, I can show you some moves. Here, watch this," Alex continued then demonstrated a double forward handspring. "It's really not as hard as it looks," she continued.

During this conversation, Elizabeth, Sydney, Kate, and McKenzie watched from b›ind the trees at the side of the road. When Alex had Amberlie's full attention, the four Camp Club Girls, along with the lizard, sneaked toward cabin 8.

"Shhhhhh!" Elizabeth told her giggling friends, but she had a hard time controlling her own giggles. She removed a small jar with holes poked in the lid from her tote bag. "You all stay here and keep watch. I'll go in and put Prince under Amberlie's covers. She always brings a pillowcase with her name on it, so I shouldn't have any problem finding her bed."

"Okay, but hurry!" McKenzie told her. "I'm not sure how long Alex can keep them entertained!"

Elizabeth surprised them by standing tall and walking right into cabin 8 as if she had every right to be there. It took her only a moment to locate the pink, ribboned pillowcase with the name AMBERLIE embroidered across the top. Carefully, she turned back the covers then gently removed the small lizard and kissed him on the head. "Do your job, Prince," she said. She tucked the creature under the blankets and smoothed them back into place.

The other three girls stood in the road, trying to act casual. A few moments later, Elizabeth darted out of the building then slowed down. The four girls walked toward their own cabin, trying to control the laughter that bubbled up inside them.

Alex and Bailey caught up with them at their cabin door, and the girls circled toward cabin 8 again. They hid in the bushes outside the windows of Amberlie's cabin. This would be a show they didn't want to miss.

Missing Biscuit

The Camp Club Girls could hear the conversation from Amberlie's room drifting through the open window.

"We're going to beat those girls from cabin 12. And it's going to start tomorrow night at the talent show. After that, we'll win the horse-riding match and the canoe races, no problem," said Amberlie.

"What about the scripture memory competition? That Elizabeth is good. She's won all the practice competitions in class," said a voice Elizabeth couldn't place.

Amberlie laughed. "Yes, but she hasn't been up against me yet. My dad's a preacher, and I've memorized scripture since before I could walk. No way she'll beat me."

The girls looked at one another. "A preacher's kid? Amberlie's dad is a. . ." Bailey felt Elizabeth's hand cover her mouth.

"Shhhhh!" The other girl whispered. The light went out in cabin 8, leaving only the soft glow of a lamp. Slowly the Camp Club Girls pefied in the window, just in time to see Amberlie pull back her covers.

The girl was wearing pink satin pajamas, and her head was covered in pink hair curlers. She slid leisurely beneath the covers and reached for the lamp. She clicked it off and all went black. Not a sound.

The six girls outside the window waited for several minutes then looked at each other in the moonlight. Disappointed, they turned to go back to their cabin. They had just stepped into the shadows of the trees when they heard the loudest, shrillest, most chilling scream.

"Help! Help me! Heeeeelp! Get it off, get it off, get it off! Eeeefi! It's in my hair! Get it off! Ew, ew, ew! Heeeeelp!"

The cabin door flew open, and Amberlie dashed outside, jumping up and down and smacking herself in the head, yanking out her curlers and screaming.

The girls of cabin 12 didn't know whether to run or stay and enjoy the show. They backed a little farther into the shadows but stayed to watch the scene play out.

A counselor soon emerged, saying, "Amberlie, be still or I can't help you."

"I can't be still! There's a giant snake, or a big spider, or something crawling in my hair! *Get it off!*"

The girls saw that Amberlie was truly terrified. They almost felt sorry for her.

Almost.

Later, after the Camp Club Girls had climbed into their own beds and switched off the lamp, Elizabeth said, "I feel kind of bad."

"Yeah, me, too," said McKenzie.

Silence filled the room. It was interrupted first by Bailey's giggles then Kate's, and soon they were all lost in an uncontrollable combination of guilt and giggles.

Elizabeth was awakened early the next morning by Bailey, who was shaking her back and forth. "Beth! Pssssst! Beth, wake up!"

Elizabeth opened one eye. It was still dark outside. "This better be an emergency, Bales," she mumbled.

"It is, Beth! It's a big emergency!"

Elizabeth sat up groggily. "What is it?" she asked.

"The talent show is tonight! We have to practice. Now."

Elizabeth dropped back down and pulled the covers over her head again. "Go to sleep, Bailey," she grumbled.

"But we have to practice, and everyone else who is in the talent show will want to practice today, too. That means the piano and the stage will be taken all day long. If we don't go now, we may not get a chance later, Beth!"

Elizabeth moaned. Bailey had a point. But sleep was more important to her at that moment.

Unfortunately, winning was more important to Bailey, and she wasn't giving up easily. "Beth, please? Pretty please, Beth? Don't you want to beat Amberlie?"

Reluctantly, Elizabeth sat up once again. "Okay. But you owe me," she mumbled.

The two girls dressed quickly, left a note to let the others know where they were headed, and were halfway to the dining hall when the trumpet began to warble reveille. They pushed open the doors to the quiet building without paying much attention to where they were going. As they entered, someone else was exiting. A very tall someone with muddy boots and a large cup of coffee. The two girls collided with the man, spilling coffee all over the boots and the freshly mopped floor.

"Oh, I'm sorry!" both girls cried out before they realized who they were speaking to.

Mr. Gerhardt pulled a handkerchief out of his pocket and knelt to clean up the mess. "You girls are up early. Do you always wander around in the dark?" he asked.

"Oh no, sir," said Elizabeth. "We just need the piano to practice for tonight's talent show."

Mr. Gerhardt gave them each a long, steely look then turned back to refill his coffee.

"We only have a couple of days of camp left," Elizabeth told Bailey, who stared after the man.

"Yeah," Bailey said. "If we're going to solve this mystery, we need to move!"

The girls were now wide-awake and scurried through the inner doors of the dining hall. Elizabeth sat at the piano and began warming up with some scales. Bailey sat next to her and sang, "Do, re, mi, fa, so, la, ti, do." When both girls were warmed up, Bailey took the stage and began smiling at the tables and chairs.

"What are you doing?" asked Elizabeth.

"I'm practicing my smile," Bailey replied, as if it were the most obvious thing in the world.

Elizabeth chuckled and began playing the song. They ran through it three times before a line formed outside. "We'd better go," she told Bailey. "Come on, we can hold a place for the others."

The two stepped outside and took their places at the end of the short line. Before long, the rest of the Camp Club Girls joined them. "I can't believe you two got up so early," mumbled

Kate. "The rest of us overslept. Biscuit is still in the room. We didn't have time to take him to the golf course, so we'll have to do that after breakfast."

"Oh, and tell her about the socks," Sydney urged.

"Oh yeah, the room is a wreck. Biscuit got into the socks again," Kate told them. "The alarm clock didn't go off, and we woke up to Biscuit slinging Alex's smelly sock onto my head."

"Hey!" Alex protested. "My socks aren't any smellier than yours!"

"He got into the socks again? Great. What is the deal with that dog and dirty socks?" Bailey groaned.

"We need a plan. Why don't we get our breakfast to go? Kate, you and Alex take Biscuit to the golf course, and the rest of us will clean up the room."

"No, let me go instead of Alex," urged Bailey. "Maybe I can practice a few strokes!"

The other girls laughed at their youngest roommate. "Bailey, I don't know where you get all that energy, but you should bottle it and sell it," said Elizabeth.

The girls followed the rest of the line into the dining hall.

●—●—●

Kate, Bailey, and Biscuit entered the empty golf course, and Biscuit immediately ran for the pile of golf clubs stacked on the office porch. He returned with his favorite club. The handle was marked up and down with his teeth marks.

He dropped it at Bailey's feet and looked at her longingly. "Ew, sorry boy. I have to practice, and I'm not gonna do it with your slobbery club. I think I'll get a fresh one," she told him with a pat on the head. She headed over to select her own club.

Kate picked up the chewed-up golf club and looked at it. "I've never known of a dog who likes golf." She laughed. "My dad plays golf. If only I could convince him to let you be his caddy, you could come home with me." She threw the golf club, and Biscuit bounded after it.

Bailey was on her third stroke when the sound of a golf cart interrupted them. Biscuit, who seemed afraid of Mr. Gerhardt, slipped b›ind the clown attraction, tripping the wire and causing the loud, silly laughter the girls had grown used to. Kate and Bailey were relieved to see that Mr. Anzer was with Gerhardt.

"You girls sure spend a lot of time down here," said Mr. Anzer as he climbed out of the cart.

The girls laughed nervously. "Yeah, I wanna be the next Tiger Woods," Bailey told him.

The old man smiled. "Sounds great. Then the rest of us will be able to say, 'We knew her when. . .' "

Kate glanced nervously over her shoulder, looking for Biscuit. Since that first day at the golf course, the little dog disappeared every time Gerhardt came around. But he had drawn attention to himself with the clown's laughter. Gerhardt looked toward the clown then started walking that way.

"Is that the dog I ran off last wefi?" he asked. "I keep seeing his paw prints around, but I can never catch him. I've called the pound. They should be out sometime today or tomorrow."

Suddenly Biscuit took off.

"Hey, mutt! Come back here!" yelled Gerhardt, chasing the little dog. Biscuit slipped through the gate and he was gone. Gerhardt examined the gate then walked toward his office.

"I'll fix this problem. That back gate is going to be fastened for good."

The color drained out of Kate's face, and she looked like she was going to be sick. Bailey gently touched her friend's arm and whispered, "It's okay. We'll find him. He'll probably find us first."

Kate gulped then nodded. She couldn't do anything about it now.

"You girls need to get to class, don't you? You'll be late," said Mr. Anzer.

The girls nodded then headed out the gate. When they were out of earshot, Kate said, "What will we do now? Gerhardt said the pound is coming. We've got to find Biscuit before they do, or he'll be lost to us forever!"

"Well, I'd rather the pound find him than that cougar! At least they won't hurt him," said Bailey. "Come on. If we hurry, we might be able to catch the others before class. Let's see if they have any ideas."

The two girls ran back to the cabin and arrived just as the others were leaving. "Biscuit!" Kate said, stopping to catch her breath.

The girls could read the pain in Kate's eyes. "What's wrong?" McKenzie asked.

"He's gone!" exclaimed Bailey. "And the pound is coming for him today!"

Kate and Bailey took turns explaining what had happened, and the others listened with concern.

"What can we do?" asked Kate in a worried voice.

"We'll divide up right now and search the woods," suggested Alex.

"We can't miss class. We'll get in trouble," said Elizabeth.

"I know what we'll do," offered Sydney. "Mac and I go on a nature walk with our class this morning. We'll walk right through the woods where Biscuit is hiding. Why don't we each carry a backpack filled with treats. . .something he'll smell. Maybe then he'll find us. If he does, we can slip him into the backpack."

The others agreed that this sounded like a good plan—at least until later when they could search more freely.

"What kind of treat should we put in your backpacks?" Bailey asked.

The girls offered suggestions, from stale cheese crackers to leftover biscuits. But Elizabeth offered the winning solution.

Minutes later, Sydney and McKenzie left the cabin, each with a backpack filled with dirty socks.

●—●—●

"Today is our last day to practice before the big contest," Miss Rebecca told her students. "I am very pleased with how much scripture you have memorized. As you know, memorizing God's Word is one of the most important things you can do. That's why the winner of this competition will receive double points for her team. So, who's ready to get started?"

Hands shot up around the room until the counselor called on Elizabeth. Then all hands went down. "Oh come on, doesn't anybody want to compete with Elizabeth?" Miss Rebecca asked with a smile.

The class laughed. Elizabeth had a reputation for being a scriptural encyclopedia.

Finally Amberlie raised her hand. "I'll do it, Miss Rebecca," she said sweetly.

"Wonderful! Come to the front. For this first part, I'll give the reference, and then you say the complete verse with the reference at the end. Every once in a while, I may stop and ask what the verse means. Ready?"

Both girls nodded.

"Elizabeth, you first. Proverbs 20:15."

Elizabeth smiled. " 'Gold there is, and rubies in abundance, but lips that speak knowledge are a rare jewel,' Proverbs 20:15."

Good job. Amberlie, Proverbs 3:13–14."

Amberlie smiled sweetly. "Certainly, Miss Rebecca. 'Blessed are those who who find wisdom, those who gain understanding, for she is more profitable than silver and yields better returns than gold,' Proverbs 3:13–14."

"Very good, Amberlie. I'm impressed! You've been holding out on us," said the counselor.

Amberlie beamed. But when Miss Rebecca turned to address the class, the girl leaned toward Elizabeth and whispered, "You're toast, Anderson."

Elizabeth smiled. "Bring it on," she whispered back.

•—•—•

The nature hike provided some interesting clues in the search for Biscuit, but the girls couldn't find the little dog. At one point, Sydney spotted paw prints in the mud, which looked the size of Biscuit's. But the girls couldn't disrupt class by calling out for the little dog, so they just kept hiking. They tried to mark the spot in their minds so they could come back and search later.

The girls gathered at the cabin for Discovery Time, and Elizabeth said a special prayer. "Dear Lord, please keep Biscuit safe! Please help us to find him before the pound does. And please help us to solve the mystery of Mr. Gerhardt's digging. Amen."

"Amen," the girls echoed.

"We have two goals for today," said Alex. "We have to find Biscuit. And we have to find out why Mr. Gerhardt is digging at the golf course every night. We know he's probably looking for the missing jewels that were never found when his father was convicted."

McKenzie jumped in. "Perhaps we should stop concentrating on why he's digging and start digging ourselves."

The rest of the girls looked at McKenzie. "You're brilliant!" exclaimed Sydney. "Why didn't we think of that before?"

The girls divided into two teams. Kate, Sydney, and Elizabeth would search for Biscuit, and the other three would search the golf course for hidden treasure.

Kate would take her cell phone into the woods, and the other three would carry Elizabeth's cell phone with them. That way they could maintain contact in case the jewels were found.

Or in case any cougars showed up.

●━━●━━●

When they arrived at the golf course, Alex, Sydney, and McKenzie heard Mr. Gerhardt's voice from inside the office building. Sneaking to the window, they listened to the man talking frantically. There were no other voices, so he must have been talking on the phone.

"I know, I know. The golf course is a mess. But I'm. . ."

He stopped to listen to the other person. Then he started again. "I know. But trust me, I have a good reason for digging things up. I'll fix it before the next camp begins, I promise."

More silence.

"I can't tell you why."

Quiet.

"I know I can trust you, but. . ."

There was a long pause, and then Gerhardt sighed. "Okay. I'll tell you everything, but it will take awhile. I'll meet you in your office at two o'clock."

More silence.

Then he said, "Okay. I'll see you at the stables at two o'clock." They heard the man hang up. "Oh, dear God," he said, "if those jewels are here, please let me find them. Please help me prove my father's innocence."

The girls looked at one another, wide-eyed, then headed back toward the main camp. As soon as they were out of earshot, Sydney spoke. "It sounds like he's going to spill the beans to Mr. Anzer. We've got to figure out a way to listen in on that conversation!"

Golf Clubs and Socks

Alex, Sydney, and McKenzie were halfway back to the cabins when they remembered the cell phone. "Let's call and check on the others," McKenzie said.

Kate answered the phone right away. "Did you find the jewels?" she asked without saying hello.

"No, but we may be very close to solving the mystery. How about you all? Any sign of Biscuit?" asked McKenzie.

"We saw signs of him but no Biscuit. Sydney led us to where you two found his paw prints this morning. We've called and called, but we can't find him. We're headed back now. We'll search some more after lunch." Kate sounded sad.

"Don't worry, we'll find him. Meet us back at the cabin. We have a lot to discuss," McKenzie told her.

All six girls were back at the cabin within ten minutes, discussing Gerhardt's phone conversation.

"How can we listen in on that conversation? The stables are busier than the golf course. We can't just stand by the window; that would look suspicious," said Elizabeth.

"I have an idea," said Kate. "Let me see Elizabeth's phone. . . ."

●—●—●

After lunch, the girls headed to the stables. They had talked about splitting up again to search for Biscuit, but only Kate was willing to miss the conversation. And they agreed it wasn't safe for Kate to search the woods alone.

"We'll all go search as soon as we hear what Mr. Gerhardt says," Elizabeth promised.

The girls walked casually into the stable area, admiring the horses and talking about riding the trails. They each played their parts well.

"Hello, girls!" greeted Mr. Anzer. "What can I do for you today?"

"Well, um, I actually have a question," said Kate. "Could I talk to you in your office?"

The old man smiled. "Certainly, young lady." He held the door open for her then followed her inside. "What can I do for you?"

Kate took a deep breath then began talking. She fingered the telephone in her pocket, ready to press Elizabeth's number on the speed dial. "I live in the city—Philadelphia—but I'd really like to spend more time around animals. Are there any clubs I could join that would let me be around horses even though I don't have room for one at my house?"

"Why, certainly! I'm sure an equestrian organization is near you. I'll check into it and get back to you before you leave camp." Mr. Anzer smiled. "Was that all you wanted?"

Um, yes, sir. Thank you so much," she answered. As the gray-haired man stood, she pressed the button. She heard Elizabeth's phone ringing just outside the door. Suddenly she heard Amberlie's voice.

"You think you're so smart, Elizabeth! But you just wait. I'm gonna smear you in that scripture memory competition, and every other competition. You and your little team will wish you never came to Camp Discovery Lake!"

Mr. Anzer was out the door in a moment, and Kate quickly slid her phone under a corner of his desk then followed him out. Elizabeth's phone was still ringing.

"Amberlie, may I see you in my office, please?" Mr. Anzer said sternly.

Amberlie, clearly surprised, turned syrupy sweet. "Oh, hello, Mr. Anzer. Elizabeth and I were just. . ."

"I heard you, Amberlie. Now step into my office, please," he told her.

Her face held a mixture of defiance and fear as she stepped into the room. Elizabeth answered her phone just as Mr. Anzer shut the door.

The six girls didn't know what to do. They had meant to plant the phone for Gerhardt's conversation. Now they could hear Mr. Anzer's conversation with Amberlie. Sydney took the phone from Elizabeth, held her finger to her lips, and pressed the button for the speakerphone. Alex kept watch at the stable entry as the conversation was broadcast for them all to hear.

"Amberlie, I don't understand you," came Mr. Anzer's voice through the phone. "You're a smart, beautiful, talented girl. You act sweet around adults, but you don't have any of us fooled. You are mean and spiteful to the other girls your age. Why?"

"I don't know," Amberlie said softly.

There was a long silence. Then Mr. Anzer said, "You know, Amberlie, my father was a pastor. When I was a little boy, I felt like everyone expected me to be perfect. I wasn't allowed to act silly or get into mischief or make the normal mistakes that most kids made. I felt like I had to be perfect. Sometimes I envied the other kids because their lives seemed so. . .normal."

The girls heard sniffles. Then sobs. Finally Amberlie spoke. "It's not fair! Those other girls get to do whatever they want, and nobody expects anything of them! Everyone expects me to be polite, to make good grades, to be clean and tidy. I feel like I'm being judged all the time by everyone."

Mr. Anzer said, "Here is a box of tissues. I know exactly how you feel. But you know what I finally learned?"

"What?" the girl asked.

"Most people weren't judging me at all. Oh, a few were. But most of them just loved me and wanted me to be happy."

Amberlie sniffled. "Really?" she asked.

The girls outside the door were silent. None felt right about eavesdropping on this conversation. But they needed to keep the phone on so they could hear Gerhardt. Finally Elizabeth took the phone from Sydney and flipped it shut. "This is wrong," she said. "We'll just have to forget about Gerhardt. We don't need to eavesdrop. I feel almost like we're stealing something. . . ."

The other girls nodded.

"We were stealing a conversation that didn't belong to us," said McKenzie.The girls were just leaving when the office door opened again. No one looked at Amberlie as she walked past them.

Kate approached the office door as Mr. Anzer was leaving. "I left something in your office," she said and retrieved the phone. The girls left the stables in silence. They had a lot to think about.

The girls spent the next hour in the woods searching for Biscuit. But either the little dog had escaped to the other side of the woods, or else. . .well, they didn't want to think about the "or else."

Finally, tired and sweaty, they gave up. Bailey and Elizabeth decided to go back to the cabin to shower and prepare for the talent show. The others decided to snoop around the golf course and perhaps do some digging of their own.

When they arrived at the golf course, Sydney, McKenzie, and Alex started examining the piles of dirt. Kate sat on the office porch and looked at the pile of golf clubs. Biscuit's chewed-up club was on top of the pile, and she picked it up. She sat holding the club and thinking of her little lost dog when her phone rang. It was her father.

"Hello, Katy-kins! Are you still having fun at camp? Do you miss your ol' dad at all? I can't wait to see you tomorrow evening!" Her dad's voice was loving and familiar. The sound of it brought the tears that had threatened all day. Before she knew it, she was pouring out her heart.

"Daddy! I found a dog, and I named him Biscuit, and he has been my dog for the whole camp, and I taught him to sit and to stay, and he sleeps at my feet, and he's the best dog in the whole world, and. . .and. . .he's gone!"

"Whoa, there! Slow down! Why don't you back up and tell me what you're talking about," her father told her.

She sat on the porch, holding the tooth-marked golf club and telling her daddy the whole story of Biscuit. When she finished, he remained quiet.

Finally he said, "You say he's been sleeping with you in your bed?"

"Yes, sir," she answered.

"And he's not bitten or hurt you or the other girls?"

"Oh no, sir! He's the sweetest, gentlest, smartest dog in the world!" she told him.

"Well, your mother and I have talked about letting you have a dog. I'll call the camp director. If they find him, as long as he is healthy, you can keep him," her father told her.

"Really? You mean it?" Kate asked, hardly believing her ears.

As Kate hung up the phone, her spirits were lifted, but only for a moment. Right now, she had no idea where Biscuit was. She didn't know if she'd ever see him again. She picked up the golf club, walked to the fence, and tossed it into the woods. If Biscuit came back, maybe he'd find the club and bring it to her, wanting to play fetch.

●—●—●

The crowd was growing, and Bailey was getting nervous. She stood with Elizabeth behind the curtain, watching the chairs fill. "We just have to win, Elizabeth! We just have to! This could be my big break, you know?"

Elizabeth smiled at her friend, who looked ridiculous in her pink curlers and face cream. "You'll be great, Bales. Just relax. If you don't make it to Hollywood, you always have golfing to fall back on."

"Yeah," said Bailey. "Too bad there wasn't more interest in the golf course. I would have won a golfing competition for sure."

Soon the camp director was on stage testing the microphones. When she was certain all was working properly, she began her speech. "Good evening, ladies. As you know, Camp

Discovery Lake is almost over. Tonight's talent competition marks the beginning of the final competitions, which will continue all day tomorrow.

"Before we begin, I want to tell you how proud I am and how proud all the counselors are of all of you. You have been a wonderful group of ladies, and I believe you have experienced real growth here during the last two wefis. You've learned about all sorts of things, but the most important thing we've tried to teach you is that nothing is more important than your relationship with God."

The woman continued with a reminder about being supportive and polite to all the contestants, and before long, the first act was introduced.

Elizabeth and Bailey were third on the program, just after a baton twirler and before a tap-dancing duet. When their act was introduced, they were surprised by loud cheers and applause. The Camp Club Girls had a reputation for being friendly to everyone, and it was paying off.

Elizabeth began playing, and Bailey performed. The audience laughed in all the right places. When she finished, she bowed, and the room erupted in more applause. Then she gestured toward Elizabeth, who also bowed, and the girls left the stage.

They were nearly knocked over by their four roommates. "You were awesome! Bailey, you're a natural! And Elizabeth, you can really play! We'll win this for sure!"

The group was hushed by a counselor as the next act was introduced. The girls sat and politely applauded when the dance number was finished. The next act was Amberlie, and the girls held their breaths. They had a feeling she would be their main competition.

Amberlie took the stage and held the microphone. The music began, and the girl began to sing. Her voice was pure and sweet, and she sang a popular Christian song almost better than the original artist. The audience leaned forward, drinking in her voice.

Then, at a climactic point in the song, a dreadful howling noise sounded from outside the window. It got louder and louder, and more and more dreadful. At first the audience thought Amberlie had really messed up. But the Camp Club Girls knew that howl. Without thinking, Kate jumped to her feet and ran out the door, yelling, "Biscuit! You're okay!"

Her five roommates followed, creating quite a stir in the room. Amberlie, who had just sounded like an angel from heaven, stopped the song. "I can't believe this!" she yelled. "Those girls did this on purpose so they would win! This isn't fair!" She slammed her microphone into its stand and stormed off the stage.

The girls exited the dining hall just in time to see two men getting out of a large white van. It had the words ANIMAL CONTROL painted on the side. Gerhardt spoke to the men, one with a long stick and the other with a net.

"Oh no! What will we do now?" whispered Kate. The howling continued as campers and counselors poured out of the building.

Elizabeth thought quickly. "Kate, you and Sydney come with me. Alex, Bailey, and McKenzie, create a distraction."

"A distraction?" questioned McKenzie.

Alex grabbed her with one hand, Bailey with the other, and said, "Come with me!" She led them to the men beside the white truck. "Excuse me?" she interrupted.

The men looked at the girls, their eyes resting on Bailey and her silly costume.

"That howling has interrupted our talent show. What kind of animal is that?" Alex asked.

"We believe it's a dog, miss. Now if you'll. . ."

"You have such a dangerous job. It must be scary to have to catch these animals. I mean, you don't know if they have rabies or if they will attack you. Have you ever been bitten?" she continued.

As the men looked at Alex with annoyance and confusion, Kate, Elizabeth, and Sydney moved toward the howls. Biscuit seemed to be in the woods across from the dining hall. As they moved into the shadows, Kate flipped open her cell phone for light.

"Biscuit!" they called. The howls were getting closer, but they couldn't find the little dog.

"He must be stuck," said Sydney, "or he would have come to us by now."

The girls continued the search but soon heard men's voices b>ind them. A large spotlight shined on them, and Mr. Gerhardt called out, "You girls get back to the dining hall. You could get hurt out here!"

Suddenly they heard one of the men yell, "I found him! He's stuck in this hole. Poor little guy! Good thing he didn't get stuck out here a few days ago, before we hauled off that cougar. He would have eaten this little fellow for lunch!"

The man walked into the spotlight holding a very wiggly, very dirty Biscuit in his arms. When Biscuit saw Kate, he lunged out of the man's grip and ran for his beloved owner.

But Gerhardt was too quick for the dog. He stepped in front of Kate, saying, "Oh no you don't. You're not getting away again!"

Biscuit changed directions and dashed toward the dining hall. Campers and counselors squealed as the filthy dog ran into the building, followed by three men and six girls, all yelling, "Come back!"

The man with the net cornered the dog on the stage, but just as the net was coming down on him, Biscuit took off again and headed back out the door. The big man leaped for the dog and crashed into a row of chairs.

Out the door came the little dog, then Gerhardt, then Kate and Sydney, then the man with the pole, then Bailey with her curlers and face cream, then the other three Camp Club Girls. The man with the net followed, limping.

Biscuit led the group toward the golf course. The men gradually slowed, holding their sides and breathing heavily. The girls raced ahead, and as they reached the fence, they found Biscuit, tail wagging, with his favorite golf club in his mouth.

"Biscuit!" Kate yelled, and scooped the filthy dog into her arms. "I'm so glad you're safe!"

The dog clung to the golf club, and the girls laughed. "Bailey, I know you want to be the next Tiger Woods, but I think Biscuit may give you a run for your money," said Elizabeth.

Just then, Mr. Anzer's golf cart pulled up. Gerhardt sat beside him, and the two Animal Control men were in the backseat. Several of the counselors followed, including Miss Rebecca. Gerhardt jumped out of the cart and stepped toward Kate. "You need to put the dog down," he said sternly. He grabbed the golf club, but Biscuit growled and refused to let go.

The tug-of-war continued, Kate holding Biscuit, Biscuit holding one end of the golf club, and Mr. Gerhardt pulling on the other end of the club.

Suddenly, the club broke apart, and out spilled an old sock.

Everyone gasped as the contents of the sock tumbled out!

Real Treasure

No one moved. They stood in the moonlight, with the golf cart headlights casting a soft glow on the broken golf club, the old sock, and the sparkly, shiny jewels that had fallen from it.

Then Mr. Gerhardt sank to his knees. Tears trickled down his cheeks as he gathered the colorful treasures. "Thank you, God! We found them!"

The girls jumped up and down and cheered, and the man looked confused. Elizabeth stepped forward. "We know all about your father, Mr. Gerhardt. We know he was convicted of stealing these jewels and selling them on the black market. And we know he didn't do it."

The man stood up. "But. . .but how did you—"

Alex spoke up. "We were curious about your digging. We figured that the spooky sounds weren't real, and we figured you were b>ind them. So we decided to do a little investigating of our own."

"When Mr. Anzer told me about the thieves that used to hide in that old house, we put two and two together. You looked pretty suspicious for a while," Elizabeth told the man.

The adults who had followed them to the golf course were now gathered around, listening intently.

"We went to the house, as you know. There we found an old newspaper with an article about the stolen jewels. I did an Internet search and found out your father was convicted for stealing them," said Kate.

"Yeah," Sydney interjected. "But we also learned that the jury was divided. That there wasn't real proof of his guilt."

"It didn't make sense," McKenzie added her two cents. "If your father was guilty, he would have just told you where the jewels were hidden. You wouldn't have been digging those holes everywhere!"

"That's when we decided the thieves must have hidden them somewhere at the golf course. We searched but didn't find anything. And just think, all this time, Biscuit was trying to give us the answer!" Elizabeth concluded.

Gerhardt nodded. "I've been trying to prove my father's innocence for nearly twenty years. I've searched high and low, but the jewels were just gone. Then, several months ago, I found out the thieves had hidden in that old house, and I had a feeling this was my big break. I searched the area, and the golf course seemed the most logical hiding place for the jewels. After all, who would think to look at a kids' camp?

"That's why I really didn't want you girls snooping around. I was afraid you'd find them first and not tell anyone about them. I didn't mean to scare you girls." His eyes fell on Bailey. "I'm sorry I frightened you so much. I hope you'll forgive me," he said.

Bailey's cold-creamed face shone in the moonlight, and she smiled her million-dollar smile. "You're forgiven. Besides, this has been the most exciting two weeks of my life!"

The man tousled her hair then looked at Biscuit. "And you, little dog, are a hero. Just think, I've been trying to get rid of you, and you ended up finding the jewels for me!" He patted the filthy dog on the head, and Biscuit let out a friendly bark.

Kate laughed. "He has a thing for smelly old socks. That explains why he was so drawn to this golf club! All this time we were trying to solve the mystery at Discovery Lake, and Biscuit had the answer the whole time!"

Mr. Anzer approached Kate, examining the dog in her arms. "So this is the little guy who caused such a stir around here. He is quite the mystery maker, leaving evidence of his presence all over camp. But we could never find him! Now we know why. You were hiding him!"

Kate smiled sheepishly.

"I spoke with your father on the phone this evening, Kate," he continued. "I called him to discuss an equestrian society I located in Philadelphia, and he wanted to talk about dogs!" The group laughed, and Mr. Anzer reached for Biscuit. "You can keep this little fellow, but tonight he needs to go with the Animal Control men. They'll make sure he is healthy and is caught up on his shots. They'll probably even give him a bath before they bring him back to you!"

"Good luck with that!" said Sydney, and all the girls laughed.

Miss Rebecca stepped forward. "This explains the strange smells from your room. I just thought you girls were really stinky," she said with a wink. "And the socks! He must be the one who kept your room in a mess!" She knelt down, and Biscuit licked her on the nose.

The Camp Club Girls told Biscuit good-bye, and Kate

held him tightly before handing him to Mr. Anzer. "I'm so glad you're safe, Biscuit. You really had me worried! After tomorrow, we'll never have to be apart again!"

Biscuit wagged his tail and covered her face with sloppy kisses before being carried to the Animal Control men. The limping man took him gently and slid into Mr. Anzer's cart. "Would you mind giving us a lift?" he asked the old gentleman.

The group of girls and counselors followed the golf cart back to the dining hall, and the talent show was soon back under way.

●—●—●

The girls awakened early the next morning, listening to the annoying trumpet reveille for the last time. They stretched and groaned. Bailey clutched her oversized panda under one arm and her blue ribbon in the other hand. She had been thrilled to win first prize in the talent show and had fallen asleep with the ribbon under her pillow.

"Okay, girls. Today is the day we win or lose," said Sydney. "Even with Bailey's points, we're still b›ind. Biscuit made sure we didn't win the cleanest cabin award. We have to win almost all of the competitions today or we won't walk away as champions."

"We'll win. We have to win. We're the Camp Club Girls," said McKenzie.

Alex bounced to the center of the room. "Remind me again who is doing which competition?"

Kate sat up in her bed. "I took the nature studies quiz yesterday, and we'll find out our scores today at breakfast."

"I'm competing in scripture memory," said Elizabeth.

"Mac, aren't you doing the horse-riding competition?"

"Yes," McKenzie replied. "I signed up yesterday."

"Alex, will you compete with me in the canoe races?" Sydney asked. "I really want to do that, but I need a partner."

"That sounds like fun. I think we really have a chance to win!" Alex said.

A short time later, as the girls sat at their usual breakfast table, the camp director took the microphone. "Good morning, ladies. May I have your attention?"

Miss Barr continued. "I hope you're ready for an exciting, fun-filled last day of camp. As you know, the Camp Club Girls of cabin 12 took the winning points last night at our talent competition." She paused for applause. "But the Princess Pack from cabin 8 is still in the lead. They had the cleanest cabin almost every day!" She paused again, but not as many people clapped.

"I have just received the results from the nature studies quiz taken yesterday," the woman continued. "Believe it or not, we have a three-way tie! Equal points will be given to Grace Collins of the Princess Pack, Rachel Smith of the Shooting Starlets, and Kate Oliver of the Camp Club Girls. Congratulations to each of you and your teams!"

The room erupted into a combination of applause and disappointed groans. "The first competition this morning will be barrel racing. The races begin at 9:00 a.m., so I suggest you all finish your breakfast and head that way." The woman replaced the microphone into the stand and stepped down from the stage.

The Camp Club Girls congratulated Kate, who seemed

unaffected by her win. She simply smiled, thanked them, and continued devouring her bacon-filled biscuit.

The girls finished their breakfast and headed toward the stables. "Are you nervous?" Elizabeth asked McKenzie.

"Not really," Mac replied. "I love to ride. I just hope I get the horse I want."

"We'll cheer for you!" called Sydney as McKenzie headed for the corral.

She was relieved when she saw that Spirit didn't yet have a rider. She walked over to his stall and began saddling him.

"I've seen you ride. You're good," came a voice from the next stall. McKenzie was surprised to see it was Taylor, one of Amberlie's roommates.

"Thank you," she responded.

"Well, good luck out there," the girl called as she rode into the paddock.

McKenzie stared after the girl. She had assumed that all of Amberlie's friends were just as mean as Amberlie. But this girl had been. . .friendly. "I guess that will teach me to make snap judgments," she told Spirit.

The dozen girls that competed in barrel racing lined up their horses. Most of them did a good job, but few had McKenzie's expertise. The Camp Club Girls' cheers could be heard above all others as they watched their friend effortlessly guide Spirit around the barrels and to the finish line, taking nearly a minute less than anyone else.

Mac smiled proudly, and her blush was almost darker than her auburn hair as she accepted the blue ribbon.

•—•—•

Elizabeth held a little white index card, reading the verse over and over. The other girls were confident that Elizabeth would win, but she wasn't so sure. Philippians 2:3–4 always tripped her up: "Do nothing out of selfish ambition or vain conceit. Rather, in humility value others above yourselves, not looking to your own interests but each of you to the interests of others."

She always messed up on the "selfish ambition or vain conceit" part. She could never get those phrases in the right order. Taking a deep breath, she offered a silent prayer.

Miss Rebecca took the stage. "Welcome to the scripture memory competition. Round one will begin with verses you all have learned here at camp. I will give the reference for the verse. Then contestants must recite the complete passage word for word and repeat the reference. Any questions?"

No one spoke, and the two dozen contestants formed two lines on the stage.

"This will take awhile," whispered Kate, settling in her chair. But the contestants dropped like flies, and by round four, only three girls were left. Elizabeth stood at one end of the line and Amberlie at the other, with a quiet girl named Caitlyn in the middle.

Miss Rebecca began the round with Elizabeth. "Philippians 2:3–4," she said.

Elizabeth took a deep breath and briefly closed her eyes in concentration. Her five roommates held their breath as their friend began to speak.

"Come on, Beth, you can do it," whispered Bailey.

Elizabeth spoke. "Do nothing. . .out of. . .selfish conceit

131

or vain ambition, but in humility consider others better. . ."
She stopped and looked directly at Miss Rebecca. "That wasn't
right, was it?" she asked.

The counselor shook her head but smiled. "No, I'm sorry,
Elizabeth. But you aren't disqualified yet. Remain on stage
until another contestant correctly says the verse."

Caitlyn began to recite the verse but messed up in the
middle. The audience leaned forward as Amberlie took the
microphone. She smiled the sweet smile that was reserved for
public use and began the verse. Without missing a beat, she
recited it perfectly, and her team cheered.

Miss Rebecca said, "Congratulations to each of our
contestants. We are proud of all of you, and I hope you will
continue to memorize God's Word. And a special congrat-
ulation goes to Amberlie and the Princess Pack for winning
this competition."

The audience applauded politely and dispersed for the
next competition.

•—•—•

Sydney and Alex stood on the bank of the pond, looking
fiercely competitive. They had to win this race if they had any
hope of winning the championship.

"When the whistle blows, you will climb into your boats,
paddle to the marker in the center of the pond, and then turn
around and canoe back," the counselor instructed. "At no time
during the race can you exit the boat. If you fall or jump out
of the boat, you'll be disqualified. Please make sure your life
jackets are securely fastened."

Sydney and Alex checked each other's life jackets. "I think

we can win," whispered Alex.

"We have to win," Sydney responded.

"On your marks. . .get set," the counselor called then blew the whistle.

The two Camp Club Girls launched their canoe with skill and speed, and easily floated into first place. "One—two, one—two," shouted Sydney. They had spent more than a half hour after breakfast, sitting on dry ground, practicing their timing and technique. Both girls were naturally athletic, and the strokes came easily. In no time, they reached the marker in the center of the lake and rowed around it.

Elizabeth, Kate, McKenzie, and Bailey stood on shore, cheering as loudly as they could. The two girls in the center of the pond paid no attention, however. They concentrated on paddling as fast as they could. When they were within yards of the finish line, Sydney turned around to give Alex a high five. "We did it!" she called out.

Alex, caught off guard, was thrown off balance. She leaned to one side, trying to regain control, but it was too late. The boat tipped.

Splash! Two girls fell ungracefully into the water only inches from the finish line.

Sydney stood and yelled, "No! No way! This cannot be happening!" just as two girls from another cabin sailed past them to win the race.

Alex sputtered and pushed hair out of her eyes. The four remaining Camp Club Girls stood in shock until McKenzie broke into laughter.

"That was the funniest thing I've ever seen!" she called out.

"That moment made losing the race worth it!"

Sydney and Alex frowned at her. But then they looked at themselves and their overturned boat, mere inches from the finish line, and the humor of the situation began to sink in. They had to laugh.

"Here, let me give you a hand," said McKenzie, holding out her arm. Alex and Sydney both reached out, grabbed their auburn-haired friend, and pulled her into the water with them. "Hey!" McKenzie yelled.

"Now that," Sydney said with laughter, "was the funniest thing I have ever seen!"

●—◆—●

Elizabeth watched out the window as buses lined up to transport girls to the airport. The Camp Club Girls sat near the back of the room, frantically jotting down phone numbers and e-mail addresses. Kate cuddled Biscuit, who had been returned to her just moments before.

The camp director, Miss Barr, took the stage, and the noise died down.

"Saying good-bye is always the most difficult part of the camp experience. I know you all have developed some lasting friendships during the last two wefis. I hope each of you will return next year. And now, let's announce this year's Discovery Lake champions. As you know, teams have built points during the entire camp. But the greatest source of points comes from the counselors' award, which is given to the team that has shown loyalty, friendship, and humility throughout the camp. This year, one special group of ladies has exhibited these characteristics in an outstanding way. Camp Club

Girls, would you join me on stage?"

The girls looked at each other in shock and rose from their chairs. When they arrived on stage, Mr. Anzer and Mr. Gerhardt joined them.

"These girls have been friendly, sweet, and supportive during the past two wefis. But they have also gone above and beyond what anyone could expect of our campers," said Mr. Anzer.

Mr. Gerhardt took the microphone. "Girls, you helped me solve the mystery at Discovery Lake, and because of it, my father's name will be cleared, and he'll be set free. I'm pleased to award the Camp Club Girls with the title Team Discovery Lake. You deserve it!"

The room erupted in cheers. Elizabeth looked at the audience, and even Amberlie was clapping. Biscuit wiggled in Kate's arms, and the girls gathered into a group hug.

"We did it!" they called out, whooping and hollering.

"I wonder what mystery we'll solve next," Elizabeth said with a smile. Just then her cell phone rang. It was her father, and she stepped away from the cheering group so she could hear.

"How's my girl?" asked her dad, and she filled him in on their win. "That's great," he told her. "I have a surprise for you. When you get home, you won't even need to unpack your bags!"

"What do you mean?" she asked him.

"We're going to Washington, D.C.! We leave on Monday."

Elizabeth had always wanted to visit the capital, and now she had a friend there. After hanging up the phone, she went to find Sydney.

As the girls said their final good-byes and promised to keep in touch, they had no idea that another mystery was already beckoning the Camp Club Girls. From their various corners of the United States, soon they'd be embroiled in *Sydney's D.C. Discovery.*

"It was great to find the jewels for Mr. Gerhardt," Elizabeth commented as the girls hugged each other. "But the real treasure I found. . ." Elizabeth paused as she looked, in turn, into the faces of Kate, Bailey, Sydney, McKenzie, and Alex. "The real treasure is finding friends like you!"

Camp Club Girls
Sydney's D.C. Discovery

Jean Fischer

Go 64

Splaaaashhh! Whoosh!

"Watch out!" someone called near Sydney's ear.

But it was too late. The pent-up explosion of the water landed square against Sydney's back, knocking her to the ground.

Dazed, she rolled onto her back and looked up into the hot summer sky. The water swirled around her whole body. From a distance she heard happy shouting and water gushing onto the street.

A fireman's face appeared above her. "Are you okay, little girl?"

Little girl? Little girl! I'm twelve years old! I'm not a little girl, mister.

The indignation snapped Sydney out of her dazed condition. She looked up and saw that two firemen were now looking at her anxiously. Carefully they helped her to her feet.

"Are you okay, little girl?"

She looked in the fireman's face. He seemed so worried that her irritation melted.

Sydney looked down at her soaked gray tank top and shorts. "Yes, sir, I'm fine," she said. "Thank you," she added, remembering her manners.

Sydney Lincoln had been talking to one of her neighborhood friends. She hadn't even noticed the firemen at the fire hydrant b›ind her. And she sure hadn't realized she was in the direct line of the nozzle the men were releasing.

Still out of breath from the shock of the water, Sydney dropped onto the curb in front of her house. She tore off her running shoes and socks and stuck her bare feet into the gutter. She watched as the water from the hydrant down the street shot into the air and out the nozzle. The neighborhood kids laughed and splashed in its flow.

As Sydney's clothes began to dry in the torrid sun, the water rushed along the curb like a river. It streamed between Sydney's toes and sent goose bumps creeping up to her knees.

Sydney lived in the middle of a row of brick houses. The two-story houses were connected so they looked like one long building. The only windows were in the front and the back. The houses were close to the street, and each had a narrow front porch with three steps leading to a tiny front yard and the sidewalk.

The screen door on Sydney's house swung open, and her mom stepped outside. "Sydney, have you seen your aunt Dee yet?" Her curly black hair was pulled back with a blue band to keep it off of her face.

"No, Mom," Sydney answered. "I ran past the Metro station looking for her, but she wasn't there."

"Well, when she gets here, you two come inside. Dinner's ready."

Sydney dipped her fingers into the water and splashed some onto her long, thin arms.

"Don't you want to come in by the air-conditioning?" Her mother fanned herself with a magazine. "Aren't you hot in the sunshine?"

"No, Mom," Sydney answered. She didn't think it was necessary to tell her mom about her little brush with the explosion of water.

The cell phone in the pocket of her pink shorts buzzed. Sydney took it out and found a text message from one of her best friends, Elizabeth Anderson. It said: ALMOST PACKED.

Sydney tapped a reply on her keypad: CAN'T W8 TIL U GET HERE.

Sydney and Elizabeth had met at Discovery Lake Camp, and although Elizabeth lived in Texas, they talked every day. Four other girls had been with Sydney and Elizabeth in Cabin 12B. They were Bailey Chang, Alexis Howell, McKenzie Phillips, and Kate Oliver. When camp ended, Kate set up a website so the girls could stay in touch. It was password protected, so it was like their own secret cabin in cyberspace. They'd all bought webcams with babysitting money, chore payments, and allowances so they could see each other and talk online. The Camp Club Girls—as they liked to be called—made webcam calls, sent IMs, and frequently met in their own private chat rooms.

Sydney continued typing her message: WILL PIC U UP @ D APORT @ 4 2MORO.

"Sydney, I really wish you'd come inside." Sydney's mother crossed her arms.

"Okay, in a few minutes, Mother!" Sydney said without looking up.

The screen door slammed shut.

This was the worst heat wave Washington, D.C., had seen in twenty-five years. Everyone had air conditioners blasting. The energy load was way too much, and the night before, the power had gone out. Sydney hated being in total darkness. She was relieved that today seemed normal.

PACK SHORTS, she typed. REALLY HOT HERE!

While she sat texting, Sydney heard the *thump, thump, thump* of music getting closer and closer. A green jeep raced around the corner, and the booming bass from its stereo echoed inside Sydney's chest. In the passenger seat, Aunt Dee held on to her tan park ranger hat to keep it from flying off of her head. The jeep screeched to a halt in front of Sydney's house, and her aunt hopped out.

"Thanks for the ride, Ben!" she yelled over the music. "See you tomorrow."

The young driver waved and drove off.

GOTTA GO, BETH, Sydney wrote. ANT D'S HOME.

Sydney stood and wiped her feet on the grass. "You're late again," she said. "Mom's mad."

"I know," Aunt Dee apologized. "There was trouble at the Wall." She took off her ranger hat and perched it on Sydney's head. Aunt Dee always blamed her lateness on her job at the Vietnam Veterans Memorial. Sydney didn't understand how she could be so enthusiastic about a long black wall with a bunch of names carved onto it.

"So what was the trouble?" Sydney asked.

"I'll tell you at dinner," said Aunt Dee. She linked her arm through Sydney's. "It's hot out here, girlfriend. Let's go inside."

By the time Sydney washed and sat at her place at the table, Mom and Aunt Dee were already eating. Sydney had learned at camp to pray before every meal. So she bowed her head and said out loud, "Dear Lord, make us truly grateful for this meal and for all the blessings of this day." She noticed that her mom and Aunt Dee stopped eating and bowed their heads, too. "And please keep Dad safe," she said. Sydney always added a blessing for her dad, who was serving in the military overseas.

"Amen!" Mom and Aunt Dee chimed.

Sydney poured iced tea into her tall glass and scooped pasta salad onto her plate. "So what happened at the Wall?" she asked, reaching for a piece of French bread.

"Someone spray-painted the sidewalk last night," Aunt Dee replied. "Graffiti."

Sydney's mom got that look on her face—the one where her for>ead turned into wrinkled plastic wrap. "You mean *vandalism*," she said. "I think it's just terrible what kids do these days—"

"How do you know it was kids?" Sydney interrupted. Her mouth was full of creamy macaroni. "Kids aren't the only ones who do bad stuff."

"Don't talk with your mouth full," said Aunt Dee.

"Most times it is," her mom argued. "Just look around our neighborhood." She waved her hand toward the kitchen window. "Vandalism everywhere! Who do you think did all that? Not the adults. The kids don't care about our community. Do they care that this neighborhood used to be a military camp to help slaves that escaped from the South? No! They just want to mess up the nice things that good folks worked so hard to build." Sydney's mother sighed and took a long drink of her iced tea.

Mrs. Lincoln worked at the local historical society, and she was very protective of the neighborhood and its landmarks. She liked to talk about how, in the old days, kids had manners and didn't do anything wrong. Sydney hated it that her mom blamed everything on the kids in the neighborhood.

"There are good kids, too," Sydney argued. "You don't see my friends and me running around spray-painting everything. Give us some credit!" She looked at her plate and pushed the rest of her pasta salad into a neat little pile. "We care what happens."

"We don't know who did it," said Aunt Dee, trying to stop the argument. "Someone painted 'GO 64' in front of panel 30W—in orange paint. Ben and some other volunteers scrubbed it this morning. They'll work on it again tonight when the air cools off some. They're having a hard time cleaning it. Pass the bread, please."

"What does 'GO 64' mean?" Sydney asked, handing her the basket of bread.

"That's what we're trying to figure out," Aunt Dee answered. "We're wondering if the number 64 is a clue to who did it. Ben said that in some rap music, 64 means a 1964 Chevrolet Impala. Another volunteer plays chess and said 64 is the number of squares on a chessboard. We don't know what it means."

"Maybe it's Interstate 64," Sydney's mom suggested. "There's construction on that freeway and plenty of orange construction cones. Maybe the orange paint is to protest all that."

"But if it's about the freeway or a car or a chessboard, why would they complain by painting graffiti at the Vietnam Wall? Besides, Interstate 64 is in Virginia," Aunt Dee said.

"Yes, but there's some military bases out that way," Mother said. Then she added, "It's probably just kids."

The air-conditioning kicked in again, and a cool draft shot from the air vent, making the kitchen curtains flutter.

"The Wall's lighted at night," Sydney said. "And the park police keep an eye on all the monuments. So why didn't anyone see who did it?"

"The lights were out," Aunt Dee reminded her. "The whole city went dark for a while, and the park police were busy with that. That's when it happened, I'm sure. Anyway, it's a mess, and we have to clean it up fast. The TV stations are already making a big deal out of it." She dipped her knife into the butter container and slathered butter onto her French bread. "I had such an awful day at work. Everybody blamed everyone else for letting it happen. Like we would *let* it happen! People don't know how hard the Park Service works—"

"May I be excused?" Sydney asked, swallowing her last bite of pasta.

"You may," her mother answered.

Sydney put her dishes into the dishwasher. Then she went upstairs to her room.

The computer on Sydney's desk was on, and her screensaver cast an eerie blue glow on her yellow bedroom walls. Syd's bedroom had no windows, so it was always dark. That was the trouble with living in a row house. If your room was in the middle of the house, you had no windows. She

145

flipped the switch on her desk light and tapped the spacebar on the computer. The monitor lit up, and Sydney noticed that McKenzie Phillips was online. She sent her an IM: *Talk to me?*

The phone icon on the computer screen jiggled back and forth. Sydney clicked on it, and McKenzie's freckled face appeared. She was sitting at the work island in her family's kitchen. "What's up?" she asked.

Sydney turned on her webcam. "Not much," she said. "I just finished dinner."

"Me, too," McKenzie replied. "Well, almost." She held a slice of cheese pizza in front of her face so Sydney could see it. "We ate early because Dad and Evan have to drive some cattle to pasture. Then they want to practice for the rodeo this wefiend." She pointed to the blue baseball cap on her head. Its yellow letters said SULFUR SPRINGS RODEO.

"I didn't want to hang out downstairs," Sydney told her. "Someone spray-painted graffiti by the Vietnam Wall last night, and Mom blamed it on kids again."

McKenzie took a bite out of her pizza. "I saw it on the news. Why did she blame it on kids? I mean, anyone could have done it."

"She blames *everything* on kids," Sydney answered. "I think it's because a lot of the kids around here get into trouble. I try to tell her that we're not all like that, but she doesn't listen. Lately she doesn't listen to anything I say."

"My mom's like that, too," McKenzie said. "Nothing I do is ever right." Her face lit up. "Hey, the news said it was *orange* paint, right?"

"Yeah," Sydney said, fidgeting with her cornrows. "Orange

graffiti that said 'GO 64.' So what?"

"So maybe it's some crazy nutcase with Agent Orange."

"Agent who?" Sydney asked.

"Agent Orange!" said McKenzie. "Agent Orange was a chemical they used in Vietnam. I read about it in school. It made some Vietnam soldiers really sick, and some even died. So maybe it wasn't a kid who wrote it. Maybe it's a guy who got Agent Orange, who's mad at the government and wants to get even. By the way, I can't see you well."

"You think too much," Sydney answered. She pulled her desk light closer to her computer and bent it toward her face. "They're trying to figure out what 'GO 64' means. My aunt and mom think it could be about some sort of car or highway or maybe even a chessboard—"

"A chessboard!" McKenzie screeched. "A person who plays chess won't spray-paint a national monument."

"I know," Sydney said. "Some gang member probably wrote it. Anyhow, I don't care. I don't want to talk about it anymore."

"I can see you fine now," McKenzie said, changing the subject. "So when is Elizabeth coming?"

"She and her uncle Dan are flying in from Texas tomorrow," Sydney answered. "Aunt Dee and I are going to pick them up at the airport at four. We'll take her uncle to his hotel, and then Elizabeth will come here to stay with us."

"Can Elizabeth's uncle Dan get around all by himself?" McKenzie asked. She twisted a strand of her shoulder-length hair around her fingers. "I mean, he's in a wheelchair and everything."

"As far as I know, he can," Sydney answered. "Elizabeth said he plays wheelchair basketball and competes in wheelchair races, so I suppose he gets around just fine by himself. I'm sure once he gets to the hotel, his Vietnam buddies will help him out if he needs help."

McKenzie reached for a gallon milk container on the kitchen counter. She poured herself a glass. "Well, at least you and Elizabeth don't have to hang around with him the whole time. He'll be busy with his reunion stuff, right?"

"Right," Sydney agreed. "We'll see him Monday at the Vietnam Wall. Aunt Dee wants to give him the tour, and she thinks that Elizabeth and I should be there. Otherwise, we're on our own." Sydney heard strange sounds coming from her computer speakers. "Is that mooing?" she asked.

"Can you hear it?" said McKenzie. "That's Olivia, our old milk cow. About this time every day, she wanders up to the kitchen window and talks to us. I'll move the camera, and you can see her."

McKenzie's face disappeared from the screen. Sydney watched her friend's bare feet move across the kitchen floor as she carried the webcam to the window. Then a big, black-and-white cow head appeared. Olivia stood chewing her cud and looking at Sydney with huge brown eyes.

"Earth to Mac! Earth to Mac!" Sydney called into her computer's microphone. "Come back, Mac!"

Sydney watched McKenzie's bare feet walk back to the computer. Then her face showed up on the screen.

"Isn't Olivia awesome?" she said. "You really should come to Montana, Syd. We have tons of animals. I know you'd love it, and we could ride horses and hike, just like we did at camp."

"Maybe I will someday," Sydney replied. "But right now, I'm signing off. I want to clean up my room before Elizabeth gets here from Texas. All of my junk is piled on the other bed. If I don't move it, she won't have a place to sleep."

"Okay then," McKenzie said. "I'll sign off, too—and eat more pizza." She picked up the gooey slice from her plate and took another bite. "I'll talk to you tomorrow."

"See ya," Sydney answered, switching off her webcam.

Everything in her room looked neat except for the other twin bed. It was hardly ever used, so that was where Sydney stored most of her stuff. It held boxes filled with colorful papers and art materials, magazines, piles of clothes, and posters she planned to put up in her room. Sydney had so much stuff stored there that she didn't know what to do with it all. *Under my bed, I guess,* she thought.

Before long, the bed was cleaned. Sydney changed the sheets. Then she went to her closet and pulled out a new black and tan bedspread that matched her own. She threw it on top of the bed and tucked it neatly around the pillow.

"Sydney?" Aunt Dee stood in the doorway. She held a long white envelope. "This came for you."

The letter was from Elizabeth. Sydney tore open the flap and found a note taped to an information sheet.

Uncle Dan wanted me to send you this so your mom can keep track of him. Just in case of an emergency. It's his reunion schedule.

Sydney Lincoln read the heading on the sheet of paper. It said, "Annual Reunion—64th Transportation Company, Vietnam."

The Wall

Thunderstorms in Texas delayed Elizabeth's flight. By the time Aunt Dee, Sydney, and Elizabeth dropped Uncle Dan off at his hotel and got back to Sydney's house, it was almost midnight.

After the girls got ready for bed, Elizabeth handed Sydney a small package wrapped in polka-dot-covered paper. "I got this for you," she said.

Sydney grinned. She loved getting presents. Carefully she peeled the tape off the paper. Then she reached in and pulled out a square gray box. On the top of it, gold script letters spelled out HIS WORLD, AMARILLO, TEXAS. Sydney opened the lid and found a thick, coppery bangle bracelet. Etched all around it was a scripture verse: *Be strong and courageous. Do not be afraid; do not be discouraged, for the LORD your God will be with you wherever you go. Joshua 1:9.* "This is so cool!" Sydney exclaimed. "Thank you, Beth." She slipped the bracelet over her left wrist.

"My uncle gave me a pendant with that scripture," Elizabeth said. She reached for the pendant on a long silver chain around her neck. Then she held it up so Sydney could see. "It has a special meaning."

Sydney settled into her bed and covered herself with the

cool white sheet. "What's the meaning?"

"Well, when Uncle Dan was in Vietnam, he always carried a small Bible in his hip pocket. When he got shot, the bullet went through his pocket and right through the Bible. The doctors said that the Bible slowed down the bullet. If it hadn't, he might have died instead of being paralyzed." Elizabeth stretched out on her own bed and got under the covers. She switched off the light next to her bed. "And do you know what else? In the hospital, Uncle Dan opened his little Bible with the bullet hole, and it fell open to the words, 'Be strong and courageous. Do not be afraid; do not be discouraged, for the Lord your God will be with you wherever you go.' It was Joshua 1:9!"

"Wow," said Sydney. "What a coincidence, huh? Good thing he had the Bible in that pocket."

"Coincidences don't exist," Elizabeth answered. "That was God."

Sydney shut off the light on her nightstand. "Your uncle is lucky to be alive. Maybe he can't walk, but he sure does seem to get around fine. He just zipped around the baggage carousel and grabbed that suitcase. It was—"

"Not that great." Elizabeth finished Sydney's sentence. "Because he still can't walk. I pray every night for God to make him well again. But so far, nothing has happened. If it weren't for you, I wouldn't even have come here with him. Aren't there a lot of statues of soldiers and reminders of wars here? I don't like statues like that. They make me think of Uncle Dan."

Sydney heard tears in her friend's voice. "Washington's not so bad," she said. "We'll go to the Wall first thing tomorrow when Aunt Dee shows your uncle around. Then, the rest of the time, we can do fun stuff."

Elizabeth said nothing.

"Good night, Elizabeth," Sydney said. "Thanks for the bracelet."

"Good night, Sydney," Elizabeth whispered.

●—●—●

The girls got up early the next morning and were glad to find the weather had cooled and left a beautiful, sunny day. They ate breakfast, and then they walked from Sydney's house to the Metro station. From there, they took the Metro, the name everyone called the subway system, to L'Enfant Plaza. They transferred to another train and ended up in a neighborhood west of downtown called Foggy Bottom.

Elizabeth was impressed by how easily Sydney got around. "I'm glad I'm not doing this alone," she said. "You know how directionally disabled I am!"

"Do I!" Sydney replied. "Remember at camp when we were in the woods, and we scared off that cougar? You didn't have a clue where we were. And *you* were the one who'd been to Discovery Lake Camp before!"

They ran up the stairs from the train platform to the street.

"And who got us out of that one?" Sydney added.

"You did!" Elizabeth laughed. "Like I said, I'm directionally disabled."

Quickly they walked a few blocks to the Vietnam Wall.

Elizabeth was surprised to see that the Wall was in a big, grassy park with lots of trees. The girls had agreed to meet Sydney's aunt at the Three Servicemen statue near the west entrance. By the time they got there, Aunt Dee was already telling Uncle Dan and two of his buddies about the memorial. "The total length of the Wall is 493 feet and 6 inches," Aunt Dee said in her park ranger voice. "Its two arms meet at the central point to make a wide angle of 125 degrees, creating a V shape. One end points toward the Washington Monument and the other end toward the Lincoln Memorial. The wall is ten feet three inches high at the center and is made of black granite—Oh, hello, girls!"

Uncle Dan and his friends turned to look at Sydney and Elizabeth standing b›ind them. "Hi, Elizabeth," Uncle Dan said. "Boys, this is my niece, Elizabeth Anderson, and her friend Sydney Lincoln."

The men shook hands with Sydney and Elizabeth. "Are you any relation to Abraham Lincoln?" one of them asked jokingly.

"Not that I know of," said Sydney.

They moved toward the wall as Aunt Dee continued her tour. "The Wall was designed by a young American sculpture artist named Maya Lin."

"Violin," Sydney whispered into Elizabeth's ear. The girls giggled, and Aunt Dee frowned.

"The names of 58,220 men and women are etched into these panels," she said. "You already know these were the men and women killed in the Vietnam War, or listed as missing in action. If you'd like to find specific names, I can help you with that, and our volunteers have tracing paper if you'd like to make tracings of any names. Also, feel free to leave a note or other memento at the Wall. People leave things here every day, like these—" She hesitated. "Oranges?"

A row of oranges lined the base of the Wall. Actually, they

were tangerines, but Sydney kept that fact to herself. Aunt Dee got annoyed when Sydney corrected her about such facts. The tangerines were neatly placed about three feet apart, stopping halfway down the west part of the Wall.

"We've had some strange things left here lately," Aunt Dee said. "Last wefi, it was lemons."

"Lemons?" Uncle Dan chuckled. "That does seem strange."

"I know," Aunt Dee answered. "They were arranged in a neat little pyramid in front of panel 4E. The wefi before that, a box of blueberries was left by 48W; and the wefi before that, a row of limes led to panel 14W. They were set there just like these oranges."

"Tangerines!" Sydney corrected her. She couldn't help herself.

"Whatever," Aunt Dee replied. "And then, of course, the other day some vandals struck."

"I heard about that on the news," said one of the buddies. "It made me mad that someone disrespected the Wall like that. Did they catch them yet?"

"No," Aunt Dee answered. "Since it was graffiti, we think it was kids, probably some gang members. Most cities seem to have that problem."

Sydney and Elizabeth walked away, leaving the adults to discuss gang activities and whatever else people their age talked about.

"This place is so quiet and depressing," Elizabeth observed.

Sydney agreed. "A lot of people treat it like it's a cemetery. I don't come here unless Aunt Dee needs me to. . . . Too many sad people. But we have to hang around until your uncle and his friends leave."

"I guess," said Elizabeth.

"Then we can walk to the Tidal Basin and ride the paddle boats," Sydney continued. "That'll be fun."

The girls wandered along the Wall with groups of tourists. They noticed all the different things left by people who wanted to remember the dead soldiers: a teddy bear here, a pair of combat boots there, letters addressed to loved ones, identification tags soldiers had worn in Vietnam, and plenty of tiny American flags. Nearby a man was busy making a rubbing of one of the names on the Wall. Not far from him, an old woman laid a red rose on the brick walkway in front of one of the panels.

When they were about halfway down the west side of the Wall, Elizabeth noticed her uncle and his friends b›ind them. Uncle Dan had his head in his hands. He seemed to be crying, and each buddy had an arm around him. Elizabeth looked away. She couldn't stand to see her uncle being sad. Bitter anger crept up inside of her. "*Refrain from anger and turn from wrath; do not fret—it leads only to evil,*" she reminded herself. *Psalm 37:8.* The shiny granite wall reflected images like a mirror, so Elizabeth stopped to put a clip in her long blond hair.

Sydney was next to her by panel 30W, setting up a little American flag that had toppled over. She saw a tall man approaching them. He looked about the same age as Tyler, Sydney's brother, who was away at college. The man's fair chefis and chin were almost hidden by his bushy red beard, and Sydney noticed that he smelled like cigarette smoke. His blue T-shirt was stained and his black cargo shorts were too big for him. He wore shabby brown sandals at the ends of his long, sunburned legs. Each was decorated with a silver peace sign about the size of a quarter.

The man read the names on the wall. Then he picked up the last tangerine in the long row of them. He tossed it into the air and caught it in his right hand. "This is the place, Moose," he said.

A big, burly guy had sauntered next to him. His head was shaved and his walnut-colored eyes darted about as he scanned the names on panel 30W. His gray T-shirt showed the picture of a fierce bulldog with the words NICE DOGGY.

"You're right, Rusty," he said. "Looks like they got the sidewalk cleaned up already. Good thing there was a picture in the paper." He took a handkerchief out of his pocket and blew his nose.

"Yeah, these guys work fast," Rusty muttered. "Bet it took a lot of scrubbing." He reached down and picked up a note someone had attached to a flag by the wall. He read it aloud. "Patience is bitter, but it bears sweet fruit." He laughed. "The Professor has a sense of humor. I think I'll eat my orange now."

Sydney wanted to say that they were tangerines, not oranges. Instead she and Elizabeth listened while trying not to be obvious.

Moose retied the laces on his dirty tennis shoes. "This one was a little different from green, blue, and yellow," he said. "But I didn't have to look long before I found it, Rusty. You saw it, too, right?"

Rusty peeled the tangerine and stuffed the peelings into

his pocket. Then he gave the fruit to his friend. "Yeah, I saw it, Moose. Right away."

"Saw what?" Elizabeth whispered to Sydney.

Sydney shrugged.

Moose bit into the tangerine. Juice ran down his chin, trickled onto his hairy arms, and dripped onto his shirt. When he finished eating, he wiped his sticky hands on his jeans. "We should probably leave something for The Professor, so he knows when—"

"Shut up," Rusty grunted.

"But we have to—"

"Shut. . .up!" Rusty whispered, spitting out each word. He tipped his head slightly toward Sydney and Beth. Then he nodded toward the other tourists.

"I get it," Moose said. He sounded like he'd just discovered the answer to a riddle. He faced the Wall. Then, after about thirty seconds and a quick jab in the ribs from Rusty, he saluted. "We should leave something nice for our dearly departed fellow soldier," he said loudly.

Rusty picked up another tangerine and tossed it to Moose. "Let's go sit down and have a snack," he directed.

The two men walked away.

"What do you think that was about?" Elizabeth asked.

"Beats me," Sydney answered. "But we should walk; otherwise they might think it's weird that we're standing here for so long."

The girls strolled toward the center of the Wall, the place where the West Wall met the East. Uncle Dan and his buddies were halfway down the East Wall, and one of the buddies was kneeling on the ground making a tissue paper rubbing of a name.

"I think those guys were creepy," Elizabeth said. "They were obviously looking for something and found it. Who do you think The Professor is?" Elizabeth was so busy thinking and talking that she almost bumped into a lady in front of her.

"And that stuff about this one being different from green, blue, and yellow," Sydney added. "You're right. They were kind of creepy."

"Maybe we should tell your aunt," said Elizabeth. "I think they're up to something. Maybe they're the guys who painted the graffiti on the sidewalk."

Sydney stopped in front of panel 10E and pretended to search for a name. "No, I don't think so, Beth. I hate to admit it, but kids probably did the graffiti. And I don't think we should tell my aunt. I mean, they weren't doing anything wrong."

"But they were acting suspicious," Elizabeth argued as she joined Sydney and pretended to look for a name on the shiny black panel.

"Think about it. *We* might look suspicious," Sydney suggested. "We've been standing here for five minutes acting like we're looking for a name. Not exactly what a couple of kids would do."

The girls walked to Elizabeth's uncle and his friends.

"There you are!" Uncle Dan said. "Listen, we're almost done. Would you girls like to have lunch with the boys and me?"

Sydney looked at Elizabeth.

"I'm buying," Uncle Dan said, smiling.

"Well, okay," Elizabeth replied. "How about if we meet you

by the statue of the ladies when you're done?"

"You mean the statue of the *nurses*," one of the buddies corrected her. "We can tell you some stories about them over lunch." He grinned and winked at Uncle Dan.

"Okay, we'll meet you over there," Sydney said. "Let's go, Elizabeth!" She linked her arm with her friend's and tugged on it, pulling Elizabeth back toward the center of the Wall.

"What?" Elizabeth balked.

"Look." Sydney pointed toward the middle of the West Wall. Moose and Rusty were back, putting something near the bottom of panel 30W.

"Slow down," Elizabeth said. "Let them leave it, and then we'll see what it is."

The girls stopped walking and pretended again to look for a name on the Wall.

"Okay, they're leaving," Elizabeth reported. "Let's *slowly* walk down there so we don't draw attention to ourselves."

The girls strolled toward panel 30W. When they got there, they found a note written on lined notebook paper. It was stuck onto the thin plastic stick of a small American flag. Elizabeth knelt down and read it aloud. "Meade me in St. Louis, July 1."

"Huh?" Sydney bent down to see.

"That's what it says," Elizabeth told her. "All in capital letters. 'MEADE ME IN ST. LOUIS, JULY 1.'" She hesitated for a few seconds. "Sydney? Do you know how it is when God puts a thought in your head and you know that it's true? Well, I just got one of those thoughts, and it's not good!"

Elizabeth felt a heavy hand rest on her shoulder.

"It's time to go, little girl," a man's voice ordered.

The Lincoln Memorial

Elizabeth's heart jumped to her throat. She whirled around. Uncle Dan waited b›ind her.

"Did I scare you, honey?" he said. "I'm sorry. Are you ready to go to lunch?"

Elizabeth brushed some dirt from the knees of her new blue jeans. "You know what, Uncle Dan? I think Sydney and I will skip lunch today. I really want to see stuff in Washington, D.C., and we're only here for a wefi."

What? Sydney thought. She was looking forward to a free lunch in the city. Most of the time when her family went out to eat, it was to a place in her neighborhood called Ben's Chili Bowl. Anywhere else was a treat.

Uncle Dan looked disappointed but didn't try to persuade the girls any further.

The girls walked with Uncle Dan and his friends to the west end of the Vietnam Wall to say their good-byes.

"Check in with me this wefi," Uncle Dan told his niece. "Your mom will be furious if I don't take good care of you."

One of his buddies, Al, chuckled. "And we'll take good care of your uncle," he said. Al was the one who had corrected Elizabeth about the nurses' statue. Elizabeth didn't like something about him.

She kissed her uncle on the for>ead. "Don't worry, Uncle Dan. I'll be fine."

The men had barely walked away when Sydney said, "You know, a free lunch sounded pretty good to me."

Elizabeth took Sydney's arm and pulled her. "We have to find Rusty and Moose," she said. "I think they went that way." She pointed toward the Lincoln Memorial.

The girls started walking along Henry Bacon Drive toward the big white building with the famous statue of Abraham Lincoln.

"When I read the words 'Meade me in St. Louis,' well, I got a thought," Elizabeth said. "If I'm right, those guys are terrorists."

"What!" Sydney shrified. "They're weird and creepy, but they don't look like terrorists."

A police car rushed past them, weaving through traffic on the drive. Its siren briefly interrupted their conversation.

"Remember that Bible verse: 'Outside you look good, but inside you are evil and only pretend to be good'?" Elizabeth asked.

"No," Sydney answered. "Why do you know so much scripture?"

"Because just about everybody in my family is a minister or a missionary," Elizabeth said.

The girls split up and walked around two ladies pushing baby strollers.

Elizabeth had to run a few steps to catch up with Sydney. "As soon as I read those words, 'Meade me in St. Louis,' I thought about a few years ago when terrorists tried to assassinate President Meade. Do you remember? It was at the Smithsonian, at the National Air and Space Museum. Slow down a little, please."

Sydney never did anything slowly. Her friends often had a hard time keeping up with her fast, long legs. "Oh yeah," she answered. "The president was there to celebrate some sort of anniversary."

"The anniversary of Charles Lindberg's flight across the Atlantic in his plane, The Spirit of St. Louis," Elizabeth added.

"I almost forgot about that," Sydney continued. She walked a little slower. "That was the first year that Meade was president. Someone tried to shoot him but got away, and the government said it was terrorists. The Spirit of St. Louis. . . President Meade. . . Elizabeth! You don't think the note was about that?"

"They never caught who did it," Elizabeth reminded her. "I think Rusty and Moose might at least know something about that."

The girls passed a crowd of people at a food cart near the Lincoln Memorial. Sydney suddenly realized how hungry she was.

"You and the rest of the Camp Club Girls always accuse me of jumping to conclusions," she said. "But this time, I think *you're* jumping to conclusions. Even if you *are* right, Moose and Rusty are gone by now. We'll never find them in this crowd. And since you cost me a free lunch today, let's get in line and buy some sandwiches."

"Okay," Elizabeth replied. "But I wish I knew where they went."

When the girls finally got their food and drinks, they sat on a bench facing the street. The Lincoln Memorial towered to their left, almost one hundred feet tall. Its huge white columns made it look like an ancient Grefi temple.

Sydney peeled the paper off her BLT wrap and took a bite. "As long as we're here, do you want to tour the memorial?" she asked.

"Not really," Elizabeth said as she opened her chocolate milk. "Did you know that a long time ago, Vietnam War protests went on at the Lincoln Memorial? Being here reminds me of what happened to my uncle Dan."

"Elizabeth," Sydney groaned. "You can't visit Washington, D.C., and not see the monuments. Sure, there have been protests here, but that's not what it's all about."

Elizabeth said nothing. It was just like the night before when they'd been talking about Uncle Dan before going to bed.

"This place is a memorial to the president who freed the slaves. Martin Luther King Jr. made his famous 'I Have a Dream' speech here, and Marian Anderson sang here when they wouldn't let her sing in Constitution Hall because she was black. I like the Lincoln Memorial, Elizabeth. Some really good things happened here!"

Sydney didn't like being annoyed with her friend, but she couldn't understand Elizabeth's attitude. She was always easygoing and understanding, but since she'd arrived, she just didn't seem to be herself.

"I'm sorry," Elizabeth apologized. She picked at her burrito with a black plastic fork. "I just don't understand why people have to fight in wars where good folks get hurt—like my uncle."

Sydney thought hard for something to say. "Wars have happened since way back in Old Testament times, Beth. Remember when David fought Goliath? Can you try not to think about bad stuff and just have a good time?" She offered her friend a dill pickle.

Elizabeth screwed up her face. "No, thank you," she said.

A shiny black limousine pulled up in front of them. It stopped on the wrong side of the street and held up traffic. The driver got out and walked briskly toward the back door.

"Wow," said Elizabeth. "Who do you think is in there?"

Sydney took the last bite of her wrap and tossed the container into a trash can by the bench. "Probably a senator or a congressman. You see tons of limos in the District."

The driver opened the back door, and a short, dark man in a black suit got out. His crisp white shirt gleamed against his tan skin, and a thin black necktie hung neatly inside the front of his suit jacket. His mirrored sunglasses reflected the image of Sydney and Elizabeth sitting on the bench nearby. "Twenty minutes," he said to the driver. He walked toward the memorial, and the limo drove off.

Sydney turned around to look at him. "Elizabeth!" she gasped.

"What?"

"There are Rusty and Moose."

Sure enough, Moose and Rusty stood on the sidewalk, not far from where Sydney and Elizabeth sat. The girls watched the man in the suit approach them. Moose stuck out his hand for the man to shake it, but the man ignored him. Then all three walked briskly toward the Lincoln Memorial.

"Let's see what they're up to," Sydney said.

"But you think they're good, upstanding citizens," Elizabeth reminded her.

"I didn't say that," Sydney argued. "I said that they don't look like terrorists. It won't hurt to check them out. Maybe you're right. Maybe they did have something to do with the graffiti."

The men were a good distance ahead of them now. The girls wove through the crowd trying to keep them in sight. Sydney, being taller than Elizabeth, focused on Rusty's shaggy red hair. The short man was impossible to see. He was dwarfed by Moose's big, hulking body.

"Do you see them?" Elizabeth asked. She walked a few steps on her tiptoes.

"I see the top of Rusty's head bobbing up and down," Sydney answered. "Looks like they're heading for the stairs."

The Lincoln Memorial had fifty-six wide marble stairs leading to the statue of the sixteenth president of the United States. People sat on the staircase talking and reading. Tourists climbed to the top to gaze at the Reflecting Pool on the Mall and, beyond it, the Washington Monument and the United States Capitol Building.

The men started to climb the stairs.

"Now what?" Elizabeth asked.

"We should try to get close enough to listen and find out, once and for all, if they're up to something," Sydney told her. "But we'll have to be careful that they don't see us. They might remember us."

"How about if we split up?" Elizabeth suggested. "They're less likely to recognize us if we're not together."

The men were halfway up the stairs now.

"Good idea," Sydney agreed. "But let's keep an eye on each other. Just in case."

The girls split up. Elizabeth ran up the left side of the staircase, and Sydney ran up the right.

At the top of the stairs, a sign read QUIET, RESPECT PLEASE. Just beyond it was the nineteen-foot-tall statue of President Lincoln. He towered over the tourists, looking relaxed but alert, sitting in his chair, watching over the nation's capital. Moose, Rusty, and the short man didn't seem to notice the president. They whisked past him as if he weren't even there.

The memorial was surrounded by thirty-six huge columns. They were thirty-seven feet tall and fat enough to hide b‹ind. Sydney saw the men hurry to the column farthest to the right of the president. They disappeared around it.

Sydney searched for Elizabeth and saw her standing at the foot of the Lincoln statue. She was watching Sydney like a hawk. Sydney pointed to herself and then toward the column where the men went, showing Elizabeth that she would follow them. Elizabeth put her right index finger to her lips.

Silently, like a shadow, Sydney slipped from one marble column to the next. Finally she was just one column away. It would be tricky to shift to the last column where the men were standing. If the men changed their position, she would be caught. Sydney pefied around the column to be sure the coast was clear. She said a short prayer and took a deep breath. Then she slithered to the column hiding the men.

With her back plastered against the pillar just a few feet from where they stood, Sydney listened.

"We left a note for you," Moose was saying, "because we didn't expect you to show up."

The short man snickered. "You never know when I'll show up." His deep voice didn't fit his small, slim body. "That's why you'd better do exactly what you're told."

"We are, boss!" Rusty spoke this time. His voice was almost a whisper, nervous and hushed. "We're doing it just like you told us to."

"That's good," said the man. "Otherwise, we might have to send you on the trip with Meade."

What does that *mean?* Sydney wondered. She pressed tighter against the marble pillar and shifted, ever so slightly, to her left. She tried to listen even harder.

"*Waaaaaaaaaa!*" A high-pitched shrifi filled the air. Sydney's heart stopped as she looked toward the Lincoln statue. A woman near Elizabeth was trying to calm her unhappy little boy. As Elizabeth and Sydney watched, the mother led her screaming child down the steps and away from the president's statue. Sydney sighed.

"Who came up with the tattoo idea?" The short man was talking now. Sydney had missed part of the conversation.

"I did, boss," Moose said uncertainly.

There was a short pause.

"Good work," he said. "I didn't think you had it in you, Percival."

Percival! Sydney thought to herself. *Moose's real name is Percival?* She stifled a laugh. What a funny, old-fashioned name!

168

"Thanks, boss!" Moose's voice relaxed.

"Don't you want us to go check out the place?" asked Rusty. "We could go right now."

"I warned you about being impatient," the short man snapped. "I'll talk it over with him first. If it's a go, then we'll move up to the next level. When that happens, *then* you can go and check it out."

"Tomorrow?" Rusty asked.

"Tomorrow," the man said.

Sydney saw Elizabeth with her right arm in the air. Beth was frantically making counter-clockwise circles with her right hand. Sydney heard footsteps on the opposite side of the pillar. The men were leaving. She inched her way counter-clockwise around the gigantic column, making sure she was opposite of where they were. If they saw her, she couldn't imagine what would happen.

Sydney held her breath and didn't let it out until she was sure they were gone. She pefied around the back of the column and looked toward Elizabeth. The men were almost to her, but she had her back to them. She was talking with a group of old ladies, trying to edge her way in front of them as she pointed up at the Lincoln statue.

She's acting like a tour guide so they won't recognize her,

Sydney thought. The men walked by, not seeing Elizabeth, and continued down the stairs.

Sydney came out from her hiding place and hurried toward her friend.

"And if you'd like to learn more about the Lincoln Memorial, you can ask one of the park rangers down there."

Elizabeth pointed down the steps toward the Reflecting Pool where a ranger, wearing a uniform like Aunt Dee's, was talking with tourists. The women started down the stairs.

"So what did they say?" Elizabeth asked.

"I don't have a good feeling about them," Sydney confided. "Moose and Rusty called the suit guy 'Boss,' and they seemed afraid of him. They were extra polite. The suit guy said Meade is taking a trip, and if Moose and Rusty don't do what they're told, they might go with him. They talked about a tattoo and taking things to the next level, and they asked the boss if they should go check someplace out. But I don't know where that is. Something's happening tomorrow, too, but I don't know that either. And would you believe that Moose's real name is Percival?"

"*Percival!* Do you think the suit guy is The Professor?" Elizabeth asked.

"I don't know," Sydney said. "But I think it's too late for us to go to the Smithsonian now. And I think we should tell the other Camp Club Girls what's going on and see what they think. Let's text McKenzie and ask her to schedule a group chat for tonight."

"Great idea," Elizabeth responded. "Especially since all the time I watched you, I felt someone was watching *me!*"

Colors of Danger!

Promptly at 6:55 that night, Sydney was waiting at her computer with Elizabeth seated next to her. She entered the Camp Club Girls' chat room, and right away, the messages began to arrive.

> Alexis: *Are you guys ok? I got an uncomfortable feeling about you today and prayed for you.*
> Sydney: *When everyone logs on, we'll explain all.*
> McKenzie: *I'm here. I bet something to do with Agent Orange is involved.*
> Alexis: *Let's hope it's just kids playing a prank and not something worse. However, I did see a mystery movie last wefi that had terrorists masquerading as kids.*
> Kate: *Biscuit started barking like crazy as soon as I pulled up this screen. I think he knows it's you guys, and is trying to tell you he misses you.*
> Sydney: *How is Biscuit? I wish he could text with us.*
> Kate: *He's wanted to play ball with me all day.*
> Bailey: *I'm here! Just got home from a day with Mom in*

Chicago. Good thing we came home early. We're an hour b›ind you here in Peoria.

McKenzie: *I was beginning to wonder if you were home when I sent an e-mail and didn't hear from you.*

Sydney: *Okay, since we're all here, let's get started. . . .*

●—●—●

Sydney spent the next few minutes telling the girls about all that had happened that day. She told them about Moose and Rusty and everything that had gone on at the Wall that morning. Then she explained how she had listened to their conversation at the Lincoln Memorial.

Elizabeth took the keyboard and slid it over to where she sat next to Sydney at her desk.

Elizabeth: *When I read the note,* "Meade me in St. Louis, July 1," *the Lord gave me the memory of President Meade and when he was almost shot a few years back. It was at the National Air and Space Museum at the Smithsonian Museum, here in Washington. The president was there to honor Lindberg's flight in his plane, the Spirit of St. Louis. So I've been wondering, do you think they could be planning something evil at the same place on July 1st?*

Alexis: *Are you sure that the thought was from God, Elizabeth? Sometimes Satan gives us thoughts to throw us off track. You probably know where the Bible says that.*

Elizabeth: *It's in 2 Corinthians: "Even Satan tries to*

172

make himself look like an angel of light. So why does it seem strange for Satan's servants to pretend to do what is right?" But, Alex, I know that this thought was from God. Oh, and I forgot to tell you about the fruit.

Bailey: *Fruit? This is beginning to sound really crazy, Lizzybet.*

Elizabeth: *I know. Someone has been leaving fruit at the Vietnam Wall: a small pyramid of lemons, a box of blueberries, and rows of limes and oranges.*

Sydney took the keyboard back.

Sydney: *Tangerines!*

McKenzie: *I think the fruit is important. That one guy found the note about patience being bitter and bearing sweet fruit.*

Kate: *I looked that up online. It's a Turkish proverb. Whoever wrote it might want those guys to be patient about whatever they're up to.*

Bailey: *That one guy's name is Red. Why? What do they look like?*

Elizabeth: *Moose and* Rusty, *that's his name, look messy, like they haven't combed their hair or washed their clothes in a while. The short guy. . . well. . .think of an FBI agent. He looks like that.*

McKenzie: *Rusty said, "This one is different from green, blue, and yellow." Think about it. Limes are green, blueberries are blue, lemons are yellow.*

Sydney: *And* tangerines *are orange! But what do those colors mean. . .if anything?*
Kate: *Was the fruit always left in the same spot?*

Sydney turned to Elizabeth. "Do you know?"

Elizabeth twisted the pendant on her necklace. "It wasn't in the same spot," she said. "I remember your aunt told Uncle Dan where they left it, but I wasn't really listening. Why don't you ask her? But don't be too obvious about it."

"Okay," Sydney replied. "I'll get a banana from the kitchen. Then I'll use that to start a conversation. I'll say that it reminded me of the fruit at the Wall. Aunt Dee will love it if I ask her. She likes talking about her work."

Sydney pushed the keyboard back to Elizabeth and hurried downstairs to find Aunt Dee.

The other girls chatted for a while as they waited for Sydney to return. Elizabeth told them a little about her uncle and that he had been wounded in Vietnam. She asked them all to pray that the Lord would heal Uncle Dan's legs so he could walk again.

Suddenly Sydney burst back into the room repeating, "4E, 48W, 14W." She took the keyboard from Elizabeth.

Sydney: *Write this down. 4E lemons, 48W blueberries, 14W limes.*
Kate: *And the oranges were where?*
Elizabeth: *They were in a long row from the beginning of the Wall to the same place where the graffiti was painted on the sidewalk—panel 30W.*

Kate: *Everyone go to* www.viewthewall.com. *Let me know when you're there.*

Sydney: *We're there.*

McKenzie: *Me, too.*

Bailey: *And me.*

Alexis: *Hang on. My browser is acting up. I have to try it again. Okay, I'm in. Now what?*

Kate: *Click on any panel number and it will take you to a photograph of that panel on the Wall. Then you can zoom in and read the names on the panel. I think that's what we need to do. We need to read each panel where the fruits were left, and look for clues.*

McKenzie: *That will take forever! I think we should research Agent Orange. That's the obvious answer.*

Alexis: *Maybe the obvious answer isn't the one we need. I think we should check out Kate's idea. Then, if that doesn't work, we can check out Agent Orange.*

Sydney clicked on panel 4E. A photo popped up of that panel on the Vietnam Wall. She and Elizabeth began reading the hundreds of names on the panel.

Sydney: *There are 136 rows. Why don't we divide them up? It'll go faster that way.*

She assigned each girl a group of rows.

Bailey: *What am I supposed to be looking for?*

Sydney: *Any name that might connect with lemons.*
Think about what they look like, how they taste,
that sort of stuff.

"I don't like doing this," Elizabeth told Sydney. "All of these names represent someone who was killed in Vietnam. This is more than just a list of names; it's real people."

"I know," Sydney agreed as she searched the rows. "I don't like doing it either."

Bailey: *I think I might have found something. I see*
someone with the last name Gold *in row 34.*
Lemons are sort of gold.
Alexis: *That's great work, Bailey! I wrote that down.*
Lemons, gold, row 34, panel 4E.
Kate: *Did anyone else find anything? If not, let's move*
to the next panel, 48W. Look for anything that
connects to blue or blueberries.

Again Sydney assigned rows, and she and Elizabeth searched their lists of names. Before long, McKenzie's name popped on the screen.

McKenzie: *I think Bailey might be on to something.*
A soldier is on my list with the last name Blue!
Kate: *I'm looking on panel 14W, where the limes were.*
There's a Green on my list.

Sydney shrugged her shoulders and looked at Elizabeth.

"If there's a soldier named Tangerine on panel 30W, I'll make your bed the rest of the time you're here," she promised. Sydney figured that it was a safe promise to make, because no one, especially not a soldier, would be named Tangerine.

Bailey: *I'm on 30W. And guess what? I found a guy named Orange.*

Sydney: *Oh, come on, Bailey. No one is named Orange. I mean, have you ever met any Oranges?*

Alexis: *Bailey is right. And this one is different from Green, Blue, and Yellow. . .I mean Gold. Orange is his* first *name.*

Sydney clicked to the photograph of panel 30W. Sure enough, there was a man named Orange.

McKenzie: *And do you see* where *it is? Row 64. That's what 64 means in* "GO 64." *It was a clue for Rusty and Moose to look at that row. The leader must have thought that they needed some extra help, since this name is a little different from the others.*

Elizabeth took the keyboard from Sydney.

Elizabeth: *So we know the boss, or professor, or whoever he is, was telling Rusty and Moose to look for colors. But why?*

Kate: *You'll never believe this. I was doing a search for colors, and Biscuit put his red ball in my lap.*

Bailey: *Pet Biscuit for me!*

Sydney: *What's hard to believe about Biscuit putting his ball in your lap?*

Kate: *The ball is red. I pushed it out of my lap as I was typing a search for the colors we talked about. When I saw the red ball bouncing, I accidentally typed in red, too. Guess what! These colors are the colors of the Homeland Security Terror Alert System. Green is a low risk of terrorist attacks. Blue is a general risk of attacks. Yellow means a significant risk of attacks. And orange is a high risk. There's only one more level above that, and it's red—a severe risk of terrorist attacks!*

Elizabeth looked at Sydney, and Sydney knew what she was thinking.

Elizabeth: *That's what the short man meant when he told Moose and Rusty that they'd be taking things to the next level.*

Sydney grabbed the keyboard back.

Sydney: *Oh my goodness! They really are terrorists!*

A Plan to Track Trouble

The next morning, Sydney and Elizabeth were at Union Station in Washington, D.C., waiting for Kate Oliver to arrive. She was on the ten o'clock train from Philadelphia. During their group chat the night before, Kate had come up with a brilliant idea that involved a piece of electronic equipment. Since Philadelphia was only a few hours away and trains ran frequently up and down the coast, the girls had decided she would join Sydney and Elizabeth. If all went well, they would put her idea into action before the terrorists stepped up their plan to Level Red.

The old, cavernous train building was alive with activity. Its white marble floors echoed with the footsteps of tourists, people on business, and government workers as they rushed to and from their trains. Music drifted from stores on the upper level, adding to the chaos.

Sydney stood by the doors nearest the train tracks to the Philadelphia–Washington, D.C., line. Kate's train would arrive at that platform.

Sydney and Elizabeth opened the big glass doors that led out to the tracks. A blast of air, heavy with the smell of diesel fuel, swept past the girls' faces. They waited and watched while some trains sat idle on the tracks and others chugged in and out of the station.

Sydney soon spotted a single headlight on the Phila-delphia track. Slowly an enormous, shiny, bullet-shaped engine chugged into the station pulling six cars b›ind it. It stopped at the platform where the girls waited. The doors slid open, and passengers spilled out and scurried into the building like ants toward a crumb.

"Do you see Kate?" Sydney asked.

"Not yet," Elizabeth replied.

The crowd was thinning out. Only a dozen or so people remained. The girls worried that Kate had missed her train, but then they saw her. She waved to them as she exited the third car and stepped onto the concrete platform. She ran toward them, her sandy-colored hair bouncing. With her yellow T-shirt, fuchsia backpack, and bright green shorts, she looked as if she'd stepped off a tropical island.

"Hi, Syd. Hi, Elizabeth," Kate said. She briefly hugged each friend.

"We were afraid you missed the train," Sydney said as they walked into the crowded station.

"I was listening to Casting Crowns on my iPod," Kate answered. "I decided to hang out on the train until most people got off. It was a zoo in there."

Sydney led the girls down the escalators to the street level of the station. Then they walked toward the Plaza exit. "We'll go to West Potomac Park," Sydney announced. "Then we can talk."

Kate and Elizabeth scurried, trying to keep up with Sydney's long stride.

"I have the equipment ready," Kate announced. "I just have to show you how to use it. Do you have the rest of the stuff?"

"Yes. In my backpack," Elizabeth answered.

They were outside Union Station now and walking across the Plaza. They passed the Columbus Memorial Fountain where the statue of Christopher Columbus stared steely-eyed into the distance. To the right of him was a carving of a bearded man, sitting. To the left of him was a carving of an American Indian from long ago, crouching b›ind his shield and reaching for an arrow.

The friends caught a city bus on Constitution Avenue. Cars, taxis, and delivery vans whizzed beside them as they traveled west to 15th Street. They got off on 15th and walked toward the Washington Monument. Then they covered the short distance to the Tidal Basin in the park.

The girls found a quiet bench under the cherry trees. Nearby, children and grown-ups rode paddleboats through the cool, clear water in the Tidal Basin. In the peaceful setting, no one could have known that Kate, Elizabeth, and Sydney were worried about a terrorist attack on President Meade.

Kate unzipped her backpack and pulled out a small black cell phone. "Here it is," she said. "I've programmed it so any of us can access the data from our computers. It works like this: We have to make sure that this phone is with Moose all the time. From what you said, he's the dumber of the two, so it'll be easier to get him to take it. As long as he has this phone, we can track him wherever he goes."

Kate handed Sydney and Elizabeth each a slip of paper with some writing on it. "When you get home, just go to this

URL and type in your password. Elizabeth, yours is 'Indiana.' Sydney, yours is 'Jones.' Once you do that, you'll see a screen with a map on it. It will show you exactly where Moose is. He'll appear as a little green blip on the screen."

Sydney laughed when she thought of the big, hulking Moose as nothing more than a small green blip.

Elizabeth opened her yellow backpack and took out the box that Sydney's bracelet had come in. Then she pulled out a brown paper lunch bag, a pair of scissors, and a roll of tape. "I have everything we need," she said.

Kate handed Elizabeth the phone, and carefully Elizabeth placed it into the box. She cut the paper bag and made it into a piece of wrapping paper. Then she folded it around the box and sealed it with tape.

"Now we have to create the note," Sydney began. "I know what we should say."

"You dictate and I'll write," Kate offered, taking a black permanent marker out of her backpack.

"Okay, here goes." Sydney dictated the words and Kate wrote them on a leftover scrap of the paper bag:

Moose, it is very important *that you keep this package with you at all times. DO NOT OPEN IT or talk to anyone about it, including people you trust—not even the person giving you this! You will be asked for this package at the end of your mission. Keep it safe, keep quiet, or else!*

"That sounds good!" Kate said, smiling.

"I think so, too," Elizabeth agreed. "From what Sydney overheard at the Lincoln Memorial, Moose seems to want to please the guy in the suit. So he'll probably take very good care of this package."

She folded the note in half, hiding the message inside. Then she wrote "Moose" on the blank side and taped it to the top of the wrapped box.

"We should go now," she said. "Idle hands are the devil's playground."

"Is that in the Bible?" Sydney asked.

"No, but it's a good proverb," Elizabeth replied.

Within moments, the girls arrived at the Vietnam Wall. When the friends got there, they found the place crowded with visitors.

The girls hid near the trees at the south yard of the Wall.

"Kate, I think you should do this alone," Sydney suggested. "Moose and Rusty have never seen you. So if you run into them, it'll be no big deal. Plus, if my aunt is around and she sees us, she'll wonder why we're here."

"I think you're right," Kate said. She dropped her backpack on the ground. "Watch my stuff."

Elizabeth handed her the small package wrapped in brown paper. Then Kate went toward the Wall.

Sydney and Elizabeth stayed hidden in trees. Sydney had brought a pair of binoculars she liked to use for bird watching. She was peering through them, watching Kate.

Kate purposefully looked indifferent as she casually strolled past the panels etched with names. On the west end, the panels began with the number 70. Only five names were etched onto that first panel. It was the shortest one on the west part of the Wall. Each panel beyond it stood a little bit taller until the east and west walls met in the middle at their highest points. Kate walked on past panels 61. . .60. . .59. . .58. . . 57. Then something caught her eye. She hurried to a spot five panels down.

"Hey, she's stopping!" said Sydney, squinting through the binoculars.

"She must be there," Elizabeth added.

"No. She's a long way away from it still," Sydney disagreed.

Sydney watched as Kate stopped in front of a quart-sized box of huge red strawberries on the ground at the center of panel 52W.

"She's at the wrong panel!" Sydney exclaimed. "Didn't we agree that she'd leave the box by panel 30W?"

"Yes," Elizabeth confirmed.

"Well, she's a long way from there," Sydney said, focusing her binoculars.

"What's she doing now?" Elizabeth wondered. She could see Kate crouching down in front of the Wall.

"I don't know. I can't tell, because she has her back to me. I think she might be leaving the package there," said Sydney.

"But it's the wrong place!" Elizabeth said with exasperation.

"Oh, Elizabeth! What are we going to do? Come on, girl!" Sydney said under her breath. "You're at the wrong spot!"

The girls watched as Kate set the package down.

"I'm going in," Sydney exclaimed, handing the binoculars to Elizabeth.

"Do you think that's a good idea?" Elizabeth asked nervously.

"Probably not, but I'll be careful. If that phone gets into the wrong hands, we're sunk. Keep an eye on us." Sydney sprinted across the grass toward the Wall.

Just as Kate stood up, she felt someone grab her arm. She jumped.

"What are you doing?" Sydney whispered. "This is the wrong place."

"No, it's not!" Kate whispered back. "Let's not talk about it here."

"But this isn't 30W!" Sydney reminded her. "It's down that way." She pointed to her left.

"Don't point!" Kate scolded. "Someone might be watching us. Let's get out of here."

Sydney was about to cut across the grass again.

"Uh-uh," Kate said. She took Sydney by the arm. "You'll show them where we're hiding!" Kate was right. Obediently, Sydney followed her to the entrance to the memorial. They doubled back toward the trees where Elizabeth was.

"I knew what I was doing!" Kate said when they were away from the crowd. "As I walked to panel 30W, I saw a box of strawberries by panel 52W. I had to check it out."

The girls were approaching Elizabeth now. She was still watching the Wall through Sydney's binoculars.

"Hey, Beth, Kate found some strawberries!" Sydney didn't mean to startle her friend, who swung around, dropping the binoculars on the ground.

"Don't do that to me!" Elizabeth said.

"I'm sorry," Sydney apologized. "But Kate found some strawberries by panel 52W."

Elizabeth picked up the binoculars and handed them to Sydney.

"That's not all I found," Kate said. "A soldier on that panel had the last name Redd. You know what that means, don't you? They've accelerated their plot to Level Red. Anytime now, they could put their plan into action—and we have to find out what it is before someone gets hurt!"

Kate picked her backpack up off the ground and took out her notepad and marker. She printed the words *Hail to the chief at the twilight's last gleaming*. "There's a note with the strawberries, attached to a small American flag. This is what it says," Kate told them.

Elizabeth read the words. "Were the letters all capitalized like you've written them here?" she asked.

"I didn't really pay attention," Kate answered. "But no, I don't think so. I'm almost sure that they weren't all caps."

"Then this note must be from The Professor, or the guy in the suit," Elizabeth decided. "The note that Moose and Rusty left for him was written all in capital letters, the one that said 'Meade me in St. Louis.' "

Kate reached into her backpack and took out a plastic bottle of water. She plopped down on the ground and drank some. "Who do you think The Professor is?" she wondered. "Do you think it's the suit guy?"

"I doubt it," Sydney said, watching the Wall with her binoculars. "At the Lincoln Memorial, Rusty wanted to go and check out *the place*, whatever that meant, and the suit guy said no, that he'd have to talk it over with *him* first. I think *him* might mean The Professor."

"So, we think they might be plotting to do something to President Meade," Kate sighed, "but we don't know who the *him* is or where the place is."

"You've got it," Sydney replied, still watching through her binoculars. "But if your plan works, we'll know soon. Hey, Elizabeth, isn't that your uncle Dan's friend?"

"Huh?" Elizabeth answered.

"I think I see that Al guy," Sydney went on. "The one who asked me if I was related to President Lincoln. He's over by the center of the Wall."

"Let me see." Elizabeth took the binoculars from Sydney. She focused them until she could see clearly. "Yeah, that's him," she said. "He's just standing there leaning against the Wall." She moved the binoculars away from her uncle's friend and scanned the east part of the Wall and then the west. She saw no sign of Uncle Dan or of the other man who had been with them yesterday morning.

"He's looking all around now," Elizabeth reported, "like he thinks someone might be watching him. There he goes. He's walking along the west part of the wall. Still looking around. Acting sort of nervous."

"I see him," Sydney said. "He's too far away to see what he's up to, though, so keep telling us."

"Who are we looking at?" Kate wondered as she put the water bottle inside her backpack.

Sydney explained, "Yesterday morning Elizabeth's Uncle Dan and two of his friends met us here at the Wall. My Aunt Dee showed them around, and we hung out, too, just to be polite. That man was with us. His name is Al."

Kate was still confused. "Which man? Where?"

"He's walking past 30W now," Elizabeth informed them.

"The guy in the white shirt and khaki cargo shorts," Sydney told Kate. "See, he's almost to where the strawberries are."

"And he's stopping there," Elizabeth reported. "He's looking at the berries. . . . Now he's looking around again. I wonder what he's doing. . . . He's kneeling. Is he praying? No. . . . He's reading the note that's on the flagpole. Hey! He's picking up our package!"

"Oh no!" Sydney cried. "What's he going to do with it?"

"Is he one of the bad guys?" Kate asked in disbelief.

"Now he's lifting the tape on our note. I think he's reading it," Elizabeth continued. "Yeah, he *is* reading it. I knew yesterday that I didn't like something about him."

"He's leaving," Kate observed. "And he seems to be in a hurry. Did he take our box?"

"No, it's still there," replied Elizabeth.

"Let me have the binoculars," Sydney said. She took them from Elizabeth and scanned the Wall from right to left. "Look over there, where the two walls meet. It's Rusty and Moose!"

"We've Got Legs. . . ."

"I'll follow your uncle's friend," Kate announced. She stood and grabbed her backpack. "I'll meet you guys at Union Station before my train leaves at two, at that little café on the upper level. If Moose takes our package, send a text message to the Camp Club Girls so they can track him online."

Kate ran off to follow the guy named Al.

Sydney watched Moose and Rusty through her binoculars. The two men walked slowly, looking at all the items that visitors had left to honor the fallen soldiers. They worked their way, panel by panel, along the west part of the Wall, obviously looking for a clue.

"They're getting closer," Sydney reported to Elizabeth. "I don't think they've seen the berries yet. . . . They're almost there. Oh, Rusty sees them! There they go. They're nearly to panel 52W now. Okay, they've stopped."

Elizabeth could see the men in the distance, but she relied on Sydney to tell her what was happening. "What's going on with our package?" she mused.

"Nothing yet," Sydney answered. "It looks like they're reading the names on the panel. At least Rusty is. Moose is bending over. Oh, wouldn't you know it? He's eating one of the strawberries."

Moose had picked out the biggest and best strawberry of the bunch and popped the whole thing into his mouth.

As Moose reached for another berry, Sydney watched his focus land on the brown-paper-wrapped package.

"He's reading our note, Elizabeth!" Sydney watched through the binoculars. "He's turning sideways now so Rusty can't see what he's doing. Yeah, he's reading it!"

"Can I have a turn, please?" Elizabeth asked.

Reluctantly Sydney shared her binoculars.

Elizabeth peered at the men through the strong, thick lenses. "Oh, now he's putting the package into the back pocket of his shorts. Yuck! He has the hairiest legs that I've ever seen."

"Elizabeth!" Sydney said.

"Well he does," Elizabeth confirmed. "Rusty looks upset, and Moose is grinning. He's probably thrilled that the boss gave him such an important job. Moose is picking up another strawberry now. He's giving it to Rusty. Hey! Rusty just hit Moose on the arm. I wish we could hear what they're saying," she added.

"He just hit Moose again," Elizabeth observed. "Just before that, Rusty wrote something on a piece of paper and stuck it on the little flag. Now they're leaving."

"Just like yesterday," Sydney said. "They've left a note for The Professor. We have to go see what it says."

Elizabeth gave the binoculars back to Sydney. "But shouldn't we wait and watch for The Professor to come? I mean, at some point he or the suit guy is going to read it, right?"

"Probably," Sydney answered. "But if The Professor is smart, he won't take that note in broad daylight. If anything, he'll just stroll by, looking like a tourist. He'll take a quick look at it, like anyone else being curious. I think he does his dirty work at night, Elizabeth. That's when the graffiti happened, and no one saw him do it."

"I guess you're right," Elizabeth answered. "I'm going to send a text message to the girls." She took her cell phone out of her pocket and typed: MOOSE HAS PHONE. TRACK HIM! BETH.

Then Elizabeth turned to Sydney and said, "So how do we go over there and look at the note without being seen?"

"Girl! You don't see the forest for the trees," Sydney exclaimed. "Look at that crowd. There are so many tourists that it'll be easy for us to blend in. We'll just get in line and go with the flow. Come on!"

The girls walked to the Vietnam Wall and joined the crowd. Surprisingly, though many people gathered there, the noise level was low. The Wall that morning reminded Sydney of being in church just before the service began. People talked but in hushed voices.

As they neared panel 52W, Sydney and Elizabeth heard children laughing. When they got closer, they saw the reason. Two squirrels were busy eating the strawberries. Each squirrel sat with a berry in its tiny front paws and nibbled at it until it was gone. Soon, just one berry was left. Both squirrels lunged for it, but only one got it. The lucky squirrel raced away with the berry in its mouth. It ran across the grassy area toward the trees where the girls had been hiding. Then the second squirrel tore Rusty's note off the little flag. Off it went, in pursuit of the first squirrel, with the precious note in its mouth.

"Oh my goodness!" Elizabeth gasped. Sydney sprinted across the grass, chasing the squirrel. She ran at lightning speed, almost catching up as the squirrel scampered for the trees.

By now, a crowd of people stood watching. Hurriedly Elizabeth followed Sydney.

"Sydney! Where are you?" Elizabeth was annoyed by the time she got to the trees.

"Up here," came a voice from overhead. Elizabeth looked up and saw Sydney sitting on a thick lower limb of the tree. Sydney grinned as she waved the note at Elizabeth. "The squirrel dropped it, and I caught it."

Far up in the tree branches, the angry squirrel sat on a branch, shaking its tail and scolding.

"What does the note say?" Elizabeth asked.

Sydney unfolded the paper and read: " 'LIEUTENANT DAN, WE'VE GOT LEGS.' In all capital letters—"

"Girls! What are you up to?" Aunt Dee stood b›ind Elizabeth, looking very official in her park ranger's uniform.

"Hi, Aunt Dee," Sydney said brightly. "We were just goofing off." She slid down the tree trunk and brushed herself off. "We were in the neighborhood and decided that we'd visit the Wall again. How are things going?"

Aunt Dee stood with her hands on her hips. "Sydney Lincoln, did I just see you chasing a squirrel across the lawn by the Wall? With a whole bunch of people watching you?"

The smile disappeared from Sydney's face. She had no idea

that she'd made such a scene. "Yes, ma'am," she answered.

"Girlfriend!" Aunt Dee said. "This is a national monument where people come to pay their respects. I'm glad that you and Elizabeth want to come here, but it's not a place to play."

As Elizabeth looked beyond Aunt Dee toward the Wall, she saw Moose and Rusty by panel 52W. They were too far away to tell what was going on, but Rusty was holding the little flag and pointing toward the trees. Had they seen Sydney run off after the squirrel?

"We're sorry, Miss Powers," Elizabeth said. "We were just about to leave. Sydney wants to take me to Union Station." She shot Sydney a desperate look. Sydney had no idea why.

"That's a good idea," Aunt Dee said. Her voice was less stern when she spoke to Elizabeth. "I have some tour buses coming soon, so I'll see you girls at supper. Have fun!"

As soon as Aunt Dee left, Elizabeth grabbed Sydney's arm. "Look!" she said, pointing toward the Wall. Rusty and Moose were walking across the grass toward the trees. "I don't think they see us yet. Drop the note on the ground, and let's get out of here."

"Why should I drop the note?" Sydney questioned.

"I'll tell you later!" Elizabeth exclaimed as she tore the paper from Sydney's hand and threw it to the ground. "Run!" she said.

They ran as fast as they could, through the trees and away from the Wall. They ran until they were almost to the Tidal Basin.

"Why did you leave the note b›ind?" Sydney asked.

"So they'd think the squirrel got it!" Elizabeth dropped to

the ground and stretched out on her back, trying to catch her breath. "What if they saw you chasing the squirrel, Syd? At least if they find the note, they might think you never saw it. What if Moose and Rusty were watching the whole time? We could be in big trouble."

Sydney plopped on the grass and sat cross-legged with her head in her hands. "I didn't stop to think," she said. "When that squirrel took off with the note, I just started running. Did other people see me?"

Elizabeth sighed. "I can't believe you just said that. Do you know how fast you can run? Everyone was watching you. You were amazing!"

Sydney looked at Elizabeth. "What if they did see? We're not talking about some common thugs here, Elizabeth. These guys are out to get President Meade."

Elizabeth sat up. "We'll have to be extra careful now," she said. "We'd better get going. Kate's train leaves in an hour."

The girls walked to the bus stop on 15th Street. They watched for Rusty and Moose. Before they paid the fare on the bus and walked to their seats, they looked around to be sure that the men weren't on board. By the time they got to Union Station, they were reasonably sure that they hadn't been followed.

Kate was waiting for them at a café on the upper level of the station. She sat at a small white table with three chairs, sipping a cold soda. Elizabeth and Sydney both noticed that Kate looked serious.

"Hi, you two," she said. "You'd better sit down. I have a

lot to tell you."

"We have a lot to tell you, too," Elizabeth replied.

"I'll buy some sodas," Sydney told them. "They don't like it if you sit without buying something."

By the time Sydney returned, Elizabeth had told Kate about the new note that Rusty and Moose left on the little flag and what had happened with Sydney and the squirrel. Sydney placed two Cokes on the table and sat down. "We might be in big trouble," she said.

"Maybe more trouble than you know," Kate responded. "I followed that guy, Al, to a hotel on East Street Northwest."

"That's where the Vietnam Veterans' Reunion is," Elizabeth said. "My uncle is staying there."

"I know," Kate said. "I think I saw him. What does he look like, Elizabeth?"

"Well, he's in a wheelchair. . . ," said Elizabeth.

"A flashy one with lots of chrome," Sydney added.

"He has blond hair, a little on the longish side," Elizabeth continued, "and big muscles on his arms, because he wheels himself around in the chair. He won't use one of those motorized ones. And he usually wears khakis or camouflage, especially when he's with his Vietnam friends. Oh, and I forgot, he has a bushy mustache."

"That was him," Kate said. She took a long drink of her soda. "You're not going to like what I have to tell you."

"What?" Elizabeth said cautiously.

"Well, I followed Al to the hotel. He got on an elevator, and

I watched to see what floor he got off on. It was the third. So I ran up the stairs, and by the time I got there, he and your uncle were going into one of the rooms. When they shut the door, I went to the door and listened."

"Kate! Are you out of your mind?" Sydney asked. "What if someone had seen you?"

"I was okay, because the room was next to a broom closet. If I had to, I could have hidden in there," Kate said. "Beth, they were talking about the stuff at the Wall. Al told your uncle about every place that you've been. He knew about the 'Meade me in St. Louis' note and about your going to the Lincoln Memorial and that Sydney listened to those guys b›ind the pillar. He even knew that you met me at the station this morning, but he doesn't know who I am. And, of course, he knew about the latest note. The one the squirrel got."

Elizabeth said nothing.

Sydney remembered, "At the Lincoln Memorial you thought you were being followed, Elizabeth. I guess it wasn't your imagination. It was your uncle's friend. He's been watching us!"

"I can't believe that," Elizabeth said. "Why would he do that? And why would Uncle Dan let him?"

"There's more," Kate said. "Your uncle said something about talking to a man named Phillips. He said Phillips was watching the situation closely. Then your uncle said, 'If the girls get too involved in this, we might have to—.' I didn't hear the rest because someone around the corner turned on a vacuum cleaner."

Elizabeth spilled her soda, and Sydney hurried to get napkins to wipe it up.

"Beth," Kate said softly, "I think your uncle Dan might be one of the terrorists."

CHAPTER 7

Suspicions

"My uncle is *not* a terrorist!" Elizabeth exploded.

Kate looked at her solemnly and handed her a sheet of folded-up notebook paper. "Stick this in your pocket," she whispered. "Don't lose it, and don't open it until you get back to Sydney's house."

By three o'clock, Sydney and Elizabeth were back in Sydney's bedroom. Elizabeth read Kate's note aloud:

> *Elizabeth,*
>
> *I think a tracking device might be hidden in your backpack. That might be how Al knows where you are all the time. From now on, leave your backpack at Sydney's house, but not in your room where a mic could pick up your discussions. Be careful what you say in public, too. Someone might be listening.*
>
> *Kate*

Elizabeth flopped down on her bed as Sydney booted up the computer. "I don't care what anyone says. My uncle is *not* plotting to do something terrible to the president."

Sydney watched the monitor screen turn from black to blue. "You're probably right, Beth, but we have to be careful until we find out what's going on."

"And do you know what else?" Elizabeth continued. "We need to pray. In 1 Timothy the Bible says to pray for those in authority. So we should be praying for President Meade. In Matthew scripture says we should pray for our enemies. We should be praying for Rusty and Moose, the suit guy, and The Professor. And most of all, we should be praying for ourselves that we're doing the right thing."

Sydney clicked on the icon to bring up her e-mail program. "You're right, Beth. We'll form a Camp Club Girls prayer group. If we all join together to trust God, I know He'll help us save the president."

"*If* the president needs saving," Elizabeth reminded her. "We don't know what this is all about yet."

Sydney clicked her mouse a couple of times to bring up a list of new mail messages. Only two waited: one from Bailey and the other from McKenzie. "Elizabeth, even before I agreed with you, you'd decided those guys were terrorists."

"I know," Elizabeth answered, "but now it's getting personal."

Sydney opened Bailey's e-mail.

I've been tracking Mr. Green since I got your text message. He went from the Wall a little bit south. Then he turned around and went north. He's been a little northwest of the White House all afternoon. He hasn't moved at all. I hope you guys are okay!

Let me know what's happening.

"I'm going to log on to Kate's tracking site," said Sydney. "My password's Jones, and you're Indiana, right?"

"Right," Elizabeth said. She got up from the bed and walked across the room to sit with Sydney at the desk. Sydney typed the password into the log-in box. Soon a map appeared. A little off from the center of it was a small, glowing green dot. Sydney clicked the zoom icon. The map morphed into a bird's-eye view of Washington, D.C. You could see the tops of trees and buildings as if you were looking down at them from an airplane. All the important streets, highways, buildings, and monuments were labeled.

"This is so neat!" Elizabeth exclaimed. "Kate's outdone herself this time."

"And Bailey's right with her directions," said Sydney. "Moose is northwest of the White House, in Foggy Bottom. From this view, it looks like they're in an apartment house."

Elizabeth remembered that she and Sydney had gotten off the train in Foggy Bottom, but she had no idea that it was northwest of the White House.

"Well, now we know that Moose and Rusty didn't follow us," Sydney said. "According to Bailey's e-mail, they walked from the Wall a little bit south. That must have been when they were coming after us, just before we ran."

Sydney minimized the map screen and brought up her e-mail program. "Then if they turned and went north, they must not have seen that we ran to the Tidal Basin."

Sydney typed her reply to Bailey:

Great work, Bailey! That area northwest of the
White House is called Foggy Bottom. Keep watching,
OK? In a little while, we'll set up a schedule so we
all can take turns watching Moose. We're fine. More
later. Syd.

"Did you notice that the blip didn't go anywhere near where my uncle is staying?" Elizabeth asked. "I just know that he's not a part of this."

"You're right; it didn't," Sydney replied. Then she opened McKenzie's e-mail.

Call me online as soon as you get this. Kate has
texted me the whole time she's been on the train. She
told me everything that's going on. Call me!

Before Sydney could respond, the videophone rang. It was McKenzie. Sydney turned on the webcam and picked up the call.

McKenzie sat at the computer desk in her bedroom. She wore a pink baseball cap with a picture of a rac>orse embroidered on the front. Her orange tomcat, Andrew, lounged on the back of her desk chair.

"We were just going to call you," Sydney said.

"I couldn't wait," McKenzie replied. She twisted a lock of her hair between her thumb and her index finger. "Do you realize what a big deal this is if you've uncovered a plot to assassinate the president? I couldn't believe half the stuff that Kate told me."

"Believe it," Sydney said. "It's all true."

Elizabeth slid her chair closer to Sydney's. "Hi, McKenzie," she offered.

"Hi, Elizabeth," McKenzie answered. "Listen, I've been thinking. That first note you found said 'Meade me in St. Louis, July first,' right?"

"Right," Elizabeth confirmed.

"Get off!" Andrew had jumped from the chair onto McKenzie's keyboard. He loved to act up when she was online. "I just Googled the president to find out where he'll be on July first. He's not anywhere near St. Louis. He's going to be in Baltimore. So could you be on the wrong track with all of this?" She picked up Andrew and put him on her lap.

"Your guess is as good as ours," Elizabeth said. "The first of July is Friday. That gives us two days to find out if we're right. If nothing happens by the end of the weefend, I'll have to help out from Amarillo. We're going home on Sunday night. Uncle Dan has a class starting on the fifth."

Sydney picked up a red fine-point marker and scribbled the word *Baltimore* on a scrap of paper. She doodled all around it. Drawing flowers and animals som›ow helped her concentrate.

"What kind of class is your uncle taking?" McKenzie asked.

"He's not taking it; he's teaching it," Elizabeth replied.

Sydney penned the words: *Teaching. . .Teacher.*

"My uncle teaches American history at Amarillo Community College," Elizabeth continued.

Sydney scribbled the words: *Teacher. . .College. . . Professor!*

Oh my goodness, she thought. She decided not to say what she was thinking. As Elizabeth and McKenzie talked, Sydney tore the paper into little pieces and tossed it into the trash can under the desk.

"So what's the president doing in Baltimore on Friday?" she asked. She tried hard not to let her feelings show. Inside her brain, a voice shouted, *"Oh no! Kate's right! Elizabeth's uncle is The Professor, the top guy in the plot to kill the president!"*

McKenzie was feeding Andrew now. She held his bowl of food while he sat on the desk and scarfed it down. "He's going to be at Fort McHenry for some Fourth of July wefiend concert thing. I can't remember exactly what it's called. Just a minute, I wrote it down." McKenzie set the cat's dish on the desk. The girls heard paper rustling as she looked for the note she'd jotted about the president. "Here it is. It's called a Twilight Tattoo."

Elizabeth gasped.

"What?" McKenzie asked.

"That was Moose's big idea," Elizabeth said. "He made a plan that involved a tattoo, and the suit guy couldn't believe that Moose was bright enough to think of it—"

Sydney interrupted, "Only we thought he meant tattoo, as in a picture branded on your skin."

"Tattoos aren't *branded* on people," McKenzie corrected her. "You brand cattle."

"Obviously that's not what it means," Elizabeth said. She found a dictionary in Sydney's bookcase. She opened it to the *T* section and searched. "Tattle. . .tattler. . .tattletail. . . *tattoo!* Here it is. Oh girls, listen to this: 'an outdoor military exercise given by troops as evening entertainment' and 'a call sounded shortly before taps as notice to go to quarters.' It all fits! Taps is a bugle call that's sounded at the end of a day and at military funerals. They plan to assassinate the president at the tattoo!"

McKenzie leaned back in her chair and put her hands on top of her baseball cap. "I can't believe this is happening," she said. "What are you guys going to do? I mean, if you say something and we're wrong, can you imagine all the trouble it will cause?" She took off her hat and set it on the desk. "Just a second, I'm getting an IM from Alexis. She wants to know what's going on—"

"Listen, McKenzie," Sydney said. "We have to go. Will you tell Alexis and the rest of the girls what we just talked about?"

Elizabeth got up and started unpacking her backpack. "Tell her to get a prayer group going, too," she said as she looked through her backpack for anything odd, like a tracking device.

"I heard," McKenzie said. "Will do, and I'll tell the girls to try to figure out more of this. We'll be in touch with you later." McKenzie waved at the camera and signed off.

Elizabeth had everything out of her backpack now. Her camera, a tube of sunscreen, her hot-pink iPod, a pair of socks, lip gloss. . .all of it lay in a pile on her bed. She turned the yellow backpack upside down and gave it a few hard shakes. Nothing fell out. "See," she said. "No tracking device. If anyone is tracking me, it's not with this backpack."

Sydney sat quietly at her desk pretending to straighten papers and organize her bookcase. There was one important clue that she and Elizabeth hadn't discussed, and they couldn't avoid it any longer. "That note we left b›ind," Sydney said. "The one that said 'Lieutenant Dan, we've got legs.' What do you think it meant, Beth?"

Once again, Elizabeth said nothing.

Sydney felt anger inside of her. She didn't want to be mad at her friend, but something was very different about Elizabeth. She wasn't acting like the same girl Sydney knew from Discovery Lake Camp.

"What's going on with you?" Sydney asked. "Every time I try to talk about your uncle, you clam up. Don't you know you can talk to me if something's bothering you?"

Elizabeth sighed and sat down on the edge of the bed. "My uncle saved his whole company of men in Vietnam by putting himself in the line of fire," she said. "He got shot, and he might never walk again, and, Sydney, that's not right! I get mad at God sometimes because bad things happen to good people. I get mad at my uncle's Vietnam buddies because they can walk and he can't. Then I get mad at myself for feeling that way. I know what kind of a man my uncle is, and now you want me to believe he's a bad guy and is trying to kill the president. Well, he's *not*! I don't know what the note means, but it isn't what you think."

Sydney walked across the room and sat on the bed next to Elizabeth. "I don't want your uncle to be a bad guy, Beth, and he probably isn't. Help me prove that he isn't, okay? I'm on your side. I really mean that."

Elizabeth held the pendant that hung around her neck. It was a habit that helped her to remember the scripture verse

205

engraved on it: *"Do not be afraid; do not be discouraged, for the Lord your God will be with you wherever you go."*

"I want your uncle to walk again," Sydney continued, "but sometimes bad things do happen to good people, and you just have to accept that."

As Elizabeth held the pendant, it came off the chain. The pendant remained in her hand, and the chain slipped to the floor. "Oh," she said. "I can't believe that happened. Uncle Dan just took this to the jewelry store the day before we came out here. He had it matched to this nice silver chain." She picked up the chain and checked out the clasp. "That's strange. It doesn't look broken. I guess I must not have fastened it right. Will you do it, please?" Elizabeth held up her long blond hair while Sydney fastened the clasp.

"There," Sydney said. "It's as good as new. And how about us? Are we good as new?"

Elizabeth smiled. "We are," she said softly. "Let's make a pact to prove that my uncle Dan isn't a terrorist. Agreed?"

"Agreed!" Sydney said.

Just then, Sydney's cell phone began to buzz. She took it from her pocket and found a message from Bailey: MR. GREEN IS ON THE MOVE! LOG ON NOW AND WATCH WHERE HE GOES.

Quickly Sydney and Elizabeth logged on to Kate's tracking site. The green blip was moving steadily away from Foggy Bottom. Its rate of speed told the girls that Moose was not traveling on foot. The blip was on New York Avenue heading northeast out of town. Elizabeth and Sydney sat at the desk and watched for more than an hour as it slowly traveled to the Baltimore-Washington Parkway, on to Maryland 295 North, and along I-95 North. Then it stopped.

"Why is he stopping?" Elizabeth wondered. "Isn't he in the middle of a freeway?"

"Maybe a toll booth or traffic," Sydney answered.

"So now we know he's in a car," Elizabeth added.

"Or a taxi or a bus," Sydney said.

Soon the green blip left I-95 and began weaving through the streets of Baltimore.

"Either he's lost, or he's looking for something," Sydney observed. "It doesn't look like he knows where he's going."

Eventually the green blip traveled east of Baltimore's Inner Harbor and stopped again. The girls waited for about twenty minutes, wondering if the blip would move. It didn't.

"I know that neighborhood," Sydney said. "It's just across the harbor from Fort McHenry. I've been there with my aunt Dee; sometimes she fills in at the fort when a ranger is on vacation. Anyway, that neighborhood where Moose is now was once upon a time a place where pirates hung out."

"Interesting," Elizabeth said. "So now what do we do?"

Sydney was busy typing an e-mail to the Camp Club Girls.

Subject: Camp Club Girls Unite
Moose has moved from Washington, D.C., to
Baltimore's Inner Harbor. (Rusty is probably with
him.) Let's group chat tonight at 8:30. We need
to make a plan to save President Meade, and we
have to pray for guidance and safety. Tomorrow
Elizabeth and I will go to Baltimore to check out
Fort McHenry and to find out more about the

Twilight Tattoo. We'll meet you in the chat room.

"We're going to Baltimore?" Elizabeth exclaimed. "How will we get there?"

"That's easy," Sydney answered. "Aunt Dee! The National Park Service has a van that travels from the Wall to Fort McHenry every day. I'll tell Aunt Dee that I want to take you to see the fort, and we can hitch a ride with a ranger. We can spend the whole day in Baltimore sleuthing things out. Plus, we can get into the fort for free."

"What if we run into Moose and Rusty?" Elizabeth asked.

"We won't as long as the girls are tracking them," Sydney replied. "They can let us know if Moose and Rusty are near, and then we can ditch them. Right now, we have other things to think about. The Camp Club Girls need to get organized. We're on a mission to save the president."

On the Move. . .

The girls wasted no time getting to the chat room at 8:30. None of them had much of an appetite at supper that night. Their minds were on how to solve the mystery of Moose, Rusty, and President Meade.

Alexis Howell was the first to "talk." She had been working on the latest clue left by the Wall.

Alexis: *Have any of you seen the movie* Forrest Gump?
   That note, "Lieutenant Dan, we got legs," is like a line from the movie. The line goes: "Lieutenant Dan, you got new legs."
   In one part of the movie, Forrest Gump is a soldier in Vietnam. His platoon gets ambushed and Forrest saves his wounded officer, Lieutenant Dan. Afterwards, the lieutenant is real mad at Forrest.
Bailey: *Why is he mad at him?*
Alexis: *Because Dan wanted to die in battle as a hero. Instead he lost his legs and was disabled for the rest of his life. He figured he'd be better off dead.*

Elizabeth and Sydney sat at the computer watching the words flash across the screen.

"Some of it is like what happened with my uncle," Elizabeth said to Sydney. "But Uncle Dan never complains that he lost the use of his legs, and I'm sure that he doesn't think he'd have been better off dead. The clue has to have another meaning."

Sydney typed on her keyboard.

Sydney: *Then what happened?*

Alexis: *Forrest and Dan went into shrimping together and got rich. Years later, when Forrest got married, Lieutenant Dan showed up at the wedding walking. Forrest said, "Lieutenant Dan, you got new legs." The Lieutenant showed Forrest his new metal legs and said, "Custom-made titanium alloy. It's what they use on the space shuttle."*

McKenzie: *I'm sorry, Elizabeth, but this seems to point right to your uncle Dan. He was wounded in Vietnam and can't use his legs. So Moose and Rusty are using their legs to help him. I bet that's what it means: Lieutenant Dan, we got legs!*

Alexis: *McKenzie, we can't jump to conclusions. Elizabeth's uncle is innocent until he's proven guilty.*

An uncomfortable pause filled the chat room and Sydney's bedroom. Neither Sydney nor Elizabeth said a word. The only sounds were the soft hum of the computer and the gentle patter of rain on the roof.

Bailey: *What's titanium alloy?*
Kate: *It's a metal made of titanium and other chemical
    elements. It's super-strong, lightweight, and it can
    withstand high temperatures. The military uses it
    to make stuff, like planes and weapons.*

The storm was getting stronger. The girls heard the rain falling harder on the roof.

Sydney: *Let's make a plan for tomorrow when
    Elizabeth and I go to the fort. A storm's coming,
    and we'll have to shut down the computer soon.*
Kate: *It's been here already. Would you believe Biscuit
    was outside digging in the pouring rain? He tracked
    mud all through the house. He's never done that
    before.*

As the storm raced toward Sydney's neighborhood, the girls made a plan for the next day. Kate told Sydney and Elizabeth how to set up their cell phones to view the tracking site. That way Sydney and Elizabeth could see where Moose was at any given time.

Bailey and Alexis would be their backup. They'd watch Moose, too, and would report to Kate and McKenzie what was going on. Meanwhile, Kate and McKenzie would dig deeper into the clues to look for any new leads.

Before they signed off, Sydney and Elizabeth promised to stay in touch with the girls by texting them from the fort, and all the girls promised to pray.

Rain poured down on the brick row house. A huge clap of thunder exploded over the house, making the girls jump.

Just then Elizabeth's cell phone rang. She looked at the caller ID and pressed the answer button.

"Hi, Uncle Dan," she said.

"Hi, honey," her uncle replied. "I'm just checking on you. There's quite a storm outside. Are you girls all right?"

"We're fine," Elizabeth answered. "We were just getting ready for bed. I'm glad Sydney's room doesn't have any windows. I'd rather not see all the lightning."

"So what's on your agenda for tomorrow?" Uncle Dan asked. "Do you and Sydney have something fun planned?"

"We're going to Baltimore to see Fort McHenry," Elizabeth said.

Sydney sat on her bed waving her arms to get Elizabeth's attention. "No!" she whispered. "Don't tell him!"

But the damage was already done.

"I have to go now," Elizabeth said abruptly. "It's probably not a good idea to talk on the phone in a storm. Good night, Uncle Dan."

She ended the call before her uncle could ask anything else about their plans. "I'm sorry. I forgot," Elizabeth said. "Besides, I won't treat my uncle like he's a criminal. Like Alex said, he's innocent until he's proven guilty."

As the wind howled outside, the two girls shared a time of prayer. They asked God to guide them and protect them. They prayed for their friends and family, and especially for President Meade. Elizabeth asked the Lord to do something soon to prove that her uncle Dan was innocent, and she prayed that her uncle might walk again.

Then Sydney and Elizabeth climbed into their beds and said good night.

• — • — •

Sydney awoke the next morning to someone gently shaking her. It was Aunt Dee. The room was dark and quiet, and Elizabeth was still asleep.

"What time is it?" Sydney groaned.

"It's 7:00 a.m.," Aunt Dee answered. "If you girls are going to catch a ride to the fort, you have to get up soon. The power went out for a while overnight, so your alarm clocks are b›ind."

Elizabeth stirred in her bed across the room. "What's going on?" she asked, sitting up and rubbing her eyes.

"It's time to get up," Sydney told her. "We have to leave in an hour to go with Aunt Dee to the Wall."

The girls got dressed and logged on to Kate's tracking site. The green blip was still in the same spot as the night before, just east of Baltimore's Inner Harbor.

"I'm going to e-mail the girls," Sydney said.

> *We're leaving in a few minutes to go to the Wall with Aunt Dee. Catching a ride to the fort at 10:00 a.m. Make sure you let us know if Moose moves, in case we're not looking at our phones.*

• — • — •

At ten o'clock, Sydney and Elizabeth met Ranger Hank Ellsworth at the Visitor Center at the Vietnam Memorial. As they rode along in the backseat of his white park service van, Ranger Hank told them about the fort.

"My great-great-great-grandpa fought at Fort Mc-Henry," the ranger said, scratching the short, gray beard on his tan, weathered face. "But you girls probably aren't interested in hearing about that."

He turned the van onto the highway into heavy traffic.

"No, we want to hear," Sydney said. "We want to learn as much as we can about the fort."

The ranger checked his rearview mirror and changed lanes. "Well, when you get there, you'll have to use your imagination," he said. "The story goes like this: Way back in the 1700s, Baltimore was afraid of being attacked by the British. We were at war with Britain. So the people decided to build a fort to protect themselves. They picked a site called Whetstone Point. It was a good place to build a fort, because it was near the city and was surrounded on three sides by water."

"A peninsula," Elizabeth said.

"Right," the ranger agreed. "And it was smart to build the fort on a peninsula, because any ships sailing in to attack Baltimore had to pass it. When they first built the fort, it was just big mounds of dirt. But later a politician named James McHenry raised money for a new and better fort."

A car cut in front of the van, and Ranger Hank maneuvered to another lane. "The people named Fort McHenry after him because he was so generous and also because he was President George Washington's secretary of war."

Sydney took her cell phone out of her pocket and flipped it open.

"The fort is built in the shape of a five-pointed star," Ranger Hank explained. "They did that so each point of the star could be seen from the point on either side. It only took five men to guard the whole thing. One man could watch from each point of the star."

"That was smart," said Sydney. "Then they could see if the enemy was coming by land or by boat."

"Right," said the ranger. "And the new fort was strong. It was made of brick to protect the soldiers who lived inside. When you get there, you'll see how they lived in houses called barracks. There's the Commanding Officer's Quarters, the Junior Officers' Quarters, and two buildings for the enlisted men. That's where my great-something grandpa lived.

"And don't forget to check out the magazine—that's the strong room where the soldiers stored their gunpowder. They added it to the fort during the Civil War to keep ammunition safe from any sparks or explosions. There's a guardhouse on the grounds, too, with some jail cells. That's where they locked up prisoners."

Sydney checked her cell phone, and Elizabeth leaned in toward her to take a look. The green blip hadn't moved.

"Do you know why the fort is so famous?" asked Ranger Hank.

Sydney flipped her phone shut and slipped it into her pocket.

"It's because of 'The Star-Spangled Banner,'" Elizabeth said. "That's where the song was written."

"And the Battle of Baltimore," Ranger Hank added. "That was the one my great-grandpa fought in."

They came to a stretch of highway that was lined with orange barrels and construction cones, slowing traffic even more.

"Sydney, it's a good thing that you didn't live here back then," said Ranger Hank. "If you had, you'd have seen most of Washington, D.C., burned by the British. Thunderstorms, like the ones we had last night, dumped rain and helped to put the fires out. But the White House and the Capitol Building were destroyed.

"After that, the British sailed toward Baltimore. They planned to take Fort McHenry and then sail into the Baltimore Basin and attack the city. They made it to where Key Bridge is today. From there, they fired on the fort, and that was the start of the battle. My grandpa and the other soldiers were ready for them and put up a brave fight."

Elizabeth was looking out the window, watching the traffic inch along. "That's where Francis Scott Key comes in," she said. "I studied about him. When the Brits attacked Washington, they took an old doctor prisoner. He was being held on a British ship, and his friends worried that he would be hanged. So they asked Francis Scott Key for help because he was a lawyer. He and another guy were allowed to get on the enemy ship and make a deal with them to release the doctor."

"A dangerous proposition," inserted Ranger Hank. The traffic was thinning, and he increased the van's speed. "The British agreed to release the doctor, but not until the battle was over. They figured that Key and his friends knew about their battle plans, so they were stuck on a ship that was shooting bombs at Fort McHenry."

He turned the van onto I-95 North and headed into Baltimore.

"So how does 'The Star-Spangled Banner' fit in?" Sydney asked.

"Well, there was a huge battle," said Hank. "For twenty-five hours the British attacked Fort McHenry. They used bombs that weighed two hundred pounds and had lighted fuses that made them explode when they reached their targets. The Brits used cannons on their ships and fired fifteen hundred bombs at the fort. All the while, Francis Scott Key was on the enemy's ship watching Fort McHenry under attack."

"Key was a religious man," Elizabeth said, "so he was probably praying as the bombs flew through the air. He was a writer, too, so while he watched, he wrote a poem about what he saw. He didn't know what was going on at Fort McHenry, because it was all smoky from the bombs. But when the smoke cleared over the fort, the big American flag was still there. Baltimore had won the battle."

"If they hadn't won," said Ranger Hank, "Key would have seen the British flag flying over the fort instead."

They turned off of I-95 onto Exit 55. The fort was only a couple of miles away now.

"And that poem that he wrote," said Hank, "was 'The Star-Spangled Banner.' "

The Ranger picked up the yellow ranger hat on the seat next to him and put it on his head. Then he entertained the girls by singing:

"Oh, say, can you see, by the
dawn's early light,

217

What so proudly we hail'd at the
twilight's last gleaming?
Whose broad stripes and bright
stars, thro' the perilous fight,
O'er the ramparts we watch'd,
were so gallantly streaming?
And the rockets' red glare, the
bombs bursting in air
Gave proof thro' the night that
our flag was still there.
Oh, say, does that Star-Spangled
Banner yet wave
O'er the land of the free and the
home of the brave?"

Just as he finished the song, they turned left onto Fort Avenue. As they drove down the road, soon the girls saw Fort McHenry and the huge American flag towering over it, blowing in the wind. Ranger Hank drove the van to the Visitor Center.

"Here we are, girls," he said. "Come inside and I'll set you up with free passes. They'll get you in here today and for the next seven days, if you want to come back."

"What about the tattoo tomorrow?" Sydney asked. "Will the pass get us into that, too?"

"It will," the ranger answered. "Are you coming to the tattoo, then? Probably with your aunt, since she has to work here tomorrow. Lots of us got called in because the president is coming. It'll be special for you girls to see

President Meade. Most people never get to see a real, live president."

"And we hope to keep him that way," said Sydney.

Elizabeth elbowed her. "Thanks for the ride," she said. "What time should we meet you back here?"

"Closing time is 4:45," said the ranger. "I'll be here to pick you up."

As the girls walked out of the Visitor Center, they checked their cell phones. The green blip was moving on water!

"Sydney, he's headed this way," Elizabeth said. "What will we do when they get here?"

Sydney grinned at Elizabeth. "We're going to follow them," she said. "I was hoping that this would happen. Following them is the only way we're really going to find out what's going on."

"But it's too dangerous," Elizabeth protested.

"We'll be careful," Sydney replied. "We can hide in any of the points of the star, and we'll always know where Moose is. We'll be fine."

As the girls walked toward the entrance to Fort McHenry, their cell phones began to vibrate. It was a text message from Bailey: MR. GREEN IS ON THE MOVE. HEADED RIGHT AT YOU. ON THE WATER. IN A BOAT? B CAREFUL.

Fort McHenry Fiasco

Sydney and Elizabeth walked on the weathered brick pathway into the arched entranceway of Fort McHenry. The short, dark hallway was flanked by vaulted doors.

"This is awesome," Elizabeth said. "These doors are ginormous!"

The hallway opened into the bright sunshine and the fort's grassy parade grounds. Just beyond this grassy area were red brick buildings, the barracks that Ranger Hank had told them about. The barracks were two stories high with red roofs, white balconies, and green shutters on the windows. Red-white-and-blue banners hung from the balconies in honor of the Fourth of July, and actors dressed in costumes wandered the grounds making the fort seem more like 1814 than the twenty-first century.

"I just got an idea," Sydney said. "Follow me."

Elizabeth followed Sydney toward a short, stout lady who was one of the actors. She sat on a wooden bench outside the barracks wearing a floor-length, blood-red dress with a tan bonnet. It seemed like way too much clothing for the hot summer day.

"Good day," the lady said as the girls approached her.

"Good day," Sydney and Elizabeth said in unison.

The woman gave each girl a tour map of the fort. "Is this your first visit to Fort McHenry?" she asked.

"It is," Elizabeth answered.

"Nice dress!" said Sydney enthusiastically. "Do you have to get dressed like that at home, or do you change into your costumes here?"

The woman smiled and said, "Oh my! We don't dress like this at home. All our volunteers change here at the fort."

"Neat!" Sydney said. "Elizabeth and I took drama classes at summer camp."

Elizabeth smiled and nodded.

"We had a big room where we stored all the costumes," Sydney continued. "I suppose you do, too?"

"We do," the woman answered. "In that enlisted men's barrack." She pointed to a building across the courtyard. "All kinds of costumes are stored there. You can take a look, if you'd like."

"Oh, that would be great," Sydney said. "Do you think we could try some on, too? My aunt is Deandre Powers, the park ranger. I promise we'll be careful."

The woman thought for a minute. "I know Dee," she replied. "You must be Sydney. She talks about you all the time. Well, I suppose it wouldn't hurt, but make sure you put everything back the way you found it."

"We will," Sydney answered. "Thank you!"

Sydney grabbed Elizabeth's arm and hurried toward the barracks.

"Sydney, what are you up to?" Elizabeth asked.

"We can dress like the volunteers," Sydney answered. "Moose and Rusty will never recognize us, and we can get right up to them and find out what's going on. Then we'll put them back before we go."

The girls opened the door to the enlisted men's barracks and went inside. It was like walking through a time warp into the 1800s. The air smelled musty, and cobwebs hung from the rafters. The cobwebs glowed in rays of sunshine that streamed through the only window in the room. It was made up of twenty-five little glass squares, and in front of it sat a small wooden table and chair. An old military jacket hung over the back of the chair, and an inkwell was on the table with some yellowed writing paper and an old oil lamp.

The stuffy room held three rows of simple wooden bunk beds. Each uncomfortable-looking bed had a thin straw mattress and a single flat pillow. Soldiers' shoes hung from several of the bedposts, and muskets stood in their holders, ready for troops to grab them as they hurried out the door. The wooden plank floor creaked as the girls walked on it.

At the back of the barracks was a door marked WARDROBE. Sydney opened it, and the girls found a room filled with racks of costumes: soldiers' uniforms as well as costumes that citizens wore in the early 1800s. The girls went inside and bolted the door b›ind them.

"So do you want to be a soldier or a lady?" Sydney asked.

"A lady, definitely," said Elizabeth. She picked out an apple green dress and a white bonnet. Sydney helped her pull the dress on over her sleeveless top and shorts. It fit perfectly. Its hem was even long enough to cover the tops of her sandals.

"I'll roast in this!" Elizabeth complained as she pinned her long blond hair on top of her head and tied the bonnet over it. "What will you be?"

"A soldier," Sydney replied. She wiggled into the soldier's uniform—white pants and a dark blue coat with long sleeves and brass buttons. A white sash crisscrossed the front of the jacket, and the jacket's blue-and-gold collar fit snugly against Sydney's neck. She pulled on a pair of tall, black boots. Then she set a blue soldier's hat on top of her cornrows, pulling the visor down just below her eyebrows. "There," she said. "How do I look?"

"Like you're ready for a winter storm," Elizabeth said. "Sydney, you'll be too hot."

"I'll be fine," Sydney argued. "Don't forget to take your cell phone with you. I'll take my binoculars, too. And we should hide my street clothes and our backpacks in here somewhere."

Sydney searched for a place to hide their things.

"Why don't we just hang them up neatly with the costumes?" Elizabeth said. "There are so many clothes in here that no one will notice ours."

"Good idea," Sydney agreed.

The girls made sure that no one was coming. Then they left the barracks through a back door. As soon as they got outside, they checked their phones. The bright green blip was just offshore now, and they saw a string of messages from Bailey and an urgent message from McKenzie: I THINK HE'S ON A WATER TAXI. LOOKS LIKE IT'S LANDING NEAR THE FORT. BE CAREFUL!

"What's a water taxi?" Elizabeth asked, looking prim and

proper in her old-time dress.

"It's a tour boat that shuttles visitors around the Baltimore Harbor," Sydney said. "Listen. It says here on the Fort McHenry tour map that each point of the star-shaped fort is called a bastion. We can walk out on the bastions to look all around the fort. It says the big park we saw around the fort is often used for recreational purposes, like hiking, picnicking, and looking out at the harbor. Let's go to the bastion that faces the water taxi dock. Maybe we can see Moose from there."

Elizabeth and Sydney, wearing their costumes, walked onto the long, raised, grassy area that made up one point of the star-shaped fort. The sides of the bastion had strong brick walls, and several old cannons faced outward, reminders of days when soldiers defended the harbor. Sydney took out her binoculars and looked in the direction of the boat landing.

"Perfect timing!" she said. "There they are." She handed the binoculars to Elizabeth.

Moose and Rusty walked toward the fort. Elizabeth noticed that Moose carried a long slender case strapped over his shoulder. "What do you think he's carrying?" she said. "A gun?"

"I don't think they'd be that obvious," Sydney answered. "Watch where they go."

"They're not coming into the fort," Elizabeth reported. "It looks like they're going to hang out in the park instead. They're walking by the water now. . . . They're sitting down on a bench near some trees."

Sydney's cell phone vibrated like crazy. It was another message from Bailey: PERCY ALERT! HE'S WALKING AROUND

OUTSIDE OF THE FORT! WATCH OUT!

Sydney sent a reply: WE SEE THEM. NO MORE TEXT MESSAGES UNTIL YOU HEAR FROM US. WE'RE GOING TO FOLLOW THEM.

"Let's go," said Sydney. "I want to get close so we can hear what's going on."

"I still don't like the idea of this," Elizabeth said, following Sydney, careful not to trip on the hem of her dress.

The girls walked back to the fort entrance. They went through the brick hallway and then followed a brick path toward the waterfront. They saw Moose and Rusty sitting on the bench. Moose had opened the long slender case and was putting together some sort of contraption. It resembled a weed trimmer.

"What's that?" Sydney asked.

"I don't know," Elizabeth replied. "Let's see what he does with it."

Moose had the thing put together now, and it looked like he was plugging headphones into its handle.

"What in the world is he doing?" Sydney wondered.

Moose got up and put the headphones over his ears. He started walking with the contraption in one hand. He waved it back and forth over the grass while he listened through the headphones.

"I'm calling Kate," Elizabeth said. "She'll know what it is." Elizabeth took out her cell phone, took a picture of the contraption, and transmitted it to Kate. Then she dialed Kate's number. Kate answered on the first ring.

"Are you okay?" she asked. "Bailey said you're following them!"

"We're fine—don't worry," Elizabeth replied. "We need your help."

Since the picture hadn't come out well, Elizabeth described to Kate what Moose was doing with the tool.

"It's a metal detector," Kate told her. "He's waving it over the ground looking for something that's buried there. If the thing detects something metal underground, it gives a signal through the earphones."

When Elizabeth hung up, she told Sydney what Kate said.

"Let's split up," Sydney suggested. "You walk over there, like you're playacting. Say 'good day' to them, and see if you can discover anything."

"I can't do that!" Elizabeth said. "You want me to talk to them?"

"Yes!" said Sydney. "Do it for President Meade."

"You'd better protect me," Elizabeth warned as she walked toward Rusty and Moose.

As she approached the bench, Elizabeth heard Rusty giving Moose instructions. "Try ten paces east. . . . Now go ten paces north. . . ."

Moose walked along, counting to himself.

Elizabeth walked right up to Rusty. She saw that he was holding some sort of map. "Good day!" she said brightly. She startled Rusty, and he gave a little jump.

"Yeah," he said gruffly.

"Are you enjoying your visit?" Elizabeth asked. She leaned in to get a better look at the map.

"Humph." Rusty grunted, almost ignoring her.

Elizabeth saw a big red X on the map.

"Is there anything you'd like to know about the fort? Anything that I can help you with?" Elizabeth bravely sat on the bench near Rusty to get a closer look at the map. Under the red X was the word *BUM* in all capital letters.

"You can help by leaving me alone, lady," said Rusty.

His steely gray eyes gave Elizabeth the creeps. She got up quickly. "Well, good day then," she said. But instead of walking back toward Sydney, she circled around the park and met her friend near a grove of trees.

"He's creepier than you could imagine," Elizabeth said.

"So what did you find out?" asked Sydney.

Elizabeth told her all about the map, the red X, and the word *BUM*. Then she texted the other Camp Club Girls to let them know what was going on.

All afternoon, Sydney and Elizabeth watched as Rusty and Moose wandered around the park with the metal detector. Whatever they looked for didn't seem to be there, or maybe they were even more directionally disabled than Elizabeth. Then, just as the park was about to close, something happened.

Sydney watched through the binoculars. The men were searching back where they'd started, near the bench. Moose stopped by a tree about twenty feet from the shoreline. Rusty hurried to Moose. Then he went back to the bench and picked up his backpack. He took it to where Moose was standing and pulled out a small folding shovel. He knelt down and dug in the dirt beneath the gnarly old tree. After a few minutes, Rusty pulled out a metal box about the size of a box of animal crackers.

"I'm heading over there to see what's going on," Sydney

said. "Watch me." She gave the binoculars to Elizabeth.

Sydney walked like a soldier, steadfast and straight, toward Rusty and Moose. She slowed her pace as she neared them. Then she stopped, turned her back to them, and pretended to look across the harbor. Rusty and Moose were so excited about the box that they didn't seem to notice her.

"Handle it real careful, Rusty," Moose was saying. "We don't need accidents."

Rusty opened the lid of the box and pefied inside. Just then, an enormous explosion rocked the ground and rumbled across the water. Sydney nearly jumped out of her boots.

"What time is it?" Rusty asked Moose.

What time is it? Sydney thought. *Something just exploded inside the fort, and you're wondering what time it is?*

She turned around just long enough to see Rusty close the box and carefully place it in the backpack.

"It's 4:30," Moose said. "When that cannon goes off, it means the fort's closing, doesn't it, Rusty?"

Sydney sighed with relief.

"Yeah," Rusty said, sounding annoyed. "And because you took so long to find this, now we'll have to take it with us."

"But the boss said we should get it done today," Moose protested. "I don't think he wants us hauling that thing all over Baltimore."

"We don't have time," Rusty snarled. "The last boat leaves at five o'clock, and we have to be on it. We'll come back tomorrow. What the boss doesn't know won't hurt him."

Sydney followed b›ind the men as they walked toward

the Visitor Center. They passed Elizabeth on the pathway near the fort's entrance. Sydney saw Elizabeth curtsy. When Sydney caught up to Beth, she told her what was going on.

"The fort closes in fifteen minutes, and we have to return these costumes," Sydney said. "The girls will track Moose. They can tell us where he goes."

The girls scurried back to the wardrobe room and bolted the door. Elizabeth was grateful to get out of the long, heavy dress. Even the stuffy, humid air in the back room felt good against her skin. She hung the dress on a rack and offered to hang up Sydney's uniform while Sydney slipped on her street clothes. Elizabeth was about to return Sydney's cap to a cabinet near the door when she heard a familiar voice.

"Well, here we are, the last stop. A bed for two and nobody sleeps waiting for the alarm," the voice said. "We've been to every room inside the fort."

"Yeah," said an unfamiliar voice. "And the minutes are ticking down."

There was shuffling outside the door. The visitors seemed to be searching for something.

"I can't imagine where they went," said the first voice. "Maybe they've given up spying on our friends."

"Hey, what do you think is in here?" the second voice asked. The doorknob rattled.

"Hide!" Elizabeth whispered. She pulled Sydney toward the racks of clothes.

"No! Out the window!" Sydney exclaimed.

The girls rushed to the only window in the room. Just as they were about to climb out, Elizabeth felt the silver pendant fall from the chain on her neck.

"My pendant!" she gasped.

"Leave it!" said Sydney. "Let's get out of here."

Caught!

The girls barely said a word on the ride home with Ranger Hank. Elizabeth's heart was so heavy that her chest hurt. She was horrified at losing her favorite necklace. But even worse, with a dull ache, Elizabeth had to admit to herself that she knew that first voice they'd heard in the barracks. It was Uncle Dan. And she suspected that Sydney had recognized his voice, too.

When the girls finally returned to Sydney's room, Elizabeth dropped down on the bed and cried.

Sydney booted up the computer and e-mailed the Camp Club Girls. Soon they were all talking in the chat room about the voices near the wardrobe room. The girls agreed that in some way Uncle Dan was involved.

> McKenzie: *You know that note you found: "Hail to the chief at the twilight's last gleaming"? "Hail to the Chief" is the song they play when the president shows up. "Twilight's last gleaming" could mean the end of the Twilight Tattoo. Those words are in "The Star-Spangled Banner," too. They plan to kill the president at the end of the tattoo.*

Sydney doodled on a sheet of paper as she remembered something Aunt Dee had said.

Sydney: *The president isn't scheduled to appear until just before the fireworks start. There's a concert and marching presentation at twilight. When that's over, the president will show up and make his speech. When he's done, it'll be dark, and then the fireworks start.*

"In more ways than one," Elizabeth said. She had come to sit next to Sydney at the desk and was reading the words on the screen.

Kate: *I'm almost certain a weapon is in that little metal box they dug up. Maybe a bomb.*

Sydney scribbled words from "The Star-Spangled Banner" on her paper: *the rocket's red glare. . .the bombs bursting in air. bombs. bomb. BUM!*

"Bum!" she said out loud. She grabbed the keyboard.

Sydney: *Elizabeth saw the word BUM on the map near the red X. Maybe it meant bomb. Maybe whoever wrote it couldn't spell.*
Bailey: *So Percy has a bomb in his backpack?*
Sydney: *I think so. And it's your job to keep an eye on him. Let us know the minute he moves.*
Alexis: *I've been thinking about The Professor.*

*I remember a story about Sherlock Holmes,
the English detective. His worst enemy was this
guy named Professor Moriarty. In the story, the
professor was a mastermind criminal. He knew
about a secret hiding place for storing bombs
during World War II. So maybe our Professor has
a secret hiding place inside the fort.*

Sydney: *Maybe you're right. We're going to Fort
McHenry with Aunt Dee tomorrow afternoon. She
has to work there from five o'clock until the tattoo
is done. We won't have much time to find the
bomb.*

"Find the bomb?" said Elizabeth. "Oh, Sydney."

"We have to," Sydney said. "Remember, we're not sure any of this is true. We might be way off track, but if we're not—"

The Camp Club Girls agreed to follow the green blip while Sydney and Elizabeth were at the fort. Only very important text messages would be sent, and those would come through Kate.

•—•—•

The next afternoon, Sydney, Elizabeth, and Aunt Dee arrived at Fort McHenry when it closed, at about a quarter to five. Guests for the tattoo wouldn't be allowed in until six. Aunt Dee gave the girls permission to wander around, but she told them to be back at the Visitor Center by nine o'clock, when President Meade was scheduled to speak.

As they walked through the arched hallway into the fort, the girls took out their cell phones and logged on to Kate's tracking site.

"Moose hasn't moved since they took the water taxi back to the Inner Harbor," Elizabeth observed. "So they probably still have the bomb."

"Not necessarily," Sydney replied. "Maybe Rusty brought it back here overnight; we wouldn't have known if he did."

"I hadn't thought of that," said Elizabeth.

When the girls entered the parade grounds, they saw uniformed troops practicing drills. In the distance they heard drummers and buglers r›earsing for the tattoo.

"Elizabeth," Sydney said. "I think you should call your uncle."

"Why?" Elizabeth asked.

"Because we need to know where he is," Sydney responded. "But don't let on where *we* are."

Reluctantly Elizabeth took out her cell phone and called her uncle's number. It rang several times before Uncle Dan answered.

"Hey, Beth!" he said. "How are you doing?"

"I'm fine, Uncle Dan," Elizabeth said. "Just checking in to see what you're up to. Do you have plans with your friends for tonight?"

Her uncle paused before answering. "We're going fishing," he said. "And where are you going?"

Elizabeth thought quickly. "Oh, we're hanging out with Sydney's aunt Dee."

Sydney put her index finger up to her lips.

"Well, I'm glad to hear that," said Uncle Dan. "Stay close to Aunt Dee tonight, all right?"

What a strange thing to say, Elizabeth thought. "I will," she promised. "I have to go now. I'll talk to you tomorrow." She ended the call.

"So what did he say?" Sydney asked.

"They're going fishing tonight," Elizabeth answered.

Sydney spoke without thinking, "Fishing for President Meade."

As a line of soldiers marched past them wearing 1800s uniforms, Elizabeth said, "I have faith in my uncle, Sydney, almost as much as I have in God."

Sydney didn't say a word.

For the next hour, the girls searched Fort McHenry for the mysterious metal box. First they checked each of the bastions. As they walked on the ramparts, they looked into the gun barrels of the cannons along the way. They checked the magazines on the bastions—storage areas built into mounds of earth used for stockpiling gunpowder and weapons. Then they moved inside the fort near the barracks and looked underneath the wooden platform that surrounded the enormous flagpole. Above them, they could hear the huge American flag, a replica of the one from the Battle of Baltimore, flapping in the breeze.

Next the girls went to the barracks, searching each one. Starting on the upper level, they looked under each bed, through every drawer, and inside all the wooden barrels that held supplies. They left no door unopened and explored every nook and cranny. Nothing!

The last place they checked was the enlisted men's barracks. While Sydney searched, Elizabeth decided to go back to the wardrobe room and look for her pendant. She found the door bolted shut. Inside, she heard men's voices.

"Look alive, boys!" a man shouted.

"Ready arms. By twos!" shouted another.

As Elizabeth listened, she heard the sound of heavy boots moving toward the door. Quickly she crouched b›ind some barrels in a corner of the barracks. The door to the room opened and several actors dressed as 1800s soldiers came out. They walked across the wooden floor, past where Elizabeth was hiding, and out the front door.

Elizabeth slipped inside the wardrobe room. Methodically she scanned every square inch of the floor but found nothing. She also kept her eyes open for the important metal box.

"It's not here."

Elizabeth sucked in her breath and her heart skipped a beat. "Don't scare me like that," she told Sydney.

"The metal box isn't here," Sydney repeated. "I looked everywhere."

"Neither is my pendant," said Elizabeth. "Maybe we should just give up."

"We're not giving up," Sydney protested. "Not until we can prove that nothing evil is going on."

Just then, both girls' cell phones began to vibrate. It was a message from Kate: MOOSE IS ON THE MOVE. ON THE WATER AGAIN. HEADING FOR THE FORT.

"So what do we do now?" Elizabeth asked.

"We hide outside of the fort and wait," said Sydney. "When they get here, we follow them. Only this time, we have to be careful not to be seen."

Elizabeth and Sydney hid near some trees between the Visitor Center and the fort entrance. Before long, crowds of people arrived. They lined up four or five deep to walk into the fort.

"We'll be lucky to see Moose and Rusty in this crowd," Sydney said. "What if we miss them, Beth? Then what?"

Elizabeth had her cell phone out and was busy watching the tiny screen. "We won't. Not as long as we rely on Kate's website. We just have to watch where the green blip goes and keep following it. Even if we can't see them with our own eyes, we'll know where they are."

"And we have to be careful that they don't see us," Sydney added.

The girls watched the blip come onshore. It traveled slowly past the Visitor Center and along the pathway toward the entrance.

"There they are!" said Elizabeth.

Moose and Rusty shuffled along in the middle of the mob. Sydney almost missed them. They looked oddly respectable. Each wore a pair of neat blue jeans and a polo shirt, and Rusty sported a neatly trimmed beard. They blended well with the patriotic crowd.

"Let's go," Sydney said.

Both girls apologized as they cut into the line a few steps b›ind Rusty and Moose.

"Keep them in sight," Sydney whispered. She fixed her eyes on Rusty's red hair.

The crowd squeezed into the narrow hallway and then swarmed toward the bleachers set up around the parade grounds. Sydney and Elizabeth were pushed along, forced to go with the crowd. When they exited into the fading sunlight, they saw that someone was missing.

"Where's Moose?" Sydney asked.

Elizabeth checked the green blip on her cell phone. "He's still in the hallway," she said.

They found a bench near the barracks and watched Rusty as he sat on a lower tier of the bleachers. They waited for Moose to come out. But he didn't!

"Something's wrong with Kate's website," Elizabeth complained. "We've lost Moose."

"I'm going to check out the hallway," Sydney told her. "I'll be right back."

Cautiously Sydney walked to the entrance hall. The crowd had begun to thin out, and Moose was nowhere in sight. She hurried back to Elizabeth. "He's not there," she said. "Tell Kate. Maybe she can fix the website."

Elizabeth sent a text message to Kate telling her what was going on.

EVERYTHING SEEMS TO BE WORKING FINE, Kate answered. BUT I'LL DOUBLE CHECK.

"Now what?" Elizabeth asked.

"We wait," Sydney told her. "Keep your eyes on Rusty. Sooner or later, Moose will show up."

"I hope so," said Elizabeth.

The girls watched as the troops marched onto the field. Some soldiers played fifes and others played drums. All marched as if they were going to the battlefield. Swords hung from their belts and some carried muskets.

The troops surrounded the parade grounds and then stood at parade rest. Soon the United States Army Band marched to a stage on the far end of the field. They sat on metal chairs and opened folders of sheet music on their music stands. An announcement boomed over the loudspeaker: "Ladies and gentlemen, please stand for 'The Star-Spangled Banner.' "

Then the concert began. Sydney and Elizabeth had no choice but to sit, listen to the music, and watch Rusty. Kate sent several text messages insisting that the website was not broken. Still, no sign of Moose.

After about an hour, the sunset faded to dusk, and the dim crescent moon hung almost overhead.

"Sydney," Elizabeth gasped. "Look!"

Moose came sneaking out of the hallway. He carried the metal box as he prowled close to the fort's brick wall. Just then, Rusty got up and left the bleachers.

The girls' cell phones were vibrating with Kate's message: HE'S ON THE MOVE. EXITING THE HALLWAY NOW.

Elizabeth sent a quick reply: WE SEE HIM.

"You follow Rusty, and I'll take Moose," said Sydney. "I have a feeling we'll end up at the same place."

With their hearts pounding, Sydney and Elizabeth took off.

Quietly and carefully, Sydney stayed close to the fort's wall. She watched Moose slinking from barracks to barracks in the shadow. Finally he paused at an old guardhouse not far from the podium where President Meade was supposed to speak. Sydney saw Elizabeth hiding b›ind whatever she could find as she followed Rusty. Both girls watched as the men entered the guardhouse, leaving the door open b›ind them.

The girls met at the open door. Sydney stood on the left and Elizabeth on the right. They could hear the men talking.

"I didn't think you were ever coming out from that secret room," said Rusty. "It's about time!"

"Sorry," Moose answered. "It was dark in there, and I couldn't see my watch. I didn't know what time it was."

"Come on!" Rusty ordered. "That old jail cell is just around the corner. There's a bucket inside where the boss wants us to put it."

Carefully Sydney pefied into the room. The men had disappeared around a corner b›ind an old jailer's desk. She motioned for Elizabeth to follow her inside. Elizabeth took a deep breath. Then the girls slipped into the guardhouse.

Silently Sydney walked across the room. She pefied around the corner. Straight ahead was a short hallway. At its end was an old jail cell with a heavy iron door. The cell was made of thick brick walls, with no windows. Moose and Rusty were both inside, and Sydney noticed that the cell door had a lock. She watched Rusty take an old tin pail from one corner of the cell, and then Moose gingerly placed the metal box inside.

"We'd better get out of here fast," Moose said.

"I don't think so!" Sydney shouted.

Elizabeth watched with horror as her friend leaped into the hallway and rushed the jail cell. She slammed the door, locking Moose and Rusty inside. Rusty's steely eyes glared at her.

"Who are *you*?" asked Moose.

"I'm your worst enemy," Sydney snapped.

Elizabeth dashed beside her.

"It's those girls from the Wall," Rusty said. "I told you I didn't like something about them." Rusty's voice echoed inside the dark, musty cell. The only other sound came from the tin pail. It was ticking!

"You'd better tell us what you're up to," said Elizabeth. "Or else."

"Or else, what?" Rusty laughed.

In the dim light from the hallway, the girls saw sweat pouring down Moose's face. He stuttered, "There's a b–bomb in here. It's going to g–go off when the f–fireworks start. P–please, let us go. We all g–gotta get out of here." He looked nervously at the pail, inches from his feet.

Through the doorway, the girls heard the loudspeaker announce that President Meade would soon be at the podium.

"You'd better let us go, or we'll all die!" said Rusty. "This is a high-tech military bomb made from titanium alloy. It'll blow this place to smithereens." He took the metal box out of the pail and held it menacingly in front of the girls.

"Run and get help," Sydney told Elizabeth. "Hurry! Go!"

"You come, too!" Elizabeth said.

"*Just go!*" Sydney commanded.

Elizabeth raced out of the short hallway, around the corner, and past the jailer's desk. She bolted out the door and into the darkness. She was almost to the parade grounds when she felt one strong arm wrap around her waist. Then a hand covered her mouth, and someone was dragging her away from the fort and toward the water. The kidnapper pulled her onto a pier and into a small boat. Only then did she get a look at him. It was her uncle's friend Al.

The Rockets' Red Glare

Elizabeth struggled with her kidnapper until she saw Uncle Dan sitting in the boat. Al let her go, and she ran into her uncle's arms.

"I can't believe you're involved in this!" she sobbed. "I always thought you were a good man who loves the Lord."

Uncle Dan hugged her. "I am, and I do," he said. "Now listen to me."

A stranger appeared from the darkness in the back of the boat. He was dressed in black and carried a gun!

"We think there's a plot to assassinate President Meade right here, tonight—and very soon. This is Agent Phillips from the FBI. If you know anything, Elizabeth, tell him right now! It's a matter of life and death. Why were you running, and where is Sydney?"

Elizabeth's heart pounded.

"Sydney has Moose and Rusty locked in a jail cell in the guardhouse." She pointed in the direction from which she'd run. "They have a bomb and it's set to go off when the fireworks start. Sydney told me to run for help. She insisted on staying there to guard them."

Al stood b›ind Elizabeth and put his hands gently on her

242

shoulders. "See, I knew there was a bomb," he said. "I could sense it from our combat days in Vietnam."

"Tell me exactly what the bomb looks like," Agent Phillips said. "And who are Rusty and Moose?"

"Rusty and Moose work for the boss and The Professor," said Elizabeth. "They're the bad guys. The bomb is in a small metal box that they dug up yesterday afternoon over there." She pointed to the area. "I don't know what's inside the box, but it's ticking, and Moose is nervous. He said if they don't get out of that jail cell, everyone is going to die."

Agent Phillips jumped from the boat onto the dock. He ran as fast as he could toward the guardhouse.

"I'm going, too," Elizabeth demanded. "I have to save Sydney!"

She started to move, but Al and Uncle Dan held her back.

"Let Agent Phillips handle this, Elizabeth," Uncle Dan said. "He knows what he's doing. Sydney will be all right."

Al had one big, strong arm around her shoulder now. This time, instead of it making her feel terrified, she felt safe.

"I'm sorry, Elizabeth," he said. "I didn't mean to scare you back there. We knew that something was going on, but we weren't sure what it was. If you had screamed, who knows what might have happened. I had to get you to the boat so you'd be safe. I don't know what your uncle would do if he lost you."

Uncle Dan took something from the pocket of his jeans and held it in his closed fist. "And speaking of losing things," he said, "did you lose this?" He opened his hand and revealed Elizabeth's pendant.

"Oh," Elizabeth gasped. "You found it."

"After you and your friend climbed out the window yesterday," he said. Uncle Dan read the inscription out loud: " 'Be strong and courageous. Do not be afraid; do not be discouraged, for the Lord your God will be with you wherever you go.' Joshua 1:9. I gave you this pendant for times like this, Beth. The Lord is with us. He'll save President Meade and your friend. Just you wait and see."

Uncle Dan fastened the chain around Elizabeth's neck. "And by the way," he said. "What were you and Sydney doing in the wardrobe room?"

Elizabeth explained how they had dressed in costume and followed Rusty and Moose. She also told her uncle about the package Moose was carrying, and she showed them Kate's website and the green blip that was inside the jail cell.

●—●—●

Meanwhile, Agent Phillips rushed into the guardhouse. He passed the old jailer's desk and turned the corner into the shallow hallway. Sydney was standing guard over the prisoners, and Rusty was pleading, "Kid, just go and get the key!"

The FBI agent flashed his badge. "Phillips, FBI!" he said. "Sydney, get out of here. I'll handle this."

Sydney stood straight and tall. "No," she said. "Where's Elizabeth?"

"She's safe," said Agent Phillips. "Get out!"

Sydney didn't move.

"Unlock this door!" Rusty thundered. "We have less than a half hour before this thing blows."

Moose stood next to Rusty, hanging on to the bars. His

eyes were glazed, and his face was an odd gray color. "I think I'm going to throw up," he said.

"Sydney, where's the key?" the agent asked calmly.

Sydney felt like she was in an old spy movie, the kind that Alexis was always talking about. "I don't know," she answered.

Agent Phillips stayed calm when he spoke. "We have to find the key. The only thing that might stop that bomb from going off is to drown it in water. We need to get it out of this jail cell and into the harbor. *Now!*"

Agent Phillips began searching the guardhouse. Sydney helped. They dumped the contents of all the drawers in the jailer's desk and found nothing. They looked in cabinets, under a pile of books, and beneath the mattress of the jailer's cot in the corner. Then Phillips got on his radio and called for help. Within seconds five men wearing black suits burst through the door.

"Oh!" Sydney gasped.

One was the short, dark man she and Elizabeth had seen at the Lincoln Memorial—the boss.

"Arrest that guy!" Sydney cried. "He's the boss!"

The man looked at her as if she were crazy. "Peter Daniels, Secret Service," he said to Agent Phillips.

"Daniels, get President Meade out of here right now!" The FBI agent commanded. "He's in danger."

The Secret Service agent bolted out of the room.

"But you can't let him get away!" Sydney said. "He's the boss!"

Everything was so mixed up. Sydney had no time to tell Agent Phillips the whole story, and he had no idea what she meant. Meanwhile, she watched the boss get away.

"Elizabeth and I were spying on Moose and Rusty," she blurted out. "At the Lincoln Memorial. That guy is the one who was giving them the orders. He's part of the plan to get President Meade!"

Agent Phillips looked at her with disbelief.

"Oh please, just trust me," said Sydney.

Phillips nodded toward the other men, and two of them ran into the darkness.

"Sydney, I need your help," said Agent Phillips. "Run as fast as you can to the Visitor Center and see if you can find where they keep the key. Radio the information back to me." He handed her a small walkie-talkie. "Whatever you do, don't come back here. Get as far away from Fort McHenry as you can."

Sydney Lincoln took the walkie-talkie in one hand and started to run. She ran faster than she ever had. Everything was at stake now: the president's life and the lives of everyone in the fort, including her own.

●—●—●

In the Visitor Center, Aunt Dee sat at a desk watching the fort entrance on a security monitor. The entrance was deserted. All of the visitors were in the bleachers waiting for President Meade. Dee looked at a wall clock. It was a few minutes past nine o'clock, and the president was late getting to the podium. The loudspeaker played patriotic music as the visitors waited for him to appear.

Aunt Dee glanced back at the monitor just in time to see Sydney dash through the entrance from the fort. It didn't seem at all odd that she was running. After all, Dee had told her and Elizabeth to be back at the Visitor Center by nine. And they were late.

Sydney ran through the front door.

"Aunt Dee! Aunt Dee! Help!"

Dee jumped up from her desk and hurried to Sydney. "What's the matter?" she demanded. "Did something happen to Elizabeth?"

"Aunt Dee, an FBI agent sent me. There's a bomb in the guardhouse, and we need the key to the jail cell!"

"What?" Aunt Dee asked doubtfully.

Sydney held the walkie-talkie up to her mouth and pushed a button. "Agent Phillips? Please tell my aunt what's going on. I don't think she believes me."

The walkie-talkie crackled. "This is Agent Phillips from the FBI," the voice said. "We have a code red situation in the guardhouse, and we need the key to the jail cell right away!"

"There's a plot to kill the president," Sydney added.

Sydney's aunt rushed into a back room and returned with a big, black skeleton key hanging on a bigger metal ring. "Tell him I've got it," she said.

Sydney tore the key from her aunt's hand and took off.

"Sydney, no!" Aunt Dee shouted. But it was too late. Sydney charged through the darkness grasping the key. As she ran, she remembered the scripture verse on the bracelet Elizabeth had given her: *Be strong and courageous. Do not be afraid; do not be discouraged, for the Lord your God will be with you wherever you go.*

By now, fifteen minutes had passed. A quarter of an hour

was all that was left to drown the bomb and get to safety. As the loudspeaker played "Stars and Stripes Forever," Sydney cut across the parade grounds, past the barracks, and into the night. Several Secret Service agents, not knowing who she was or what she was up to, chased her. Sydney was faster than they were. She didn't dare slow down by looking over her shoulder to see if any of them was the boss. Instead she ran with all her might to the guardhouse.

Sydney slammed through the door. "Here!" she gasped, pushing the key to Agent Phillips.

"Leave her alone!" Phillips ordered the agents who were about to tackle Sydney. Phillips ran to the jail cell with Sydney b›ind him. "Get out of here!" he told her.

"No!" Sydney exclaimed. "I can help."

Moose was lying on the floor. He had passed out from fear. Rusty clung to the cell bars, his face ashen. He was no longer the gruff character who talked down to Moose and made demands. Instead he looked like a frightened boy.

"You'd better say your prayers," Sydney told him as Phillips put the key into the lock.

"I don't know any prayers," Rusty answered.

As Agent Phillips tried to unlock the door, Sydney prayed out loud: "After this manner therefore pray ye: Our Father which art in heaven, Hallowed be thy name. Thy kingdom come, Thy will be done in earth, as it is in heaven. Give us this day our daily bread. And forgive us our debts, as we forgive our debtors. And lead us not into temptation, but deliver us from evil: For thine is the kingdom, and the power, and the glory, for ever. Amen."

"Amen," Rusty echoed.

The cell door creaked open, and a team of FBI agents tackled Rusty. Another agent snapped handcuffs onto Moose as he lay unconscious on the cold brick floor. A third agent reached for the metal box with the bomb, but Sydney was faster. She grabbed the box and ran.

"Sydney!" Agent Phillips shouted.

"Let her go," another agent said. "She's faster than any of us. We can't do anything about it now."

On the boat, Elizabeth waited with her uncle and his friend. In the distance, they could hear "Stars and Stripes Forever" playing on the parade grounds loudspeakers.

"It's almost time for the fireworks to start," Elizabeth said. "I suppose that by now Agent Phillips has canceled them and they've dismantled the bomb. Where in the world is Sydney?"

Uncle Dan smiled weakly. "They'll probably have the fireworks anyway," he said. "It's all done by computer these days."

The two-way radio on the boat started to crackle. Agent Phillips's anxious voice came through: "Dan, Sydney has the bomb, and she's running toward the harbor. As soon as she drops it in the water, get her into the boat and get as far out in the harbor as you can—as fast as you can. Good luck!"

Elizabeth had a sick, sinking feeling in the pit of her stomach.

Al started the engine and untied the boat from the dock. Then a shadowy figure appeared on the crest of the hill near the harbor. It almost flew toward the boat docks.

"There she is!" Elizabeth cried. "She's running to that dock!" She pointed to a boat dock south from where they were. Immediately Al backed the boat out and sped in that direction.

"Run, Sydney! Run!" Elizabeth cried. "We're coming to get you!"

As Sydney ran, clutching the metal box, she prayed that the bomb wouldn't go off. Her heart was pounding when her feet hit the wooden dock. Although it was at most thirty feet long, to Sydney it seemed like a mile. Finally she reached the end of the dock. She dropped the box into the water.

"Swim to us!" Uncle Dan shouted.

Sydney dove in and swam to the boat. Elizabeth helped pull her inside. Then, with Al at the controls, the powerboat sped out into the Baltimore Harbor.

Sydney lay on her back on the boat's floor, wet and gasping for air. "W—we. . .d—did it," she said. "We s—saved P—President Meade."

Elizabeth held her friend's hand. "No, Sydney," she said. "*You* did it."

As the boat sailed a safe distance into the harbor, Elizabeth sent Kate a text message: WE'RE ALL RIGHT. TELL THE OTHER CAMP CLUB GIRLS THAT WE'LL HAVE A LONG STORY TO TELL AROUND OUR CYBER CAMPFIRE.

Kate texted: MOOSE IS ON THE MOVE AGAIN. HE'S HEADING TOWARD THE FORT'S ENTRANCE NOW, REALLY SLOW.

Elizabeth typed back: I KNOW. HE'S IN HANDCUFFS AND SHACKLES.

Kaboom! Pow! Bang! Several explosions thundered across the water making the boat rock.

"Oh no," Sydney said, still lying on the floor. "Did it go off?"

In the following seconds, Elizabeth only saw the stars and the crescent moon in the black sky. Then several bright dots shot into the air over the fort, leaving smoke trails b›ind them. One exploded into a silver fountain, another into long golden spider legs, and a third showered the fort with sparks of red, white, and blue. "It's only the fireworks starting," she said.

The radio crackled again. "All suspects are in custody," said Agent Phillips. "Percival Malone, Rusty Gates, and also the Secret Service guy Peter Daniels. A fourth suspect is in Washington, D.C., and our agents have him surrounded. Good work, Sydney and Elizabeth. But if you ever do anything this dangerous again, I might have to arrest you!"

Uncle Dan looked at the girls and nodded in agreement. Then they all laughed, happy that the whole thing was b›ind them.

"Do you think that Agent Phillips will tell us the whole story?" Sydney wondered as she accepted a blanket Uncle Dan found in a seat. "I mean, we still don't know why those guys wanted to kill the president or who The Professor is."

Al settled back in his captain's chair and watched as fireworks spilled over the fort. "I'm sure he'll tell us what he can," he said. "Your uncle and I would like to know the whole story, too."

Sydney sat looking toward the fort. The exploding fireworks cast a strange flickering light on the huge American flag flying near the barracks. Sydney couldn't help but imagine what it was like for Francis Scott Key as he stood on the deck of an enemy ship in the Baltimore Harbor, watching bombs explode over Fort McHenry. She thanked God that tonight's rockets' red glare came from the fireworks.

According to His Plan

The next morning, Elizabeth and Sydney went to the police station to tell everything they knew about Moose, Rusty, and the plot to kill President Meade. Uncle Dan and Al went, too, and Agent Phillips was there to help.

●—●—●

Meanwhile, Alexis, Bailey, McKenzie, and Kate were all in the chat room waiting for them to return. The only information they had came from an e-mail that Sydney sent after she and Elizabeth got back from the tattoo. It told everything that had happened at the fort, but there were still lots of missing pieces.

Finally Sydney and Elizabeth logged in.

> Bailey: *So tell us what you found out at the police station. And don't leave anything out.*
> Alexis: *Yeah. I'm dying to know what happened. I've had "The Star Spangled Banner" playing in my head ever since I read your e-mail. Sometimes I hate it that my brain is so musical.*
> McKenzie: *I didn't see anything about it on the news this morning. Why not?*

Sydney and Elizabeth sat at Sydney's desk. In front of them was an open box of chocolates, a gift from Agent Phillips. Two pieces of candy were missing from the box, and Sydney reached for another. On the shelf near Elizabeth sat a big glass vase filled with two dozen red roses. A white card with gold lettering hung from it, reading: WITH SINCERE GRATITUDE— PRESIDENT WILSON MEADE.

Sydney: *They're keeping the assassination plot quiet. The visitors to the tattoo had no idea that anything was going on, because the FBI didn't want them to panic. It was quicker to get the bomb away from the crowd than to get the crowd away from the bomb. When it was all over, President Meade made his speech as if nothing had happened, and then the tattoo ended with the fireworks.*

Alexis: *So you're not going to be on the news?*

Sydney: *Not unless someone leaks it to the media. The FBI hopes it won't happen. They don't want other bad guys to get ideas.*

Elizabeth borrowed the keyboard from Sydney.

Elizabeth: *You can't say a word to anyone about what we're going to tell you. This is a Camp Club Girls secret. Let's do a cyber pinkie-promise that we'll take it to our graves.*

Bailey: *I promise.*

Alexis: *And me.*

McKenzie: *I'm in.*

Kate: *Me, too. Biscuit promises, too.*

Sydney and Elizabeth linked their pinkie fingers and promised to keep the secret forever.

McKenzie: *So who was The Professor?*

Kate: *And what was up with the Secret Service guy, the boss?*

Elizabeth: *One thing at a time. We have to start at the beginning, way back in 1967 in Vietnam. The boss—his real name is Peter Daniels—was a soldier then in the United States Army. He was the Dan in the note, "Lieutenant Dan, we've got legs," not my uncle.*

Alexis: *I'm glad, Elizabeth. None of us wanted your uncle to be one of the bad guys.*

Elizabeth chose a square piece of chocolate from the box before she continued.

Elizabeth: *Peter Daniels had a twin brother named Adam, and they fought together in the Vietnam War. They were both in a platoon called White Skull, and they were in the worst of the fighting.*

Sydney took over the keyboard while Elizabeth ate the chewy caramel.

Sydney: *One day, there was a terrible battle. The White Skull troopers were under attack, and they were outnumbered. So their leader, Sergeant Kuester, told them to retreat. He figured if he didn't get his men out of there, they'd all get killed.*

McKenzie: *How do you know all this?*

Sydney: *Because Sergeant Kuester is here in D.C. at the Vietnam Veterans' Reunion, the same one Beth's uncle is at. The FBI found out that Sergeant Kuester had been Daniel's platoon leader, and they figured he might have an idea why Daniels wanted to kill the president. It was his information that got Peter Daniels to confess.*

Bailey: *So why did he want to kill the president?*

Sydney: *President Meade was in the White Skull platoon, too, when he was a young soldier. When Sergeant Kuester told his men to retreat, Meade froze. Adam Daniels, the boss's twin brother, tried to get Meade out of there, but Meade went crazy. He started fighting with Adam, like he was the enemy or something—*

McKenzie: *It was Agent Orange, wasn't it? I've thought from the beginning that whoever we were looking for was sick from that.*

Sydney: *Sorry, McKenzie, but you were wrong about that. It had nothing to do with Agent Orange. Meade just froze in fear.*

Sydney helped herself to another piece of candy before

going on with the story.

Sydney: *Sgt. Kuester realized that two guys were missing, so he went back to get them. When Peter Daniels found out that one of the missing guys was his brother, he went to help.*

Of course, when they got to them, they found Meade fighting with Adam Daniels. Adam was trying to drag Meade out of there while they were under attack. Kuester managed to get between them and wrestle Meade to the ground. But the enemy fired at them. The sergeant got shot in the leg and Adam Daniels fell to the ground—dead. Kuester managed to get out and Peter Daniels rescued Meade, but secretly he blamed Meade for the death of his twin brother.

Sydney pushed the keyboard toward Elizabeth. "You tell the next part," she said.

Elizabeth: *After he got out of the army, Peter Daniels became a police officer in Washington, D.C. He worked his way up to the rank of lieutenant.*

Kate: *And that's why they called him Lieutenant Dan in the note.*

Elizabeth: *Right. Wilson Meade became a politician and was elected to the United States Senate. He and Peter Daniels were friendly, but Daniels was just like Jesus' disciple Judas. He pretended to be*

Meade's friend, but in the end, he betrayed him.

When Meade got elected president, he wanted Peter Daniels as one of his Secret Service guys, because he trusted Daniels with his life. In fact, we found out today that it was Daniels who saved President Meade when he was almost shot at the National Air and Space Museum.

Kate: *So the boss saved Meade's life twice. Once in Vietnam and again at the Spirit of St. Louis thing.*

Elizabeth: *Meanwhile, Daniels was getting angrier that his brother was dead. He hated it that Meade was not only alive, but had also become the president of the United States. He just couldn't get it out of his head that Meade was responsible for Adam's death.*

McKenzie: *So he decided to get even.*

Elizabeth wiped her chocolaty fingers on a piece of scrap paper.

Bailey: *What about The Professor?*

Alexis: *And how do Moose and Rusty fit into all this?*

Sydney asked Elizabeth to go down to the kitchen to get some bottles of water. They needed something to wash down the chocolates. In the meantime, she went on with the story.

Sydney: *Daniels knew a scientist who had helped create the space shuttle. He was a troublemaker and hated the government, so he got kicked out of NASA. Daniels figured he'd be more than willing to help get rid of Meade, so he got Professor Hopkins to create a miniature smart bomb made of titanium. It was tiny enough to fit into that little metal box Moose and Rusty had but powerful enough to destroy all of Fort McHenry and most of the peninsula it's built on.*

Alexis: *So Hopkins was the mastermind professor, like Professor Moriarty in the Sherlock Holmes stories.*

Elizabeth returned with two bottles of water. Sydney opened hers and took a drink.

Sydney: *The Professor was the brains b›ind it all. Plus, he knew his way around the fort, so he decided where the best place was to plant the bomb. When they arrested him last night, he confessed to his part in the plot, but he blamed it all on Daniels.*

Bailey: *And what about Moose and Rusty?*

Sydney gave the keyboard to Elizabeth.

Elizabeth: *Daniels and The Professor turned out to be cowards. They didn't want to get killed if the bomb went off too soon, and they didn't want to be connected with the assassination, so they got Moose and Rusty to do their dirty work.*

Moose and Rusty were both in trouble for not

paying their taxes, and Daniels promised they wouldn't go to prison if they helped him plant the bomb. As much as possible, Daniels tried to stay out of it. That's why he left those messages at the Wall. He didn't want to be seen with Rusty and Moose.

Kate: *So did Moose and Rusty confess?*

Elizabeth: *They sure did. They told the FBI a lot of stuff. They said since Daniels was a Secret Service agent, he was allowed at Fort McHenry to bury the box with the bomb. He told the park ranger he was checking the place ahead of the president's visit.*

McKenzie: *Then he's the one who made the treasure map.*

Elizabeth: *He made the map. But Rusty and Moose messed up. They were supposed to plant the bomb that afternoon. The Professor wanted them to put it in a secret room in the fort's hallway, the one that Moose hid in last night. But Daniels wanted it closer to where President Meade was supposed to give his speech. He told Moose and Rusty to hide it in the jail cell. It was all supposed to be done the day before the tattoo. But it got too late and Moose and Rusty took the bomb with them. They weren't supposed to be anywhere near the fort on the night of the tattoo. Kate, if not for your tracking device, last night would have been a disaster.*

McKenzie: *What did your uncle say, Elizabeth?*

Kate: *And what about his friend Al? Was he following you?*

Elizabeth took a drink from her bottle of water.

Elizabeth: *That first day at the Wall, when I found the "Meade me in St. Louis" note, my uncle was suspicious. When I didn't want to go to lunch, he figured something was going on. He was worried because I'd told him about our sleuthing at camp. So he asked his friend Al to keep an eye on me for a while. He was afraid I wouldn't be safe in the city.*

Kate: *Was I right that they put a GPS in your backpack?*

Elizabeth: *No. There was no tracking device. But Al soon figured out that we were on to something. He was reading those notes at the Wall, too. None of them made sense to him and Uncle Dan, but they figured out, like we did, that something was going on with President Meade.*

Elizabeth helped herself to one more piece of candy.

Elizabeth: *Uncle Dan called Agent Phillips from the FBI. Phillips was Uncle Dan's old army buddy. My uncle told Phillips about the notes at the Wall and also the two suspicious-looking guys who left them there.*

Kate: *So that's what I heard when I was listening*

outside their hotel room that day.

Elizabeth: *Right. Phillips wasn't sure what was
going on but decided that by following us they
would keep us safe, and maybe find out what, if
anything, we knew. I'd accidentally told my uncle
we planned to go to Fort McHenry, so he, Al, and
Agent Phillips followed us. But they lost us when
we changed into costumes. They saw us go into
the enlisted men's barracks but didn't see us come
out. When I heard them outside the door to the
wardrobe room, it sounded like they were looking
for something. Turns out that they were looking
for us!*

She pushed the keyboard over to Sydney's side of the desk
and asked her to finish the story.

Sydney: *By the time Uncle Dan found Elizabeth's
pendant, we had already left the fort. Agent
Phillips figured we'd gone out the window.
So Al went looking for us, and guess what he
found instead—Rusty's map. He must have
dropped it on his way to the water taxi. And
guess what it was written on—the back of a flyer
announcing the Twilight Tattoo. So that's how
Uncle Dan and his friends found out that maybe
something was going to happen at the tattoo. Then
when they found out that we were there last night,
they were doubly suspicious.*

Alexis: *It's a good thing they followed you last night. You both might have been killed.*

Sydney: *I don't think so. I think we'd have found a way to save the president. I don't know how, but the Lord would have helped us.*

Alexis: *He did help you! It all worked out according to His plan. By the way, what does your mom think about all of this?*

Sydney put the lid on the box of candy. She and Elizabeth had decided to save some for later.

Sydney: *Mom didn't know anything about it until we got home last night. Aunt Dee brought us here in one of the ranger's vans. Uncle Dan and Al came along and explained the whole thing to my mom. At first she was mad. But then she understood that we saved President Meade's life. She cried and hugged us because we were safe. Then I couldn't believe my ears. She said kids like us made the world a better place!*

McKenzie: *All right! Let's hear it for the Camp Club Girls!*

A soft knock sounded on Sydney's bedroom door and her mom peeked inside. "I'm sorry to interrupt," she said, "but I just invited Elizabeth's uncle and his friend over for some barbeque. Dee's starting the grill. Would you girls come help us get ready, please?"

"Sure, Mom," Sydney answered. "We'll be down as soon as we've said good-bye to our friends."

Sydney's mom smiled and closed the door.

Elizabeth: *We have to go. Uncle Dan and Al are coming over for a cookout.*

Bailey: *Have a safe trip home.*

McKenzie: *We'll keep praying that your uncle Dan will walk again real soon.*

Elizabeth: *Do you know what? I'm not angry about that anymore. This whole adventure taught me that Psalm 37:8 is true: "Refrain from anger and turn from wrath; do not fret—it leads only to evil."*

Camp Club Girls
McKenzie's
Montana Mystery

Shari Barr

CHAT ROOM TERMS:

2 – too, to

4 – for

B – be

BFF – best friends forever

GF – girlfriend

G2G – got to go

Kewl – cool

LOL – laugh out loud

LTNC – long time no see

RU – are you

Sum – some

Thx – thanks

TTFN – ta ta for now

TTYL – talk to you later

U – you

WTG – way to go

Y – why

A Surprise for McKenzie!

Aaaaaahhhh!

McKenzie screamed and clutched the reins with sweaty palms. She tugged firmly, trying to control her horse.

Please, God, help me, she prayed as Sahara bolted down the arena.

McKenzie's heart pounded and her auburn hair whipped b›ind her.

Something's wrong! she thought.

She leaned forward and pulled the reins with all her strength. The tightness she usually felt in the reins was missing. She had no control over her horse! Sahara raced straight toward the barrel in the middle of the arena.

"McKenzie!" a voice screamed from the sidelines. "Hold on."

The reins slipped between her fingers. McKenzie started to slide from the saddle. She grasped the saddle horn, but Sahara's galloping bounced her up and down until she could hold on no longer.

McKenzie hit the ground with a thud as thundering hooves barely missed her. She laid with her face on the ground. Sahara raced by and finally slowed to a trot.

"McKenzie! Are you okay?" A pair of cowboy boots appeared in front of her face.

Rolling over, McKenzie pushed herself into a sitting position. She coughed from the dust Sahara had stirred up and looked into the eyes of Emma Wilson, her riding instructor. "I—I don't know yet," she stammered as she stretched her legs.

She felt a strong hand support the back of her head. Turning, she saw Emma's hired hand, Derfi, holding up two fingers. "How many?" he asked.

"Four," McKenzie answered.

Emma and Derfi stared at her. No one said anything for a minute.

"But two fingers are bent over," she added.

After a second, Derfi's face broke into a grin. He unbuckled her riding helmet and slipped it off her head.

"She's okay," a familiar voice announced. The girl with a fringe of black bangs fluttering on her olive skin popped a red gummy worm into her mouth.

"Bailey! What are you doing here?" McKenzie screeched as the girl approached her. "Hey, can I have one of those?"

"Yep, she's definitely okay," Bailey said as she dangled a green and orange worm in front of McKenzie.

McKenzie grabbed the worm and pulled her legs forward, trying to stand up. But Emma placed a firm hand on her shoulder. "Not so fast. Sit for a minute."

"What happened anyway?" McKenzie watched as her horse sauntered back across the arena and nuzzled her face. "I had no control over Sahara. I just couldn't hold on."

Derfi reached his hand out to the chocolate brown mare.

"Here's the problem," he said as his fingers touched a dangling strap. "Her bridle is broken."

McKenzie tried again to stand. Emma and Derfi each put a hand beneath her arms and helped her to her feet. Feeling slightly light-headed, she stepped forward and grabbed Bailey in a tight hug.

"So, how did you get here?" McKenzie asked.

"When you told me you were coming to Sunshine Stables to train for the rodeo and help with Kids' Camp, I convinced Mom and Dad to let me fly out with Uncle Troy on a business trip. He rented a car and drove me out from the airport. He didn't have time to stick around, so he's gone already."

"Why didn't you tell me you were coming?" McKenzie asked.

"Well, I signed up for the camp, since I'm not that good on horses. When Miss Wilson found out we were friends, she invited me to stay here, but she wanted to surprise you. Then after camp, she's going to train both of us for the rodeo." Bailey's dark eyes flashed.

"Oh, Emma, this is the best surprise ever!" McKenzie turned to her instructor.

"Think of it as a thank-you for coming to Kids' Camp on such short notice," Emma said with a smile. "I didn't expect so many kids to sign up. You'll be a big help with the younger ones. But, let's get you up to the house to sit for a minute. If you can walk, that is."

"I'm fine," McKenzie assured Emma as she brushed dirt from her face with the sleeve of her T-shirt. "I'd better take care of Sahara first, though."

"I'll do that," Derfi said as he grabbed Sahara's halter. "I'll take her to the stable and find her a new bridle. You go on to the house."

Emma and the girls walked to the large, white farmhouse. A sign reading SUNSHINE STABLES stood in the front yard. Several sheds and a huge red barn stood beyond the house. The riding arena was next to a matching red stable. A dozen or so horses grazed in the lush, green pasture.

McKenzie sighed with contentment. She had met Bailey at Camp Discovery, where they had shared a cabin with four other campers. The six girls, or the Camp Club Girls, as they called themselves, had become fast friends by solving a mystery together. Though they all lived in different parts of the country, they had kept in touch and gone on to solve another mystery together. Bailey was the youngest of the group at nine years old, four years younger than McKenzie.

The girls stepped onto the huge porch that wrapped around the house. They dropped onto the porch swing while Emma slipped inside. Emma quickly returned with cold drinks.

"Emma, this is so perfect." McKenzie reached out to pet Buckeye, Emma's brown and white terrier. "This will be so fun having Bailey here. Now, we can work on barrel racing together."

"Don't forget you have to save time for the Junior Miss Rodeo Queen contest, too," Emma said as she ran her fingers through her short blond hair.

McKenzie groaned. She wasn't sure she wanted to compete in the contest. Emma had competed when she was younger and had told McKenzie's mom what a wonderful experience it had been. Now, Mom had talked McKenzie into competing. McKenzie didn't like the thought of wearing fancy riding clothes for the contest. And she especially dreaded the thought of standing on stage in front of hundreds of people.

McKenzie got slightly nervous in riding competitions, but just thinking about the queen contest made her want to throw up.

"Are your parents coming for the rodeo and the queen contest?" Bailey scratched Buckeye's ears.

"Yes, they'll be here," McKenzie answered, sipping her lemonade. "My family doesn't live too far away. I usually come over here and train a couple of days a wefi. But now that I'm helping with Kids' Camp, I get to stay here until the rodeo next wefi. I'll have a lot of extra time to train."

After the girls finished their lemonade, Emma asked McKenzie to show Bailey their bedroom. The girls stepped inside the front door where Bailey had left her bags. She grabbed her pink-and-green-striped pillow and tucked it under her arm along with a monster-sized, black-and-white panda. McKenzie grabbed the two bags and led the way upstairs to their bedroom. A set of bunk beds stood against one wall.

McKenzie turned to her friend. "I knew you were hoping to visit, but I didn't think you'd be able to come."

"I didn't either." Bailey dropped her pillow and panda on the floor. "When Uncle Troy found out about his trip, Mom and Dad decided at the last minute that I could come along."

"We'll have a blast." McKenzie pointed to Bailey's bags. "Do you have cowboy boots in there somewhere? And you might want to change into jeans so we can go horseback riding as soon as Derfi finds a new bridle for Sahara."

Bailey changed her clothes. Then the girls headed back downstairs and went outside with Emma.

"I'll help you saddle your horses," Emma said as she led the way across the yard. "Bailey, you can ride the Shetland pony, Applejack. Then you two can go for a ride while I work. How does that sound?"

"Great," McKenzie said. "When do we need to be back for chores?"

"About an hour or so," Emma said as they walked through the stable to Applejack's stall.

First Emma helped saddle the horse for Bailey, while McKenzie put the bridle on. Emma grabbed a riding helmet for the younger girl and led Applejack out of the stable.

Derfi met them at the doorway holding Sahara, who was fitted with a new bridle. Derfi was Emma's newest stable hand. He had only been working at Sunshine Stables for two months. Even though Derfi was an adult, he reminded McKenzie of her eight-year-old brother, Evan. Both were always full of mischief.

"You look better than you did awhile ago," Derfi told McKenzie. "You're not even limping."

"Nope. I told you I was fine." She patted Sahara's neck.

"McKenzie, why don't you introduce your friend to Derfi? I didn't have a chance to do that when you were taking your wild ride," Emma teased.

McKenzie pulled Bailey to her side. "Bailey Chang, meet Derfi McGrady. Bailey lives in Peoria, Illinois."

"Nice to meet you, Bailey. You ready to hop on Applejack? He's ready for you." He grabbed the horse's reins and opened the gate.

McKenzie followed with Sahara. She placed her boot in the stirrup and swung herself up onto the saddle. Then with ease, Bailey hopped onto Applejack's back.

"Your mom said you've done quite a bit of riding, Bailey. Is that right?" Emma asked as she closed the gate b›ind them.

"Yes. But I'm not as good as McKenzie." Bailey swept her long bangs away from her for›ead and slipped on her helmet. "I've done some racing at county fairs but never a rodeo."

"You're a lot younger than she is. You have plenty of time to improve." Emma smiled at Bailey.

"Is it okay if we ride to Old Towne?" McKenzie put her helmet on and fastened the chinstrap.

"Sure. You have your cell phone with you, right?" Emma asked. "After you look around for a while, head back for chores. Both of you can help with Diamond Girl when she comes in from pasture."

Diamond Girl was Sunshine Stable's most famous horse. She was Emma's prize horse and a rodeo winner. For the last three years, Emma had ridden Diamond Girl in the barrel-racing competition, and each year Emma brought home the first-place trophy. McKenzie couldn't wait to show Diamond Girl to Bailey.

Eager for a ride, the girls waved to Emma and Derfi and headed for the dirt track b›ind the house. A warm summer breeze rustled the pine trees lining the trail.

"What is Old Towne?" Bailey asked as her horse plodded

beside McKenzie's.

"It's a bunch of Old West buildings. There's an old-time Main Street with a general store, post office, and stuff like that. But it's more like a ghost town now. It belongs to Sunshine Stables and is open during June, July, and the first wefi of August. It's closed now for the season. But we can still go look around." McKenzie shielded her eyes against the sun and peered into the distance.

Pointing her finger, she continued, "See that old wooden windmill way out there? That's Old Towne."

"It looks kind of creepy." Bailey wrinkled her nose.

"You know, there is a spooky story about Old Towne." McKenzie flicked her reins at Sahara who had stopped to munch some grass. "A long time ago, a mysterious rider was seen riding out there at dusk. Some people say it was a ghost rider."

Bailey looked quizzically at McKenzie. "Is that for real?"

McKenzie chuckled. "That's what they say."

"Has anybody seen the ghost rider lately?" Bailey nudged Applejack forward.

"I haven't heard anything about it. Emma said the ghost rider story started years before she bought Sunshine Stables. She says someone just made it up to get visitors to come to Old Towne. It worked. Old Towne used to rake in the money. People paid to ride horses from the stables, hoping to see the ghost rider."

"That's spooky. A fun kind of spooky, that is," Bailey said as she leaned over and scratched Applejack's neck.

"Well, let's go check the place out. I've never been here

after it was closed for the season."

McKenzie nudged Sahara with her heels. The girls galloped down the trail. The horses' hooves stirred up little puffs of dust.

"Here we are," McKenzie said as she arrived at the top of a small hill. She halted Sahara and waited for Bailey to catch up.

"Wow! This is neater than I thought it would be!" Bailey exclaimed, her eyes wide.

The girls continued down the trail leading to Main Street. Old storefronts lined both sides of the dirt street. A weathered school building and a church were nestled on a grassy lawn at the edge of town, away from the other buildings.

"Let's tie our horses at the hitching post and look around." McKenzie hung her helmet on the post and fluffed her sweaty curls.

After tying both horses, the girls stepped on the wooden sidewalk. Bailey ran ahead, her boots thumping loudly on the wood. She stopped and peered through a streaked windowpane. A tall red-and-white barber pole stood beside it.

"I can just imagine a cowboy sitting in there getting his hair cut," Bailey said with a giggle.

"Yeah, and then he could head across the street to the general store for a piece of beef jerky and a new pair of chaps." McKenzie stuck her thumbs in her belt loops and walked bow-legged across the street.

Bailey laughed and raced to catch up with McKenzie. She stopped suddenly in the middle of the street and looked at the dusty ground. "Hey, did cowboys eat candy bars?"

McKenzie picked up the wrapper and shoved it in her

pocket. "Maybe the ghost likes the candy. Whooo-ooooh!" McKenzie wailed eerily.

The girls headed to the general store and peered through the window. McKenzie pointed out different items in the darkness. They saw old wooden rakes, hand plows, and row after row of tin cans on the shelves. A headless mannequin wore a long, lacy white dress, and a pair of men's bib overalls hung from a hanger.

Both girls jumped when McKenzie's cell phone rang. She pulled the phone from her pocket, answered, and listened to the caller for a minute. Then she quickly said, "Okay. Bye," and flipped the phone shut.

"That was Emma," she said. "She wants us to hurry home. Diamond Girl is missing!"

Missing!

As the girls rode back to the house, McKenzie prayed that they'd find Diamond Girl. Not only was she a treasured rac>orse, but Emma also planned to use her as a therapy horse once her racing days were over. McKenzie had helped at a horse therapy center the year before. She'd watched angry kids calm down as they worked with, rode, and took care of the horses. She'd also seen the horses have a good affect on disabled people and adults who were dealing with problems. Diamond Girl's calm nature made her perfect to work with disabled or troubled kids and adults.

Since Diamond Girl was already older than most rac>orses, Emma had said that this might be Diamond Girl's last year to race in the rodeo.

God just has to keep her safe, McKenzie thought. *Too many people depend on her.*

When the girls arrived back at Sunshine Stables, McKenzie hoped to see Diamond Girl safely in her stall. But she only saw three stable hands cleaning out the stables, refilling the stalls with fresh hay.

"Has anybody found Diamond Girl yet?" McKenzie called as she hopped off Sahara's back.

Ian, a kindly, middle-aged man, shooed a fly away from his dark brown face as he walked to the girls. "No sign of her yet. Emma and Derfi are still searching. Looks like somebody left a gate open. She's been out to pasture all afternoon, so there's no telling how far she's gone by now."

McKenzie couldn't believe someone would leave a gate open. All stable hands knew to close the gates b›ind them. She met Bailey's worried gaze. "Can we help look for her?" McKenzie asked.

"Emma wanted you girls to take care of your horses and put them up for the night," Ian said as he stuck his pitchfork into a hay bale.

McKenzie held the reins as Ian removed Sahara's heavy saddle. Then Ian removed Applejack's saddle while McKenzie and Bailey removed the horses' bridles.

After McKenzie turned the horses into the corral, she turned to Bailey. "We'll leave them out here while we clean their stalls. Then we'll bring them in for the night."

McKenzie and Bailey each grabbed a pitchfork and pitched dirty hay and manure into wheelbarrows. McKenzie heard the stable hands quietly talking to each other. Everyone seemed anxious, McKenzie thought. She guessed the workers were eager to finish chores and help look for Diamond Girl.

When the girls had cleaned the stalls, they covered the floor with fresh, sweet-smelling hay and filled the water troughs and feed bunks. McKenzie rested for a moment, leaning on her pitchfork as she wiped her sweaty for›ead with a T-shirt sleeve.

She looked at her young friend, struggling to keep up. McKenzie knew Bailey had asthma, so she got winded easily. Fortunately the hay didn't seem to be bothering Bailey at the moment. "Let's take a break. I'll grab a couple of sodas."

McKenzie went to a fridge in a small room at one end of the stable and grabbed two cans of strawberry pop.

After handing Bailey a pop, McKenzie popped the top of her can and enjoyed the cold drink trickling down her throat. She listened to the soft whinnies of the horses and smelled the musty mix of hay and horses. A horse in the next stall snorted.

"We'd better bring Sahara and Applejack in now." McKenzie swallowed the last of her drink. "It's almost their suppertime."

McKenzie and Bailey soon had the halters back on the horses. After giving the horses a quick rinse with a hose, the girls led them into the stable.

The stable hands were feeding the last of Emma's horses, and by the time McKenzie and Bailey finished with their horses, the chores were all done. McKenzie felt as though she hadn't helped much. She hoped Emma wouldn't regret asking her to stay and help. The two younger girls couldn't work nearly as hard as Emma's older employees.

Ian approached the girls as they put their pitchforks and wheelbarrows away. He lifted his worn cowboy hat and scratched his black curly hair. He looked at the girls as if he wanted to say something.

"Emma's been gone a long time. Haven't they found Diamond Girl yet?" McKenzie asked, again offering a silent prayer.

Ian hesitated and then answered. "Emma called awhile ago. She found no hoof prints at the open gate. Emma doesn't think Diamond Girl wandered off. Every other gate in the pasture is locked. She thinks the mare was stolen."

McKenzie felt her heart pounding. "Stolen! Who would steal Diamond Girl?"

Ian shrugged as the girls followed him out of the stable. "Emma and Derfi are on their way back, and the sheriff is on his way out to talk to the stable hands. Emma said you girls should go to the house and get something to eat. It could be a long night."

Though she wanted to wait for the sheriff, McKenzie agreed they should have supper. She led Bailey across the yard and up the back steps of the house.

"Do you think somebody really stole Diamond Girl?" Bailey asked as she kicked off her cowboy boots.

"Ian seems to think so." McKenzie splashed cold water on her face from the sink in the mud room. "I've been praying that she's safe ever since I heard she was missing."

"Yeah, me, too," Bailey said as both girls headed into the kitchen. "I've never even seen Diamond Girl. What's she like?"

McKenzie took packages of sliced ham and cheese from the fridge. "She is the prettiest horse you ever saw. Shiny black with a white diamond shape on her for›ead, and she's the fastest runner around here. When Emma rides her in the rodeo, no other horse stands a chance of winning."

After pouring two glasses of milk and making sandwiches,

the girls carried their plates to the front porch. As McKenzie said the blessing for the meal, Buckeye sat at their feet to beg bread crusts.

While they ate, the girls saw Emma and Derfi ride in from the pasture on their four-wheelers. The sheriff's dirty white pickup truck pulled in the driveway, and he headed toward the stables. McKenzie wished she could hear what the sheriff was saying, but she knew it wasn't any of her business.

The sun was low in the western sky when the sheriff drove off and the stable hands left. Emma approached the house and sank into a wooden chair on the porch with a deep sigh.

"What a day!" Emma said as she stretched her legs and closed her eyes. "I can't believe everything that's happened."

"Did someone really steal Diamond Girl?" McKenzie asked as she tucked her legs beneath her on the porch swing.

For a second she thought Emma wasn't going to answer. When Buckeye laid his head on Emma's lap, she opened her eyes. "It looks that way. I had hoped and prayed it wasn't true, but we see no signs that Diamond Girl ran off."

Emma looked so sad that McKenzie wanted to cheer her up, but she didn't know what to say or do. She knew Emma would be devastated without Diamond Girl.

"Do you think the sheriff can find her before the rodeo?" McKenzie asked. She didn't want to think about Diamond Girl not being able to compete, but she couldn't help it.

"I certainly hope so," Emma said. "But I just hope that wherever she is, she is okay. Competing in the rodeo isn't that important as long as I get Diamond Girl back safe and sound."

McKenzie nodded. Surely no one would hurt a horse as gentle as Diamond Girl. She couldn't imagine anyone being that mean.

"Can we help do something?" McKenzie asked softly. "We can get things set up for Kids' Camp tomorrow."

"I could fix you a sandwich." Bailey swatted a mosquito on her arm.

"You girls are great." Emma smiled as she rose from her chair. "Everything is pretty much ready for the kids tomorrow, but I'll take you up on that sandwich, Bailey."

As the sun dipped below the horizon, they all stepped inside. While Emma washed up, Bailey and McKenzie fixed her a light supper.

"Would you mind if we use your computer for a few minutes, Emma? We usually go to a chat room about this time each night." McKenzie poured a glass of iced tea and set it on the table for Emma. "I can't wait to tell the other girls that Bailey is here."

"Of course," Emma said. "Make yourselves at home. If I'm not using the computer, feel free to e-mail or chat or whatever."

As the girls headed to Emma's office, the phone rang. "Hi, Maggie," McKenzie heard Emma say. McKenzie could tell Emma was talking with Maggie Preston, the owner of a neighboring stable, Cedar Crefi Ranch. "You won't believe what's going on around here." Emma informed Maggie of Diamond Girl's disappearance.

The girls continued down the hall and into the office. After pulling an extra chair up to the desk, McKenzie logged on to the Camp Club Girls chat room. She found their four friends already chatting.

Alexis: *Hey, Mckenzie, where've U been?*

Alexis wrote from her home in Sacramento, California. Sydney was online in Washington, D.C. Kate lived in Philadelphia and Elizabeth in Texas. Though the girls lived in different parts of the country, they tried to chat online frequently. And when they were on a case, like they'd been with the mystery at Camp Discovery and Sydney's adventure in D.C., they also texted and used other forms of communication to solve mysteries together.

Sydney: *Everybody's here but Bailey.*

McKenzie typed as fast as she could: *R U ready for this? She's here with me. Big surprise! She's staying 2 train for the rodeo with me.*

Kate: *WTG Bailey. How kewl! Tell McKenzie 2 teach U sum of her trix. She really knows how 2 ride.*

After the girls had chatted for a few minutes, Bailey reached over and typed a quick message: *Sunshine Stable's prize horse has been stolen. The sheriff was here. Hope 2 find her.*

Alexis: *Y would someone steal her?*

McKenzie: *Dunno. Guess sheriff will figure that out.*

A message popped up on the screen from Elizabeth, who at fourteen was the oldest: *McKenzie and Bailey, maybe God brought U 2 together this summer 4 a reason. Maybe He wants*

U 2 figure out what happened 2 the horse.

McKenzie and Bailey looked at each other. Elizabeth always seemed to remember to turn to God for the right answers. McKenzie often wished she were more like Elizabeth. She often forgot that with God, everything happens for a reason.

McKenzie: *Maybe U R right, Elizabeth. Maybe there's more work 2 do here than train 4 rodeo.*

Sydney: *Hey, another mystery 2 solve. Wish I was there.*

McKenzie: *Time 2 go. TTYL.*

While McKenzie logged off, she glanced out the window. A sliver of moon shone in the sky. Pale streaks of violet and pink were all that remained of the sunset. She shoved the extra chair back against the wall and heard Emma's voice in the kitchen. McKenzie could tell she was still on the phone with Maggie.

"Did you see a light out there?" Bailey asked as she peered out the window.

McKenzie returned her gaze to the window. The trees and shrubs were shadowy shapes in the darkness. "I don't see anything except some lightning bugs."

Bailey looked again out the window. "I thought I saw a light clear out there in the pasture." She pointed. "But I don't see it now."

The girls watched awhile longer, but when the light didn't reappear, McKenzie stepped away from the window and turned off the desk light. As they walked into the kitchen, Emma was just hanging up the phone.

"News sure travels fast." Emma placed dirty dishes in the dishwasher. "Maggie, over at Cedar Crefi, saw the sheriff go by and wondered if something was wrong. I asked her to watch for any unusual activity around here. I'd hate to think horse thieves are in the area."

"Do you think the thieves will come back?" Bailey asked.

"Oh, I didn't mean to frighten you, Bailey." Emma placed an arm around the younger girl's shoulders. "The sheriff suggested we keep a close eye on things. Maggie volunteered to have one of her men patrol the area at night, and I agreed. I can't ask my team of workers to work a night shift when Kids' Camp is starting tomorrow."

McKenzie knew Diamond Girl's disappearance was serious, but knowing the sheriff had asked Emma and the neighbors to patrol their ranches worried her even more. McKenzie had never heard of horse thieves in this area, and the thought scared her. What if the thieves did come back?

"I've scared you both," Emma said as she slung her other arm around McKenzie's shoulder. "I'm sorry this had to happen when you were here, but with God's help, everything will work out. We have to trust Him on this." Emma yawned. "It's been a long day. Why don't you two head on upstairs. I'll clean up down here."

Both girls flung their arms around Emma's neck and told her good-night. McKenzie was tired and ready for bed. She knew the next day would be a busy one. When the campers left in the afternoon, she and Bailey needed to practice for the rodeo. In less than two wefis, the competition would begin.

As McKenzie showered, she thought of Sahara and all the rodeo events she needed to work on. Not only that, but she'd also be responsible to help Bailey. By the time she had slipped into her pajamas, she felt better about Diamond Girl's disappearance. Surely the sheriff would have some news soon.

When she stepped into the bedroom, she saw Bailey leaning on the windowsill. Bailey turned to McKenzie, and her voice trembled. "I just saw another flash of light in the pasture. Something is out there!"

The Clue at the Crefi

McKenzie's heart quickened. She dashed to the window. "Where did you see the light?"

Bailey pointed toward a cluster of trees at the far edge of the pasture. "It was there a minute ago," she said. "It really was."

"I believe you." McKenzie peered into the darkness. "Maybe it's some of Maggie's workers patrolling the area."

Bailey sighed and moved away from the window. "I just hope it's not the horse thieves returning."

"They wouldn't hang around. They know people will watch for them now. I'm sure they're long gone." McKenzie picked up her brush from the dresser and yanked it through her thick, wet hair.

"Do you think we can help find Diamond Girl?" Bailey asked as she unpacked her bags into a couple of dresser drawers.

McKenzie climbed onto the top bunk and dangled her legs over the side of the bed. She had wanted to offer to look for the horse, but she figured Emma would want the sheriff to handle it. But after Elizabeth had mentioned it in the chat room, and now Bailey, it seemed like a good idea.

"Maybe so," McKenzie said. "If the sheriff doesn't find out

something by morning, let's ask Emma if we can investigate."

"How will we have time to do everything? We're at Kids' Camp every morning. Then in the afternoons, we'll train for the rodeo," Bailey said as she pulled out a bag filled with bottles of nail polish of every color.

"We'll find time," McKenzie said. "We won't practice all afternoon. Then we'll have evenings, too. And since Kids' Camp is only for a few days, we'll have more free time after that."

"But you'll have to get ready for the Junior Miss Rodeo Queen contest sometime, too," Bailey said with a frown. "I wish I could be in the contest."

McKenzie wished she hadn't agreed to compete. It was the last thing she wanted to do this summer, and Bailey wanted nothing more than to be in it. It didn't seem fair that Bailey couldn't enter when she wanted to so badly.

"I wish you could, too," McKenzie stretched on her stomach and hung her head over the bunk. Her hair hung down as she looked at Bailey. "But the Junior Miss Rodeo Queen contestants have to live in Montana. I wish I could trade places with you."

Bailey's eyes grew wide. "You're kidding! How come you're entering it then?"

McKenzie shrugged her shoulders, as well as she could while hanging upside down. "Because Mom wants me to."

"Did you tell her you don't want to be in it?" Bailey asked as she alternated painting her toenails orange, yellow, and purple.

McKenzie swung herself back up on the bed. She stretched

her leg and pulled the chain for the ceiling fan with her toes. "No. I didn't have the nerve. She thinks I wanted to enter. She'd be disappointed if I backed out now."

"I don't believe you don't want to be a rodeo queen." Bailey shook her head as she waved her feet around to dry the polish. "I would love to be queen almost as much as I'd love to find Diamond Girl."

McKenzie wished she had the enthusiasm for the contest that Bailey had. All she really cared about now was finding the stolen horse. Winning a contest didn't seem to matter much.

She shut off the light and thought about the horse thief. Maybe she should pray for him instead of just Diamond Girl. She asked God to be with the person who had taken the horse. Whoever had stolen her must have a horrible problem to do something like that. As she asked God to help her forgive that person, she drifted off to sleep, dreaming of Diamond Girl's safe return.

●—●—●

At breakfast the next morning, Emma told the girls she had heard nothing new from the sheriff about Diamond Girl. He had spoken with all the neighbors, but no one had seen anything out of the ordinary.

"We're pretty good at solving mysteries. Would it be all right if we try to figure out what happened?" McKenzie asked through a bite of cinnamon roll.

"I don't see why not," Emma said. "Maybe you can find a clue the sheriff overlooked. The campers leave at 2:00. After you practice with Sahara, you can do what you want."

Shortly before nine o'clock, the kids began arriving for

camp. Emma gathered everyone under a large, shady oak tree in the front yard. The more experienced riders, including Bailey, would train with Emma. McKenzie would help Derfi and Ian with the beginning and average riders.

First the campers helped feed and groom their horses. Then the younger kids learned to mount and ride. As McKenzie worked, she watched Emma helping Bailey and the other riders learn how to barrel ride.

Barrel riding was McKenzie's favorite rodeo event. Three barrels were set up in the arena in the shape of a large triangle. Each contestant raced to the first barrel and made as tight a turn as possible around it before moving on to the second and third barrels. After turning around the last barrel, the rider raced her horse across the finish line. The rider with the fastest time would be the winner.

Bailey handled the horse well. Soon she had Applejack galloping around the barrels.

Applejack had been trained in the rodeo event, so he could almost run the course without a rider. He was a gentle horse who ran only as fast as Bailey urged him.

The day flew by, and at two o'clock, the campers went home. Applejack had worked most of the morning, so Bailey led him to his stall to rest. Since McKenzie hadn't ridden all morning, she brought Sahara to the paddock.

Sahara stood still as McKenzie mounted her. McKenzie combed the horse's thick brown mane with her fingers, feeling her warm, velvety back rippling beneath her touch. Sahara twitched her head and neighed, telling McKenzie she was eager to run.

"I think Sahara's ready," Emma hollered across the arena as she leaned against the white fencing. "Take her for a few laps. Then we'll work on the barrels."

McKenzie flicked the reins and Sahara leaped forward. McKenzie let her body move with the motion of the horse. Together they flew around the arena with McKenzie's hair flying b›ind her like a streamer. Round and round they sailed.

After warming up for a few minutes, McKenzie slowed the horse to a walk, but Sahara wasn't ready to rest. She wanted to run.

Emma signaled McKenzie to begin, so she dug her heels into Sahara's side. The horse leaped forward as they flew toward the first barrel. McKenzie pulled on the reins, guiding Sahara in a tight circle around it.

Then she raced toward the second barrel. After circling the third barrel, McKenzie squeezed Sahara's side with her calves, urging her to go faster. As they crossed the finish line, Emma clicked the stopwatch.

"Great run, McKenzie," Emma called out. "You beat your last time by half a second."

McKenzie rode over to the fence where Emma and Bailey waited. Her face flushed with pride. She knew she had to work hard if she wanted to win at the rodeo. "Do you think I stand a chance of winning?" McKenzie asked.

"Sure," Emma said as she patted Sahara's back. "But you have a lot of tough competition. Last year's winner will be racing against you. If you push yourself, you can easily make the top three. But remember, McKenzie, doing your best is what matters the most. God doesn't expect any more than that, and neither does anyone else."

McKenzie knew that, but it was hard to believe sometimes. She knew God wanted her to do her best, but by winning she would know she had done that. If she didn't even place in the top three, she would always feel as if she hadn't tried hard enough.

This would be her third year to compete in barrel racing at the rodeo, and she had finished in the bottom half each time. This year she was determined to get at least second or third place.

"Let's try it a few more times," Emma said.

Again, McKenzie and Sahara flew through the course. The sun beat down on them, and McKenzie felt the sweat trickling down her back. She tried to make as tight of turns as she could around the barrels. Every split second counted in barrel racing. When Emma shouted that it was quitting time, both horse and rider were relieved.

"You had some great runs, McKenzie," Emma said as she approached Sahara.

Bailey had said nothing while McKenzie practiced. When McKenzie glanced at her, she turned away. Was Bailey upset about something? She seemed almost sad. McKenzie wondered if she was homesick.

"I need to call Sheriff Danby. Hopefully he will have some news about Diamond Girl," Emma said as she glanced at her watch. "You can start your investigation if you want, but why don't you get some cold drinks while the horses rest?"

McKenzie gave Sahara a quick rinse to cool her off, and then the girls grabbed two bottles of water from the supply room. Fifteen minutes later, they rode into the pasture b>ind Sunshine Stables.

"You really did good on Applejack this morning, Bailey." McKenzie adjusted her riding helmet.

"Not really," Bailey said with a frown. "You're lots better than I am. You'll win for sure."

So that's what's bothering her, McKenzie thought. She remembered how she had felt when she had first begun barrel racing. She had thought everyone was better than she was.

"You were great, Bailey," McKenzie said cheerfully. "I've been racing for years. This is your first time. You're better than I was when I started."

Bailey shrugged her shoulders. "You're just saying that. There's still no way I'll win anything."

McKenzie pulled on the reins to stop her horse. "It doesn't matter if you win. You're probably the youngest person in our division. You've only been riding horses for a little while, and you're already competing in a rodeo. How many kids get to do that? You were great. I mean it."

Bailey smiled but didn't answer as she reached over and scratched Applejack's neck. The horse whinnied softly as he plodded beside McKenzie and Sahara.

"Let's head to the gate that was hanging open." McKenzie led the way across the pasture. "Emma and Derfi said Diamond Girl didn't go through it because there were no hoof prints, but maybe we can find a clue there, anyway."

McKenzie knew the gate that had been left open was on the far side of Sunshine Stable's land. Soon McKenzie turned to Bailey and pointed to a gate about a hundred yards away.

"There's the gate we're looking for."

As the girls approached the gate, McKenzie slid off Sahara's back. She looped the reins around a fence post and patted the horse. Sahara leaned across the fence and began munching the tall, green grass on the other side. McKenzie turned to the gate, which opened onto a dirt road.

"Emma and Derfi are right. The ground is soft and no tracks are here. The grass hasn't been trampled and there aren't any tire tracks either. So, no one parked on the road and hauled her off in a trailer." McKenzie searched the ground looking for clues.

"So who opened the gate? And why?" Bailey dismounted Applejack and walked to McKenzie.

"I don't know. It's really weird. The gate has a solid latch, so someone had to open it on purpose." McKenzie leaned against the fence, staring into space. "It's almost like someone wanted us to think Diamond Girl escaped through the gate."

"Hey, maybe that's it." Bailey's dark eyes sparkled. "The thief could have parked on the road and walked over to open the gate. That's why there are no hoof prints or tire tracks."

"I think we're on to something," McKenzie said with excitement. "The thief could have stolen Diamond Girl from another part of the pasture. Then he could have opened this gate to throw everyone off."

"So what do we do now?" Bailey asked with a frown.

"Well, the thief must have taken her through a gate. Right? So, we need to check the other gates to the pasture." McKenzie pulled Sahara's reins from the fence post and mounted her.

"How many gates are there?" Bailey asked as she pulled

herself onto Applejack's saddle.

McKenzie thought for a minute. "Three other ones, I think. And this pasture is big, so it'll take awhile to get around to all of them."

As they rode, McKenzie tried to think of people who might want to steal Diamond Girl, but she couldn't imagine anyone doing something that awful. Almost everyone in the rodeo business had heard about the prize-winning horse, so anyone might have done it. The horse would bring a large sum of money if the thief sold her. Surely the thief wasn't someone she knew.

McKenzie couldn't stand the thought of never seeing Diamond Girl again, so she knew how Emma must feel. Her instructor would be devastated if they didn't find Diamond Girl.

McKenzie led the way across the valley b›ind Sunshine Stables. As they approached the next gate, she quickly checked the ground beyond it.

"No trailer has backed up here, that's for sure," McKenzie said with a sigh. "She must have been stolen through one of the last two gates. Let's check them out."

But the girls didn't find any evidence at either of the other gates. McKenzie was not only disappointed, she was also confused. How could Diamond Girl have been stolen? No tracks of any kind disturbed the ground beyond the gates.

"I don't get it," Bailey remarked. "She couldn't have disappeared into thin air."

McKenzie sat in the saddle. "The only other opening into the pasture is next to the stable," she told Bailey. "Surely

Diamond Girl didn't leave that way. Surely a thief couldn't just walk out the front gate with her without anyone seeing them."

"This just doesn't make sense!" Bailey said.

McKenzie wiped the sweat from her for>ead with the back of her hand. "These horses need a drink. Let's head to the stream, and then we'll head back. I'm hot."

The girls rode slower now that the late afternoon sun was beating down on them. At the top of the rise, McKenzie stopped and gazed at the stream below them. After leading the horses to the crefi bank, the girls dismounted to let them drink. McKenzie pulled off her boots and socks. She rolled up her jeans and waded into the stream, letting the cool water bubble around her ankles as it tumbled over rocks from high in the mountains.

"Come on in," McKenzie called to Bailey. "The water's great."

As the horses drank, the girls splashed in the foaming water. Within minutes they were laughing and playfully shoving each other.

"We'd better head back," McKenzie said through her laughter. "Emma will wonder what happened to us."

Bailey walked up the bank, with water streaming down her legs. Her black hair was plastered to her head. Water trickled down her face onto her red tank top. Little globs of mud stuck to her like an explosion in a chocolate bar factory.

"You look like a river rat," McKenzie teased as she wiped her face with her T-shirt hem.

Bailey stuck her tongue out at her friend. "I can't look as bad as you, can I?" she kidded McKenzie.

"All right. That does it. You're getting dunked." McKenzie laughed as she lunged toward the younger girl, grabbing her arm.

Bailey twisted out of her grasp and fell into the shallow crefi. Even with Bailey on her knees, the water only reached the tops of her thighs. "Hey, look what I found," she said as she reached into the water. "An old horseshoe."

With water dripping from her elbows, she stood and handed it to McKenzie, who examined it.

"Bailey," McKenzie said as she scrutinized the horseshoe. "You're a genius! This isn't any old horseshoe. It's Diamond Girl's!"

A Wild Ride!

"How do you know the horseshoe is Diamond Girl's?" Bailey asked as the girls walked up the grassy bank.

"Emma had custom horseshoes made for her. See the little diamond shapes on the arch." McKenzie traced her finger along the engravings. "But I guess it really doesn't mean anything. It just means she came down here to drink, and all the horses do that."

"I think we should consider this a clue," Bailey said. "Detectives should take every piece of evidence very seriously. She had to lose the shoe yesterday before she disappeared or someone would have noticed, right? We just need to figure out where she went from here."

"You've got a good point. Maybe she wandered out through a hole in the fence." McKenzie surveyed the barbed wire fence stretched across the shallow part of the crefi, looking for a broken wire. But every wire was secured tightly.

"What about tracks?" Bailey asked. "Wouldn't it be easy to track a horse with one missing shoe?"

McKenzie looked up with a grin. "Great idea, Bailey."

Both girls returned to the crefi's edge, looking for tracks in the dirt.

"You mean, not so great," Bailey grumbled after a few minutes. "All the hoof prints around here have been washed away from our splashing."

McKenzie continued to look, searching for tracks farther up the crefi. All the tracks seemed to come from horses with all four shoes in place. She sighed hopelessly. "I feel like we've overlooked a clue, but I don't know what else to do."

"Detectives take pictures of the crime scene to go over later. Maybe you could do that," Bailey suggested. "Your cell phone takes pictures, doesn't it?"

"Brilliant!" McKenzie said as she pulled her phone from her jeans pocket. "I hope it didn't get too wet."

She flipped open the phone. It seemed dry, so she quickly snapped pictures of the ground. She didn't really know what she hoped to find, but maybe they would see a clue they had missed when they reviewed the pictures later.

Applejack and Sahara had waded into the stream to cool off and waited patiently. After leading their horses up the bank, the girls slipped into their boots and headed for home. Though the sun was still hot, the breeze felt almost cool against their wet clothes.

After arriving back at the stables, the girls removed the horses' tack and led them to the corral and the watering trough.

"Let's find Derfi or Emma and show them the horseshoe," McKenzie suggested.

They found Derfi at the far end of the stables and showed him their find. They explained their theory to him.

"It's Diamond Girl's all right," Derfi said. "I'm sure she went to the crefi yesterday to drink, but that part of the crefi has a lot of large rocks to catch a horse's shoe. I really don't think it's a clue to her disappearance. I'm sorry, girls."

McKenzie's face fell at Derfi's remark. She had convinced herself that the horseshoe was the first real lead they had found. Now she was beginning to think it didn't mean a thing.

As Derfi left with a wheelbarrow full of old hay and manure, the girls headed through the stable.

"I was hoping the horseshoe was a clue," McKenzie said with a sigh.

"Me, too," Bailey said dismally. "But maybe we'll find a real clue soon."

McKenzie suddenly stopped and peered into the nearest stall. "Let me show you one of Emma's special horses. Her name is Krissy, and you'll like her. But first I need to get Derfi to help."

The girls stood to the side as the stable hands hauled wheelbarrows of hay to the stalls. Nightly feeding and grooming had already begun. McKenzie would quickly show Krissy to Bailey, and then they would need to help with chores.

McKenzie hurried to the supply room and grabbed a handful of baby carrots from the fridge. She asked Derfi to help with Krissy. Then she returned to Bailey's side.

McKenzie opened the stall door and stepped inside. An older black horse covered with white splotches lifted its head at the sound of the girls' voices.

Bailey gasped and flung her hands over her mouth while her dark eyes gleamed. After a few seconds she finally spoke, "An Appaloosa! This is my favorite breed of horse. I've always wanted one!"

McKenzie laughed as she stepped to Krissy's side and patted her back. "See the big white spots that look like snowflakes? They look like Christmas snow, so Emma named her Krissy, like Kris Kringle."

Bailey ran her hands through Krissy's mane. The horse tipped her head toward Bailey and whinnied. Krissy obviously loved the attention. The horse stood still as Bailey stroked her spotted back.

Soon Derfi arrived carrying a stack of bright cardboard signs.

"Are you ready for the good part?" McKenzie asked as she untied Krissy's lead rope. "This horse is very talented."

McKenzie turned the horse around and held on to the rope. "We're ready if you are," she said to Derfi.

He held up three cards and looked at the horse. "Okay, Krissy. How many signs am I holding? Count for me," Derfi said.

Bailey looked skeptically at McKenzie. Then she turned her gaze back to Krissy. The horse lifted her head and nodded one, two, three times. Bailey's mouth fell open as she turned back to McKenzie.

"Did that horse just count?" Bailey asked with surprise.

"Yep, she sure did," McKenzie assured her as she offered Krissy a carrot.

"Do you want to try it?" Derfi asked Bailey.

"Sure," Bailey said eagerly.

Derfi handed Bailey the stack of cards then grabbed a pitchfork and stepped into the next stall.

Bailey held up four cards. "Okay, Krissy. How many cards am I holding?"

The horse simply looked at Bailey, refusing to nod. Again, Bailey asked Krissy to count.

This time the words "one, two, three, four" came out of Krissy's mouth. Bailey jumped back, dropping the signs. For a minute she stood speechless, staring at the horse.

Finally McKenzie could control herself no longer. She burst out laughing and cried, "Derfi, that's a mean trick to play on your new friend."

Derfi's head popped over the top of the stall, and his laughter filled the stable. "Haven't you ever seen a talking horse before?" he said, though his mouth didn't move.

Bailey stared at him for a minute then grabbed a handful of straw and threw it at him, laughing. "Are you a ventriloquist?"

He dodged the straw and turned back to Bailey. Again, his mouth didn't move as he spoke, "Only when I need to be."

"Wow, you are really good," Bailey exclaimed. "How do you do it? And how did you get the horse to count by nodding her head?"

Derfi continued to scoop hay and manure. "I've been practicing ever since I was a kid. I performed in a few talent shows when I was younger. As for teaching Krissy to count, that's my little secret." He turned to McKenzie and winked.

Though McKenzie had tried to get Derfi to tell her the secret, he wouldn't let her in on it. McKenzie turned to Krissy and secured her lead rope. After grabbing a brush from the ledge, she began stroking the horse's back. "I wish you could talk, Krissy. Then maybe you could tell us what happened to Diamond Girl."

No one answered for a few seconds. Derfi leaned on his

pitchfork and took off his cowboy hat. He pulled a bandana from his back jeans pocket and wiped the sweat from his face. "I know you girls are worried about that horse. But there's really not much anybody can do."

McKenzie grew worried at his words. Did he think no one would ever find Diamond Girl? Surely he didn't really believe that.

Bailey seemed to read McKenzie's mind. "Can't the sheriff find her?" The younger girl pulled a tube of watermelon lip balm from her pocket and ran it across her lips.

"He's called all the auction companies in the area, but no thief would try to sell a prize horse like Diamond Girl around here. She would be easily recognized. But some thieves know how to disguise a horse, so she could be sold anywhere. No one would ever find her." Derfi shook his head dismally.

McKenzie stared at Derfi. Surely God wouldn't let Diamond Girl just disappear off the face of the earth. They just had to find her, and she would keep trying until they did.

McKenzie wanted to tell Derfi and Bailey not to give up hope, but as soon as she opened her mouth, a figure at the end of the stables caught her eye. She turned as a woman approached them.

McKenzie recognized Maggie Preston—the neighbor Emma had been on the phone with the night before. She owned Cedar Crefi Ranch, which was next to Sunshine Stables. McKenzie wondered how long Maggie had been standing there. Had the woman been listening to their conversation?

"Derfi, I'm surprised to see you're still around here. I thought you'd be gone by now." The woman flicked a piece of straw off her red T-shirt. "Is Emma around? I need to talk to her."

Derfi pushed the wheelbarrow to the next stall. "She ran into town to pick up a load of feed. Can I do anything for you?"

Maggie handed Derfi a flyer. "Would you mind posting this somewhere so your riders can see it? I'm offering calf-roping sessions for teams who want to practice for the rodeo, and I only have two time slots left."

Derfi took the flyer and looked it over as Maggie continued. "I mainly wanted to ask her about Diamond Girl, though. I'm so worried that something awful might have happened to her. I came by to tell her I'll do anything I can to help. If she doesn't feel up to taking on all those kids this wefi, she can feel free to send them my way. After all, Emma owes me."

Without another word, she turned and marched out of the stable. Derfi shook his head as he watched her leave.

"Why was she surprised to see you here, Derfi? Are you leaving Sunshine Stables?" McKenzie asked.

"No. I'm not leaving. Not yet, anyway. But I would like to start my own stable someday, and I need to save a lot of money before I can do that," Derfi said as he stepped back into a stall.

McKenzie hoped Derfi wouldn't leave. She'd had so much fun since he had come to Sunshine Stables.

"What did she mean by saying Emma owes her?" McKenzie grabbed another pitchfork and began scooping old hay and manure from another stall.

"Several of Maggie's riding students dropped out and are going to Emma's Kids' Camp instead. I guess she's a little upset about that," Derfi said.

McKenzie couldn't believe anyone could be angry with Emma. She was such a sweet person. McKenzie had often thought that if she had an older sister, she would want her to be like Emma. Could Maggie really be upset because she had lost a couple of her young riders to Kids' Camp? It was just a one-wefi program. McKenzie wondered if something else was bothering the woman. *Could Maggie know something about Diamond Girl?*

"Well, Emma would never take Maggie's riders on purpose." Bailey folded her arms across her chest as she defended her instructor.

Derfi nodded. The three raked old hay out of the stalls in silence. After they had filled several wheelbarrows, Derfi stood up and stretched.

"Emma wanted that lean-to off the barn cleaned today," he said. "Some old machinery is in there, but everything else can be thrown on the trailer to be hauled off. It shouldn't take long. Would you girls do that?"

"Sure," McKenzie agreed. She loved messing around in the hayloft of that old red barn. Emma's cat, Cheetah, often had a litter of kittens up there. Working in the barn sounded good.

On their way out of the stable, McKenzie stopped in the supply room for a pair of binoculars. From the hayloft in the barn, a person could see the countryside for miles. She thought Bailey might enjoy the view.

McKenzie led Bailey through a gate leading to the back of the barn. She swung the door open and stepped inside, breathing the musty smell of old hay. Sunlight streamed through the cracks in the walls.

The barn was a large, tall building supported by heavy wooden beams. The hayloft stretched across one end of the barn and was piled with hay bales. An old, wooden ladder stood at one side reaching to the floor of the loft.

McKenzie hung the binoculars around her neck by the leather strap and tugged on Bailey's arm. "Do you want to go up?" McKenzie asked as she headed toward the ladder.

Bailey stood at the foot of the ladder and peered up, frowning. "Oooh, I don't know about this," she said in a trembling voice. "It's awful high up."

"Oh, you'll love it once you get up there," McKenzie said, stepping onto the first rung. "I'll go first."

McKenzie continued climbing until she stepped onto the loft. She knelt and peered down over the edge. "Come on. It's really neat up here."

Bailey wrinkled her brow as she stared at McKenzie. "I don't like high places. I don't think I can do it."

"Sure you can. Step on the first rung and take it one step at a time, but don't look down. You'll do fine." McKenzie held out her arm toward Bailey.

Taking a deep breath, Bailey stepped on the ladder. Climbing slowly, she finally reached the loft as McKenzie clutched her arm.

Bailey glanced around at the bales. "Wow, this really is cool," she said, brushing the dust from her hands.

"Come to this window." McKenzie scampered to a pile of bales and climbed almost to the top of the barn. She turned and leaned out the open window as the breeze brushed her chefis. She could almost reach out and grab a branch in the treetop.

Bailey's hands trembled as she held the binoculars to her eyes. She gasped. "Hey, I can see the old windmill turning at Old Towne and the barber shop and. . .I see someone in the woods b›ind Old Towne."

McKenzie grasped the binoculars and peered into the distance. "I see it, too," she said as a flash of red moved slowly through the trees. But whoever it was disappeared quickly into the timber.

Bailey wrinkled up her nose and sneezed. "Ooh, it's dusty in here," she said as she covered her nose with her hand.

McKenzie knew that because of Bailey's asthma, sometimes hay and dust bothered her. "Why don't you go outside? I'll start carrying out those boxes."

Bailey frowned. "I have my inhaler. I can help."

McKenzie didn't want to take the risk of her friend having an asthma attack. "I'll do it," she assured Bailey. "But see those two horses near the fence. Bring the brown mare, Molly, in here through that other gate. Grab a brush and give her a rubdown, and she'll love you forever."

The girls climbed down the ladder and headed outside, Bailey to get Molly and McKenzie to the lean-to.

As McKenzie's eyes adjusted to the darkness, she saw the shapes of old machinery at one end. Boxes and cans littered the other end. She grabbed a box filled with old leather straps and tack and loaded it onto the trailer parked outside the door.

She carried box after box, and as she was finishing, something furry rubbed against her leg. She shrified and jumped back.

After glancing nervously at her feet, she chuckled. "Cheetah, you scared me half to death." McKenzie bent over to pet the cat's soft fur.

As she stood up, she noticed several crates b›ind an old wooden horse cart. The crates were crammed into the corner, so she would have to move the cart to get to them. McKenzie grabbed the cart and rolled it outside.

"This is a great horse, McKenzie," Bailey called out as she brushed the mare's back. "She's as gentle as a bunny."

"I thought you'd like her. Her eyesight is going bad, but she can still run," McKenzie said as she headed back for the crates. They were heavier than they looked, so she rearranged the contents before she could lift them. She looked up as a shadow filled the doorway.

"Hey there, Buckeye. How are you doing, boy?" she asked as the dog trotted to her side.

Buckeye sat beside her, content to have his ears scratched. Until he saw Cheetah.

With a leap and a yowl, he was on his feet. Cheetah's back arched. She hissed and spat before she sprang for the door with Buckeye close b›ind. Within seconds, McKenzie heard a frantic neigh and a piercing scream.

McKenzie raced to the door. As Molly lunged against the gate, the latch slipped, and the horse raced into the open pasture. McKenzie was surprised to see that Bailey had hitched the old horse cart to her.

McKenzie scanned the corral to find Bailey. She couldn't

see her anywhere. But then she spotted Bailey, her black hair flying b›ind her as she clung to the sides of the old horse cart! It dangerously careened from side to side as the nearly blind horse ran uncontrollably! Bailey screamed again, hanging on for dear life!

The Stranger

"Bailey!" McKenzie screamed. "Hold on!"

She ran to the chestnut horse grazing nearby. Since she had no time to saddle the horse, she climbed the fence, and with a quick jump she was on his back. Clinging to his mane, McKenzie clucked and dug in her heels.

The horse leaped forward and McKenzie raced after Bailey and the runaway horse. She leaned forward until she was almost lying on the horse's neck, urging the horse to run faster. Soon she gained on the old brown mare. Bailey shrieked more, spurring Molly to go even faster.

The wind whipped McKenzie's hair and curls flew in her face, but she didn't let go. Her only choice was to get close enough to the mare to slide onto her back. McKenzie prayed that the mare would slow down. With the extra weight of the cart and Bailey, Molly finally showed signs of tiring. McKenzie urged her horse onward, slowly gaining on the mare.

When she was neck and neck with Bailey's mare, McKenzie called out in a soothing voice, "Hey there, Molly. It's okay. Easy, girl."

Soon the mare slowed. McKenzie glanced at Bailey still gripping the sides of the horse cart. The younger girl's eyes were wide with fear.

It's now or never, McKenzie thought as she inched closer to Molly. She leaned over to the mare and grabbed the halter. With all her strength, McKenzie pulled herself onto the mare's back.

McKenzie tugged on the reins to slow down the mare, talking softly to Molly until she slowed to a walk. With another tug on the reins, McKenzie finally brought the mare to a halt.

"You okay, Bailey?" McKenzie asked. Bailey still gripped the horse cart.

Bailey didn't answer for a moment; then she pushed her tangled black hair out of her face. "I think so," she whispered.

McKenzie leaned forward, feeling Molly pant beneath her. She couldn't believe she had just ridden bareback and jumped onto a moving horse! She was glad it was over and that Bailey was all right.

"Wow, that was some ride," McKenzie said after she caught her breath.

Bailey sat cross-legged and still in the cart. Her face was pale with little pink spots on both chefis.

"You can get out now," McKenzie continued as she patted the mare. "This old girl's not going anywhere for a while."

"I don't think I can," Bailey mumbled. "My legs are scared stiff. They won't move."

McKenzie laughed. "You think you were scared? I can't pry my fingers off these reins."

Bailey pulled her legs from beneath her and stretched. "You were great, McKenzie. I can't believe you did that! It was just like in the movies!"

"Well, if that's Hollywood, I've had enough," McKenzie said as she sat up straight. "Hey, where did my horse go?"

The girls glanced around the pasture and spotted the horse about a hundred yards away.

McKenzie took a deep breath. "We'd better go round him up and head for home. I'm going to have a talk with Buckeye when I get back. No more scaring cats around the horses."

"I don't have to ride back here, do I?" Bailey asked from her seat in the horse cart.

"No way. You can ride Molly back. She should be okay now that there aren't any cats around." McKenzie hopped off and helped Bailey onto the mare's back. Her knees felt wobbly after her daring ride. She grabbed the reins and led the mare toward her horse.

The girls didn't speak as McKenzie walked beside Molly and Bailey. She glanced up at her young friend who was staring straight ahead, slouched in the saddle. McKenzie knew the runaway horse had frightened Bailey, but now that the incident was over, Bailey seemed more embarrassed than scared.

McKenzie knew that her younger friend was a talented rider, especially for someone with as little training as she'd had. But Bailey had little confidence in herself when she was around the older Camp Club Girls. McKenzie knew how important it was for Bailey to be a good horseback rider, but this incident sure wouldn't help matters.

As the girls approached McKenzie's chestnut horse, Bailey exclaimed, seemingly forgetting the runaway horse episode. "Hey, look. Someone else is out riding. His horse is gorgeous."

McKenzie looked across the fence, about fifty yards away,

at a young man struggling with his horse. He was clearly frustrated with the animal, so he didn't notice the girls. But Bailey was right, the horse was beautiful.

McKenzie had never seen a horse like this one. She looked like a brown American paint horse with large white splotches and stockings.

"Hey," McKenzie called out. "Do you need some help?"

The young man looked up, apparently surprised to see them, but he didn't answer. His horse bounded closer to the fence, snorting loudly. The man jerked on the reins, but the horse reared on her hind legs.

McKenzie stared in disbelief. He seemed to have no clue as to how to handle the animal. She felt sorry for the poor horse. The horse acted like she wanted to throw her rider.

No animal deserves to be treated like that! McKenzie thought angrily.

As McKenzie looked at the horse, she thought the horse looked familiar, but she knew if she'd seen a horse with that coloring before she'd remember it.

"I can help you calm your horse, if you'd like," McKenzie called out. "I've worked with horses quite a bit."

The young man glared at her and snapped, "I don't need your help. I've got it under control."

McKenzie winced. It was clear he didn't have things under control. He acted as if he'd never ridden a horse before.

"Your horse is beautiful. What's her name?" Bailey called, her eyes glistening.

"Would you two just leave?" he stammered in a raised voice, ignoring her question. "Can't you see you're scaring my horse?"

McKenzie looked sheepishly at Bailey. "I think we'd better go. Can you handle Molly by yourself? Then I'll ride my horse."

Bailey patted Molly affectionately. "Sure. We're friends now, aren't we Molly?"

McKenzie stepped up on the fence to mount her horse. The young man had gained some control of his horse. She clucked at her horse and headed back toward Sunshine Stables.

In the distance, she saw a rider on horseback racing toward them. As he drew nearer, she recognized Derfi. Within minutes, he pulled up alongside them, holding his battered white cowboy hat against his chest.

"You two okay?" he asked breathlessly. "I heard screaming, and then I saw Molly flying across the pasture with Bailey in the cart. I was unloading feed, or I would have been here sooner."

Bailey looked down as a flush came over her chefis. "I'm fine. I did a dumb thing, I guess."

Derfi flashed a grin at Bailey but didn't scold her. Apparently, he figured out what had happened.

"Well, at least nobody was hurt. I don't think I even want a ride that wild," he said as he jumped off his horse. "Why don't you take my horse, Bailey, and I'll take Molly and the cart."

Bailey gave Derfi a relieved look and slid off Molly. "I like that idea."

After Derfi helped Bailey onto the saddle of his horse, he turned to McKenzie. "Are you all right riding bareback?"

McKenzie assured him she would be fine. Then she asked, "Do you know that guy back there?"

Derfi looked to where she was pointing. "I don't see anyone."

316

McKenzie looked back and sighed. Where could he have gone so quickly? "He was there a minute ago. He was riding a beautiful brown paint horse with white spots."

"And his horse wanted to throw him off," Bailey piped up.

Derfi shrugged his shoulders. "I don't know anyone around here with a horse like that. Maybe one of the riders at Cedar Crefi brought his own horse."

McKenzie hadn't thought of that, but Derfi was probably right. The rider had been on Maggie's land, and he looked and acted like a beginning rider. McKenzie knew lots of adults who wanted to learn to ride and took lessons.

McKenzie and Bailey led the way back while Derfi followed them with Molly and the cart. As they rode back, McKenzie mentioned the flyer Maggie had brought over earlier.

"I entered the calf-roping contest at the rodeo last year and it was a lot of fun. Would you want to be my partner? I would show you how to do it," McKenzie swatted at a mosquito perched on her arm.

"That sounds like fun, but how would we practice? Emma doesn't have calves," Bailey asked.

"Maybe we could sign up for one of Maggie's calf-roping sessions." McKenzie urged her horse as they approached the backside of the old barn. "What do you think?"

"I think it's a great idea," Bailey said. "I just hope Emma will let us."

Emma was waiting at the barn for the girls when they returned. "Thank God you two are all right," she said, giving each one a hug. "You had me worried for a minute."

They told Emma the whole story as they groomed, fed, and

watered the horses. They asked their instructor if they could sign up for calf-roping sessions at Maggie's place.

Emma thought for a minute and then said, "I don't see why not. I'll call her after supper. I'm starved. Let's go inside. We're finished here."

The girls fixed the toppings for a pizza while Emma made the crust. After placing the pizza in the oven, Emma went to call Maggie.

The girls slipped out to the front porch as the sun dipped low in the western sky. Soon it would disappear b>ind the nearby mountains.

McKenzie loved living near the mountains and had lived here all her life. With the mountains practically in her backyard, she could go skiing and snowboarding in the winter whenever she wanted. Sunshine Stables was in the valley about thirty miles from her home and had been a perfect place for her to train with Sahara.

Buckeye came up the steps, stopping to sniff a baby kitten. Cheetah hissed at him from her perch on the porch railing. Bailey scooped up her little orange kitten and dove onto the porch swing, cuddling the tiny bundle in her arms.

"Oh no you don't, you big mean dog," she scolded playfully.

McKenzie called Buckeye to her side and scratched his ears. Soon he laid his head in her lap and closed his eyes, while McKenzie daydreamed about the rodeo. Every year she looked forward to competing, but this year it was hard to get excited. A part of her looked forward to it, but she felt almost guilty with Diamond Girl missing. If no one could find the horse, Emma couldn't enter the rodeo. McKenzie couldn't imagine the rodeo without Emma and Diamond Girl.

McKenzie jumped when Emma opened the screen door with a loud creak. A wonderful smell of sausage and seasonings floated out.

"Pizza's ready," Emma said. "I called Maggie, but she's already filled the last two time slots. She did say you could go over and watch the other teams practice, though. McKenzie knows how to rope, but it would help you, Bailey, to watch the event a few times."

"When can we go?" Bailey slid into a chair at the kitchen table.

"I told her Friday afternoon. Kids' Camp will be over, so that will give you more time. How does that sound?"

"Great," McKenzie said. "Then we'll have the other afternoons this wefi to work with our horses."

During supper the girls talked back and forth, but Emma said little.

"You miss Diamond Girl, don't you?" Bailey asked with her mouth full of pizza.

Emma looked up suddenly. "I guess I do," she said with a sigh. "I just hope she's okay."

"We're still working on the investigation," McKenzie said. "We're good at finding clues others miss."

Emma reached out and grabbed McKenzie's hand. "I think this is an investigation for the sheriff, but you can keep trying if you want. Don't forget the main part of this investigation is prayer, and we all need to remember that we have to accept God's will in all this. He wants us to learn from this, no matter what happens, okay?"

McKenzie knew Emma was speaking the truth. Her parents had always told McKenzie and her little brother that with God, everything happened for a reason. When bad things happened, it was to bring them closer to Him. God promised never to give them more than they could handle as long as they had faith.

Emma pulled away and changed the subject. "Oh, by the way, McKenzie. Your mom called and said your outfit for the Junior Miss Rodeo Queen contest came in. I picked it up at Boots and Buckles when I was in town." Emma disappeared into the dining room.

She returned a minute later holding an outfit on a hanger. Bailey gasped and her eyes widened as she stared at the pants and top.

McKenzie loved the outfit. In fact, it seemed prettier than when she and her mom had picked it out. The crisp black western style jeans looked perfect with the emerald green riding blouse, while dozens of matching green sequins on the cuffs and collar flickered in the light.

"You'll look gorgeous in this," Emma said as she touched a sparkling sequin. "You'll be the prettiest girl on the stage."

McKenzie said nothing. Usually she liked trying new things. But now heaviness settled in her stomach. If only she hadn't let her mom talk her into entering the rodeo pageant. She stared at the riding outfit. Emma had told her she would have a lot of fun, but McKenzie was seriously starting to doubt that. She knew she would only embarrass herself as well as her family if she got up there on stage.

She decided right then and there that she wasn't going to

let that happen. Competing in a rodeo queen contest wasn't her thing. It was okay for Emma and okay for her mom, but there was absolutely no way she would wear that outfit. Not in the Junior Miss Rodeo Queen contest. Not ever! She'd figure some way out of it!

The Ghost Rider Returns?

"What's the matter, McKenzie?" Emma asked. "Isn't this the outfit you and your mom picked out?"

McKenzie's mouth felt dry as a cotton ball. "Oh, it's the one we ordered, all right," she stammered as she placed her elbows on the table and cupped her chin.

Emma laid the outfit over the back of a kitchen chair. "Then what's wrong?" she asked with concern.

"She doesn't want to be in the contest," Bailey answered then slapped her hand over her mouth. "Oops. I'm sorry, McKenzie. I didn't mean to tell."

Emma pulled out the chair next to McKenzie and sat down. "Is that right, McKenzie? Do you really not want to be in the contest?"

McKenzie folded her arms on the table and put down her head. "Yes," she mumbled. "I mean yes then no."

Emma gently stroked McKenzie's hair as she asked softly, "But why? I thought you wanted to be in it."

McKenzie answered sullenly. "I don't want to get all dressed up and stand in front of a bunch of people with judges staring at me. But I have to do it because Mom wants me to."

Emma stopped stroking McKenzie's hair for a second.

Then she started in again. "Ah. I see. Does your mom know you don't want to be in it?"

"Nope," Bailey answered again with a sigh. She held the blouse up to her chest and checked the sleeves for length against her own arms. "She doesn't want to hurt her mom's feelings."

"Oh McKenzie, you need to talk to her if you feel that way. I'm sure she wouldn't want you to compete if she knew you really didn't want to." Emma patted McKenzie's arm. "But why don't you sleep on it and call her tomorrow. You know, I was really nervous, too, the first time I competed. But I'm so glad I did. You might change your mind, too."

McKenzie looked up and thought about Emma's words. Her instructor might be right, but McKenzie wasn't ready to admit it just yet. It wouldn't hurt to wait one more day to call her mom. Besides, she didn't want to upset her mom this late in the evening.

McKenzie stood up and began clearing the table.

"Isn't it about time to chat with your camp friends? Why don't you see if anyone is online while I clean up the kitchen?" Emma gathered the remaining dishes and carried them to the sink.

The girls headed into the office. After logging on, they noticed their other four friends were already chatting.

Kate: *Where have U 2 been?*

Alexis: *Have U found the horse yet?*

McKenzie: *Still working on it. Not many clues yet. Tho we did find Diamond Girl's horseshoe in creek.*

Sydney: *Maybe DG disappeared from that spot.*

McKenzie: *We thot of that, but there was no gate and the fence across the crefi had no holes.*

Elizabeth: *It's only been 2 days. Something will turn up. Remember Ecclesiastes 3:6 says, "a time to search and a time to give up." I think God wants U 2 search longer. Don't give up on DG yet.*

McKenzie knew the Bible verse Elizabeth was talking about. The scriptures talked about how there was "a time for every purpose under heaven." McKenzie knew that everything happens for a reason, but right now she couldn't imagine what that reason could be.

Elizabeth: *Hey, McKenzie, R U ready 2 B rodeo queen?*

McKenzie cringed. *I want 2 drop out. I'll get 2 nervous.*

Elizabeth: *U can't do that. U have 2 enter. U'll do great.*

Alexis: *Yeah. I would luv 2 B queen. U can't quit!*

After the Camp Club Girls chatted a few more minutes, McKenzie agreed to seriously reconsider the queen contest. Maybe it wouldn't be so bad after all.

As she logged out of the chat room, she turned to Bailey. "I almost forgot the pictures I took with my cell phone. Let's put them on the computer and see if we find a clue."

McKenzie loaded the pictures onto the computer, magnifying each picture one at a time. With their heads together, the girls studied them, hoping to see something that looked out of place. McKenzie's eyes grew tired staring at the screen, and she was almost ready to give up when something caught her eye.

"Look." McKenzie touched her finger to the screen, pointing out a yellow object on the ground. "What is that?"

Bailey peered closer. "I can't tell. Is it a wrapper or something?"

"I'm not sure," McKenzie said. "It's too late to check it out now, but maybe we can go back to the crefi tomorrow afternoon. Hopefully it's not paper and won't blow away."

After scanning the remaining pictures, the girls saw nothing else that looked unusual. McKenzie wondered what detectives looked for. She hoped she didn't miss a clue that was right in front of her eyes.

McKenzie stretched her arms above her head and yawned. "Let's be done for the night. Okay?"

McKenzie logged off the computer and stepped out of the office. When she saw the rodeo outfit draped over a chair, she felt a sudden urge to try it on. Maybe Emma and the Camp Club Girls were right. A spark of excitement began to form deep inside her.

Minutes later, the girls were in their room. Bailey flung herself onto her bunk, hiding her face in her pillow.

"Tell me when you're ready." Bailey's voice sounded muffled. "I don't want to look until I see the whole package."

McKenzie changed out of her clothes and slipped into the new black jeans and shimmering green blouse. She added her new black cowboy hat and boots then finished off the outfit with a matching black belt with a large silver buckle.

"Ta-da!" McKenzie posed with one hand on her hips.

Bailey pulled her face from her pillow and gasped. Then her lip trembled as she stared at McKenzie.

"What's the matter?" McKenzie asked as she glanced down at her outfit. "Do I look stupid?"

Bailey turned away and said nothing. Without looking at McKenzie, she finally answered, "It's not fair."

McKenzie didn't understand. "What's not fair?"

"You don't even want to be queen and I do, but I can't because I don't live here." Bailey's voice cracked as she spoke.

For a minute, McKenzie didn't know what to say. Maybe she should drop out of the competition after all. The last thing she wanted to do was to hurt Bailey's feelings.

But as soon as the thought went through her mind, she knew she couldn't do that. She had already promised her mom, and after talking with the Camp Club Girls, she had decided to go ahead with the competition as planned.

Now that McKenzie knew Bailey's true feelings, she needed to figure out a way to include her younger friend.

McKenzie glanced in the mirror over the dresser at her shoulder-length auburn curls flowing beneath the cowboy hat and wondered how she should wear it for the contest—a low ponytail maybe, or she could just let it hang loose.

She frowned as she rubbed her chefis, wishing she could simply rub away the sprinkling of freckles across her nose. With a sigh she turned to Bailey. "I might get through this queen thing after all, that is if you'll help me with my hair and makeup. Mom got me a kit and said I could wear a little but only for the contest. But you're better at doing hair and makeup than I am. Would you help me with it?"

Bailey sniffed and turned around. Her eyes were red. "I guess I could do that. Everything has to look just right, you know. You can borrow my nail polish, too. It matches your top perfectly." Bailey tried to smile as she held out her neatly painted green fingernails.

The girls said little as they changed into their pajamas and slipped into their bunks. McKenzie heard a coyote howl outside and Buckeye barked an answer, but she was so tired the howling didn't bother her. Before she could finish her prayers, she had fallen asleep.

●—●—●

McKenzie didn't wake up until she smelled blueberry muffins baking the next morning. Within minutes, both girls were dressed and sitting at the kitchen table. McKenzie had just finished her third muffin when the first of the campers arrived for the day.

McKenzie and Bailey hurried outside to meet them as a woman in a van dropped off three kids. All of them were rowdier than usual.

"My older brother's girlfriend saw the ghost rider last night," one young boy exclaimed to his friend.

"Your brother's just making it up," another boy argued.

A girl who looked about Bailey's age said, "No sir. My grandpa says the ghost rider is back. Several people saw him riding around last night. Kind of like a ghost—at dusk." The girl made a high-pitched, eerie ghost sound.

McKenzie and Bailey exchanged glances.

Did several people really see the ghost rider? McKenzie wondered. She thought it was just a story someone had cooked up years ago.

The girls had little time to listen to the story. After the campers had all arrived, McKenzie gathered her group and Bailey went off with her group. She was learning fast under

Emma's teaching. Since arriving at Sunshine Stables, she had her horse making tighter turns around the barrels, and she had also improved on her time.

After Kids' Camp, McKenzie worked diligently with Sahara. They ran through the course several times as she worked on perfecting her turns. After turning around the third and last barrel, she squeezed her calves together, urging her horse faster and faster. Emma said she was improving every day, but McKenzie wasn't sure. She hoped she placed higher in the standings than she had the previous year.

McKenzie practiced until a pickup pulled into the driveway next to the arena. She rode over to the fence, watching Maggie Preston climb out and stride toward Emma.

"Looks like you're keeping busy training your girls," Maggie said as she flipped her hair over her shoulder. "Honestly, Emma, I don't know how you can concentrate with all the commotion going on around here. I would be a basket case if my prize horse was stolen."

"I figure I have to keep busy. I just can't sit and worry, or I'd go nuts," Emma explained. "I have faith that God will return Diamond Girl to me. If I didn't have faith, I could never get through this."

Maggie shook her head and scoffed. "You need a little more than faith, Emma. It sounds to me like you need a little luck on your side. Has the sheriff found anything yet?"

"He's working on it, but so far there's not much to go on," Emma said dismally, ignoring Maggie's comment.

"It's such a shame. Unless the sheriff finds your horse soon, you'll have to drop out of the competition, and I would sure hate to see that happen. Let's see, you've brought home the first-place trophy for three years now, right?" Maggie said as she stared intently at Emma.

"Just barely," Emma said with a smile. "You were only a fraction of a second b›ind me, remember?"

"How could I forget?" Maggie mumbled as she pulled her ringing cell phone from its case.

Seconds later Maggie excused herself and headed back to her pickup. She was needed back at the stables, she said.

Emma turned to the girls and said they had worked enough for one day, so they watered the horses and turned them into the corral.

By the time they finished, a few clouds had rolled in, bringing a cool breeze with them. McKenzie suggested that she and Bailey walk to the spot in the back pasture where they had found the horseshoe earlier.

"Hopefully that yellow thing we saw in the picture is still there," McKenzie said after stopping at the house for a couple of popsicles.

"We definitely need a clue to solve this mystery, that's for sure." Bailey licked a grape popsicle. Her lips and tongue turned purple. "We don't have much to go on yet."

"Just the horseshoe," McKenzie said, "and the yellow thingy on the ground."

"Don't forget the funny guy we saw yesterday on that gorgeous horse. That could be a clue. Maybe."

"I guess there are a few more possible clues than I thought. It would help if we could figure out if any of them are connected." McKenzie dropped a piece of strawberry popsicle on her white T-shirt. When she tried to wipe it off, the red stain grew bigger.

The fence by the crefi was over a mile away, and by the time the girls reached it, sweat was dripping down McKenzie's neck. She cupped the cool water and splashed her face and arms. While Bailey dipped her arms in the crefi, McKenzie walked to the fence. Hopefully the yellow object they had seen in the photo hadn't blown away.

McKenzie stared at the ground as she walked but soon stopped and turned to her friend. "Bailey, the yellow thing is still here."

Scurrying the last few steps, McKenzie knelt and grabbed the piece of yellow plastic. She turned it over in her hand as Bailey came up b›ind her.

"What is it?" Bailey asked.

McKenzie looked up at Bailey, whose bangs were plastered to her head with sweat. "It's a clip used to fix a barbed-wire fence."

McKenzie stood and examined the fence beside her. Farmers and ranchers used these kinds of clips all the time. She looked up and down the fence row and saw clips on every post, securing the wire to the post. All of the other clips had faded from the sun, but the one she held in her hand was shiny and new. She looked at the post directly in front of her. All of the clips on that post looked brand-new, too.

"I think I know how Diamond Girl got out. Someone has recently fixed this fence. I can tell because this post has all new clips," McKenzie explained to Bailey. "The horse thief or thieves took down this stretch of fence that crosses the shallow part of the crefi. After they took Diamond Girl through the opening, they fixed the fence."

Bailey's eyes lit up. "That's why there are no tracks. The thief led Diamond Girl up the crefi."

McKenzie nodded. "Right. The thief struggled with Diamond Girl on the rocks in the crefi. That made her lose her horseshoe back there."

"I think our detective work is paying off," Bailey said excitedly. "It's a good thing you took those pictures. Otherwise we never would have seen that clip on the ground."

McKenzie's heart beat faster as a sudden thought came to her. Someone had fixed Emma's fence, but who? Was it one of her workers? If so, did that mean someone at Sunshine Stables had stolen Diamond Girl?

McKenzie swallowed as she thought about it. All of Emma's employees were also her friends and surely none of them would steal Diamond Girl—would they?

Danger Nearby!

"Do you really think someone at Sunshine Stables stole Diamond Girl?" Bailey asked after McKenzie explained her idea.

"I don't want to believe that," McKenzie said firmly. "Everyone there loves Emma and Diamond Girl too much. At least I hope they do."

The thought that the thief might be someone McKenzie knew made her sick to her stomach. She had known most of Emma's workers for several years, except for Derfi. Surely none of them would steal Emma's prize horse. But she knew she couldn't overlook this possible clue if they wanted to find Diamond Girl.

"Didn't Derfi say he wanted to open his own stable someday? He said he needed a lot of money. You don't think he'd—" Bailey stopped abruptly.

"No. Derfi would never steal Diamond Girl," McKenzie said as convincingly as she could. But she had also only known Derfi for a couple of months. McKenzie shook her head as she brushed the thought from her mind.

"What are we going to do?" Bailey asked.

"I don't know. I know it's wrong to accuse someone of a

crime when we can't prove it, but this sure looks suspicious. I think we need to tell Emma about it." McKenzie headed up the bank toward home.

"Too bad Elizabeth's not here," Bailey said. "She would know what to do."

Besides being the oldest, Elizabeth knew her Bible much better than McKenzie did. When McKenzie read her Bible, she often didn't understand what God was saying. Elizabeth, however, always seemed to know what the scripture meant.

McKenzie sighed. "Maybe we should e-mail Elizabeth when we get back. We can tell Emma what we've found later."

McKenzie gazed across the pasture to Sunshine Stables in the distance. She wished they had ridden horses. Not only were her legs tired, but the breeze from earlier had died. A timber ran along one edge of the pasture, stretching all the way to the stables. Though walking through the trees was a longer route home, at least it was shade. So she made a quick decision.

McKenzie looked at Bailey's red, sweaty face and said, "Let's go to the woods and cool off a little. Then we'll walk home through the trees."

Bailey eagerly agreed and in a few minutes the girls stepped into the cool shade of the timber, slumping onto a fallen log.

McKenzie laid back on the rough bark and closed her eyes. She breathed the fresh smell of grass and wildflowers and listened to the rustle of the leaves overhead. She heard the crackling sounds of rabbits and squirrels scurrying over dried twigs and grass.

The air in the timber was so still she started to doze. Then she was startled by a loud voice and the heavy clomping footsteps crunching through the brush.

McKenzie sat up and peered through the overgrown brush. Across the fence, she saw a horse and rider going through the timber. As the pair drew nearer, the horse whinnied softly.

McKenzie recognized the rider as the young man she and Bailey had seen the day before. At least McKenzie thought it was the same man. Today he wore a black cowboy hat pulled down low over his for>ead, and though the day was hot, he wore a dark brown, long-sleeved shirt. His collar was pulled up to his chin, so it was hard to see his face. He was definitely riding the same horse, but he seemed to have more control of her.

Bailey whispered into McKenzie's ear, "Why is he riding out here?"

McKenzie turned to her friend. "I don't know. This is a weird place to learn to ride. I wonder if Maggie knows he's out here. I'd think she'd want her new riders to stay on open land, not in timber."

McKenzie wanted to call out to the man, but then she remembered how he had treated them. She was afraid he'd get angry again, so she decided to keep quiet. Slipping to the ground as quietly as she could, she motioned for Bailey to do the same. From b>ind bushes, the girls peered at the man on the spotted horse.

Again McKenzie thought there was something familiar about that horse. Why couldn't she figure out where she had seen it before?

The crunching twigs and dried leaves beneath the horse's

hooves echoed through the timber. Slowly the man guided the horse around stumps and fallen logs, staring at the ground, first one side and then the other.

He acted as if he'd dropped something and was looking for it. He continued searching the ground but finally gave up. With a flick of the reins, he disappeared through the trees.

McKenzie stood and brushed the dirt from the knees of her jeans. "I wonder who that guy is." She picked a bramble off her shirt. "I think it's the same guy we saw before, but I'm not sure."

Bailey nodded. "But it's definitely the same horse."

"That horse is one of a kind, that's for sure," McKenzie said as she glanced at her watch. Chore time had probably already started, but if they hurried they would get there in time to help with most of the jobs. The girls started back toward Sunshine Stables, hurrying through the trees, dodging bushes and low-hanging branches.

As they hurried single file through the woods, Bailey lagged b›ind. "Hey, McKenzie, wait up," she called through jagged breaths. "I found something." McKenzie turned and went to Bailey's side. The younger girl took a deep breath and handed McKenzie a piece of paper.

McKenzie looked at the words scrawled across it, "Willow Ridge Horse Therapy Ranch. 555-9814."

"I wonder if this was what that guy lost," McKenzie said as she studied the handwriting.

McKenzie had never heard of Willow Ridge Horse Therapy Ranch. In fact, she didn't know of a horse therapy farm around here. She stuffed the paper in her jeans and continued through the timber. Soon they arrived at Sunshine Stables. The stable hands had just begun chores, so the girls weren't late after all.

They rinsed their horses in the wash area, and McKenzie let the cold water splash her arms and face. Usually washing the horses wasn't her favorite part of grooming, but today she enjoyed the job. The cool spray of water felt good on her sweaty skin. She didn't care that she was nearly soaked when they finished.

When the chores were finally done, the girls changed into dry shorts and T-shirts and settled in the porch swing. McKenzie pushed her toes against the wooden floor, setting the swing in motion. The heavy chain hanging from the ceiling creaked with each sway. Cicadas sang their shrill song in the nearby trees.

McKenzie leaned her head back remembering the stories the young campers had told that morning. Several of them knew people who had seen the ghost rider recently.

"I wonder if the ghost rider really has returned." McKenzie tucked one leg beneath her.

"Lots of people seem to think so." Bailey slapped a mosquito on her leg.

"I think it's funny that no one has seen this ghost rider for years. Now, all of a sudden he shows up again, right after Diamond Girl disappears. Don't you think it's weird?" McKenzie looked skeptically at Bailey.

Bailey nodded. "Yeah, I guess it is. It's all a part of the mystery."

McKenzie thought about Bailey's words. Maybe the ghost rider was a part of Diamond Girl's disappearance. It seemed more than coincidence that the mysterious rider had shown up this wefi. Did he know something about the horse? McKenzie was still wondering about that when Emma called them in for supper.

While they ate, McKenzie told Emma what the campers had told them that morning. "Do you think the ghost rider could be back?"

Emma laid down her hamburger before speaking. "Oh, I'm sure those people really did see someone. There are several riding stables around here, you know. Old Towne belongs to Sunshine Stables, but some people forget it's private property. I wouldn't be surprised if someone was riding out there, but I think it's just the old story coming back to life. I suppose I need to put up some new 'No Trespassing' signs, though."

The three continued eating in silence.

"Have you heard anything new from the sheriff about Diamond Girl?" Bailey interrupted the silence as she set down her milk glass.

Emma shook her head. "Instead of branding my horses, I have microchips embedded in their necks. Now, if the thief tries to sell Diamond Girl at a horse auction, the microchip will be scanned, and it will show that she has been stolen. Authorities can then be called to make an arrest. The sheriff is hoping the thief will eventually show up at one of these auctions. He doesn't really have any other leads on the case."

Bailey stuffed her last bite of hamburger into her mouth. "I sure hope we find her soon."

Emma nodded as she stared at her plate. "The longer it takes to find Diamond Girl, the farther the thief can take her."

"Keep praying about it, Emma," Bailey encouraged.

"Doesn't God answer all our prayers if we have faith?"

McKenzie hadn't noticed the dark circles beneath Emma's eyes until now. McKenzie knew how much her instructor loved her horse, and she could tell Emma hadn't been sleeping much. McKenzie felt a lump form in the bottom of her stomach.

"You're right, Bailey," Emma said after a moment. "God does answer all prayers, but He doesn't always give us what we ask for. He gives us what He knows is best for us."

McKenzie stacked the empty plates and carried them to the sink. She knew Emma's words were true. But she felt God was directing her to keep searching for Diamond Girl.

"Emma, would you care if Bailey and I go out to Old Towne before it gets dark?" McKenzie rinsed the dishes and placed them in the dishwasher.

"Sure, go ahead," Emma said with a slight smile. "But you girls have done enough walking for one day. Since the horses are put away for the night, why don't you take the four-wheelers? You have driven one haven't you, Bailey?"

"I drove one several times at the stable where I practice back home," Bailey said.

"Good." Emma turned to McKenzie. "You can show Bailey the smaller four-wheelers. Be careful and don't be gone long."

Minutes later McKenzie led the way to the machine shed and stepped inside. She grabbed two helmets, giving one to Bailey.

McKenzie pointed to a small four-wheeler. "That one's for you," she said. She hopped on the seat of a red ATV that she had ridden many times before.

Bailey climbed onto the blue four-wheeler. As the girls pressed the starter buttons, the engines roared to life. McKenzie steered her ATV through the large doorway and motioned for Bailey to follow. Soon, both girls were headed down the tree-lined path that led to Old Towne.

The sun hung low in the sky, casting long, dark shadows. Mosquitoes buzzed around their heads while vultures hovered on the ground ahead of them. They flapped their heavy wings and soared into the sky when they heard the roar of the engines.

At the top of the hill overlooking Old Towne, McKenzie steered her ATV into a small thicket of trees and parked.

"Why did you want to come out here?" Bailey asked as she turned off her four-wheeler.

"I thought maybe we could watch for the ghost rider or find signs that someone has been here." McKenzie set her helmet on the seat of the four-wheeler and headed down the slope. "Our four-wheelers are pretty much hidden here in the trees. Let's go on down and look around. We don't have much time before dusk, and that's when everyone has seen the ghost rider."

"Where are we going to hide so we can watch for him?" Bailey jogged to catch up with McKenzie.

"See that slope just past the old schoolhouse? I thought we could crouch low on the other side. Nobody could see us there." McKenzie pointed to an area about 100 yards away.

Soon the girls were walking down the only street in Old Towne. The Old West setup reminded McKenzie of ghost towns she had seen in movies. The town was eerily quiet in the gloom. The entire street was shrouded in shadows. Old shutters banged on upstairs windows, and the old windmill creaked as the wind turned its blades. McKenzie felt goose bumps ripple up her arms.

"This is creepy," Bailey whispered as she edged closer to McKenzie.

"I agree," McKenzie whispered back. "Let's get to our lookout."

Eager to get out of Old Towne, the girls scurried down the street past the schoolhouse. McKenzie reached the top of the slope first and stopped. The ground before them had suddenly dropped off. She instinctively flung out her arm to keep Bailey from falling over the edge.

McKenzie peered over the edge. Something was strange about this place. She knew there were no cliffs out here, so what caused this drop-off? Then an idea came to her as she scurried down the side of the hill. Soon she was standing below Bailey looking up at her friend.

"Bailey, come down here," McKenzie called. "You've got to see this. It's an old pioneer dugout. You're standing on the roof."

Bailey giggled and scurried to McKenzie's side. "Wow. Is this ever cool."

"I don't think it was used as a house, though," McKenzie said. "Look at the wide double doors. I think it was a stable."

McKenzie stepped to the old rickety door and pulled on it.

It creaked on rusty hinges as McKenzie peered inside. It took her eyes a moment to adjust to the darkness and then she exclaimed, "Look Bailey. There's fresh hay in here."

"Do you think someone is keeping a horse here?" Bailey whispered.

McKenzie eyed an old wooden feed bunk. Bits of leftover feed lay in it, and a large bucket of clean water stood in the corner. McKenzie's heart fluttered as she glanced about the dark, musty stable.

"It sure looks like it," McKenzie said. She poked around in another bucket and found a lead rope, curry comb, and other grooming supplies. A larger third bucket held empty diet pop cans, candy, and fast food wrappers, an empty bottle of hair dye, and dirty stained rags.

McKenzie jumped as a gust of wind blew the stable door shut. Her heart thumped loudly in her chest as she put a finger to her lips. "Did you hear that?" she whispered.

"I just heard the banging door." Bailey clutched McKenzie's arm. "What did you hear?"

"It sounded like a horse neighing." McKenzie pushed the door open and peered out cautiously. After glancing in all directions, she stepped outside.

The sun had sunk below the horizon, deepening the shadows and darkness. For a moment she thought she heard rustling in the nearby timber. She squinted but saw nothing besides trees and a meadow. Yet, something didn't feel right. She had the feeling something or someone was watching her.

Suddenly, waiting for the ghost rider didn't seem like such a good idea.

McKenzie reached into the dugout and clutched Bailey's arm. She suddenly sensed that danger lurked nearby.

"Let's get out of here before someone sees us!"

A Disturbing Discovery

McKenzie pulled Bailey away from the stable and headed up the hill. When she reached the top, she turned and looked back. The woods looked dark and scary in the fading light.

"Let's run," she said, tugging Bailey after her.

McKenzie ran as fast as she could toward Old Towne, her feet barely touching on the dirt street. In the dusk, the stores lining Main Street reminded her of a tunnel. She raced past the general store and the old wooden windmill and didn't stop until she reached the thicket of trees at the top of the hill.

She bent and placed her hands on her knees, panting as she waited for Bailey to catch up.

Bailey breathed heavily as she slowly climbed the slope, holding her side when she reached the top. "I need to rest," she said as she pulled her inhaler out of her pocket and took several deep breaths.

"I'm sorry, Bailey, but as soon as you can drive we need to get out of here," McKenzie said nervously.

"What's the hurry?" Bailey asked as her breathing slowed.

"I'll tell you when we get home. Let's go." McKenzie hopped on her four-wheeler and steered it onto the dirt track. McKenzie looked b›ind to make sure Bailey was following;

then she sped up the path.

Lightning bugs flickered in the twilight while the beams from her headlight cast eerie shadows along the path. A chilly wind had replaced the heat from earlier in the day, making McKenzie wish she had worn a sweatshirt. Within a few minutes she saw the lights of Sunshine Stables.

Driving into the machine shed, she flipped on the overhead light. When both girls had parked their ATVs, they settled onto some old wooden crates. McKenzie rubbed her arms to chase away the chill.

"Okay, tell me now." Bailey pulled her knees to her chest and stretched her T-shirt over her legs. "Did you see something? Did you see the ghost rider?"

"Well, I know I heard a horse. It sounded like it was coming from the timber by the dugout. I know we went out there to try to see the ghost rider, but then I decided it might not be a good idea," McKenzie explained.

"But why?" Bailey looked quizzically at McKenzie. "That was the whole point of going to Old Towne."

"I know, but if we see the ghost rider and he knows we saw him, he won't come back. Right? I think there's a connection between the ghost rider and Diamond Girl's disappearance. We need to find out more about him and why he's hanging around Old Towne. If we scare him off, we'll never solve this mystery."

"I guess you're right," Bailey said as she stepped off the crate. She picked up Cheetah who had wandered into the shed. The cat settled into her arms and closed her eyes. "So, what now?"

"I don't know." McKenzie sighed and then added, "Maybe that note you found earlier has another clue on it."

"Yeah," Bailey said as she stroked Cheetah's back. "You put it in your pocket."

"I sure hope Emma didn't do laundry this evening." McKenzie hopped off the crate and headed for the door. "I'd better go find it."

Within minutes the girls were in the house and racing up the stairs to their bedroom, McKenzie taking them two at a time.

"Oh, good. They're just where I left them." She grabbed her jeans off the floor and pulled the scrap of paper out of the pocket.

She unfolded the crumpled paper and turned it over. "All it says is Willow Ridge Horse Therapy Ranch and the phone number. There's nothing written on the back either."

She opened the dresser drawer and tucked it under her socks for saffieeping. The note must be important if the man was looking for it. But then she thought maybe it wasn't even his. Maybe he had been looking for something else.

McKenzie sighed. If the sheriff had no clues to Diamond Girl's disappearance, would Bailey and she really be able to help? She wondered if searching for clues was a waste of time. It was only a few more days until the rodeo, and then she would leave Sunshine Stables. What if she left before finding out what happened to Emma's horse? She promised herself she wouldn't let that happen.

"Do you think we should tell Emma we suspect Derfi?" Bailey asked, interrupting McKenzie's thoughts.

McKenzie frowned. She still didn't want to think Derfi was involved with Diamond Girl's disappearance. "We were going to ask Elizabeth about that, weren't we?" she asked

"Why don't you call her instead?" Bailey asked.

McKenzie agreed and quickly called their friend in Texas, explaining the situation to Elizabeth.

"I don't think you should mention Derfi's name to anybody yet," Elizabeth said. "After all, you don't have any evidence against him, just hunches. You shouldn't wrongfully accuse him or anyone else."

McKenzie knew Elizabeth was right, so they chatted a few more minutes. She was just hanging up as Emma called up the stairs. She had popped popcorn and invited them to watch a movie with her before bed. The girls readily agreed and scampered downstairs.

During the first commercial break, McKenzie planned to ask Emma about the dugout at Old Towne, but when she glanced over at her instructor in the recliner, she noticed Emma's eyes were closed. Her breathing was soft and regular. McKenzie knew Emma was exhausted, so she dimmed the lights and turned off the TV. She put her finger to her lips and motioned for Bailey to follow her upstairs.

When the girls woke the next morning, Emma had already gone to the stables to prepare for the last day of Kids' Camp. After a quick breakfast, McKenzie and Bailey headed outside to help feed Sahara and the other horses that weren't used for camp. When the young campers arrived, they fed and groomed the horses they used for camp.

At two o'clock the campers went home. Emma had

told McKenzie and Bailey they could ride the four-wheelers across the meadow to Cedar Crefi Ranch to watch the roping class. The girls arrived early, hoping to walk through the stables and see Maggie's horses. They were eager to see if the beautiful spotted horse was in one of her stalls.

After parking their four-wheelers, the girls spotted Maggie outside the stables.

"Hi, Maggie," McKenzie called out as they approached Cedar Crefi's owner.

"Hi, girls. You're early. The riders won't be here for another twenty minutes," she said, glancing at her watch.

"We know," McKenzie replied. "We were wondering if we could look at your horses."

Maggie hesitated but then said, "I suppose that would be okay, but I don't have time to take you on a tour. I have to get the calves into the corral for the couple coming to practice. You can go by yourselves if you keep out of the way of my workers."

The girls promised they wouldn't bother anyone and set off toward the stable. McKenzie led the way inside and headed down the first aisle, glancing in the stalls as she walked. They passed quarter horses and paint horses with beautiful white splotches on their coats. They saw spotted Appaloosas and sturdy Morgans. She recognized Maggie's black mustang in a stall at the end.

"This is Maggie's prize horse, Frisco." McKenzie stepped aside so Bailey could see in the stall. "She's almost as fast as Diamond Girl."

"Yeah," Bailey said. "Maggie made it clear yesterday that Emma always beats her."

McKenzie nodded. "But second place is really good, too."

"You don't know what it's like to always come in second, or worse. I never win anything." Bailey frowned.

At first, McKenzie didn't know what to say. She knew how Bailey felt. "Bailey," McKenzie finally said softly, "you'll win lots of things. It's just that I've been riding a lot longer than you have, and I'm older. I did awful at last year's rodeo, so I do know how you feel. But you have lots of talents and abilities. I've seen some of your drawings and they're great. I can't draw a good stick man."

Bailey sighed but didn't answer. The girls continued down the aisle as McKenzie pointed out several breeds of horses to Bailey. She hoped to see the beautiful spotted horse they had seen in the pasture, but it wasn't in the first row of stalls. When they walked up the second aisle, they saw no sign of her there either.

Disappointed that they hadn't seen the unusual horse, McKenzie began to wonder who owned it. And why was the rider on Maggie's land if the horse wasn't stabled there? McKenzie was puzzled as she glanced at her watch and moved quickly through the stable.

The girls arrived back at the arena as Maggie turned the calves into the ring. McKenzie climbed the fence and sat on the top rung, while Bailey stood beside her.

A pair of girls, a little older than McKenzie, sat on a brown stallion. They chased a calf around the arena, the rider in front holding a lasso. As they approached a calf she flung the lasso, catching it around the calf's neck. Then she jerked the rope flinging the calf to the ground.

Bailey jumped and cried out, "Doesn't that hurt the calf?"

"Nope, not at all," McKenzie assured her as they watched the girls slip to the ground and loop the other end of rope around the calf's legs. "Just wait a sec and you'll see."

Moments later, after the calf laid still, Maggie stepped out and loosened the rope. After Maggie removed the lasso, the calf hopped up and ran around the arena unharmed.

"Maybe I could do that," Bailey said with a grin. "Now that I know it doesn't hurt the calf."

"Great," McKenzie said. "Maybe I can find an old rope around here, and I can practice throwing a lasso."

McKenzie glanced b›ind her, looking for Maggie. She heard voices coming from an old garage, so she tugged on Bailey's arm and headed in that direction. As they stepped inside she saw stacks of cardboard boxes, with the contents written with black marker on the outside. Two workers carried the boxes out the back door and loaded them into a trailer parked nearby. They paid no attention to the girls but continued hauling the boxes out.

McKenzie turned to Bailey and whispered, "I wonder what's going on in here."

Bailey pointed to the men cleaning out the garage. "Where do you think they're taking all that stuff?"

"I don't know, but it looks almost like they're getting ready to move." McKenzie eyed all the busyness around her. "Surely Maggie's not moving. Emma hasn't said anything about it."

"I bet they're just cleaning out the garage," Bailey said as she stepped away from the garage.

"Could be," McKenzie said skeptically. "They look too busy to help us find a rope. We should probably head back anyway, but I need to find Maggie and thank her for letting us come over."

McKenzie glanced around the arena looking for Maggie. She was nowhere in sight, so the girls headed toward the stables to look for her. Stable hands were doing nightly chores. McKenzie pulled Bailey into the supply room to let two workers pass with wheelbarrows full of hay.

McKenzie turned and noticed the shelves were nearly bare and cardboard boxes lined the floor. All of them were filled with horse supplies.

She jumped at a harsh voice b›ind them. "What do you need, girls?"

McKenzie turned to see Maggie standing in the doorway. The woman drained the last of her diet cola can and tossed it into the trash can.

"Uh, we just wanted to thank you for letting us come over," McKenzie stammered.

"Yeah, it was really nice of you," Bailey agreed. "I think I can do the calf-roping thing after watching those girls. Will you be at the rodeo to watch us?"

Maggie shooed the girls out of the room. She smirked at Bailey and replied, "Oh, I think I'll be there, all right."

"Are you moving, Maggie?" McKenzie asked as she glanced at the boxes.

Maggie hesitated and peered around as though to see if anyone was standing nearby. Then she pulled the girls closer and said in a near whisper, "I have someone coming over to look at the place and want it to look nice, so I'm cleaning out some junk. Nothing is definite yet; so don't say anything about it, not even to Emma. Okay?"

The girls looked at each other but agreed not to say anything. McKenzie wondered why in the world Maggie wanted to keep it a secret, especially from Emma. She thought the two women were friends. Another thought crept into McKenzie's mind. *Maggie acts like she's got something to hide. Would she have stolen Diamond Girl to keep Emma from winning the rodeo?*

Then Maggie motioned for the girls to step outside and continued, "I'm glad I could help you girls, but you better go home." Before the girls could respond, the woman turned and started to walk away.

"Oh, I almost forgot," Maggie said. She turned back to the girls and pulled a folded newspaper page from her back pocket. "Would you give this paper to Derfi? I circled an ad I thought he might want to see."

McKenzie assured Maggie she would give the paper to Derfi, and minutes later the girls headed for home. After parking the ATVs, McKenzie unfolded the newspaper and glanced at the ad Maggie had circled in bright red ink.

"Look at this, Bailey." McKenzie pointed to the ad. "Maggie wanted Derfi to see this ad about a stable for sale in northern Montana."

Bailey skimmed the ad. "I thought he wasn't going to buy a stable until he'd saved more money."

"I thought so, too," McKenzie agreed.

Bailey was silent for a moment. Then she spoke softly. "Maybe he sold something worth a lot of money."

McKenzie looked up. "You don't think Derfi stole Diamond Girl and sold her, do you?"

"I know you like him, McKenzie," Bailey said. "But he has a reason to steal her. He wants money to buy a stable. Remember the other day when he said certain thieves knew how to disguise a horse. He knows how to do all those tricks with horses. Maybe he's disguised Diamond Girl."

McKenzie knew Bailey was right about one thing. She did like Derfi. He had always been so nice, helping her feed and groom Sahara. He always seemed happy to have her around the stables.

Though she hated to admit it, he did have a reason to steal Diamond Girl. But that didn't mean he was the thief, did it? More than anything, she wanted to prove Derfi was innocent, but she didn't know how. All the clues seemed to point toward his guilt.

She felt torn inside. What if she accused Derfi and he was innocent? Could she forgive herself? But more importantly, would God forgive her?

The Nighttime Adventure

The weekend passed with no news or leads to Diamond Girl's disappearance. McKenzie began to wonder if she would ever learn what had happened to the prize horse. She knew God wanted her to help solve the mystery, but she also knew He expected her to not wrongly accuse anyone. Part of her was scared to meet the thief face-to-face. What if he was someone she knew and trusted? Would she be able to continue loving that person as God would want her to?

After church on Sunday, McKenzie pushed the thoughts from her mind as she headed to the arena to practice for the rodeo. She watched Bailey as she raced the barrel course with Applejack. Bailey had improved much since coming to Sunshine Stables, and McKenzie hoped she would do well at the rodeo. Placing in the top three would mean a lot to Bailey.

Soon it was McKenzie's turn to race with Sahara. As she leaned forward, the warm evening air caught her ponytail, slapping it up and down. Again and again she raced. Each time she worked on tightening her turns. Then she took a break and it was Bailey's turn again.

Finally Emma said the girls had practiced enough for one night. McKenzie sighed with relief. It had been a long day and she was ready to go inside. She hadn't chatted online with the Camp Club girls for a couple of days, so she wanted to fill them in on all the happenings.

Minutes later McKenzie and Bailey sat in front of Emma's computer. The other four Camp Club girls were already chatting online.

McKenzie: *LTNC.*

Elizabeth: *Where have U 2 been?*

McKenzie: *Busy with horses and trying to figure out what happened to Diamond Girl.*

Alexis: *Do you have any clues?*

McKenzie: *We found a fence clip near the place in the crefi where we found the horseshoe. Someone cut the fence and fixed it with clips. The thief could've stolen DG from that spot and led her up crefi.*

I don't want 2 suspect Derfi, but he has a reason to steal DG. He needs $$ 2 buy his own stable.

Bailey took over the keyboard: *And twice we've seen a stranger riding that beautiful spotted horse. I've never seen one like it. He acts funny 2. Doesn't even know the horse's name and he couldn't even control her.*

Kate: *U know U can lead a horse 2 water but U can't make him drink.*

Elizabeth: *Reminds me of my mom's favorite song, "Horse with No Name."*

Sydney: *UR horse with no name is a horse of a different color, LOL.*

McKenzie thought about her friends' remarks. From the first time she saw the strange horse, she thought it looked familiar. Now she knew why.

McKenzie: *U guys made me realize something. If that horse was black and didn't have spots, she could B DG!*

Kate: *Could someone have dyed DG's coat?*

McKenzie and Bailey looked at each other. Both wondered if it could be possible. McKenzie remembered the bottle of hair dye in the dugout.

McKenzie: *Dunno. How could we tell?*

Kate: *If u can get some hairs from horse I could test it with my kit.*

McKenzie knew Kate loved anything technical. She saved all her birthday and Christmas money to buy the latest gadgets. Kate was a whiz with computers and electronics. McKenzie knew Kate could test the horse hair, but she wondered how she could get the hair in the first place.

"Girls, it's getting late," a voice b›ind them called.

McKenzie glanced b›ind her. Emma was leaning against the door frame, smiling at them.

"Okay, we'll sign off," McKenzie said.

McKenzie: *G2G. Thx GFs. TTFN.*

After the girls logged off, they headed upstairs.

"Do you think the spotted horse could actually be Diamond Girl?" Bailey asked as she slipped into her pajamas.

McKenzie climbed onto the top bunk. "I suppose it's possible. Everybody assumes the thief would take Diamond Girl far away. But what better way to hide her than in plain sight."

Bailey crawled beneath the covers. "Do you think the thief is hiding the spotted horse in the dugout stable at Old Towne?"

"I've wondered about that. It sure looked like someone was keeping a horse there." McKenzie flipped onto her stomach and peered over the edge of the bed. "If so, I bet it's bedded down there at night."

Bailey peered up at McKenzie with questioning eyes. "What are you getting at?"

McKenzie flung her hair out of her eyes and grinned. "I think we need to see if a horse is out there!"

Bailey's eyes grew wide. "You mean now?"

"If that horse is actually Diamond Girl, the thief won't keep her there forever. We need to find out before she disappears again." McKenzie felt her pulse quicken. She wasn't sure she wanted to go to Old Towne after dark, but she knew they had to. In just a few short days, they would leave Sunshine Stables to go back to their homes. If they wanted to solve the mystery of Diamond Girl's disappearance, they had to hurry. "Hopefully, the spotted horse is there, and we can snip some hairs to send to Kate."

Bailey stared at McKenzie. "Well, if you're going, I'm not going to wait here," she said.

It was just after ten o'clock. If they took the horses, they could go to Old Towne, check the place out, and easily be back in less than an hour. She jumped from the top bunk. In a couple of minutes both girls had changed into jeans and sweatshirts.

The house was dark when they stepped into the hallway. They paused outside Emma's bedroom door, but no sounds came from within. McKenzie knew they should ask for permission, but she hated to wake Emma.

McKenzie made a quick decision. She motioned for Bailey

to follow her as she tiptoed down the stairs. The yard light cast a soft glow through the windows, so they could make their way through the house.

McKenzie flipped on the light over the kitchen sink and pulled a pair of small scissors, a zippered sandwich bag, and a pocket flashlight out of a drawer. She shoved them into her sweatshirt pocket as she stepped into the mud room. After grabbing a battery-powered lantern, the girls quietly slipped outside.

McKenzie shivered in the cool breeze. She was glad she had worn her sweatshirt. The yard light cast eerie shadows in the corners of the yard. Leaves in the treetops rustled in the wind, and the bushes scratched against the house.

The girls ran to the stable and slipped inside as McKenzie flipped on the light switch. She heard the steady breathing of the horses, their bodies thumping against the dividers as they settled in their stalls. McKenzie wished she could sit down right here to spend the night, but she knew she had to finish what they intended to do. After grabbing Sahara's saddle from the tack room, McKenzie lugged it into the stall.

Sahara blinked sleepily at McKenzie as she stepped inside. McKenzie talked to the horse as she set the saddle on her back. "It's okay, girl. We're going to go for a ride." McKenzie reached beneath the mare and secured the saddle. She patted the horse's head and led her out of the stall.

"Let's both ride Sahara," McKenzie suggested. "It'll be quicker. Then you can hold the lantern. Okay?"

Relief flooded Bailey's face. "Good. I didn't really want to ride after dark by myself."

McKenzie continued down the hallway and out the stable door with Sahara. She put her foot in the stirrup and mounted the horse. Then she pulled Bailey into the saddle b›ind her. They headed out of the lot and onto the trail.

After they passed b›ind the pine grove away from the yard light, she could see the sprinkling of stars in the black sky. The half-sized moon cast enough light so they could find their way without using the lantern. Twisted shadows from a maze of trees fell across the ground. McKenzie shivered beneath her sweatshirt. She felt Bailey wrap her small arms around her waist.

"Are you sure we should do this?" Bailey asked softly. "It's creepy out here."

McKenzie agreed with Bailey. This was the spookiest thing she had ever done. But with all the confidence she could gather, she said, "We have to do this, for Diamond Girl and for Emma."

"Okay, but let's get this over with as fast as we can," Bailey said. "I don't like it out here."

McKenzie turned her head toward Bailey. "We're almost there," she whispered as she saw the buildings of Old Towne.

Main Street, with its tall empty stores on either side, surrounded them in a blanket of darkness. Sahara plodded down the street, her thumping hooves the only sound in the gloom. As they rounded the curve outside of the town, McKenzie headed up the slope overlooking the dugout. She slid to the ground and looped Sahara's reins around a tree branch.

McKenzie felt as if they were in the middle of nowhere with

meadow in all directions. The mountains on the horizon made her feel even more isolated. Coyotes yipped in the distance and an owl hooted. Bailey clutched McKenzie's arm.

"Let's see if the horse is in the dugout," McKenzie whispered as she led Bailey down the slope.

McKenzie put her ear to the open window of the dugout, straining to hear if something was inside. The heavy breathing of a large animal as it shifted positions came from the far corner of the dugout. Peering through the window, McKenzie flicked on her pocket light.

"It's the spotted horse," she whispered as she flicked off her light. "Someone *is* hiding her here. Let's go around front and go in."

"Oooh, McKenzie. I don't like this," Bailey said with fear in her voice.

McKenzie glanced in both directions as she pulled Bailey to the dugout door. The rusty hinges squeaked loudly as McKenzie opened it and slipped inside.

The spotted horse stood in the corner of the dirt room. She blinked as McKenzie turned on the lantern light.

"She's even prettier up close," Bailey said with awe.

McKenzie walked cautiously to the horse's side and held out her hand, talking to her in a soothing voice. The horse nuzzled McKenzie's hand.

"Oh, Bailey. Her eyes look just like Diamond Girl's. She acts like her, too."

McKenzie stroked the large white spot on the horse's forۥead. She examined it closely. Had someone dyed the hair brown and turned the diamond shape into an uneven splotch?

Were the other spots dyed onto the horse? If so, the person had done a good job. In the dim light, the splotches of color looked natural.

She flung her arms around the horse's neck, feeling as though God had led her here for a reason. Squeezing her eyes shut, she murmured, "Dear God, let this be Diamond Girl. Please."

For a minute, McKenzie forgot her real purpose for coming here, and then she pulled away from the horse as uneasiness settled over her. Though the girls were alone in the dugout, she felt as if they shouldn't be here. "Let's get this done and get back home," she said. "Do you want to hold the light or snip the hairs?"

"I'll hold the light," Bailey answered.

McKenzie dug into her pocket and pulled out the scissors. Her hands trembled as she lifted the mane and snipped some strands on the underside. After rolling the length of hair around her hand, she tucked it into the plastic bag.

McKenzie's heart leaped as a scratching sound came from outside the stable door. She stuffed the bag into her pocket and spun around. Goosebumps rippled up her arms and the scratching grew louder. Someone or something was trying to get in.

Bailey screamed and flung one hand over her mouth. She held up the light and pointed to the bottom of the stable door. A growling animal with hairy paws was digging under the door!

"What is it?" Bailey's voice trembled. She grabbed McKenzie's arm.

Before McKenzie could answer, the animal stuck its paw

farther under the door. Her heart raced as she scurried to the window and cautiously stuck her head out. She pointed her pocket light at the door and gasped. Then she let out a big sigh as she yanked open the door. A bundle of fur jumped on her.

"Buckeye! You goofy dog," she said with a laugh. "Why did you follow us? You scared us half to death!"

The dog danced about their feet, yipping. He ran circles around her ankles, excited to see the girls. Bailey dropped McKenzie's arm and shook her head as she stroked Buckeye's head.

McKenzie scratched the dog's back and turned to Bailey. "We need to get going. I don't want whoever's hiding this horse here to come back and catch us."

McKenzie gave the horse a quick pat before Bailey turned off the lantern light. Buckeye scampered around their feet as they stepped outside and made their way in the moonlight to Sahara.

She couldn't wait to get away from here, back to the warmth of Emma's house. Taking a deep breath to help her relax, McKenzie mounted her horse. Then she pulled Bailey on b›ind her.

"I hope we don't get caught," Bailey whispered dismally. "I'm scared."

"Me, too." McKenzie turned Sahara around and headed back through Old Towne. "This place gets creepier all the time."

Buckeye ran beside the horse as the girls galloped down the dark, dusty street. Som›ow McKenzie felt safer with the dog beside them. They raced up the trail as fast as they dared in the shadowy darkness.

The dirt track seemed to go on forever, but McKenzie leaned forward, urging Sahara faster. The pounding of the horse's hooves thundered in the windy night. McKenzie sighed with relief when they crested the top of the hill and saw the yard lights of Sunshine Stables.

Emma's house was still dark. Feeling guilty for sneaking out, McKenzie moved as quickly as she could, returning Sahara to her stall. After settling her in again for the night, they scurried toward the door. McKenzie switched off the light, engulfing the stable in darkness.

As the girls stepped outside, McKenzie latched the door. She turned to follow Bailey when a movement next to the stables caught her eye. Something was there! Whirling around, she stifled a scream. A tall, dark figure stepped out of the shadows and grabbed her arm.

The Mysterious Message

McKenzie's heart raced. She heard Bailey muffle a shrift.

"Don't tell me you two can't stay away from your horses all night. You scared me silly."

McKenzie stared at the face looking down at her in the darkness, her voice quivering. "Derfi, you scared *us* half to death. What are you doing out here? I thought you went home hours ago."

"I told Emma I'd patrol the ranch tonight. I just got back from making the rounds. I was heading back to my cot in the supply room, and I saw the lights in the stable go out. I thought for sure the horse thieves were back. Lucky for you I decided to check things out before calling the sheriff. Now you two better get back to bed before Emma finds out you're gone." Derfi put his arms on the girls' shoulders and pushed them gently toward the house. "And stay in bed this time. I'm taking care of things out here, so you don't need to check on the horses. Good night."

The girls sighed with relief as they whispered their "good nights" to Derfi and hurried into the house. They crept upstairs to their bedroom as silently as possible. McKenzie took the bag of horse hairs from her pocket and laid it on the dresser.

"Boy, that was close," Bailey said as she climbed into bed. "Do you think Derfi knows we went to Old Towne?"

"I don't think so, or he would have told us. He was making rounds, so I don't think he saw a thing." McKenzie climbed into her bunk and flipped off the light switch with her foot.

Bailey whispered, "Do you think that horse was Diamond Girl?"

"I don't know, but I hope so," McKenzie said as she pulled the covers to her chin. "We need to get to town tomorrow and send those hairs to Kate by overnight mail. If it's stolen, the thief won't keep the horse there forever, so we have to move fast before he decides to move her."

"Why is that guy hiding the horse there?" Bailey asked. "If he wants her for the money, why hasn't he sold her?"

"Maybe he doesn't want to sell her. Maybe he wants to keep her for himself. She is a prize-winning rodeo horse, you know. She brings in quite a bit of money," McKenzie answered.

"Maybe he'll enter her in the rodeo," Bailey suggested. "If the horse is really Diamond Girl, no one would recognize her. She would win for sure."

The moonlight cast a soft glow about the room. McKenzie peered over the top bunk and saw Bailey's black hair framing her pale face in the dark.

McKenzie thought for a moment. "That's possible, but Emma will be at the rodeo. Surely the thief knows that. Emma would recognize Diamond Girl even if she's been dyed brown and covered with white splotches. I think we've overlooked a clue, but I don't know what it is."

"Do you think we should tell Emma that we found a horse

at Old Towne?' Bailey asked.

"Yes," McKenzie agreed. "She needs to know someone is hiding a strange horse on her land. Let's tell her first thing in the morning."

●—●—●

Sunlight was beaming through the window when McKenzie woke up. She flung the covers off and stretched her legs, listening to Bailey's soft, steady breathing coming from the bottom bunk.

Her eyes opened wide when she glanced at the digital clock on the desk. "Bailey," McKenzie exclaimed. "It's after nine o'clock!"

Bailey rolled over and rubbed her eyes. "We're supposed to be doing chores. How did we sleep this late?"

McKenzie jumped out of bed and reached for her jeans. "I can't believe Emma didn't wake us. We have a lot of work to do today."

Within minutes both girls scrambled down the stairs to the kitchen. The house was quiet, so McKenzie knew Emma had probably been up for hours. Though the girls usually woke on their own, McKenzie couldn't help wondering why Emma hadn't awakened them. The girls downed some orange juice, grabbed a couple of bagels, and hurried to the stables.

At first McKenzie didn't see any stable hands. But then she saw Derfi leading a caramel-colored Thoroughbred into the stable.

"Hey, Derfi," McKenzie called out as she hurried down the aisle toward him. "Have you seen Emma?"

"You girls are a couple of sleepyheads. I've been waiting for you to get up." He closed the stall door b›ind the horse. "Why don't you ride into White Sulfur Springs with me when I go get feed. Emma had a little accident this morning."

McKenzie caught her breath. "What happened? Is she hurt bad?"

Derfi opened the stable door for them as they stepped outside. "She was trying to break that little filly to ride. It threw her off, and she landed on her arm. You know Emma, she didn't want to go to the doctor, but I was afraid she broke it. She wouldn't let me take her, so I called her mom to come over. They left for the emergency room about an hour ago."

Bailey's eyes grew wide with worry. "Will she be okay?"

"I'm sure she'll be fine." Derfi smiled as he walked toward his black pickup truck. "Why don't we go find her now?"

Bailey opened the passenger door of the pickup and crawled inside. Then McKenzie remembered the bag of horse hair. "I need to mail a package. Can you wait a couple of minutes while I get it ready?"

"Sure, I'll be waiting," Derfi said.

McKenzie hurried toward the house with Bailey close b›ind her.

"We need an envelope for the hair. Hopefully Emma has one in the office," McKenzie said as the screen door banged b›ind her. She hurried down the hall and into the office. She opened the supply drawer and found a brown envelope. "Perfect," she said as she grabbed it and headed upstairs.

"I'll look up Kate's address." Bailey pulled her pink-and-green-striped address book out of her drawer. She not only had the Camp Club girls' addresses in it but also their phone numbers and e-mail addresses. Flipping the pages, she quickly found the address.

McKenzie printed Kate's name and address on the envelope then stuffed the bag of horse hair inside. She added a short note which read, "Please hurry. We need your help—BFF, McKenzie and Bailey."

On her way out the door, McKenzie grabbed the small backpack she sometimes carried for a purse. Overnight mail would cost a lot, and she hoped she had enough money.

The girls hurried downstairs and out the door. McKenzie had a funny feeling as she crawled in the pickup beside Derfi. She felt guilty wondering if he was a horse thief. Then she remembered that her dad had once told her that guilt was God's way of speaking to His children. Was God trying to tell her something now about Derfi?

As she leaned her head back in the seat, her mind wandered. They needed to solve the mystery of Diamond Girl's disappearance, but they also needed to focus on the rodeo that started tomorrow. In the afternoon, the judging of the Junior Miss Rodeo Queen contest would begin. She would be judged on her appearance, personality, and how well she handled her horse while riding. She shuddered at the thought of standing before the judges.

"You two are awfully quiet this morning," Derfi said, interrupting her thoughts. "Did you have too late of a night last night?"

"We just have a lot to think about," Bailey answered.

McKenzie stared out the window at the distant mountains. About twenty minutes later Derfi pulled into the parking lot of Mountainview Medical Center.

McKenzie wrinkled her nose at the smell of antiseptic as she stepped inside the hospital. Derfi stopped at the front desk and asked the receptionist about Emma. After listening to her directions, the girls followed Derfi down the hallway to a small room. A middle-aged, blond-haired woman who looked like an older version of Emma smiled at them as they entered.

Emma sat on the bed with her arm in a sling, her eyes rimmed by dark circles. "Hey girls, Derfi." She held out her uninjured arm toward the girls.

McKenzie stepped to Emma's side and put her arms around her. Emma winced.

"I'm sorry, Emma," McKenzie said. "Did I hurt you?"

"No, no," Emma said, forcing a smile to her face. "I'm fine."

"What did the doc say?" Derfi asked. "Is your arm broken?"

"Just a sprain, but I get a sling anyway." Emma shifted, holding her arm gingerly. "I also get to spend the night here. The doctor wants to make sure I don't have a concussion."

She looked apologetically at Derfi and the girls. "I'm really sorry about all this, guys. I know it's bad timing with the rodeo almost here."

"Don't worry about anything," Derfi said. "We'll take care of things at the stables."

"I'm waiting for the nurse to come back and take me to my room," Emma said with a frown.

Emma's mom, Mrs. Wilson, turned to the girls. "Emma asked me to stay with you girls tonight. If that's okay with you, I'll be out to the house after she gets settled here."

The girls told Mrs. Wilson that would be fine. They said their good-byes and headed back to the pickup. McKenzie asked Derfi if he would drop them off at the post office.

A few minutes later he pulled into a parking spot of the post office while McKenzie pulled out some money before leaving her backpack on the seat. Once inside she paid the clerk, and he told them that Kate should get the package by ten o'clock the next morning.

"Hopefully, Kate can test the hairs and call us with the results later in the afternoon. And let's hope that's soon enough," McKenzie said as they walked back to the pickup.

The girls rode in silence as Derfi drove to the feed store. McKenzie rolled down the window and let the warm air blow through her hair.

"Are you girls eager for the rodeo? I've watched you practice. You've both improved a lot since you came to Emma's." Derfi tuned the radio to a country music station.

"McKenzie will win her category. She's really good. She finishes a lot faster than me," Bailey said as she folded her arms across her chest.

"Oh, I'm not that good," McKenzie said, turning to Bailey. "There are a lot of riders who are better than I am."

"I don't know about that," Bailey said dismally. "You'll still win, and I bet you win the Junior Miss Rodeo Queen contest, too."

McKenzie didn't know what to say to cheer Bailey up. She knew how badly her younger friend wanted to keep up with her. Though Bailey rode well, McKenzie knew she would have tough competition at the rodeo. Many of the competitors had their own horses and rode daily. Bailey didn't have her own horse and had few opportunities to ride.

"Hey, why don't you enter the sheep chase, Bailey?" Derfi asked.

"That's a great idea," McKenzie said cheerfully. "I've done that before. It's a lot of fun, but I'm too old now."

"What's the sheep chase?" Bailey looked at McKenzie.

"Kids are turned loose in a pen of sheep. The first kid to catch a sheep and hold on to it is the winner. You could do that," McKenzie said with a smile.

"Sounds cool to me," Derfi said as he pulled into the parking lot of the feed store. "How about it?"

"I don't know," Bailey said reluctantly. Then she continued, "I suppose I could try. It does sound like fun."

Derfi parked at the loading dock beside a pickup with CEDAR CREEK RANCH printed across the door. He turned to the girls and handed McKenzie a few bills. "Go on in and grab a couple of drinks. My treat."

McKenzie hesitated and then thanked Derfi. Within a couple of minutes, the girls returned with icy cold drinks.

"When are we going to tell Emma about the horse in the dugout?" Bailey said after Derfi went inside the store.

"I don't know," McKenzie replied. "Now that she hurt her arm, I hate to give her something else to worry about."

Bailey nodded in agreement. "And we can't tell her we suspect Derfi when we don't know for sure," she whispered.

Derfi loaded the back of the pickup with feed. Then they headed back to Sunshine Stables. While Derfi unloaded the pickup, the girls went to the house.

McKenzie dropped her backpack to the floor, and then the girls headed back outside to the stables. They needed to help the stable hands with the extra chores because Emma was gone.

The rest of the afternoon flew by in a blur and in the early evening, they went inside and found Mrs. Wilson cooking in the kitchen.

"I found a recipe for orange chicken and fried rice on the counter," Mrs. Wilson said cheerfully. "Emma must have been planning on fixing it for supper, so I decided to try it."

Bailey's eyes lit up. "My grandma from China sent the recipe to my mom. It's my favorite. I told Emma about it and she wanted to try it."

McKenzie was glad Mrs. Wilson was staying with them. She knew Bailey was worried about not doing well in the rodeo. Ever since Emma had gotten hurt, Bailey had been quieter, but having Mrs. Wilson in the house seemed to perk her up.

After supper the girls practiced barrel racing. McKenzie and Bailey timed each other. McKenzie gave Bailey a few pointers on tightening her turns around the barrels. Soon, she had improved her time by a couple of seconds.

After heading inside the house, McKenzie noticed the backpack she had dropped earlier. As she picked it up, she noticed the zipper was partially open. She was sure she had zipped it closed before going into the post office earlier in the day. Who would have opened it? As she flung the backpack onto her shoulder, she noticed a sheet of paper stuffed inside. She pulled it out and gasped.

A handwritten message read:

"Tell no one about the mystery horse if you ever want to see it alive again."

At the Rodeo

"Who wrote this note and put it in my backpack?" McKenzie's hand trembled as she handed it to Bailey.

"Didn't you have it with you all the time we were in town?" Bailey asked.

McKenzie thought for a minute. "I left it in the pickup when I went to the hospital, the post office, and the feed store."

"Derfi waited in the pickup while we went to the post office," Bailey said as she chewed on a fingernail.

McKenzie didn't answer. Derfi was the only person who had been alone with the backpack. Had he written the note? Could he really be the thief after all?

More than anything, McKenzie wanted to talk to Emma. But that was out of the question now. The thief had threatened to kill the horse if they told anyone.

McKenzie was getting more scared by the minute. She needed time to think. She had to find some way to get help without Diamond Girl getting hurt. She clenched her eyes shut and prayed, asking God to help her and to keep the horse safe.

McKenzie was so concerned about the threatening note that she had little time to think about the Rodeo Queen contest tomorrow.

When she woke in the morning, worrisome thoughts filled her mind. She peered at Bailey, who was lying wide-awake on the bottom bunk.

"I can't believe the rodeo starts today," McKenzie said. "I am so nervous about the pageant. What if I mess up?"

"You won't, but I'll take your place if you want," Bailey said with a slight grin.

"Believe me, I'd let you if I could." McKenzie sat up and swung her legs over the side of the top bunk. "I'd rather be in the sheep chase with you."

"You're kidding," Bailey said. Then she added longingly, "I would give anything to be in the pageant."

McKenzie hopped from her bunk and pulled on a pair of jeans. After finishing chores, Derfi planned to take the horses to the rodeo grounds. He would settle them into their stalls until Mrs. Wilson brought the girls in later. That way McKenzie would have plenty of time to get ready for the pageant.

Then, after the crowning of the Rodeo Queen and the Junior Miss Rodeo Queen, Bailey would take part in the kids' sheep chase. Following that, the girls would compete in the barrel-racing and calf-roping contests.

Finally the girls finished the morning chores and helped Derfi and Ian load their horses into the trailer. They watched as Derfi pulled out of the driveway and disappeared down the road in a cloud of dust.

McKenzie glanced at her watch. "Kate should have received our package by now. I'm going to call her and see if she's found out anything about the hair yet."

She scrolled through the list of names in her cell phone and clicked on Kate's name. After a few rings, a familiar voice came on the line. McKenzie heard a dog bark in the background.

"Hi, Kate. Did you get the package?" McKenzie asked.

"I don't know. I haven't been home all morning. Mom made an appointment for Biscuit to get his shots. We won't be home till after lunch," Kate said.

McKenzie groaned. "This is really important. I have the feeling that guy will move the horse soon. We need to find out if the horse is Diamond Girl, so we can rescue her before she disappears again."

"Mom wants to stop at a sale at the shoe store, but I'll see if I can hurry her. I'll tell her it's important that we get home," Kate said.

"Thanks, Kate. Call me as soon as you get the results, okay? And give Biscuit a hug from his Auntie McKenzie." After saying good-bye, McKenzie flipped the phone shut and filled Bailey in on the conversation.

After eating a quick lunch, the girls headed to their bedroom. McKenzie pulled on her new black jeans and the sparkly green blouse. Bailey looked longingly at McKenzie as she helped apply her makeup. But a smile twitched the corners of Bailey's mouth when McKenzie asked her to french braid her hair.

As Bailey worked, McKenzie thought about the contest. Her stomach churned at the thought of the judging. She had an interview with the judges, and then she must ride her horse in a specific pattern before them.

"Are you girls about ready to go?" Mrs. Wilson hollered up the stairs.

"Just finishing up," Bailey called through the open door. Then she tied a green bow onto McKenzie's braid. "There. We're done."

The girls grabbed their backpacks filled with a change of clothes for the rodeo events. McKenzie grabbed the threatening note and stuffed it into her jeans pocket. A few minutes later, the girls tossed their bags and cowboy hats into the back seat of Mrs. Wilson's car.

Mrs. Wilson told them that Emma would soon be released from the hospital. The doctors had found no sign of a concussion. Once she'd dropped the girls off at the rodeo, Mrs. Wilson would pick up her daughter.

The girls sighed with relief at the news. All too soon they pulled into the parking lot of the rodeo grounds. Mrs. Wilson stopped the car outside the building where the judges were waiting. McKenzie agreed to meet Bailey at the stalls after the interview, and then Mrs. Wilson and Bailey went on to the stables to find Derfi and the horses.

McKenzie clutched her cowboy hat as she headed to the building where the judges held the interviews. She sat on a folding chair in the room with ten other girls. As she waited her turn, she glanced at the other competitors. She knew they were all probably wondering who would be crowned the next Junior Miss Rodeo Queen.

A young woman arrived carrying a clipboard and called McKenzie's name. After wiping her sweaty palms on her jeans, McKenzie followed the woman to a row of judges in the next room. They sat b›ind a table, staring at her. A white-haired woman with dark-rimmed glasses perched on the end of her nose asked her questions about her family and school. A chubby man with a black goatee asked her why she wanted to be crowned Junior Miss Rodeo Queen.

McKenzie managed to answer their questions, though afterward she couldn't even remember what the questions were. She breathed a sigh of relief when she finished her interview and returned to her chair in the other room. When all the contestants had been interviewed, the woman with the clipboard returned. She told them to bring their horses to the show ring in ten minutes to begin the horsemanship contest.

Sahara had the same stall every year at the rodeo, so McKenzie knew where to find her. Derfi, who had been at the rodeo grounds all day, was running a brush over the horse's backside when McKenzie arrived. Bailey was sitting cross-legged on the tack box and jumped to her feet when McKenzie approached.

"How'd you do?" Bailey asked.

McKenzie shrugged. "Not very good. I was nervous and talked too fast. I didn't know how to answer some of the questions. I really messed up."

Before Bailey could answer, Derfi spoke up. "Let's get your horse over to the arena."

McKenzie waited her turn outside the arena, wondering if her parents and brother had arrived. She hoped Emma would get here in time to see the performance, too. As she listened to the announcer's voice over the loudspeaker, she watched the faces of the other girls as they finished their routines. Some of them beamed with pride, while others hung their heads in disappointment.

McKenzie mounted Sahara, scanning the crowd outside the arena, looking for her family. When she didn't see them, she turned to Bailey. "I think I'm going to be sick."

"You can't be sick now. The announcer just called your name," Bailey said.

McKenzie prepared to enter the arena but turned as a familiar voice called her name. Emma stood several feet away giving her a thumbs-up.

McKenzie beamed. She turned and rode into the arena. She took a deep breath and began her routine, trying to remember everything Emma had taught her. The judges expected her to keep her seat in the saddle and her hands in view the entire time, and of course, she must smile constantly.

As she finished her routine, she saluted the judges. They scribbled notes on pieces of paper. Though the judges smiled back, McKenzie couldn't tell what they thought of her performance. They probably smiled at everybody. She and the other contestants would have to wait awhile longer to learn who would be crowned queen.

McKenzie led Sahara back to the stables. As she watered her horse, she heard voices shouting. Turning, she saw her mom, dad, and little brother, Evan.

"McKenzie, you did a wonderful job!" Mrs. Phillips exclaimed.

After giving her family a round of hugs, McKenzie saw Emma and Bailey approaching. Everyone told McKenzie she had done well, but she knew she had made several small mistakes. Several contestants had performed perfectly. She wished she had done better, but she was also glad the contest was almost over. Now she only had to wait.

McKenzie watched the remaining girls perform. After the contestants took their horses to their stalls, they all returned to the arena. McKenzie's palms grew sweaty as she climbed the steps of the stage at one end of the arena.

One by one, each of the girls walked across the stage to the microphone. Each girl introduced herself to the crowd then returned to her place in line.

McKenzie's heart fluttered wildly as she waited her turn. She closed her eyes and prayed, "Dear God, help me to not forget my name."

When she opened her eyes, the announcer, a middle-aged man with graying hair, was staring at her. The girl next to her nudged her with her elbow. McKenzie's legs felt rubbery as she walked to the microphone. She took a deep breath and smiled at the crowd.

A voice she didn't recognize came out her mouth. "Hi. I'm McKenzie Phillips. My parents are Dan and Jen Phillips, and I have a little brother, Evan, who is eight years old. I will be an eighth grader this fall at White Sulfur Springs Junior High."

The crowd clapped as she returned to her place in line. She felt the butterflies in her stomach settle down as she listened to the other girls' introductions.

"Well, there you have it, folks. Let's give all of these lovely young ladies a round of applause," the announcer exclaimed.

When the applause died down, he continued. "Our judges had quite a time choosing a winner. In a few minutes we'll crown our new Junior Miss Rodeo Queen. But first let's hear it for our second runner-up—Amanda Bradford!"

McKenzie clapped for the tall black-haired girl next to her. She knew she didn't stand a chance of being crowned queen, but secretly she had wished to be a runner-up. She held her breath as the announcer continued.

"Our first runner-up is—Taylor McCowen!" The announcer's voice boomed above the cheering crowd.

As McKenzie's gaze darted over the audience, she wondered who would be crowned queen. She thought about the brown-haired girl on the end. Her performance had looked almost perfect, and she had the confidence of a much older girl.

McKenzie barely heard the announcer as he continued. "And now is the moment we've all been waiting for. Our new Junior Miss Rodeo Queen is. . . McKenzie Phillips!"

McKenzie heard the cheering crowd as she forced herself to center stage. Her knees wobbled as a young woman placed a sparkly crown over her black cowboy hat and pinned a sash across her green blouse.

For a minute, McKenzie forgot the duties of the Junior Miss Rodeo Queen, but then she remembered and walked to the front of the stage. As cameras flashed, she waved to the crowd.

Before she knew it, she was whisked off stage. Soon her family, Emma, and Bailey surrounded her. Everyone talked at once, hugging and congratulating her.

Bailey stood to the back and finally came forward sheepishly. "You did great, McKenzie. I guess if I couldn't win, I'm glad you did."

McKenzie felt better knowing that Bailey was okay with her winning. Later she would let Bailey wear the crown.

After a photographer took her picture for the newspaper, the woman with the clipboard walked up to her. "We need to get you and your horse over to the arena. It's time for the rodeo to start."

McKenzie knew that the Junior Miss Rodeo Queen got to carry the Montana state flag around the arena, while the Rodeo Queen carried the American flag.

Moments later she settled onto Sahara's back, gripping the flagpole tightly in her hands. As "The Star Spangled Banner" boomed over the loudspeaker, the two flag bearers galloped around the arena. When the anthem ended, they stopped in the center of the ring while the crowd stood and cheered. Seconds later the girls rode their horses out of the ring.

After returning Sahara to her stall, McKenzie hurried back to the arena. The air was filled with the wonderful smells of rodeo foods—onion rings, hot dogs, cotton candy. She approached the fence to watch Bailey in the first rodeo event—the sheep chase. McKenzie said a silent prayer. She asked God to help Bailey do her best.

Some workers sectioned off an end of the arena, and then several sheep were herded into the ring. All the kids competing in the sheep chase stood at one end and waited. When the starting pistol cracked, they all darted forward, trying to catch one of the woolly animals.

"Go, Bailey!" McKenzie cheered.

The kids raced after the sheep that were scurrying in all directions. One boy had a sheep by the hind leg, but then it squirmed out of his grasp. Bailey ran and fell as she cornered a sheep. As she scrambled to her feet, another sheep ran by her.

She reached out and grabbed a hind leg, but the sheep was stronger. It pulled her across the ground. She held on tightly. As the sheep tried to run on three legs, Bailey reached out and grabbed the other hind leg.

The sheep struggled, but Bailey held on. She clutched the sheep until a worker clapped her on the shoulder. Bailey had won!

"Way to go, Bailey!" McKenzie shouted above the roaring crowd.

As the Junior Miss Rodeo Queen, McKenzie had the honor of presenting Bailey with her first-place blue ribbon. The younger girl beamed with pride as she followed McKenzie out of the arena.

McKenzie had little time to talk with Bailey. The younger riders in the barrel-racing contest would soon warm up. Bailey stuffed her blue ribbon in her back pocket and headed to the gate where Derfi held Applejack's reins.

Soon Bailey and the first riders galloped into the arena, warming up for the competition. Bailey sat stiffly on Applejack's back, riding faster than her competitors.

McKenzie watched from b>ind the fence. She heard the bulls snort in their pens as they waited for the bull-riding competition. A rodeo clown wearing huge, polka-dotted pants and a big, red nose teased some kids in the first row of bleachers. A toddler grabbed at his orange wig, nearly pulling it off.

As McKenzie watched the clown, a crash sounded from the bull pens. The crowd shrified. Turning back to the arena, she gasped. A huge white bull had broken out of its pen. The frightened young riders on their horses scattered about the arena.

McKenzie saw Bailey glance at the raging bull b›ind her. Terror filled Bailey's dark eyes as she dug her heels into Applejack's side. She flicked the reins, urging the horse to run faster.

McKenzie screamed when Bailey lost her balance and tumbled from her horse. The wild bull pawed at the ground, flinging dirt b›ind him. He put his head down and snorted. With his black eyes on Bailey, the bull lunged!

The Escape

Bailey screamed. The clown jumped over the fence and waved a red flag. The bull turned and pawed the ground before charging after him. The clown jumped out of the way, teasing the bull to lure it away from Bailey.

A young rodeo worker darted into the ring. He swept Bailey into his arms and lifted her over the fence to safety. Several men jumped in the ring and guided the angry bull back into his pen.

The audience cheered. McKenzie began to relax when she saw Bailey safely standing beside Applejack. Thankfully Bailey would have time to recover from her scare before her turn came.

Finally the announcer called Bailey's name, and she rode into the arena. She flicked the reins, dug her heels into her horse's sides, and darted across the starting line. She raced toward the first barrel, turning a wide circle around it.

She urged Applejack faster as she headed toward the second barrel, but she had trouble slowing down for the turn. Bailey made a near-perfect turn on the third barrel and raced for the finish line.

"Your turn is coming soon, young lady." McKenzie heard a

man beside her speak.

Turning, she saw Derfi. "I was hoping to hear the results first. I sure hope Bailey places at least third."

"It could be a close race. There was a lot of tough competition in her group. You'd better bring Sahara to the gate. It's almost time." Derfi hurried away to help Bailey lead Applejack back to the stall.

As McKenzie hurried to Sahara's stall, she heard the announcer give the results. She sighed when Bailey's name wasn't called. She hoped her friend wasn't too disappointed.

"Hey, Ian. Thanks," McKenzie said as she saw Emma's stable hand leading Sahara out of the stables.

"Go get 'em," Ian said, giving McKenzie a high five.

McKenzie grabbed the reins and headed back to the arena. Only three more riders before it was her turn. Her stomach quivered, but it wasn't like being on stage for the queen contest. She loved this kind of competition.

Finally McKenzie rode into the arena. She dug in her heels and lunged forward with Sahara. She turned the first two turns tightly around the barrels, but the third was slow and wide. On the final stretch to the finish line, she urged Sahara faster.

Her time was her best yet, but she didn't know if it was good enough to win. Several more riders had to compete.

Bailey was waiting for McKenzie in the stables when she returned with Sahara. "I've got news!"

"What?" McKenzie asked as she tied her horse in her stall.

Bailey glanced around to make sure no one was near. "The guy we've seen riding the spotted horse is here."

McKenzie stared at Bailey. "Do you know where he is now?"

Bailey glanced about the crowd and grabbed McKenzie's arm. "There he is—standing by the fence next to the grandstand. He's wearing the black cowboy hat."

As McKenzie watched, he turned and looked right at her. She turned away, and when she glanced back, he had vanished.

"He saw me looking at him. Now he's gone," she whispered.

Bailey edged closer to McKenzie. "I've been thinking. Shouldn't we have heard from Kate by now?"

McKenzie pulled her cell phone from her pocket. "I turned it off and forgot to turn it back on."

She listened to her voice mail. "Hi, McKenzie. This is Kate. Give me a call as soon as you can. I'll be home all evening. Bye."

As soon as she flipped her phone shut, the crowd around her cheered. McKenzie turned to see the last rider in her division compete. She wondered where she stood in the rankings.

The announcer's voice boomed over the loudspeaker. "That's it for the girls' barrel-riding competition. I've never seen a closer race, folks. But the young lady with the fastest time is McKenzie Phillips from White Sulfur Springs!"

McKenzie felt as if her heart would leap from her chest. She didn't even hear who came in second and third place. Bailey jumped up and down and clutched McKenzie's arm.

McKenzie felt dazed as she stepped into the arena. The crowd cheered as the Senior Rodeo Queen handed her a trophy. She had worked hard for it, but she knew she couldn't have won it without God's help.

When she stepped out of the arena, Bailey met her. The younger girl's eyes flashed with excitement.

"Wow, is that ever cool!" Bailey said as McKenzie held the trophy for her to see. "I sure hope I get one someday."

"You've still got a chance today. The calf-roping contest will start in about an hour," McKenzie said as she glanced at her watch.

McKenzie turned to her parents and Evan, who had come up b›ind her. Mrs. Phillips handed McKenzie a set of keys. "Why don't you lock your trophy up in the pickup? We parked on the side street b›ind the stables. Then you girls can meet us at Hamburger Haven before your next event."

McKenzie took the keys and turned to Bailey, "Let's call Kate when we get to the pickup and have some privacy."

The two girls headed across the rodeo grounds and past the horse stables. Cars and pickups lined the side street, while dozens of horse trailers were parked in a shaded lot beside the street.

"Hey look!" Bailey grabbed McKenzie's arm and pointed at a man carrying a bucket of water across the lot. "There's the mystery man. I wonder why he's carrying water out here."

Dusk was settling in, and McKenzie squinted at the figure walking through the shadows. "He's heading toward Maggie's pickup and trailer. Maybe he works for her. He must be carrying water to Frisco."

"Why wouldn't she be in the stables with the other horses?" Bailey asked.

"I don't know," McKenzie answered. "Maybe he's tied her in those trees b›ind the trailer."

The girls stopped when they reached the Phillips' pickup. McKenzie slid onto the backseat and pulled out her cell phone. She clicked on Kate's name and waited while the phone dialed the number.

"Hi, Kate. What did you find out?" McKenzie blurted when Kate answered.

"I didn't think you were ever going to call. There's no doubt about it. I tested the hairs you sent me," Kate said excitedly. "I can't prove they came from Diamond Girl, but the hairs have definitely been dyed."

"You're positive?" McKenzie asked as her excitement mounted.

"I'm 100 percent sure," Kate said. "Let me know if I can do anything else."

"Would you let the other Camp Club Girls know what is going on? We need all the prayers we can get."

Kate agreed and McKenzie snapped the phone shut. The girls headed back to the rodeo grounds. "We need to call Emma and tell her everything. We know the man who rode the spotted horse is here at the rodeo, so it would be a perfect time for Emma to go to Old Towne and check out the horse. She'll know if it's Diamond Girl with a dye job."

McKenzie put in a call to Emma, but she didn't answer. "Maybe she can't hear her phone with all the noise of the rodeo."

As they approached Hamburger Haven, McKenzie saw her family. "What took you girls so long? You barely have time to eat now before the calf roping starts." Mrs. Phillips handed them each a sandwich. "You'd better get Sahara ready. We'll be watching you."

McKenzie shoved the last bite of hamburger into her mouth as they stepped into the stable. She stuffed the napkin into her pocket. The stable buzzed with voices and neighing as riders prepared their horses for competitions.

"Hey, McKenzie." Bailey grabbed McKenzie's arm. "There's Frisco's stall."

McKenzie stared at the name above the stall. It read: MAGGIE PRESTON—FRISCO. McKenzie looked at the black mustang. She thought about the man carrying the bucket to the trailer. Something didn't make sense. Why was he carrying water there, when Maggie's horse was in the stable?

Suddenly McKenzie had an idea. She saw Maggie approach the stall. "Hey, Maggie, would you write down the names of those riders we watched roping calves at your stable? I want to watch them compete."

Maggie looked skeptically at the girls as she took a bite of her candy bar. *Where else have I seen that candy bar wrapper?* McKenzie thought. Maggie grabbed a pen and wrote on the napkin McKenzie gave her.

"McKenzie and Bailey, line up!" a voice called. McKenzie looked up as Derfi led Sahara up the aisle toward them.

McKenzie thanked Maggie and stuffed the napkin back into her pocket. She took Sahara's reins from Derfi. They arrived at the arena gate as the announcer was calling their names.

McKenzie had no time to get nervous. She grabbed her lasso in one hand and mounted Sahara. Bailey climbed on b›ind her.

The moment the calf came out of the chute, McKenzie darted after it. The calf kicked as it ran, but McKenzie focused and as it lifted its head, she tossed the lasso. The loop sailed through the air and landed around the calf's neck. Keeping a firm grip on the lasso, McKenzie slid from Sahara's back.

She raced to the calf with Bailey close b‹ind her. Together, the girls wrapped the other end of the rope around the calf's legs so it couldn't run away.

McKenzie had no idea whether their time was good compared to the other competitors. Right now, her thoughts were on Diamond Girl. Winning the calf-roping competition was the last thing on her mind.

They rode out of the arena while McKenzie glanced at the horses and riders lining up for the women's barrel-racing competition. Darkness had settled over the crowd, but the overhead pole lights had come on. She stopped beneath a light near a hitching post and pulled the crumpled napkin and the threatening note from her pocket.

"Look, Bailey. The handwriting is identical," McKenzie whispered to Bailey. "Maggie's pickup was in the parking lot of the feed store yesterday."

Bailey gasped. "You mean Maggie wrote both notes? So that's why you asked Maggie to write down those names."

McKenzie nodded. "Remember that candy bar Maggie was eating? That's the kind of candy wrapper that was in the dugout."

McKenzie glanced around her. Maggie stood in line for the barrel racing, adjusting Frisco's saddle. A man in a black jacket and cowboy hat stood beside her.

McKenzie gasped. He was the man who had ridden the spotted horse. As he turned away from her, McKenzie saw the red lettering on the back of his jacket: WHISPERING PINES HORSE THERAPY RANCH.

"Oh, Bailey," she whispered. "We've got trouble. Big trouble!"

The announcer's voice boomed over the loudspeaker, interrupting the girls' conversation. "The third-place trophy in the girls' calf-roping contest goes to McKenzie Phillips and Bailey Chang."

McKenzie quickly slid from Sahara's back and looped the reins around the hitching post. Bailey's eyes gleamed as the girls hurried into the arena. Bailey's hands trembled as she accepted her trophy.

The girls hurried out of the arena, not even waiting to hear the first-and second-place winners. McKenzie whispered in Bailey's ear. "Let's get out of here. We have to get back to the trailer lot. Quickly! I know a shortcut." She nodded toward a narrow street beyond the stables.

"What's going on?"

"I think I know where Diamond Girl is," McKenzie said. "We have to hurry to rescue her. But we can't look obvious. As soon as Maggie races with Frisco, she'll head out of here, taking Diamond Girl with her."

The girls quietly rode Sahara through the stable area to the back street. They could hardly hear the loud voices of the crowd and blaring music of the rodeo.

Hurrying beneath the dim streetlights, they arrived at Maggie's trailer and pickup. McKenzie slid off Sahara's back and pefied inside the trailer.

"She's not here," McKenzie whispered. "She can't be far. Wait here. Tell me if anyone comes."

McKenzie set off for the grove of trees, keeping to the shadows and calling, "Hey, girl, are you here?"

A soft whinny came from inside the grove. McKenzie pushed through the brambles. Soon she saw the white spots on the horse, barely visible in the darkness.

As she touched the horse, Bailey's cry reached her.

"Someone's coming, McKenzie. Run!"

McKenzie quickly untied the horse's reins and led her out of the trees. "Go get Derfi," she cried to Bailey.

She jumped on the horse's back and dug in her heels. McKenzie knew the spotted horse was Diamond Girl. She had to get her to safety. She raced the horse as fast as she dared. She heard hooves thunder b›ind her. She turned. In the moonlight she glimpsed the strange man chasing her on Frisco!

He screamed at her to stop. She dug in her heels, urging Diamond Girl to run faster. "Dear God, please help us," McKenzie prayed.

Where could she hide? She couldn't run forever. The hooves continued to pound the ground b›ind her. More voices shouted at her to stop. Glancing b›ind her, she saw two more figures on horses approaching. It was too dark to recognize them. She urged Diamond Girl onward. Soon the thundering hooves began to fade. She was losing at least two of them.

Suddenly, a horse came from the darkness b›ind her.

"McKenzie," a voice cried out. It was Derfi, riding Sahara. McKenzie pulled Diamond Girl to a walk.

"Ian stopped the guy who was chasing you. We've called security. You're safe and so is Diamond Girl," Derfi said.

"Bailey told us about her. But who did this to her?"

McKenzie brought Diamond Girl to a halt.

"It's Maggie," she said frantically. "Maggie stole Diamond Girl to use at a horse therapy farm. We have to stop her before she gets away."

Derfi stared at her and then snapped the reins. "Let's go!"

McKenzie and Derfi spun their horses around. They raced back to the lot where McKenzie's family and Emma had gathered.

Maggie's accomplice had broken free from Ian. He'd already loaded Frisco into the trailer. Maggie was b›ind the wheel, trying to move the pickup out of a tight parking spot.

"Don't let them go!" McKenzie screamed. "They're the horse thieves."

Mr. Phillips looked at his daughter and jumped into his pickup. Seconds later he had parked in the roadway, blocking Maggie in. The rodeo security guards arrived at the scene, ordering Maggie and her accomplice to get out of the pickup.

McKenzie hopped off Diamond Girl and led her to Bailey, Emma, and her family. Minutes later, McKenzie saw the flashing red-and-blue lights of the sheriff's pickup. A police car followed. The sheriff listened to the girls' story. After talking with Maggie and her friend, he ordered them into the police car.

Questions came to McKenzie from different directions.

She and Bailey quickly explained everything.

First, they told about finding the spotted horse at Old Towne. They explained about snipping the hairs and sending them to Kate. When the girls saw Frisco in her stall at the rodeo, McKenzie knew the strange man carrying water to the trailer lot must have a horse hidden somewhere. She had come to suspect Maggie when she saw the moving boxes at Cedar Crefi, so McKenzie had asked her to write down the riders' names so she could compare the handwriting. Then McKenzie remembered where she had seen Maggie's candy bar before. *The same kind of wrapper was in the trash at the dugout!* McKenzie thought.

Then, when she saw WHISPERING PINES HORSE THERAPY RANCH on the stranger's jacket, she realized the truth. Maggie and her friend, whose name was Chuck Hanson, had stolen Diamond Girl for their new therapy ranch.

The sheriff commended the girls on their hard work. Maggie and Chuck had confessed to everything. Maggie admitted that with Diamond Girl out of the rodeo competition, Frisco was a sure winner. She had planned to leave with Diamond Girl while Sunshine Stables staff was preoccupied at the rodeo, not only with a prize-winning rac›orse, but also a splendid therapy horse to draw customers to her new ranch.

Mr. Phillips came to his daughter's side as McKenzie watched Derfi and Ian load the horses into the trailer.

"Dad, you were right when you said that guilt is God telling us something." McKenzie looked up at her father. "I suspected an innocent person of a crime. I don't feel very good about it."

Mr. Phillips put an arm around his daughter's shoulder. "Sometimes we have to forgive ourselves just like God forgives us."

McKenzie thought about that as the sheriff drove away with Maggie and Chuck. Though she knew she would get over her anger at them, she still felt sorry for them and wondered what would happen to them next.

"You girls were amazing!" Emma's eyes lit up for the first time all wefi. "Thanks to you, Sunshine Stables will soon be back to normal!"

"You were right when you said everything happens for a reason," McKenzie said. "God had a purpose for bringing Diamond Girl back to you tonight."

Emma looked quizzically at McKenzie, "And what would that be?"

"There are more barrel-riding competitions tomorrow night. You never withdrew after Diamond Girl disappeared. Why don't you race her one more time? That is, if you feel like it."

Diamond Girl whinnied from inside the trailer. Emma laughed. "You know, McKenzie. By tomorrow, I may feel pretty well. I just might do that."

water damage warped pages

6/16/14

SG

DAMAGE NOTED

DAMAGE NOTED

We hope you enjoyed reading *Get a Clue*.
Please check out another
great young adult book series
from *Barbour Publishing*

S.A.V.E. Squad Series

Dog Daze
Book 1

When sixth-grader, Aneta Jasper, is reluctantly named one of the winners of Oakton Founders' Day poster contest, she and three girls—with nothing in common but their differences—must pull off a successful event for the first-ever Founder's Day. Will the mean girls ruin their plans to hold a Founders' Day fundraiser for homeless dogs?

The Great Cat Caper
Book 2

Three sixth-grade girls dive in to rescue doomed Dumpster cats in a parking lot. But Vee Nguyen resists. She must keep her place in the smart kids' class and has no time for wild cats. Will she finally identify with the cats and tell the S.A.V.E. Squad girls her secret?

Coming Soon....
Secondhand Horses

Available wherever books are sold.